# THE MAN IN GRAY

## A ROMANCE OF NORTH AND SOUTH

## THOMAS DIXON

1st WORLD
LIBRARY
Literary Society

# The Man in Gray

## Thomas Dixon

© 1st World Library – Literary Society, 2006
PO Box 2211
Fairfield, IA 52556
www.1stworldlibrary.org
First Edition

LCCN: 2006930801

Softcover ISBN: 1-4218-2202-4
Hardcover ISBN: 1-4218-2102-8
eBook ISBN: 1-4218-2302-0

Purchase *"The Man in Gray"*
as a traditional bound book at:
www.1stWorldLibrary.org/purchase.asp?ISBN=1-4218-2202-4

1st World Library Literary Society is a nonprofit organization dedicated to promoting literacy by:

- Creating a free internet library accessible from any computer worldwide.
- Hosting writing competitions and offering book publishing scholarships.

*The Man in Gray*
*contributed by Tim, Ed & Rodney*
*in support of*
*1st World Library Literary Society*

DEDICATED TO MY FELLOW MEMBERS
OF THE KAPPA ALPHA FRATERNITY
FOUNDED UNDER THE INSPIRATION OF
ROBERT E. LEE 1868

## TO THE READER

Now that my story is done I see that it is the strangest fiction that I have ever written.

Because it is true. It actually happened. Every character in it is historic. I have not changed even a name. Every event took place. Therefore it is incredible. Yet I have in my possession the proofs establishing each character and each event as set forth. They are true beyond question.

THOMAS DIXON CURRITUCK LODGE *Munden, Va.*

# LEADING CHARACTERS OF THE STORY

ROBERT E. LEE  - *The Southern Commander.*

MRS. LEE  - *His Wife.*

CUSTIS  - *His older Son.*

MARY  - *His Daughter.*

MRS. MARSHALL  - *Lee's Sister.*

UNCLE BEN  - *The Butler.*

SAM  - *A Slave.*

J.E.B. STUART  - *"The Flower of Cavaliers."*

FLORA COOKE  - *His Sweetheart.*

PHIL SHERIDAN  - *His Schoolmate.*

FRANCIS PRESTON BLAIR  - *Lincoln's Messenger.*

SENATOR ROBERT TOOMBS  - *of Georgia.*

JOHN BROWN  - *of Osawatomie.*

JOHN E. COOK  - *His Spy.*

VIRGINIA KENNEDY  - *Cook's Victim.*

GERRIT SMITH  - *A Philanthropist.*

GEORGE EVANS  - *A Labor Leader.*

F. B. SANBORN  - *Brown's Organizer.*

REV. THOMAS W. HIGGINSON  - *A Revolutionist.*

WM. C. RIVES  - *Confederate Senator*

GEN. E. P. ALEXANDER  - *of Lee's Artillery.*

JOHN DOYLE -  *A Poor White.*

MAHALA DOYLE  - *His Wife.*

EDMOND RUFFIN - *A Virginia Planter.*

# CHAPTER I

The fireflies on the Virginia hills were blinking in the dark places beneath the trees and a katydid was singing in the rosebush beside the portico at Arlington. The stars began to twinkle in the serene sky. The lights of Washington flickered across the river. The Capitol building gleamed, argus-eyed on the hill. Congress was in session, still wrangling over the question of Slavery and its extension into the territories of the West.

The laughter of youth and beauty sifted down from open windows. Preparations were being hurried for the ball in honor of the departing cadets - Custis Lee, his classmate, Jeb Stuart, and little Phil Sheridan of Ohio whom they had invited in from Washington.

The fact that the whole family was going to West Point with the boys and Colonel Robert E. Lee, the new Superintendent, made no difference. One excuse for an old-fashioned dance in a Southern home was as good as another. The main thing was to bring friends and neighbors, sisters and cousins and aunts together for an evening of joy.

A whippo'will cried his weird call from a rendezvous in the shadows of the lawn, as Sam entered the great hall and began to light the hundreds of wax tapers in the chandeliers.

"Move dat furniture back now!" he cried to his assistants. "And mind yo' p's and q's. Doan yer break nuttin."

His sable helpers quietly removed the slender mahogany and rosewood pieces to the adjoining rooms. They laughed at Sam's new-found note of dignity and authority.

He was acting butler to-night in Uncle Ben's place. No servant was allowed to work when ill - no matter how light the tasks to which he was assigned. Sam was but twenty years old and he had been given the honor of superintending the arrangements for the dance. And, climax of all, he had been made leader of the music with the sole right to call the dances, although he played only the triangle in the orchestra. He was in high fettle.

When the first carriage entered the grounds his keen ear caught the crunch of wheels on the gravel. He hurried to call the mistress and young misses to their places at the door. He also summoned the boys from their rooms upstairs. He had seen the flash of spotless white in the carriage. It meant beauty calling to youth on the hill. Sam knew.

Phil came downstairs with Custis. The spacious sweep of the hall, its waxed floor clear of furniture, with hundreds of blinking candles flashing on its polished surface, caught his imagination. It *was* a fairy world - this generous Southern home. In spite of its wide spaces, and its dignity, it was friendly. It caught his boy's heart.

Mrs. Lee was just entering. Custis' eyes danced at the sight of his mother in full dress. He grasped Phil's arm and whispered:

"Isn't my mother the most beautiful woman you ever saw?"

He spoke the words half to himself. It was the instinctive worship of the true Southern boy, breathed in genuine reverence, with an awe that was the expression of a religion.

"I was just thinking the same thing, Custis," was the sober reply.

"I beg your pardon, Phil," he hastened to apologize. "I didn't mean to brag about my mother to you. It just slipped out. I couldn't help it. I was talking to myself."

"You needn't apologize. I know how you feel. She's already made me think I'm one of you -"

He paused and watched Mary Lee enter from the lawn leaning on Stuart's arm. Stuart's boyish banter was still ringing in her ears as she smiled at him indulgently. She hurried to her mother with an easy, graceful step and took her place beside her. She was fine, exquisite, bewitching. She had never come out in Society. She had been born in it. She had her sweethearts before thirteen and not one had left a shadow on her quiet, beautiful face. She demanded, by her right of birth as a Southern girl, years of devotion. And the Southern boy of the old regime was willing to serve.

Phil stood with Stuart and watched Custis kiss a dozen pretty girls as they arrived and call each one cousin.

"Is it a joke?" he asked Stuart curiously.

"What?"

"This cousin business."

"Not much. You don't think I'd let him be such a pig if I could help him, do you?"

"Are they all kin?"

"Yes - " Stuart laughed. "Some of it gets pretty thin in the second and third cousin lines. But it's thick enough for him to get a kiss from every one - confound him!"

The hall was crowding rapidly. The rustle of silk, the flash of pearls and diamonds, the hum of soft drawling voices filled the perfumed air.

Phil's eyes were dazzled with the bevies of the younger set, from sixteen to eighteen, dressed in soft tulle and organdy; slow of speech; their voices low, musical, delicious. He was introduced to so many his head began to swim. To save his soul he couldn't pick out one more entrancing than another. The moment they spied his West Point uniform he was fair game. They made eyes at him. They languished and pretended to be smitten at first sight. Twice he caught himself about to believe one of them. They seemed so sincere, so dreadfully in earnest. And then he caught the faintest twinkle in the corner of a dark eye and blushed to think himself such a fool.

But the sensation of being lionized was delightful. He was in a whirl of foolish joy when he suddenly realized that Stuart had deserted him, slipped through the crowd and found his way to Mary Lee. He threw a quick glance at the pair and one of the four beauties hovering around him began to whisper:

"Jeb Stuart's just crazy about Mary -"

"Did you ever see anything like it!"

"He couldn't stop even to say how-d'y-do."

"And she's utterly indifferent -"

Sam's voice suddenly rang out with unusual unction and deliberation. He was imitating Uncle Ben's most eloquent methods.

"Congress-man and Mrs. Rog-er A. Pry-or!"

Mrs. Lee hastened to greet the young editor who had taken high rank in Congress from the day of his entrance.

Mrs. Pryor was evidently as proud of her young Congressman as he was of her regal beauty.

Colonel Lee joined the group and led the lawmaker into the

library for a chat on politics.

The first notes of a violin swept the crowd. The hum of conversation and the ripple of laughter softened into silence. The dusky orchestra is in place on the little platform. Sam, in all his glory, rises and faces the eager youth.

He was dressed in his young master's last year's suit, immaculate blue broadcloth and brass buttons, ruffled shirt and black-braided watch guard hanging from his neck. His eyes sparkled with pride and his rich, sonorous voice rang over the crowd like the deep notes of a flute:

"Choose yo' pardners fur de fust cowtillun!"

Again the quick rustle of silk and tulle, the low hum of excited, young voices and the couples are in place.

A boy cries to the leader:

"We're all ready, Sam."

The young caller of the set knew his business better. He lifted his hand in a gesture of reverence and silence, as he glanced toward the library door.

"Jes' a minute la-dees, an' gem-mens," he softly drawled. "Marse Robert E. Lee and Missis will lead dis set!"

The Colonel briskly entered from the library with his wife on his arm. A ripple of applause swept the room as they took their places with the gay youngsters.

Sam lifted his hand; the music began - sweet and low, vibrating with the sensuous touch of the negro slave whose soul was free in its joyous melody.

At the first note of his triangle, loud above the music rang Sam's voice:

"Honors to yo' pardners!"

With graceful courtesies and stately bows the dance began. And over all a glad negro called the numbers:

"Forward Fours!"

The caller's eyes rolled and his body swayed with the rhythm of the dance as he watched each set with growing pride. They danced a quadrille, a mazurka, another quadrille, a schottische, the lancers, another quadrille, and another and another. They paused for supper at midnight and then danced them over again.

While the fine young forms swayed to exquisite rhythm and the music floated over all, the earnest young Congressman bent close to his host in a corner of the library.

"I sincerely hope, Colonel Lee, that you can see your way clear to make a reply to this book of Mrs. Stowe which Ruffin has sent you."

"I can't see it yet, Mr. Pryor -"

"Ruffin is a terrible old fire-eater, I know," the Congressman admitted. "But *Uncle Tom's Cabin* is the most serious blow the South has receivedfrom the Abolitionists. And what makes it so difficult is that its appeal is not to reason. It is to sentiment. To the elemental emotions of the mob. No matter whether its picture is true or false, the result will be the same unless the minds who read it can be cured of its poison. It has become a sensation. Every Northern Congressman has read it. A half million copies have been printed and the presses can't keep up with the demands. This book is storing powder in the souls of the masses who don't know how to think, because they've never been trained to think. This explosive emotion is the preparation for fanaticism. We only wait the coming of the fanatic - the madman who may lift a torch and hurl it into this magazine. The South is asleep. And when we don't sleep, we dance. There's no use fooling ourselves. We're dancing on the crust of a volcano."

Pryor rose.

"I've a number with Mrs. Pryor. I wish you'd think it over, Colonel. This message is my big reason for missing a night session to be here."

Lee nodded and strolled out on the lawn before the white pillars of the portico to consider the annoying request. He hated controversy.

Yet he was not the type of man to run from danger. The breed of men from which he sprang had always faced the enemy when the challenge came. In the carriage of his body there was a quiet pride - a feeling not of vanity, but of instinctive power. It was born in him through generations of men who had done the creative thinking of a nation in the building. His face might have been described as a little too regular - a little too handsome perhaps for true greatness, but for the look of deep thought in his piercing eyes. And the finely chiseled lines of character, positive, clean-cut, vigorous. He had backbone.

And yet he was not a bitter partisan. He used his brain. He reasoned. He looked at the world through kindly, conservative eyes. He feared God, only. He believed in his wife, his children, his blood. And he loved Virginia, counting it the highest honor to be - not seem to be - an old-fashioned Virginia gentleman.

He believed in democracy guided by true leaders. This reservation was not a compromise. It was a cardinal principle. He could conceive of no democracy worth creating or preserving which did not produce the superman to lead, shape, inspire and direct its life. The man called of God to this work was fulfilling a divine mission. He must be of the very necessity of his calling a nobleman.

Without vanity he lived daily in the consciousness of his own call to this exalted ideal. It made his face, in repose, grave. His gravity came from the sense of duty and the consciousness of problems to be met and solved as his fathers before him had met and solved great issues.

His conservatism had its roots in historic achievements and the chill that crept into his heart as he thought of this book came, not from the fear of the possible clash of forces in the future, but from the dread of changes which might mean the loss of priceless things in a nation's life. He believed in every fiber of his being that, in spite of slavery, the old South in her ideals, her love of home, her worship of God, her patriotism, her joy of living and her passion for beauty stood for things that are eternal.

And great changes *were* sweeping over the Republic. He felt this to-day as never before. The Washington on whose lights he stood gazing was rapidly approaching the end of the era in which the Nation had evolved a soul. His people had breathed that soul into the Republic. To this hour the mob had never ruled America. Its spirit had never dominated a crisis. The nation had been shaped from its birth through the heart and brain of its leaders.

But he recalled with a pang that the race of Supermen was passing. Calhoun had died two years ago. Henry Clay had died within the past two months. Daniel Webster lay on his death bed at Mansfield. And there were none in sight to take their places. We had begun the process of leveling. We had begun to degrade power, to scatter talent, to pull down our leaders to the level of the mob, in the name of democracy.

He faced this fact with grave misgivings. He believed that the first requirement of human society, if it shall live, is the discovery of men fit to command - to lead.

With the passing of Clay, Calhoun and Webster the Washington on which he gazed, the Washington of 1852, had ceased to be a forum of great thought, of high thinking and simple living. It had become the scene of luxury and extravagance. The two important establishments of the city were Gautier's, the restaurateur and caterer - the French genius who prepared the feasts for jeweled youth; and Gait, the jeweler who sold the precious stones to adorn the visions of beauty at these banquets.

The two political parties had fallen to the lowest depths of groveling to vote getting by nominating the smallest men ever named for Presidential honors. The Democrats had passed all their real leaders and named as standard-bearer an obscure little politician of New Hampshire, Mr. Franklin Pierce. His sole recommendation for the exalted office was that he would carry one or two doubtful Northern states and with the solid South could thus be elected. The Whig convention in Baltimore had cast but thirty-two votes for Daniel Webster and had nominated a military figurehead, General Winfield Scott.

The Nation was without a leader. And the low rumble of the crowd - the growl of the primal beast - could be heard in the distance with increasing distinctness.

The watcher turned from the White City across the Potomac and slowly walked into his rose garden. Even in September the riot of color was beyond description. In the splendor of the full Southern moon could be seen all shades from deep blood red to pale pink. All sizes from the tiniest four-leaf wild flowers to the gorgeous white and yellow masses that reared their forms like waves of the surf. He breathed the perfume and smiled again. A mocking bird, dropping from the bough of a holly, was singing the glory of a second blooming.

The scene of entrancing beauty drove the thought of strife from his heart. He turned back toward the house and its joys of youth.

Sam's sonorous voice was ringing in deliberation the grand call of the evening's festivities:

"Choose-yo-pardners-fer-de-ol-Virginy-Reel!"

And then the stir, the rush, the commotion for place in the final dance. The reel reaches the whole length of the hall with every foot of space crowded. There are thirty couples in line when the musicians pause, tune their instruments and with a sudden burst play "The Gray Eagle." The Virginia Reel stirs the blood of these Southern boys and girls. Its swift, graceful action and the inspiration of the old music seem part of the heart beat of the youth and beauty that sway to its cadences.

The master of Arlington smiled at the memory of the young Congressman's eloquence. Surely it was only a flight of rhetoric.

# CHAPTER II

Phil had finally reached the boys' room after the dance, his head in a whirl of excitement. Sleep was the last thing he wished. His imagination was on fire. He had heard of Southern hospitality. He had never dreamed of such waste of good things, such joy in living, such genuine pleasure in the meeting of friends and kinfolks. Custis had insisted on every boy staying all night. A lot of them had stayed. The wide rooms bulged with them. There were cots and pallets everywhere. He had seen the housemaids and the menservants carrying them in after the dance. Their own room contained four beds and as many pallets, and they were all full.

He tried to sleep and couldn't. He dozed an hour, waked at dawn and began day-dreaming. There was no sense of weariness. His mind was too alert. The great house, in which he was made to feel as much at home as in the quiet cottage of his mother in Ohio, fascinated him with its endless menservants, housemaids, serving boys, cooks, coachmen and hostlers.

He thought of the contrast with the quiet efficiency and simplicity of his mother's house. He could see her seated at the little table in the center of the room, a snow-white cap on her head. The work of the house had been done without a servant. It had been done so simply and quietly, he had never been conscious of the fact that it was work at all. It had seemed a ministry of love for her children. Their help had been given with equal joy, unconscious of toil, her kitchen floor was always spotless, with every pot and pan and shining dish in its place as if by magic.

He wondered how Custis' mother could bear the strain of all these people. He wondered how she could manage the army of black servants who hung on her word as the deliverance of an oracle. He could hear the hum of the life of the place already awake with the rising sun. Down in the ravine behind the house he caught the ring of a hammer on an anvil and closer in the sweep of a carpenter's plane over a board. A colt was calling to his mother at the stables and he could hear the chatter and cries of the stable boys busy with the morning feed.

He rose, stepped gingerly beside the sleepers on the floor and stood by an open window. His mind was stirring with a curious desire to see the ghost that haunted this house, its spacious grounds and fields. He, too, had read *Uncle Tom's Cabin*, and wondered. The ghost must be here hiding in some dark corner of cabin or field - the ghost of deathless longing for freedom - the ghost of cruelty - the ghost of the bloodhound, the lash and the auction block.

Somehow he couldn't realize that such things could be, now that he was a guest in a Southern home and saw the bright side of their life. Never had he seen anything brighter than the smiles of those negro musicians as they proudly touched their instruments: the violin, the banjo, the flute, the triangle and castanets, and watched the dancers swing through each number. There could be no mistake about the ring of joy in Sam's voice. It throbbed with unction. It pulsed with pride. Its joy was contagious. He caught himself glancing at his rolling eyes and swaying body. Once he muttered aloud:

"Just look at that fool nigger!"

But somewhere in this paradise of flowers and song birds, of music and dance, of rustling silk, of youth and beauty, the Ghost of Slavery crouched.

In a quiet way he would watch for it to walk. He had to

summon all his pride of Section and training in the catch words of the North to keep from falling under the charm of the beautiful life he felt enfolding him.

He no longer wondered why every Northern man who moved South forgot the philosophy of the Snows and became a child of the Sun. He felt the subtle charm of it stealing into his heart and threw off the spell with an effort.

A sparrow chirped under the window. A redbird flashed from a rosebush and a mocking bird from a huge magnolia began to softly sing his morning love song to his mate.

He heard a yawn, turned and saw Custis rubbing his eyes.

"For heaven's sake, Phil, why don't you sleep?"

"Tried and can't."

"Don't like your bed?"

"Too much excited."

"One of those girls hooked you?"

"No. I couldn't make up my mind. So many beauties they rattled me."

"All right," Custis said briskly. "Let's get up and look around the old plantation."

"Good," Phil cried.

Custis called Jeb Stuart in vain. He refused to answer or to budge.

Phil found his shoes at the door neatly blacked and the moment he began to stir a grinning black boy was at his heels to take his slightest order.

"I don't want *any*thing!" he said at last to his dusky tormentor.

"Nuttin tall, sah?"

"Nuttin tall!"

Phil smiled at the eager, rolling eyes.

"Get out - you make me laugh - "

The boy ducked.

"Yassah - des call me if ye wants me - I'se right outside de do'."

The two cadets ate breakfast alone. The house was yet asleep - except the children. Their voices could be heard on the lawn at play. They had been put to bed early, at eleven o'clock. They were up with the birds as usual. The sun was an hour high, shining the glory of a perfect September morning. The boys strolled on the lawn. The children were everywhere, playing in groups. Little black and white boys mixed indiscriminately. Robbie Lee was playing rooster fight with Sid, his boon companion. The little black boy born nearest his birthday was dedicated to be his friend, companion and body servant for life.

Phil paused to see the rooster fight.

The boys folded their arms and flew at each other sideways, using their elbows as a rooster uses his spurs.

Robbie was pressing Sid against the fence of the rose garden. Sid's return blows lacked strength.

Robbie stamped his foot angrily.

"Come on now - no foolin' - fight! There's no fun in a fight, if you don't fight!"

Sid bucked up and flew at his enemy.

Robbie saw the two older boys watching and gave a star performance. As Sid lunged at him with uplifted arms, and drew back to strike a stunning blow, Robbie suddenly stooped, hurled his elbow under Sid's arm, lifted him clear of the ground and he fell sprawling.

Robbie stood in triumph over the prostrate figure.

Phil laughed.

"You got him that time, Robbie!"

Robbie squared himself, raised his spurs and waited for Sid to rise.

Sid was in no hurry. He had enough. He hadn't cried. But he was close to it.

"Ye needn't put up dem spurs at me no mo'."

"Come on again!" Robbie challenged.

"Na, sah. I'se done dead. Ye stick dat spur clean froo me. Hit mighty nigh come out on de odder side!"

"Got enough?"

The game was suddenly ended by a barefoot white boy approaching Robbie. Johnny Doyle carried a dozen teal ducks, six in each hand. They were so heavy for his hands that their heads dragged the ground.

Robbie rushed to meet his friend.

"Oh, John, where'd you get the ducks?"

"Me and daddy killed 'em this mornin' at sun-up on the river."

"Why, the duck season isn't on yet, is it?" Custis asked the boy.

"No, sir, but daddy saw a big raft of teal swingin' into the bend of the river yesterday and we got up before daylight and got a mess."

"You brought 'em to me, John?" Robbie asked eagerly.

"Jes the same, Robbie. Dad sent 'em to Colonel Lee."

"That's fine of your daddy, John," Custis said, placing his hand on the little bare sunburnt head.

"Yessir, my daddy says Colonel Lee's the greatest man in this county and he's mighty proud to be his neighbor."

"Tell him my father will thank him personally before we leave and say for all that he has given us a treat."

Custis handed the ducks to Sid.

"Take them to the kitchen and tell Aunt Hannah to have them for dinner, sure."

Sid started for the kitchen and Robbie called after him:

"Hurry back, Sid -"

"Yassah - right away, sah!"

Robbie seized John's hand.

"You'll stay all day?"

"I can't."

"We're goin' fishin' -"

"Honest?"

"Sure. Uncle Ben's sick. But after dinner he's promised to take us. He's not too sick to fish."

"I can't stay," the barefoot boy sighed.

"Come on. There's three bird's nests in the orchard. The second layin'. It ain't no harm to break up the second nest. Birds've no business layin' twice in one season. We *ought* to break 'em up."

"I'm afraid I can't."

His tone grew weaker and Robbie pressed him.

"Come on. We'll get the bird's eggs and chase the calves and colts till the dinner bell rings, ride the horses home from the fields, and go fishin' after dinner and stay till dark."

"No -"

"Come on!"

John glanced up the road toward the big gate beyond which his mother was waiting his return. The temptation was more than his boy's soul could resist. He shook his head - paused - and grinned.

"Come on, Sid, John's goin' with us," Robbie called to his young henchman as he approached.

"All right," John consented, finally throwing every scruple to the winds. "Ma'll whip me shore, but, by granny, it'll be worth it!"

The aristocrat slipped his arm around his chum and led him to the orchard in triumph.

Custis laughed.

"He'd rather play with that little, poor white rascal than any boy in the country."

"Don't blame him," Phil replied. "He may be dirty and ragged but he's a real boy after a real boy's heart. And the handsomest little beggar I ever saw - who is he?"

"The boy of a poor white family, the Doyles. They live just outside our gate on a ten-acre farm. His mother's trying to make him go to school. His father laughs and lets him go hunting and fishing."

They were strolling past the first neat row of houses in the servants' quarters. Phil thought of them as the slave quarters. Yet he had not heard the word slave spoken since his arrival. These black people were "servants" and some of them were the friends and confidants of their master and his household. Phil paused in front of a cottage. The yard flamed with autumn flowers. Through the open door and windows came the hum of spinning wheels and the low, sweet singing of the dark spinners, spinning wool for the winter clothing of the estate. From the next door came the click and crash of the looms weaving the warm cloth.

"You make your own cloth?" the Westerner asked in surprise.

"Of course, for the servants. It takes six spinners and three weavers working steadily all year to keep up with it, too."

"Isn't it expensive?"

"Maybe. We never thought of it. We just make it. Always have in our family for a hundred years."

They passed the blacksmith's shop and saw him shoeing a blooded colt. Phil touched the horse's nostrils with a gentle hand and the colt nudged him.

"It's funny how a horse knows a horseman instinctively - isn't it, Phil?"

"Yes. He knows I'm going to join the cavalry."

They moved down the long row of whitewashed cottages, each with its yard of flowers and each with a huge pile of wood in the rear - wood enough to keep a sparkling fire through the winter. Chubby-faced babies were playing in the sanded walks and smiling young mothers watched them from the doors.

Phil started to put a question, stammered and was silent.

"What is it?" Custis asked.

"You'll pardon my asking it, old boy, but are these black folks married?"

The Southern boy laughed heartily.

"I should say so. A negro wedding is one of the joys of a plantation boy's life."

"But isn't it awful when they're separated?"

"They're not separated."

"Never?"

"Not on this plantation. Nor on any estate whose master and mistress are our friends. It's not done in our set."

"You keep them when they're old, lazy and worthless?"

"If they're married, yes. It's a luxury we never deny ourselves, this softening of the rigor of the slave regime. It's not business. But it's the custom of the country. To separate a husband and wife is an unheard-of thing among our people."

The thing that impressed the Westerner in those white rows of little homes was the order and quiet of it all. Every yard was swept clean. There was nowhere a trace of filth or disease-breeding refuse. And birds were singing in the bushes beside these slave cottages as sweetly as they sang for the master and mistress in the pillared mansion on the hill. They passed the stables and paused to watch a dozen colts playing in the inclosure. Beyond the stable under the shadows of great oaks was the dog kennel. A pack of fox hounds rushed to the gate with loud welcome to their young master. He stooped to stroke each head and call each dog's name. A wagging tail responded briskly to every greeting. In another division of the kennel romped a dozen bird-dogs, pointers and setters. The puppies were nearly grown and eager for the fields. They climbed over Custis in yelping puppy joy that refused all rebuffs.

Phil looked in vain for the bloodhounds. He was afraid to ask about them lest he offend his host. Custis had never seen a bloodhound and could not guess the question back of his schoolmate's silence.

Sam entered the inclosure with breakfast for the dogs.

Phil couldn't keep his eyes off the sunlit, ebony face. His smile was contagious. His voice was music.

The Westerner couldn't resist the temptation to draw him out.

"You were certainly dressed up last night, Sam!"

"Yer lak dat suit I had on, sah?"

"It was a great combination."

"Yassah, dat's me, sah," the negro laughed. "I'se a great combination - yassah!"

He paused and threw his head back as if to recall the words.

Then in a voice rich and vibrant with care-free joy he burst into song:

"Yassah!"

> "When I goes out ter promenade
> I dress so fine and gay
> I'm bleeged to take my dog along
> Ter keep de gals away."

Again his laughter rang in peals of sonorous fun. They joined in his laugh.

A stable boy climbed the fence and called:

"Don't ye want yer hosses, Marse Custis?" He was jealous of Sam's popularity.

Custis glanced at Phil.

"Sure. Let's ride."

"All right, Ned - saddle them."

The boy leaped to the ground and in five minutes led two horses to the gate. As they galloped past the house for the long stretch of white roadway that led across the river to the city, Phil smiled as he saw Jeb Stuart emerge from the rose garden with Mary Lee. Custis ignored the unimportant incident.

# CHAPTER III

Stuart led Mary to a seat beneath an oak, brushed the dust away with his cap and asked her to honor him. He bowed low over her hand and dared to kiss it.

She passed the gallant act as a matter of course and sat down beside him with quiet humor. She knew the symptoms. A born flirt, as every true Southern girl has always been, she eyed his embarrassment with surprise. She knew that he was going to speak under the resistless impulse of youth and romance, and that no hearts would be broken on either side no matter what the outcome.

She watched him indulgently. She had to like him. He was the kind of boy a girl couldn't help liking. He was vital, magnetic and exceptionally good looking. He sang and danced and flirted, but beneath the fun and foolishness slumbered a fine spirit, tender, reverent, deeply religious. It was this under-current of strength that drew the girl. He was always humming a song, his heart bubbling over with joy. He had never uttered an oath or touched a drop of liquor amid all the gaiety of the times in which he lived.

"Miss Mary," he began slowly.

"Now Jeb," she interrupted. "You don't *have* to, you know -"

Stuart threw his head back, laughed, and sang a stanza from "Annie Laurie" in a low, tender voice. He paused and faced his fair tormentor.

"Miss Mary, I've got to!"

"You don't have to make love to me just because you're my brother's classmate -"

"You know I'm not!" he protested.

"You're about to begin."

"But not for that reason, Miss Mary -"

He held her gaze so seriously that she blushed before she could recover her poise. He saw his advantage and pressed it.

"I'm telling you that I love you because you're the most adorable girl I've ever known."

His boyish, conventional words broke the spell.

"I appreciate the tribute which you so gallantly pay me, Sir Knight. But I happen to know that the moonlight, the music of a dance, the song of birds this morning and the beauty of the landscape move you, as they should. You're young. You're too good looking. You're fine and unspoiled and I like you, Jeb. But you don't know yet what love means."

"I do, Miss Mary, I do."

"You don't and neither do I. You're in love with love. And so am I. It's the morning of life and why shouldn't we be like this?"

"There's no hope?" he asked dolefully.

"Of course, there's hope. There's something fine in you, and you'll find yourself in the world when you ride forth to play your part. And I'll follow you with tender pride."

"But not with love," he sighed.

"Maybe - who knows?" she smiled.

"Is that all the hope you can give me?"

"Isn't it enough?"

He gazed into her serious eyes a moment and laughed with boyish enthusiasm.

"Yes, it is, Miss Mary! You're glorious. You're wonderful. You make me ashamed of my foolishness. You inspire me to do things. And I'm going to do them for your sake."

"For your own sake, because God has put the spark in your soul. Your declaration of love has made me very happy. We're too young yet to take it seriously. We must both live our life in its morning before we settle down to the final things. They'll come too soon."

"I'm going to love you always, Miss Mary," he protested.

"I want you to. But you'll probably marry another girl."

"Never!"

"And I know you'll be her loyal knight, her devoted slave. It's a way our Southern boys have. And it's beautiful."

Stuart studied the finely chiseled face with a new reverence.

"Miss Mary, you've let me down so gently. I don't feel hurt at all."

A sweet silence fell between them. A breeze blew the ringlets of the girl's hair across the pink of her cheek. A breeze from the garden laden with the mingled perfume of roses. A flock of wild ducks swung across the lawn high in the clear sky and dipped toward the river. Across the fields came a song of slaves at work in the cornfield, harvesting the first crop of peas planted between the rows.

Stuart caught her hand, pressed it tenderly and kissed it.

"You're an angel, Miss Mary. And I'm going to worship you, if you won't let me love you."

The girl returned his earnest look with a smile and slowly answered:

"All right, Beauty Stuart, we'll see -"

# CHAPTER IV

The dinner at night was informal. Colonel Lee had invited three personal friends from Washington. He hoped in the touch of the minds of these leaders to find some relief from the uneasiness with which the reading of Mrs. Stowe's book had shadowed his imagination.

The man about whom he was curious was Stephen A. Douglas of Illinois, the most brilliant figure in the Senate. In the best sense he represented the national ideal. A Northern man, he had always viewed the opinions and principles of the South with broad sympathy.

The new Senator from Georgia, on the other hand, had made a sensation in the house as the radical leader of the South. Lee wondered if he were as dangerous a man as the conservative members of the Whig party thought. Toombs had voted the Whig ticket, but his speeches on the rights of the South on the Slavery issues had set him in a class by himself.

Mr. and Mrs. Pryor had spent the night of the dance at Arlington and had consented to stay for dinner.

Douglas had captured the young Virginia congressman. And Mrs. Douglas had become an intimate friend of Mrs. Pryor.

When Douglas entered the library and pressed Lee's hand, the master of Arlington studied him with keen interest. He was easily the most impressive figure in American politics. The death of Calhoun and Clay and the sudden passing of Webster had left but one giant on the floor of the Senate. They called him the "Little Giant." He was still a giant. He had sensed the approaching storm of crowd madness and had sought the age-old method of compromise as the safety valve of the nation.

He had not read history in vain. He knew that all states-manship is the record of compromise - that compromise is another name for reason. The Declaration of Independence was a compromise between the radicalism of Thomas Jefferson and the conservatism of the colonies. In the original draft of the Declaration, Jefferson had written a paragraph arraigning slavery which had been omitted:

"He (the King of Great Britain) has waged cruel war against human nature itself, violating its most sacred rights of life and liberty in the persons of a distant people who never offended him; capturing and carrying them into slavery in another hemisphere, or to incur miserable death in their transportation thither. This piratical warfare, the opprobrium of infidel powers, is the warfare of the *Christian* King of Great Britain. Determined to keep open a market where men should be bought and sold, he prostituted his negative for suppressing every legislative attempt to prohibit or restrain this execrable commerce. And that this assemblage of horrors might want no fact of distinguished dye, he is now exciting these very people to rise in arms among us, and to purchase that liberty of which he has deprived them, by murdering the people on whom he also obtruded them; thus paying off former crimes committed against the liberties of one people with crimes which he urges them to commit against the lives of another."

This indictment of Slavery and the Slave trade was stricken from the Declaration of Independence in deference to the opposition of both Northern and Southern slave owners who held that the struggling young colonies must have labor at all hazards.

Lee knew that the Constitution also was a compromise of

conflicting interests. But for the spirit of compromise - of reason - this instrument of human progress could never have been created. The word "Slave" or "Slavery" does not occur within it, and yet three of its most important provisions established the institution of chattel slavery as the basis of industrial life. The statesmen who wrote the Constitution did not wish these clauses embodied in it. Yet the Union could not have been established without them. Our leaders reasoned, and reasoned wisely, that Slavery must perish in the progress of human society, and, therefore, they accepted the compromise.

There has never been a statesman in the history of the world who has not used this method of constructive progress. There will never be a statesman who succeeds who can use any other method in dealing with masses of his fellow men.

Douglas was the coming constructive statesman of the republic and all eyes were being focused on him. His life at the moment was the fevered center of the nation's thought. That his ambitions were boundless no one who knew the man doubted. That his patriotism was as genuine and as great all knew at last.

Lee studied every feature of his fine face. No eye could miss him in an assemblage of people, no matter how great the numbers. His compact figure was erect, aggressive, dominant. A personage, whose sense of power came from within, not without. He was master of himself and of others. He looked the lion and he was one. The lines of his face were handsome in the big sense, strong, regular, masculine. He drew young men as a magnet. His vitality inspired them. His stature was small in height, measured by inches, but of such dignity, power and magnetism that he suggested Napoleon.

He smiled into Colonel Lee's face and his smile lighted the room. Every man and woman present was warmed by it.

Douglas had scarcely greeted Mrs. Lee and passed into an earnest conversation with the young Congressman when Robert Toombs of Georgia entered.

Toombs had become within two years the successor of John C. Calhoun. He had the genius of Calhoun, eloquence as passionate, as resistless; and he had all of Calhoun's weaknesses. He called a spade a spade. He loathed compromise. Three years before he had swept the floor and galleries of the House with a burst of impassioned eloquence that had made him a national figure.

Lifting his magnificent head he had cried:

"I do not hesitate to avow before this House and the Country, and in the presence of the living God, that if by your legislation you seek to drive us from the Territory of California and New Mexico, purchased by the blood of Southern white people, and to abolish Slavery in the District of Columbia, thereby attempting to fix a national degradation upon half the States of this Confederacy, *I am for disunion*. The Territories are the common property of the United States. You are their common agents; it is your duty while they are in the Territorial state to remove all impediments to their free enjoyment by both sections - the slave holder and the non-slave holder!"

He was the man of iron will, of passionate convictions. He might lead a revolution. He could not compromise.

His rapidly growing power was an ominous thing in the history of the South. Lee studied his face with increasing fascination.

In this gathering no man or woman thought of wealth as the source of power or end of life. No one spoke of it. Office, rank, position, talent, beauty, charm, personality - these things alone could count. These men and women *lived*. They did not merely exist. They were making the history of the world and yet they refused to rush through life. Their souls demanded hours of repose, of thought, of joy and they took them.

Toombs' pocket was stuffed with a paper-backed edition of a

French play. It was his habit to read them in the original with keen enjoyment in moments of leisure. The hum of social life filled the room and strife was forgotten. Douglas and Toombs were boys again and Lee was their companion.

Mary Lee managed to avoid Stuart and took her seat beside Phil Sheridan - not to tease her admirer but to give to her Western guest the warmest welcome of the old South. She knew the dinner would be a revelation to Phil and she would enjoy his appreciation.

The long table groaned under the luxuries of the season. Course succeeded course, cooked with a delicate skill unknown to the world of to-day. The oysters, fresh, fat, luscious, were followed by diamond-back terrapin stew as a soup.

Phil tasted it and whispered to his fair young hostess.

"Miss Mary, what is this I'm eating?"

"Don't you like it?"

"I never expected to taste it on earth. I've only dreamed about it on high."

"It's only terrapin stew. We serve it as a soup."

"The angels made it."

"No, Aunt Hannah."

"I won't take it back. Angels only could brew this soup."

The terrapin was followed by old Virginia ham and turnip greens. And then came the turkey with chestnut stuffing and jellies. The long table, flashing with old china and silver, held the staples of ham and turkey as ornaments as well as dainties for the palate. The real delicacies were served later, the ducks which Doyle had sent the Colonel, and plate after plate of little, brown, juicy birds called sora, so tender and toothsome they could be eaten bones and all.

When Phil wound up with cakes and custards, apples, pears and nuts from the orchard and fields, his mind was swimming in a dream of luxury. And over it all the spirit of true hospitality brooded. A sense of home and reality as intimate, as genuine as if he sat beside his mother's chair in the little cottage in Ohio.

"Lord save me," he breathed. "If I stay here long I'll have but one hope, to own a plantation and a home like this -"

Toombs sat on Lee's right and Douglas on his left. Mr. and Mrs. Pryor occupied the places of honor beside Mrs. Lee.

The Colonel's keen eye studied Douglas with untiring patience. To his rising star, the man who loved the Union, was drawn as by a magnet. Toombs, the Whig, belonged to his own Party, the aristocracy of brains and the inheritors of the right to leadership. He was studying Toombs with growing misgivings. He dreaded the radicalism within the heart of the Southern Whig.

His eye rested on Sam, serving the food as assistant butler in Ben's absence. In the kink of his hair, the bulge of his smiling lips, the spread of his nostrils, the whites of his rolling eyes, he saw the Slave. He saw the mystery, the brooding horror, the baffling uncertainty, the insoluble problem of such a man within a democracy of self-governing freemen. He stood bowing and smiling over his guests, in shape a man. And yet in racial development a million years behind the wit and intelligence of the two leaders at his side.

Over this dusky figure, from the dawn of American history our fathers had wrangled and compromised. More than once he had threatened to divide or destroy the Union. Reason and the compromises of great minds had saved us. In Sam he saw this grinning skeleton at his feast.

He could depend on the genius of Douglas when the supreme crisis came. He felt the quality of his mind tonight. But could Douglas control the mob impulse of the North where such appeals as *Uncle Tom's Cabin* had gripped the souls of millions and reason no longer ruled life?

There was the rub.

There was no question of the genius of Douglas. The question was could any leadership count if the mob, not the man, became our real ruler? The task of Douglas was to hold the fanatic of the North while he soothed the passions of the radical of the South. Henry Clay had succeeded. But *Uncle Tom's Cabin* had not been written in his day.

Toombs was becoming a firebrand. His eloquence was doing in the South what Mrs. Stowe's novel was doing in the North - preparing the soil for revolution - planting gunpowder under the foundations of society.

Could these forces yet be controlled or were they already beyond control?

# CHAPTER V

After dinner, Jeb Stuart succeeded in separating Mary from Phil and began again his adoration. The men adjourned to the library to discuss the Presidential Campaign and weigh the chances of General Scott against Franklin Pierce. The comment of Toombs was grim in its sarcasm and early let him out of the discussion.

"It doesn't matter in the least, gentlemen, who is elected in November," he observed. "There's nothing before the country as yet. Not even an honest-to-God man."

Lee shook his head gravely.

Toombs parried his protest.

"I know, Colonel Lee, you're fond of the old General. You fought with him in Mexico. But -" he dropped his voice to a friendly whisper - "all the same, you know that what I say is true."

He took a cigar from the mantel, lighted it and waved to the group.

"I'll take a little stroll and smoke."

Custis took Phil to the cottage of the foreman to see a night school in session.

"You mean the overseer's place?" Phil asked eagerly, as visions of Simon Legree flashed through his mind.

"No - I mean Uncle Ike's cottage. He's the foreman of the farm. We have no white overseer."

Phil was shocked. He had supposed every Southern plantation had a white overseer as slave driver with a blacksnake whip in his hand. A negro foreman was incredible. As a matter of fact there were more negro foremen than white overseers in the South.

In Uncle Ike's cottage by the light of many candles the school for boys was in session. Custis' brother "Rooney," was the teacher. He had six pupils besides Sam. Not one of them knew his lesson to-night and Rooney was furious.

As Phil and Custis entered, he was just finishing a wrathful lecture. His pupils were standing in a row grinning their apologies.

"I've told you boys for the last three weeks that I won't stand this. You don't have to go to school to me if you don't want to. But if you join my school you've got to study. Do you hear me?"

"Yassah!" came the answer in solid chorus.

"Well, you'll do more than hear me to-night. You're going to heed what I say. I'm going to thrash the whole school."

Sam broke into a loud laugh. And a wail of woe came from every dusky figure.

"Dar now!"

"Hear dat, folks - ?"

"I been a tellin' ye chillun -"

"I lubs my spellin' book - but, oh, dat hickory switch!"

"Oh, Lordy -"

"Gib us anudder chance, Marse Rooney!"

"Not another chance," was the stern answer. "Lay off your coats."

They began to peel their coats. Big, strapping, husky fellows nudging one another and grinning at their fourteen-year-old schoolmaster. It was no use to protest.

They knew they deserved it. A whipping was one of the minor misfortunes of life. Its application was universal. No other method of discipline had yet been dreamed by the advanced thinkers and rulers of the world. "Spare the rod and spoil the child" was accepted as the Word of God and only a fool could doubt it. The rod was the emblem of authority for child, pupil, apprentice and soldier. The negro slave as a workman got less of it than any other class. It was the rule of a Southern master never to use the rod on a slave except for crime if it could be avoided. To flog one for laziness was the exception, not the rule.

The old Virginia gentleman prided himself particularly on the tenderness and care with which he guarded the life of his servants. If the weather was cold and his men exposed, he waited to see that they had dry clothes and a warm drink before they went to bed. He never failed to remember that his white skin could endure more than their sunburned dark ones.

The young school-teacher had no scruples on applying the rod. He selected his switches with care, and tested their strength and flexibility while he gave the bunch a piece of his mind.

"What do you think I'm coming down here every night for, anyhow?" he stormed.

"Lordy, Marse Rooney," Sam pleaded, "doan we all pay you fur our schoolin'?"

"Yes, you do when I can manage to choke it out of you. One dozen eggs a month or one pullet every two months. And I don't even ask you where you got the eggs or the pullet."

"Marse Rooney!" protested Sam. "Yer know we gets 'em outen our own yards er buys 'em from de servants."

"I hope you do. Though my mother says she don't know how we eat so many chickens and eggs at the house. Anyhow I'm not here because I'm going to get rich on the tuition you pay me. I'm not here for my health. I'm here from a sense of duty to you boys -"

"Yassah, we know dat, sah!"

"Give us annuder chance an' we sho' study dem lessons -"

"I gave you another chance the last time. I'll try a little hickory tea this time."

He began at the end of the line and belabored each one faithfully. They shouted in mockery and roared with laughter, scampered over the room and dodged behind chairs and tables.

Phil fairly split his sides laughing.

When the fun was over, they drew close to their teacher and promised faithfully to have every word of the next lesson. They nudged each other and whispered their jokes about the beating.

"Must er bin er flea bitin' me!"

"I felt sumfin. Don't 'zactly know what it wuz. Mebbe a chigger!"

"Must er been a flea. Hit bit me, too!"

Sam tried to redeem himself for failing on his lessons in arithmetic. He had long ago learned to read and write and had asked for a course in history. The young teacher had given him a copy of *Gulliver's Travels*.

"Look a here, Marse Rooney, I been a readin' dat book yer gimme -"

"Well, that's good."

"Yer say dat book's history?"

"Well, it's what we call fiction, but I think fiction's the very best history we can read. It may not have happened just that way but it's true all the same."

"Well, ef hit nebber happened, I dunno 'bout dat," Sam objected. "I been suspicionin' fer a long time dat some o' dem things that Gulliver say nebber happen nohow."

"You read it," the teacher ordered.

"Yassah, I sho gwine ter read it, happen er no happen. Glory be ter God. Just 'cause yer tells me, sah!"

# CHAPTER VI

The next morning found Phil walking again between the white, clean rows of the quarter houses. He was always finding something to interest him. Every yard had its gorgeous red autumn flowers. Some of them had roses in bloom. The walks from the gate to the door were edged with white-washed bricks or conch shells. The conch shells were souvenirs of summer outings at the seashore.

In the corner of the back yard there was the tall pole on which were hung five or six dried gourds with tiny holes cut in the sides for the martins. And every gourd had its black family. The martins were the guardians of the servants' chicken yards. The hawks were numerous and the woods close to the quarters. Few chickens were lost by hawks. The martins circled the skies in battalions, watching, chattering, guarding, basking in the southern sun.

At noon the assembly bell rang at the end of the Broadway of the quarters. From every cottage, from field and stable, black-smith shop, carpenter's shop, the house of the spinners, the weavers, the dairy, the negroes poured toward the shed beside the bell tower.

"What is it?" Phil asked of Custis.

"Saturday noon. All work stops."

"My Lord, it's been raining nearly all morning. The field

hands haven't worked a lick all day. Do they stop, too?"

"It's the unwritten law of the South. We would no more think of working on Saturday afternoon than on Sunday."

"What are they gathering under that shed for?" Phil inquired.

Custis led him to the shed where Ike, the foreman, stood with Mrs. Lee beside a long table on which were piled the provisions for the week to follow.

The negroes laughed and chattered like a flock of blackbirds picking grain in a wheat field. To each head of a family was given six pounds of meat for each person. A father, mother and two children received twenty-four pounds. Their bread was never rationed. The barrel in each cottage was filled from the grist mill, a bag full at a time. They had their own garden and flocks of chickens. Sugar, coffee and molasses were given on the first of each month.

"Come right back here now all ob you!" Ike shouted, "des ez quick ez yer put yo vittles away. De Missis gwine gib ye yo' winter close now, case she gwine ter Wes' Pint next week."

The provisions were swept from the long table. Out of the storehouse came huge piles of clothing and blankets. Each package was marked with the owner's name.

To each pair, man and wife, or two children, was given a new wool blanket. This was, of course, added to the stock each house had already. A woolen blanket was good for ten years' wear. Many a servant's house had a dozen blankets for each bed. Besides the blankets, to every woman with a baby was given a quilted comfort.

To each man, woman and child were allotted two complete woolen suits for the winter, a new pair of shoes and three pairs of stockings. In the spring two suits of cotton would be given for summer. The thrifty ones had their cedar chests piled with clothes. Many had not worn the suits given out a year ago.

The heads of large families trudged away with six or seven blankets, a comfort, and twenty suits of clothes. It sometimes took the father, mother and two of the children to carry the load.

But the most amazing thing which Phil saw was the sudden transformation of the shed into a market for the sale of slave produce to the mistress of Arlington.

Mrs. Lee had watched the distribution of clothes, blankets, quilts, shoes and stockings for the winter and then became the purchaser of all sorts of little luxuries which the slave had made in his leisure hours on Saturday afternoons and at night. The little boys and girls sold her dried wild fruits. The women had made fine jellies. They all had chickens and eggs to sell to the big house. Some had become experts in making peanut brittle and fudge.

They not only sold their wares here, but they also sold them in the market in Washington. The old men were expert basket and broom makers. The slaves made so much extra money on their chickens, peanuts, popcorn, fudge, brittle, molasses cakes, baskets, brooms, mats and taking in sewing, that they were able to buy many personal luxuries. Phil observed one dusky belle already arrayed in a silk dress for the Saturday afternoon outing with her beau. A few of them had their Sunday dresses made by fashionable mantua makers in Washington.

In addition to the regular distribution of clothing, the household supplied to the servants in rapid succession everything worn by master, mistress, son or daughter. Knowing that their clothes were being watched and guarded by longing eyes, they never wore them very long. Mary Lee was distributing a dozen dresses now to the girls. They had been made within the past year.

Phil observed Sam arrayed in a swallowtail coat of immaculate cut stroll by with his best girl. She was dressed in silk with full hoop-skirts, ruffles, ribbons and flowers.

Sid annoyed Sam by calling loudly:

"Doan yer stay too late ter dat party. Ef ye do I'll hatter sing fur ye -

> "Run, nigger, run, de patterole ketch you.
> Nigger run, de nigger flew,
> De nigger loss his best ole shoe!
> Run, nigger, run. Run, nigger, run. Run, nigger, run."

Sam waved his arm in a long laugh.

"Dey won't git me, chile. I'se er conjur man, I is!"

Phil had supposed the patrol of the mysterious mounted police of the South - the men who rode at night - were to the slave always a tragic terror.

It seemed a thing for joke and ribald song.

After lunch, the negroes entered on the afternoon's fun or work. The industrious ones plied their trades to earn money for luxuries. The boys who loved to fish and hunt rabbits hurried to the river and the fields. There was always a hound at their service for a rabbit hunt on Saturday afternoons. Some were pitching horse shoes. Two groups began to play marbles.

The marketing done for the house, the mistress of Arlington, with medicine case in hand, started on her round of healing for body and mind. Mary offered to go with her but the mother saw Stuart hovering about and quietly answered:

"No. You can comfort poor Jeb. He looks disconsolate."

Into every cottage she moved, a quiet, ministering angel. Every hope and fear of ailing young or old found in her an ear to hear, a heart to pity and an arm to save.

If she found a case of serious illness, a doctor was called and a nurse set to watch by the bedside. Every delicacy and luxury the big house held was at the command of the sufferer and that without stint.

In all these clean flower-set cottages there was not a single crippled servant maimed in the service of his master. No black man or woman was allowed to do dangerous work. All dangerous tasks were done by hired white laborers. They were hired by the day under contract through their boss. Even ditches on the farm if they ran through swamp lands infested by malaria, were dug by white hired labor. The master would not permit his slave to take such risks.

But the most important ministry of the mistress of Arlington was in the medicine for the soul which she brought to the life and character of each servant for whose training she had accepted responsibility.

To her even the master proudly and loyally yielded authority. Her sway over the servants was absolute in its spiritual power. Into their souls in hours of trial she poured the healing and inspiration of a beautiful spirit. The mistress of Arlington was delicate and frail in body. But out of her physical suffering the spirit rose to greater heights with each day's duty and service.

This mysterious power caught the warm imagination of the negroes. They were "servants" to others. They were her *slaves* and they rejoiced in the bond that bound them. They knew that her body had no rest from morning until far into the hours of the night if one of her own needed care. The master could shift his responsibility to a trained foreman. No forewoman could take her place. To the whole scheme of life she gave strength and beauty. The beat of her heart made its wheels go round.

The young Westerner studied her with growing admiration

Thomas Dixon

and pity. She was the mistress of an historic house. She was the manager of an estate. She was the counselor of every man, woman and child in happiness or in sorrow. She was an accomplished doctor. She was a trained nurse. She taught the hearts of men and women with a wisdom more profound and searching than any preacher or philosopher from his rostrum. She had mastered the art of dressmaking and the tailor's trade. She was an expert housekeeper. She lived at the beck and call of all. She was idolized by her husband. Her life was a supreme act of worship - a devotion to husband, children, friends, the poor, the slave that made her a high-priestess of humanity.

The thing that struck Phil with terrific force was that this beautiful delicate woman was the slave of slaves.

As a rule, they died young.

He began to wonder how a people of the intelligence of these proud white Southerners could endure such a thing as Slavery. Its waste, its extravagance, its burdens were beyond belief.

He laughed when he thought of his mother crying over *Uncle Tom's Cabin*. Yet a new edition of a hundred thousand copies had just come from the press.

Early Sunday morning Custis asked him to go down to the quarters to see Uncle Ben, the butler, who had not yet resumed his duties. He had sent an urgent message to his young master asking him to be kind enough to call on Sunday. The message was so formal and reserved Custis knew it was of more than usual importance.

They found the old man superintending a special breakfast of fried fish for two little boys, neatly served at a table with spotless cloth. Robbie and his friend, John Doyle, were eating the fish they had caught with Uncle Ben the day before. They were as happy as kings and talked of fish and fishing with the unction of veteran sportsmen.

The greeting to Custis was profound in its courtesy and reverence. He was the first born of the great house. He was, therefore, the prospective head of the estate. Jeffersonian Democrats had long ago abolished the old English law of primogeniture. But the idea was in the blood of the Virginia planter. The servants caught it as quickly as they caught the other English traits of love of home, family, kin, the cult of leisure, the habit of Church, the love of country. It was not an accident that the decisions of the courts of the Old South were quoted by English barristers and accepted by English judges as law. The Common Law of England was the law of Southern Seaboard States. It always had been and it is to-day.

"How is you dis mornin', Marse Custis?" Ben asked with a stately bow.

"Fine, Uncle Ben. I hope you're better?"

"Des tolerble, sah, des tolerble -" he paused and bowed to Phil. "An' dis is you' school-mate at Wes' Pint, dey tells me about?"

"Yes, Uncle," Phil answered.

"I'se glad ter welcome yer ter Arlington, sah. And I'se powerful sorry I ain't able ter be in de big house ter see dat yer git ebry thing ter make yer happy, sah. Dese here young niggers lak Sam do pooty well. But dey ain't got much sense, sah. And dey ain't got no unction'tall. Dey do de best dey kin an' dat ain't much."

"Oh, I'm having a fine time, Uncle Ben," Phil assured him.

"Praise de Lord, sah."

"Sam told me you wanted to see me, Uncle Ben," Custis said.

"'Bout sumfin mos' particular, sah -"

"At your service."

The old man waved to his wife to look after the boys' breakfast.

"Pile dem fish up on der plates, Hannah. Fill 'em up - fill'em up!"

"We're mos' full now!" Robbie shouted.

"No we ain't," John protested. "I jis begun."

Ben led the young master and his friend out the back door, past the long pile of cord wood, past the chicken yard to a strong box which he had built on tall legs under a mulberry tree. It was constructed of oak and the neatly turned gable roof was covered with old tin carefully painted with three coats of red. A heavy hasp, staple and padlock held the solid door.

Ben fumbled in his pocket, drew forth his keys and opened it. The box was his fireproof and ratproof safe in which the old man kept his valuables. His money, his trinkets, his hammer and nails, augur and bits, screwdriver and monkeywrench. From the top shelf he drew a tin can. A heavy piece of linen tied with a string served as a cover.

He carefully untied the string in silence. He shook the can. The boys saw that it was filled with salt of the coarse kind used to preserve meats.

Ben felt carefully in the salt, drew forth a shriveled piece of dark gristle, and held it up before his young master.

"Yer know what dat is, Marse Custis?"

Custis shook his head.

From the old man's tones of deep emotion he knew the matter was serious. He thought at once of the Hoodoo. But he could make out no meaning to this bit of preserved flesh.

"Never saw anything like it."

"Nasah. I spec yer didn't."

Ben pushed the gray hair back from his left ear. He wore his hair drawn low over the tips of his ears. It was a fad of his, which he never allowed to lapse.

"See anything funny 'bout de top o' dat year, sah?"

Custis looked carefully.

"It looks shorter -"

"Hit's er lot shorter. De top ob hit's clean gone, sah. Dat's why I allus combs my ha'r down close over my years -"

He paused and held up the piece of dried flesh.

"An' dat's hit, sah."

"A piece of your ear?"

"Hit sho is. Ye see, sah, a long time ergo when I wuz young an' strong ez er bull, one er dese here uppish niggers come ter our house drivin' a carriage frum Westover on de James, an' 'gin ter brag 'bout his folks bein' de bes' blood er ole Virginia. An' man I tells him sumfin. I tells dat fool nigger dat de folks at Westover wuz des fair ter midlin. Dat *our* folks wuz, an' allus wuz, de very fust fambly o' Virginy! I tells him, dat Marse Robert's father was General Light Horse Harry Lee dat help General Washington wid de Revolution. Dat he wuz de Govenor o' ole Virginy. Dat he speak de piece at de funeral o' George Washington, dat we all knows by heart, now -

"'Fust in war, fust in peace and fust in de hearts o' his countrymen.'

"I tells him dat Marse Robert's mother wuz a Carter. I tells him dat he could count more dan one hundred gemmen his kin. Dat his folks allus had been de very fust fambly in Virginy. I tells him dat he marry my Missis, de gran' daughter o' ole Gineral Washington his-salf - an' en -"

He paused.

"An' den, what ye reckon dat fool nigger say ter me?"

"Couldn't guess."

"He say General Washington nebber had no children. And den man, man, when he insult me lak dat, I jump on him lak a wil' cat. We fought an' we fit. We fit an' we fought. I got him down an' bit one o' his years clean off smooth wid his head. In de las' clinch he git hol' er my lef year a'fo' I could shake him, he bit de top of hit off, sah. I got him by the froat an' choke hit outen his mouf. And dar hit is, sah."

He held up the dried piece of his ear reverently.

"And what do you want me to do with it, Uncle Ben?" Custis asked seriously.

"Nuttin right now, sah. But I ain't got long ter live -"

"Oh, you'll be well in a few days, Uncle Ben."

"I mought an' den agin I moughtent. I been lyin' awake at night worryin' 'bout dat year o' mine. Ye see hit wouldn't do tall fur me ter go walkin' dem golden streets up dar in Heben wid one o' my years lopped off lake a shoat er a calf dat's been branded. Some o' dem niggers standin' on dat gol' sidewalk would laugh at me. An' dat would hurt my feelin's. Some smart Aleck would be sho ter holler, 'Dar come ole Ben. But he ain't got but one year!' Dat wouldn't do, tall, sah."

Phil bit his lips to keep from laughing. He saw the thing was no joke for the old man. It was a grim tragedy.

"What I wants ter axe, Marse Custis, is dat you promise me faithful, ez my young master, dat when I die you come to me, get dis year o' mine outen dis salt box an' stick hit back right whar it b'long 'fore dey nail me up in de coffin. I des can't 'ford ter walk down dem golden streets, 'fore all dat company, wid a piece er my year missin'. Will ye promise me, sah?"

Custis grasped the outstretched hand and clasped it.

"I promise you, Uncle Ben, faithfully."

"Den hit's all right, sah. When a Lee make a promise, hit's des ez good ez done. I know dat case I know who I'se er talkin' to."

He placed the piece of gristle back into the tin can, covered it with salt, tied the linen cover over it carefully, put it back on the shelf, locked the heavy oak door and handed Custis the key.

"I got annudder key. You keep dat one, please, sah."

Custis and Phil left the old man more cheerful than he had been for days.

# CHAPTER VII

As the sun was sinking across the gray waters of the river, reflecting in its silver surface a riot of purple and scarlet, the master of Arlington sat in thoughtful silence holding the fateful Book of the Slave in his hand. He had promised his friend, Edmund Ruffin, to give him an answer early next week as to a public statement.

He was puzzled as to his duty. To his ready protest that he was not a politician his friend had instantly replied that his word would have ten times the weight for that reason. So deep was his brooding he did not notice the two boys in a heated argument at the corner of the house.

Robbie Lee had drawn his barefoot friend, John, thus far. He had balked and refused to go farther.

"Come on, John," Robbie pleaded.

"I'm skeered."

"Scared of what?"

"Colonel Lee."

"Didn't you come to see him?"

"I thought I did."

"Well, didn't ye?"

"Yes."

"Come on, then!"

"No - "

"What you scared of him for?"

"He's a great man."

"But he's my Papa."

"He don't want to be bothered with little boys."

"Yes, he does, too. He hears everything I've got to say to him."

"Ain't you skeered of him?"

"No!"

Robbie seized John's hand again and before he could draw back dragged him to his father's side.

Lee turned the friendliest smile on John's flushed face and won his confidence before a word was spoken.

"Well, Robbie, what's your handsome little friend's name?"

"John Doyle, Papa."

"Your father lives on the farm just outside our gate, doesn't he?"

"Yessir," the boy answered eagerly.

His embarrassment had gone. But it was hard to begin his story. It had seemed easy at first, the need was so great. Now it seemed that he had no right to make the request he had in his heart.

He hung his head and dug his big toe in the gravel.

Robbie hastened to his rescue.

"John wants to tell you something, Papa," he began tenderly.

"All right," Lee cheerfully answered as he drew one boy within each arm and hugged them both. "What can I do for you, Johnnie?"

"I dunno, sir. I hope you can do somethin'."

"I will, if I can. I like to do things for boys. I was a little boy once myself and I know exactly how it feels. What is it?"

Again the child hesitated.

Lee studied the lines of his finely molded face and neck and throat. A handsomer boy of ten he had never seen. He pressed his arm closer and held him a moment until he looked up with a tear glistening in his blue eyes.

"Tell me, sonny -"

"My Ma's been cryin' all day, sir, and I want to do somethin' to help her -"

He paused and his voice failed.

"What has she been crying about?"

"We've lost our home, sir, and my daddy's drunk."

"You've lost your home?"

"Yessir. The sheriff come this mornin'. And he's goin' to put us out. Ma's most crazy. I ain't been a very good boy here lately -"

"No?"

"No, sir. I've been runnin' away and goin' fishin' and hurtin' my Ma's feelin's and now I wish I hadn't done it. I heard her sayin' this mornin' while she wuz cryin', that you wuz the only man she knowed on earth who could help us. She was afeared to come to see you. And I slipped out to tell ye. I thought if I could get you to come to see us, maybe you could tell Ma what to do and that would make up for my hurtin' her so when I run away from my lessons this week."

The Colonel gently pressed the boys away and rose with quick decision.

"I'll ride right up, sonny, and see your mother."

"Will you, Colonel Lee?" the child asked with pathetic eagerness.

"Just as soon as I can have my horse saddled."

Lee turned abruptly into the house and left the boy dazed. He threw his arms around Robbie, hugged him in a flash and was gone. Up the dusty way to the gate the little bare feet flew to tell glad tidings to a lonely woman.

She stood beside the window looking out on the wreck of her life in a stupor of wordless pain. She saw her boy leap the fence as a hound and rushed from the house in alarm to meet him.

He was breathless, but he managed to gasp his message.

"Ma - Ma - Colonel Lee's comin' to see you!"

"To see me?"

"Yes'm. I told him we'd lost our home and he said he'd come right up. And he's comin', too -"

The mother looked into the child's flushed face, saw the love light in his eyes and caught him to her heart.

"Oh, boy, boy, you're such a fine young one - my baby - as smart as a whip. You'll beat 'em all some day and make your poor old mother proud and happy."

"I'm going to try now, Ma - you see if I don't."

"I know you will, my son."

"I'll never run away again. You see if I do."

The boy stopped suddenly at the sight of Colonel Lee swiftly approaching.

"Run and wash your face," the mother whispered, "and tell your brothers to put on clean shirts. I want them to see the Colonel, too."

The boy darted into the house.

The woman looked about the yard to see if there were any evidences of carelessness. She had tried to keep it clean. The row of flowers that flamed in the beds beside the door was the finest in the county. She knew that. She was an expert in the culture of the prolific tall cosmos that blooms so beautifully in the Indian summers of Old Virginia.

A cur dog barked.

"Get under the house, sir!" she commanded.

The dog continued to look down the road at the coming horseman.

"Get under the house, I say - " she repeated and the dog slowly obeyed.

She advanced to meet her visitor. He hitched his horse to a swinging limb outside the gate and hurried in.

No introduction was necessary. The Colonel had known her husband for years and he had often lifted his hat to his wife in passing.

He extended his hand and grasped hers in quick sympathy.

"I'm sorry to learn of your great misfortune from your fine boy, Mrs. Doyle."

The woman's eyes filled with tears in spite of her firm resolution to be dignified.

"He *is* a fine - boy - isn't he, Colonel?"

"One of the handsomest little chaps I ever saw. You should be proud of him."

"I am, sir."

She drew her figure a bit higher instinctively. The movement was not lost on the keen observer of character. He had never noticed before the distinction of her personality. In a simple calico dress, and forty years of age, she presented a peculiarly winsome appearance. Her features were regular, and well rounded, the coloring of cheeks and neck and hands the deep pink of perfect health. Her eyes were a bright glowing brown. They were large, soulful eyes that spoke the love of a mother. She might scold her husband if provoked. But those eyes could never scold a child. They could only love him into obedience and helpfulness. They were shining mother eyes.

Lee studied her in a quick glance before speaking. He knew instinctively that he could trust her word.

Thomas Dixon

"Is there anything I can do, Mrs. Doyle?"

"Oh, I hope so, sir. My man's gone all to pieces to-day. He's good-hearted and kind if I do have to say it myself. But when the sheriff come to put us out, he just flopped and quit. And then he got drunk. I don't blame him much. If I hadn't been a woman and the mother of three fine boys and two as pretty little gals as the Lord ever give to a woman, I reckon I'd a got drunk, too."

She stopped, overcome with emotion and Lee hastened to ask:

"How did it happen, Mrs. Doyle?"

"Well, sir, you see, we hadn't quite paid for the place. You know it's hard with a big family of children on a little farm o' ten acres. It's hard to make a livin' let alone save money to pay for the land. But we wuz doin' it. We didn't have but two more payments to make when my man signed a note for his brother. His brother got sick and couldn't pay and they come down on us and we're turned out o' house and home. The sheriff's give us till Wednesday to get out and we've nowhere to go -"

A sob caught her voice.

"Don't say that, Madame. No neighbor of mine will ever be without a home so long as I have a house with a roof on it."

"Thank you, Colonel Lee," she interrupted, "but you know I can't let my man be a renter and see my husband and my sons workin' other people's land like nigger slaves. I got pride. I jus' can't do it. I'd rather starve."

"I understand, Madame," Lee answered.

The two older boys came awkwardly out into the yard. One of them was fourteen years old and the other sixteen.

The mother beckoned and they came to her with embarrassed step. Her face lighted with pride in their stalwart figures and well-shaped, regular features.

"Here's my oldest boy, William, Colonel Lee."

The Colonel took the outstretched hand with cordial grasp.

"I'm glad to know you, young man."

"And glad to see you, sir," he stammered, blushing.

"My next boy Drury, sir. He ain't but fourteen but he's a grown man."

Drury flushed red but failed to make a sound.

When they had moved away and leaned against the fence watching the scene out of the corner of an eye, the mother turned to the Colonel and asked:

"Do you blame me if I'm proud of my boys, Colonel?"

"I do not, Madame."

"The Lord made me a mother. All I know is to raise fine children and love 'em. My little gals is putty as dolls."

John suddenly appeared beside her and pulled her skirt.

"What's the matter?" she whispered.

"Pa's waked up. I told him Colonel Lee's here and he's washed his face and walks straight. Shall I fetch him out, too?"

"Yes, run tell him to come quick."

The boy darted back into the house.

"Johnnie's father wants to see you, Colonel Lee," the woman apologized.

"I'll be glad to talk to him, Madame."

"He'll be all right now. Your comin' to see us'll sober him. He'll be awful proud of the honor, sir."

Doyle emerged from the house and walked quickly toward the Colonel. His head was high. He smiled a welcome to his guest and his step was straight, light and springing, as if he were not quite sure he could rest his full weight on one foot and tried to get them both down at the same time.

Lee's face was a mask of quiet dignity. The tragedy in the woman's heart made the more pathetic the comedy of the half-drunken husband. Besides, he was philosopher enough to know that more than half the drunkenness of the world was the pitiful effort to smother a heartache.

The man's smile was a peculiarly winning one. His face was covered with a full growth of blond beard cut moderately long. He never shaved. His wife trimmed his beard in the manner most becoming to the shape of his head, the poise of his neck and evenly formed shoulders. He wore his hair full long and it curled about his neck in a deep blond wave. He might have posed for the model of Hoffman's famous picture of Christ. His eyes, a clear blue, were the finest feature of his personality. In spite of his lack of education, in spite of his shabby clothes, in spite of the smell of liquor he was a personality. His clean, high forehead, his aquiline nose, his straight eyebrows, his fair skin, his tall figure spoke the heritage of the great Nordic race of men. The race whose leaders achieved the civilization of Rome, conquered Europe and finally dominated civilization.

The difference between this man and the leader who wore the uniform of a Colonel was not in racial stock. It was purely an accident of the conditions of birth and training. Behind Lee lay two hundred years of wealth and culture. The poorer man was his kinsman of the centuries. The world had not been kind to him. He had lost the way of material success. Perhaps some kink in his mind, a sense of comedy, a touch of the old wanderlust of the ages.

Lee wondered what had kept him poor as he looked at the figure approaching. It was straight and fine in spite of the liquor.

Doyle's brain was just clear enough to realize that he had been highly honored in a call from the foremost citizen of Virginia. His politeness was extreme. And it was true. It was instinctive. It leaped from centuries of racial inheritance.

"We're proud of the honor you've done us, Colonel Lee," he announced.

He grasped the extended hand with a cordial, dignified greeting.

"I only hope I can be of some service to you and your family, Mr. Doyle."

"I'm sure you can, sir. Won't you come in, Colonel?"

"Thank you, it's so pleasant outside, we'll just sit down by the well, if you don't mind."

"Yessir. All right, sir."

Lee moved slowly toward the platform of the well with its old oaken bucket and tall sweep.

His wife threw a warning at her husband under her breath.

"Don't you say nothin' foolish now -"

"I won't."

"Your tongue's too long when it gets to waggin'."

"I'll mind, Ma," he smiled.

The woman called softly to her distinguished guest:

"You'll excuse me, Colonel, while I look after the supper. I'll be back in a minute."

"Certainly, Madame."

He could not have bowed with graver courtesy to the wife of Stephen A. Douglas.

"Have a seat here on the well, Colonel," Doyle invited.

Lee took his seat on the weather-beaten oak boards.

Doyle turned his foot on a rounded stone and set down a little ungracefully in spite of his effort to be fully himself. He saw at once his misstep and hastened to apologize.

"I'm sorry, Colonel, you've caught me with the smell of liquor, sir -"

He paused and looked over his garden in an embarrassed way.

"I know what has happened to you, Mr. Doyle, and you have my deepest sympathy."

"Thank you, sir."

"I might have done the same thing if I'd been in your position. Though, of course, liquor won't help things for you."

Doyle smiled around the corners of his blue eyes.

"No, sir, except while it's a swimmin' in the veins. Then for a little while you're great and rich and you don't care which a way the wind blows."

"The farm is lost beyond hope?"

"Yessir, clean gone - world without end."

"You had a lawyer?"

"The best in the county, old Jim Randolph. I didn't have no money to pay him. He said we'd both always voted the Whig ticket and he'd waive his retainer. I didn't know what he was wavin', but anyhow he tuck my case. And I will say he put up a nasty fight for me. He made one of the greatest speeches I ever heared in my life. Hit wuz mighty nigh worth losin' the farm ter hear him tell how I'd been abused and how fine a feller I wuz. An' when he los' the case, he cussed the Judge, he cussed the jury, he cussed the lawyers. He swore they was all fools and didn't know the first principles er law nohow. I sho enjoyed the fight, ef I did lose it. I couldn't pay him nothin' yet. But I did manage to get him a gallon of the best apple brandy I ever tasted."

"What do you think of doing?"

"I ain't had time ter think, sir. I don't think fast nohow and the first thing I had to do when I come home and tole the ole 'oman and she bust out cryin' - wuz ter get drunk. Somehow I couldn't stand it."

"You've never learned a trade?"

"No sir - nothin' 'cept farmin'. I said to myself - what's the use? These damned nigger slaves have learned all the trades. They say in the old days, they wuz just servants in the house and stables, and field hands. Now they've learnt *all* the trades. They're mechanics, blacksmiths, carpenters, wagon makers and everything. What chance has a poor white man got agin 'em? They don't have to worry about nothin'. They have everything they need before they lift their hands to do anything. They got plenty to eat for themselves and their families, no matter how many children they have. All they can eat, all they can wear, a warm house and a big fire in the winter. I have to fight and scratch to keep a roof over my head, wood in my fireplace, clothes on my back and somethin' to eat on my table. How can I beat the slave at a trade? Tain't no use to try. Ef you want to build a house, your own carpenters can do it. And if you haven't enough slave carpenters of your own, your neighbors have. They can hire 'em to you cheaper than I can work and live. They're goin' to *live* anyhow. That's settled because they're slaves. They're worth twelve hundred dollars apiece. Their life is precious. Mine don't count. I got to look after that myself and I got to look after my wife and children, too. Hit ain't right, Colonel, this Slavery business. You know that as well as I do. I've heard you say it, too -"

"I agree with you, Mr. Doyle. But if we set them all free to-morrow, and you had to compete with their labor, you couldn't live down to their standard of wages, could you?"

"No, I couldn't. They would kill me at that game, too. That's why I hate a free nigger worse than a slave -"

He paused and his face knotted with fury.

"Damn 'em all - why are they here anyhow?"

"Come, come, my friend," Lee protested. "It doesn't help to swear about it. They *are* here. Not by any wish of mine or of yours. We inherited this curse from the past. We have clung to old delusions while our smart Yankee friends have shifted the responsibilities on others."

"What *can* I do, Colonel?" Doyle asked desperately. "I don't know how to do anything but farm. I can't go into the fields and work with slaves as a field hand. And I couldn't get such work to do if I'd do it. I'll die before I'll come down to it. I might rent a little farm alongside of a free nigger. But he can beat me at that game. He can live on less and work longer hours than I do. He'll underbid me as a cropper. He can live and pay the owner four-fifths of the crop. I'd starve. What am I goin' to do?"

"Had you thought of moving West into one of the new Territories just opening?"

"Yessir. I'd thought of it. But how am I goin' to get there with a wife and five children?"

Lee rose and looked about the place thoughtfully.

"How much could you realize from the sale of your things?"

Doyle scratched his head doubtfully.

"I ain't got no idee, sir. I'm afraid not much. Ye see it's just home stuff. The old 'oman's awful smart. She raises enough chickens and turkeys and ducks and guineas to eat, and she sells a few eggs and young chickens and turkeys when they brings anything in the market. I got six sheep, a cow, a calf, a mule, a couple o' pigs in the pen. But they won't bring much money. Ye see I never felt so poor ez long ez I had a *home* where I can live independent like. That house ain't much, sir. But you ain't no idea how deep down in my heart it's got."

He paused and looked at it. The Colonel followed his gaze. It was a small frame structure standing in a yard filled with trees. A one-story affair with a sharp, gabled attic. Two dormer windows projected from the high roof and a solid brick chimney at each end gave it dignity. A narrow porch came straight out from the front door. On either side of the porch were built wooden benches and behind them on a lattice grew a luxuriant rambler rose. It was still blooming richly in the warm September sun.

"Ye see, sir," Doyle went on, "what we've got that's worth havin' can't be sold. I love the smell o' them roses. I wake up in the night and the breeze brings it in the window and it puts me to sleep like an old song my mother used to sing when I was a little shaver -"

He stopped short.

"I didn't mean to snivel, sir."

"I understand, my friend. No apologies are necessary."

"And that big scuppernong grape vine out there in the garden - I couldn't sell that. I planted it fifteen years ago. Folks told us we was too fur north here fur it to grow good. But I knowed better. You can see its covered a place as big ez the house. And you can smell them ripe grapes a hundred yards before ye get to the gate. I make a little wine outen 'em. We have 'em to eat a whole month. That garden keeps us goin' winter and summer. You see them five rows of flat turnips and the ruttabaggers beside 'em? I've cabbage enough banked under them pine tops to make a fifty-gallon barrel o' kraut and give us cabbage with our bacon all winter. We've got turnip greens, onions and collards. I've got corn and wheat in my crib and bacon enough to last me till next year. I raise the finest watermelons and mushmelons in the county and it ain't much trouble to live here. I never knowed how well off I wuz till the Sheriff come and told me I had to go."

"You're in the prime of life. You can go to a new country and begin over again. Why not?"

"If I could get there. I reckon I could."

He stopped short as his wife appeared by his side. She had heard Colonel Lee's last question.

"Of course, you can begin over again. Haven't we got three of the finest boys the Lord ever give a mother? They ain't got no chance here nohow. My baby boy's one o' the smartest youngsters in the county. Ef old Andy Jackson wuz a poor boy an' got ter be President, he might do the same thing ef we give him a chance -"

"Yes, I reckon we could, ef we had a chance," Doyle agreed doubtfully. "But it would be a hard pull to leave my ole Virginy home. You know that would pull you, Colonel - now wouldn't it?"

"Yes, it would," was the earnest answer.

"You see I wuz born in this country an' me daddy before me. I like it here. I like the feel of the air in the fall. There's a flock o' ducks now circlin' over that bend o' the river. The geese are comin'. I heard 'em honk high up in the sky last night. I like my oysters and terrapin. I like to shoot ducks and geese, rabbits and quail. I like the smell o' the water. I like the smell o' these fields. I like the way the sun shines and the winds blow down here. It's in my blood."

"But you'll go if you can get away," his wife interrupted cheerfully.

Two little girls timidly drew near. Their faces were washed clean and their shining blonde hair gleamed in circles of golden light as the rays of the setting sun caught it.

Lee smiled, took them both in his arms and kissed them.

A tear softened his eyes as he placed them on the ground.

"You're darling little dolls. No wonder your mother loves you."

"Run back in the house now, honeys," the mother said.

The children slowly obeyed, glancing back at the great man who had kissed them. They wondered why their daddy hadn't kissed them oftener.

"What do you think we ought to do, Colonel Lee?" the

woman asked eagerly.

"I can tell you what I would do, Madame, in your place -"

"What?"

The husband and wife spoke the word in chorus.

"I'd go West and begin again."

"But how'm I goin' to get away, sir?" the man asked blankly.

"Sell your things for the best price you can get and I'll loan you the balance of the money you'll need."

"Will you, sir?" the woman gasped.

"I ain't got no security for ye, Colonel - " Doyle protested.

"You are my friend and neighbor, Mr. Doyle. You're in distress. You don't need security. I'll take your note, sir, without endorsement."

"Glory to God!" the mother cried with face uplifted in a prayer of thanksgiving.

Doyle couldn't speak for a moment. He looked out over the roadway and got control of his feelings before trying. There was a lump in his throat which made his speech thick when at last he managed to grasp Lee's hand.

"I dunno how to thank you, sir."

"It will be all right, Mr. Doyle. Look after the sale of your things and I'll find out the best way for you to get there and let you know."

He mounted his horse and rode away into the fading sunset as they watched him through dimmed eyes.

# CHAPTER VIII

Lee had promised Edmund Ruffin his answer early in the week. Ruffin had just ridden up the hill and dismounted.

Mrs. Marshall, the Colonel's sister, on a visit from Baltimore, fled at his approach.

"Excuse me, Mary," she cried to Mrs. Lee. "I just can't stand these ranting fire-eating politicians. They make me ill. I'll go to my room."

She hurried up the stairway and left the frail mistress of the house to meet her formidable guest.

Ruffin was the product of the fierce Abolition Crusade. Hot-tempered, impulsive, intemperate in his emotions and their expression, he was the perfect counterpart of the men who were working night and day in the North to create a condition of mob feeling out of which a civil conflict might grow. *Uncle Tom's Cabin* had set him on fire with new hatreds. His vocabulary of profanity had been enlarged by the addition of every name in the novel. He had been compelled to invent new expressions to fit these characters. He damned them individually and collectively. He cursed each trait of each character, good and bad. He cursed the good points with equal unction and equal emphasis. In fact the good traits in Mrs. Stowe's people seemed to carry him to greater heights of wrath and profanity than the bad ones. He dissected each part of each character's anatomy, damned each part, put the parts

Thomas Dixon

together and damned the collection. And then he damned the whole story, characters, plot and scenes to the lowest pit and cursed the devil for not building a lower one to which he might consign it. And in a final burst of passion he always ended by damning himself for his utter inability to express *anything* which he really felt.

With all his ugly language, which he reserved for conversation with men, he was the soul of consideration for a woman. Mrs. Lee had no fear of any rude expression from his lips. She didn't like him because she felt in his personality the touch of mob insanity which the Slavery question had kindled. She dreaded this appeal to blind instinct and belief. With a woman's intuition she felt the tragic possibility of such leadership North and South.

She saw his leonine head and shaggy hair silhouetted against the red glow of the west with a shiver at its symbolism, but met him with the cordial greeting which every Southern woman gave instinctively to the friend of her husband.

"Come in, Mr. Ruffin," she welcomed.

He bowed over her hand and spoke in the soft drawl of the Southern planter.

"Thank you, Madame. I'm greatly honored in having you greet me at the door."

"Colonel Lee is expecting you."

The planter drew himself up with a touch of pride and importance.

"Yes'm. I sent him word I would be here at three. I was detained in Washington. But I succeeded in convincing the editor of *The Daily Globe* that my mission was one of grave importance. I not only desire to wish Colonel Lee God-speed on his journey to West Point and congratulate him on the honor conferred on Virginia by his appointment to the command of our Cadets - but -"

He paused, smiled and glanced toward the portico, as if he were holding back an important secret.

Mrs. Lee hastened to put him at his ease.

"You can trust my discretion in any little surprise you may have for the Colonel."

Ruffin bowed.

"I'm sure I can, Madame. I'm sure I can."

He dropped his voice.

"You know perhaps that I sent him a few days ago a scurrilous attack on the South by a Yankee woman - a new novel?"

"He received it."

"Has he read it?"

"Carefully. He has read it twice."

"Good!"

The planter breathed deeply, squared his shoulders and paced the floor with a single quick turn. He stopped before Mrs. Lee and spoke in sharp emphasis.

"I'm going to spring a little surprise on the public, Madame! A sensation that will startle the country, and God knows we need a little shaking just now -"

He paused and whispered.

"I'm so sure of what the Colonel will say that I've brought a reporter from the Washington *Daily Globe* with me -"

Mrs. Lee lifted her hand in dismay.

"He is here?"

"He is seated on the lawn just outside, Madame," Ruffin hastened to reassure her. "I thought at the last moment I'd better have him wait until I received Colonel Lee's consent to the interview."

"I'm glad you did."

"Oh, it will be all right, I assure you!"

"He might not wish to see a reporter -"

"So I told the young man."

"I'm afraid -"

"I'll pave the way, Madame. I'll pave the way. Colonel Lee and I are life-long friends. Will you kindly announce me?"

"The Colonel has just ridden up to the stables to give some orders about his horses. He'll be here in a moment."

Lee stepped briskly into the room and extended his hand.

"It's you, Ruffin. My apologies. I was called out to see a neighbor. I should have been here to receive you."

"No apologies, Colonel, Mrs. Lee has been most gracious."

The mistress of the house smiled.

"Make yourself at home, Mr. Ruffin. I shall hope to see you at dinner."

Ruffin stood respectfully until Mrs. Lee had disappeared.

"Pray be seated," Lee invited.

Ruffin seated himself on the couch and watched his host keenly.

Lee took a cigar from the mantel and offered it.

"A cigar, Ruffin?"

"Thanks."

"Now make yourself entirely at home, my good friend."

The planter lighted the cigar, blew a long cloud of smoke and settled in his seat.

"I'm glad to learn from Mrs. Lee that you have read the book I sent you - the Abolitionist firebrand."

"Yes."

Lee quietly walked to the mantel and got the volume.

"I have it here."

He turned the leaves thoughtfully.

Ruffin laughed.

"And, what do you think of it?"

The Colonel was silent a moment.

"Well, for those who like that kind of book - it's the kind of book they will like."

"Exactly!" Ruffin cried, slapping his knee with a blow that

bruised it. "And you're the man in all the South to tell the fool who likes that sort of book just how big a fool he is!"

Lee opened the volume again and turned the pages slowly.

"Ruffin, I don't read many novels -"

He paused as if in deep study.

"But this one I have read twice."

"I'm glad you did, sir," the planter snapped.

"And I must confess it stunned me."

"Stunned you?"

"Yes."

"How?"

"When I finished reading it, I felt like the overgrown boy who stubbed his toe. It hurt too bad to laugh. And I'm too big to cry."

"You amaze me, sir."

"That's the way I feel, my friend."

He paused, walked to the window, and gazed out at the first lights that began to flicker in the windows of the Capitol across the river.

"That book," he went on evenly, "is an appeal to the heart of the world against Slavery. It is purely an appeal to sentiment, to the emotions, to passion, if you will - the passions of the mob and the men who lead mobs. And it's terrible. As terrible as an army with banners. I heard the throb of drums through its pages. It will work the South into a frenzy. It will make

millions of Abolitionists in the North who could not be
reached by the coarser methods of abuse. It will prepare the
soil for a revolution. If the right man appears at the right
moment with a lighted torch -"

"That's just why, sir, as the foremost citizen of Virginia, you
must answer this slander. I have brought a reporter from the
*Globe* with me for that purpose. Shall I call him,"

"A reporter from a daily paper with a circulation of fifteen
thousand?"

"Your word, Colonel Lee, will be heard at this moment to the
ends of the earth, sir!"

"In a newspaper interview?"

"Yes, sir."

"Nonsense."

"It's your character that will count."

"Such an answer would be a straw pitched against a hurricane.
I am told that this book has already reached a circulation of
half a million copies and it has only begun. That means already
three million readers. To answer this book my pen should be
better trained than my sword -"

"It is, sir, if you'll only use it."

"The South has only trained swords. And not so many of them
as we think. We have no writers. We have no literature. We
have no champions in the forum of the world's thought. We
are being arraigned at the judgment bar of mankind and we are
dumb. It's appalling."

"That's why you must speak for us. Speak in our defense.
Speak with a tongue of flame -"

"I am not trained for speech, Ruffin. And the pen is mightier than the sword. I've never realized it before. The South will soon have the civilized world arraigned against her. The North with a thousand pens is stirring the faiths, the prejudices and the sentiments of the millions. This appeal is made in the face of History, Reason and Law. But its force will be as the gravitation of the earth, beyond the power of resistance, unless we can check it in time."

"When it comes to resistance," Ruffin snapped, "that's another question. The Yankees are a race of damned cowards and poltroons, sir. They won't fight."

Lee shook his head gravely.

"I've been in the service more than a quarter of a century, my friend. I've seen a lot of Yankees under fire. I've seen a lot of them die. And I know better. Your idea of a Yankee is about as correct as the Northern notion of Southern fighters. A notion they're beginning to exploit in cartoons which show an effeminate lady killer with an umbrella stuck in the end of his musket and a negro mixing mint juleps for him."

"We've got to denounce those slanders. I'm a man of cool judgment and I never lose my temper -"

He leaped to his feet purple with rage.

"But, by God, sir, we can't sit quietly under the assault of these narrow-minded bigots. You must give the lie to this infamous book!"

"How can I, my friend?"

"Doesn't she make heroes of law breakers?"

"Surely."

"Is there no reverence for law left in this country?"

"In Courts of Justice, yes. But not in the courts of passion, prejudice, beliefs, sentiment. The writers of sentiment sing the praises of law breakers -"

"But there can be no question of the right or wrong of this book. It is an infamous slander. I deny and impeach it!"

"I'm afraid that's all we can do, Ruffin - deny and impeach it. When we come down to brass tacks we can't answer it. From their standpoint the North is right. From our standpoint we are right, because our rights are clear under the Constitution. Slavery is not a Southern institution; it is a national inheritance. It is a national calamity. It was written into the Constitution by all the States, North and South. And if the North is ignorant of our rights under the laws of our fathers, we have failed to enlighten them - "

"We won't be dictated to, sir, by a lot of fanatics and hypocrites."

"Exactly, we stand on our dignity. We deny and we are ready to fight. But we will not argue. As an abstract proposition in ethics or economics, Slavery does not admit of argument. It is a curse. It's on us and we can't throw it off at once. My quarrel with the North is that they do not give us their sympathy and their help in our dilemma. Instead they rave and denounce and insult us. They are even more responsible than we for the existence of Slavery, since their ships, not ours, brought the negro to our shores. Slavery is an outgrown economic folly, a bar to progress, a political and social curse to the white race. It must die of its own weakness, South, as it died of its own weakness, North. It is now in the process of dying. The South has freed over three hundred thousand slaves by the voluntary act of the master. If these appeals of the mob leader to the spirit of the mob can be stopped, a solution will be found."

"It will never be found in the ravings of Abolitionists."

"Nor in the hot tempers of our Southern partisans, Ruffin.

Thomas Dixon

Look in the mirror, my good friend. Chattel Slavery is doomed because of the superior efficiency of the wage system. Morals have nothing to do with it. The Captain of Industry abolished Chattel Slavery in the North, not the preacher or the agitator. He established the wage system in its place because it is a mightier weapon in his hand. It is subject to but one law. The iron law of supply and demand. Labor is a commodity to be bought and sold to the highest bidder. And the highest bidder is at liberty to bid lower than the price of bread, clothes, fuel and shelter, if he chooses. This system is now moving Southward like a glacier from the frozen heart of the Northern mountains, eating all in its path. It is creeping over Maryland, Kentucky, Missouri. It will slowly engulf Virginia, North Carolina and Tennessee and the end is sure. Its propelling force is not moral. It is soulless. It is purely economic. The wage earner, driven by hunger and cold, by the fear of the loss of life itself - is more efficient in his toil than the care-free negro slave of the South, who is assured of bread, of clothes, of fuel and shelter, with or without work. Slavery does not admit of argument, my friend. To argue about it is to destroy it."

"I disagree with you, sir!" Ruffin thundered.

"I know you do. But you can't answer this book."

"It can be answered, sir."

Lee paced the floor, his arms folded behind his back, paused and watched Ruffin's flushed face. He shook his head again.

"The book is unanswerable, because it is an appeal to emotion based on a study of Slavery in the abstract. If no allowance be made for the tender and humane character of the Southern people or the modification of statutory law by the growth of public sentiment, its imaginary scenes are within the bounds of the probable. The story is crude, but it is told with singular power without a trace of bitterness. The blind ferocity of Garrison, who sees in every slaveholder a fiend, nowhere appears in its pages. On the other hand, Mrs. Stowe has painted one slaveholder as gentle and generous. Simon Legree, her villain, is a Yankee who has moved South and taken advantage of the power of a master to work evil. Such men have come South. Such things might be done. It is precisely this possibility that makes Slavery indefensible. You know this. And I know it."

"You astound me, Colonel."

"Yes, I'm afraid I do. I'd like to speak a message to the South about this book. I've a great deal more to say to my own people than to our critics."

Ruffin rose, thrust his hands in his pockets, walked to the window, turned suddenly and faced his host.

"But look here, Colonel Lee, I'm damned if I can agree with you, sir! Suppose Slavery *is* wrong - an economic fallacy and a social evil - I don't say it is, mind you. Just suppose for the sake of argument that it is. We don't propose to be lectured on this subject by our inferiors in the North. The children of the men who stole these slaves from Africa and sold them to us at a profit!"

Lee laughed softly.

"The sins of an inferior cannot excuse the mistakes of a superior. The man of superior culture and breeding should lead the world in progress. What has come over us in the South, Ruffin? Your father and mine never defended Slavery. They knew it was to them, their children and this land, a curse. It was a blessing only to the savage who was being taught the rudiments of civilization at a tremendous cost to his teacher. The first Abolition Societies were organized in the South. Washington, Jefferson, Madison, Monroe, Randolph, all the great leaders of the old South, the men whose genius created this republic - all denounced Slavery. They told us that it is a poison, breeding pride and tyranny of character, that it corrupts the mind of the child, that it degrades labor, wears

Thomas Dixon

out our land, destroys invention, and saps our ideal of liberty. And yet we have begun to defend it."

"Because we are being hounded, traduced and insulted by the North, yes -"

"Yes, but also because we must have more land."

"We've as much right in the West as the North."

"That's not the real reason we demand the right of entry. We are exhausting the soil of the South by our slipshod farming on great plantations where we use old-fashioned tools and slave labor. We refuse to study history. Ancient empires tried this system and died. The Carthagenians developed it to perfection and fell before the Romans. The Romans borrowed it from Carthage. It destroyed the small farms and drove out the individual land owners. It destroyed respect for trades and crafts. It strangled the development of industrial art. And when the test came Roman civilization passed. You hot-heads under the goading of Abolition crusaders now blindly propose to build the whole structure of Southern Society on this system."

"We've no choice, sir."

"Then we must find one. Slowly but surely the clouds gather for the storm. We catch only the first rumblings now but it's coming."

Ruffin flared.

"Now listen to me, Colonel. I'm a man of cool judgment and I never lose my temper, sir -"

He choked with passion, recovered and rushed on.

"If they ever dare attack us, we won't need *writers*. We'll draw our swords and thrash them! The South is growing rich and powerful."

Lee lifted his hand in a quick gesture of protest.

"A popular delusion, my friend. Under Slave labor the South is growing poorer daily. While the Northern States, under the wage system, ten times more efficient, are draining the blood and treasure of Europe and growing richer by leaps and bounds. Norfolk, Richmond and Charleston should have been the great cities of the Eastern Seaboard. They are as yet unimportant towns in the world commerce. Boston, Philadelphia and New York have become the centers of our business life, of our trade, our culture, our national power. While slavery is scratching the surface of our soil with old-fashioned plows, while we quit work at twelve o'clock every Saturday, spend our Sundays at church, and set two negroes to help one do nothing Monday morning, the North is sweeping onward in the science of agriculture. While they invent machines which double their crops, cut their labor down a hundred per cent, we are fighting for new lands in the West to exhaust by our primitive methods. The treasures of the earth yet lie in our mines untouched by pick or spade. Our forests stand unbroken - vast reaches of wilderness. The slave is slow and wasteful. Wage labor, quick, efficient. Our chief industry is the breeding of a race of feverish politicians."

"You know, Colonel Lee, as well as I do that Slavery in the South has been a blessing to the negro."

Lee moved his head in quick assent.

"I admit that Slavery took the negro from the jungle, from a slavery the most cruel known to human history, that it has taught him the use of tools, the science of agriculture, the worship of God, the first lessons in the alphabet of humanity. But unless we can now close this school, my friend, somebody is going to try to divide this Union some day -"

Ruffin struck his hands together savagely.

"The quicker the better, I say! If the children of the men who created this republic are denied equal rights under its laws and in its Territories, then I say, to your tents, oh, Israel!"

"And do you know what that may mean?"

"A Southern and a Northern Nation. Let them come!"

"The States have been knit together slowly, but inevitably by steam and electricity. I can conceive of no greater tragedy than an attempt to-day to divide them."

"I can conceive of no greater blessing!" Ruffin fairly shouted.

"So William Lloyd Garrison, the leader of Abolition, is saying in his paper *The Liberator*. And, Ruffin, unless we can lock up some hot-heads in the South and such fanatics as Garrison in the North, the mob, not the statesman, is going to determine the laws and the policy of this country. Somebody will try to divide the Union. And then comes the deluge! When I think of it, the words of Thomas Jefferson ring through my soul like an alarm bell in the night. 'I tremble for my country when I reflect that God is just and that His justice cannot sleep forever. Nothing is more certainly written in the book of fate than these black people shall be free -'"

Ruffin lifted his hand in a commanding gesture.

"Don't omit his next sentence, sir - 'nor is it less certain, that the two races, equally free, cannot live under the same government -'"

"Exactly," Lee answered solemnly. "And that is the only reason why I have ever allowed myself to own a slave for a moment - the insoluble problem of what to do with him when freed. The one excuse for Slavery which the South can plead without fear before the judgment bar of God is the blacker problem which their emancipation will create. Unless it can be brought about in a miracle of patience, wisdom and prayer."

He paused and smiled at Ruffin's forlorn expression.

"Will you call your reporter now to take my views?"

"No, sir," the planter growled. "I've changed my mind."

The Colonel laughed softly.

"I thought you might."

Ruffin gazed in silence through the window at the blinking lights in Washington, turned and looked moodily at his calm host. He spoke in a slow, dreamy monotone, his eyes on space seeing nothing:

"Colonel Lee, this country is hell bent and hell bound. I can see no hope for it."

Lee lifted his head with firm faith.

"Ruffin, this country is in God's hands - and He will do what's right -"

"That's just what I'm afraid, sir!" Ruffin mused. "Oh, no - I - don't mean that exactly. I mean that we must anticipate -"

"The wisdom of God?"

"That we must prepare to meet our enemies, sir."

"I agree with you. And I'm going to do it. I've been doing a lot of thinking and *soul* searching since you gave me this troublesome book to read -"

He stopped short, rose and drew the old-fashioned bell cord.

Ben appeared in full blue cloth and brass buttons, on duty again as butler.

"Yassah -"

"I'm glad to see you, Ben. You're feeling yourself again?"

"Yassah. Praise God, I'se back at my place once mo', sah."

The master lifted his hand in warning.

"Take care of yourself now. No more risks. You're not as young as you once were."

"Thankee, sah."

"Ask Mrs. Lee to bring me the document on my desk. Find Sam and fetch him here."

Ben bowed.

"Yassah. Right away, sah."

Lee turned to his guest genially.

"I'm going to ask you to witness what I'm about to do, Ruffin. And you mustn't take offense. We differ about Slavery and politics in the abstract, but whatever our differences on the surface, you are an old Virginia planter and I trust we shall always be friends."

The two men clasped hands and Ruffin spoke with deep emotion.

"I am honored in your friendship, Colonel Lee. However I may differ with you about the Union, we agree on one thing, that the old Dominion is the noblest state on which the sun has ever shown!"

Lee closed his eyes as if in prayer.

"On that we are one. Old Virginia, the mother of Presidents

and of states, as I leave her soil I humbly pray that God's blessings may ever rest upon her!"

"So say I, sir," Ruffin responded heartily. "And I'll try to do the cussin' for her while you do the praying."

Mrs. Lee entered and handed to her husband a folded document, as Ben came from the kitchen with Sam, who bowed and grinned to every one in the room.

Lee spoke in low tones to his wife.

"Ask the young people to come in for a moment, my dear."

Mrs. Lee crossed quickly to the library door and called:

"Come in, children, Colonel Lee wishes to see you all."

Mary, Stuart, Custis, Phil, Robbie and Sid pressed into the hall in curious, expectant mood. Mrs. Marshall knew that Ruffin was still there, but her curiosity got the better of her aversion. She followed the children, only to run squarely into Ruffin.

He was about to speak in his politest manner when she stiffened and passed him.

Ruffin's eye twinkled. He knew that she saw him. She hated him for his political views. She also knew that he hated her husband, Judge Marshall, with equal cordiality. His pride was too great to feel the slightest hurt at her attempt to ignore him. She was a fanatic on the subject of the Union. All right, he was a fanatic on the idea of an independent South. They were even. Let it be so.

With a toss of his head, he turned toward Lee who had seated himself at the table behind the couch.

The children were chatting and laughing as they entered. A sudden hush fell on them as they caught the serious look on the Colonel's face. He was writing rapidly. He stopped and fixed a seal on the paper which he held in his hand. He read it carefully, lifted his eyes to the group that had drawn near and said:

"Children, my good friend, Mr. Ruffin, has called to-day to bid us God-speed on our journey North. And he has asked me to answer *Uncle Tom's Cabin*. I've called you to witness the only answer I know how to make at this moment."

He paused and turned toward Sam.

"Come here, Sam."

The young negro rolled his eyes in excited wonder about the room and laughed softly at nothing as he approached the table.

"Yassah, Marse Robert."

"How old are you, Sam?"

"Des twenty, sah."

"I had meant to wait until you were twenty-one for this, but I have decided to act to-day. You will arrange to leave here and go with us as far as New York."

The negro bowed gratefully.

"Yassah, thankee sah, I sho did want ter go norf wid you, sah, but I hated to axe ye."

Lee handed Sam the document.

"You will go with me a free man, my boy. You are the only slave I yet hold in my own right. I have just given you your deed of emancipation. From this hour you are your own master. May God bless you and keep you in health and strength and give you long life and much happiness."

Sam stared at the paper and then at the kindly eyes of his old master. A sob caught his voice as he stammered:

"May God bless you, Marse Robert -"

Ben lifted his hands in benediction and his voice rang in the solemn cadence of the prophet and seer:

"And let the glory of His face shine upon him forever!"

Mrs. Marshall stooped and kissed her brother.

"You're a true son of Virginia, Robert, in this beautiful answer you make to-day to all our enemies."

She rose and faced Ruffin with square antagonism.

Lee turned to the old butler.

"And Ben, tell all our servants of the estate that, under the will of Mrs. Lee's father I will in due time set them free. I would do so to-day if the will had not fixed the date."

Ben bowed gravely.

"I'se proud to be your servant, Marse Robert and Missis, and when my freedom comes frum yo' hands, I'll be prouder still to serve you always."

With head erect Ben proudly led the dazed young freedman from the hall to the kitchen where his reception was one of mixed wonder and pity.

There fell a moment's awkward silence, broken at last by Stuart's clear, boyish voice. He saw Ruffin's embarrassment. He knew the man's fiery temper and wondered at his restraint.

"Well, Mr. Ruffin," Stuart began, "we may not see as clearly as Colonel Lee to-day, but he's my commander, sir, and I'll say he's right."

Ruffin faced Lee with a look of uncompromising antagonism and fairly shot his words.

"And for the millions of the South, I say he's wrong. There's a time for all things. And this is not the time for such an act. From the appearance of this book you can rest assured the emancipation of slaves in the South will cease. We will never be bullied into freeing our slaves by slander and insult. Colonel Lee's example will not be followed. The fanatics of the North have begun to spit on our faces. There's but one answer to an insult - and that's a blow!"

Lee stepped close to the planter, laid one hand gently on his shoulder, searched his angry eyes for a moment and slowly said:

"And thrice is he armed, my friend, who hath his quarrel just. I set my house in order before the first blow falls."

Ruffin smiled and threw off the ugly strain.

"I'm sorry, sir," he said with friendly indifference, "that my mission has been a failure."

"And I'm sorry we can't agree."

"I won't be able to stay to dinner, Mrs. Lee, and I bid you all good evening."

With a wave of his hand in a gesture behind which lurked the tingling of taut nerves, he turned and left.

The beat of his horse's hoof echoed down the road with a sharp, angry crack.

# CHAPTER IX

On Sunday the whole plantation went to Church. The negroes sat in the gallery and listened with rapt attention to the service. They joined its ritual and its songs with their white folks in equal sincerity and more profound emotion.

At the crossroads the stream of carriages, carts and buggies and horseback riders parted. To the right, the way led to the Episcopal Church, the old English establishment of the State, long since separated from secular authority, yet still bearing the seal of county aristocracy. Colonel Lee was a devout member of this church. Mrs. Lee was the inspiration of its charities and the soul of its activities.

A few of the negroes of the estate attended it with the master and mistress of Arlington. By far the larger number turned to the left at the cross roads and found their way to the Antioch Baptist Church. The simplicity of its service, the fervor of its singing, and above all the emotional call of its revivals which swept the country each summer appealed to the warm-hearted Africans. They took to the Baptist and Methodist churches as ducks to water. The master made no objection to the exercise of their right to worship God as their consciences called. He encouraged their own preachers to hold weekly prayer meetings and exhort his people in the assembling places of the servants.

Nor did he object to the dance which Sam, who was an Episcopalian, invariably organized on the nights following

Thomas Dixon

prayer and exhortation.

This last Sunday was one of tender farewells to friends and neighbors. They crowded about the Colonel after the services. They wished him health and happiness and success in his new work.

The last greeting he got from an old bent neighbor of ninety years. It brought a cloud to his brow. All day and into the night the thought persisted and its shadow chilled the hours of his departure. James Nelson was his name, of the ancient family of the Nelsons of Yorktown.

He held Lee's hand a long time and blinked at him with a pair of keen, piercing eyes - keen from a spiritual light that burned within. He spoke in painful deliberation as if he were translating a message.

"I am glad you are going to West Point, Colonel Lee. You will have time for thinking. You will have time to study the art of war as great minds must study it alone if they lead armies to victory. Generals are not developed in the saddle on our plains fighting savages. Our country is going to need a leader of supreme genius. I saw him in a vision, the night I read in the *Richmond Enquirer* that you had been called to West Point. I shall not see you again. I am walking now into the sunset. Soon the shadows will enfold me and I shall sleep the long sleep. I am content. I have lived. I have loved. I have succeeded and failed. I have swept the gamut of human passion and human emotion. I have no right to more. Yet I envy you the glory of manhood in the crisis that is coming. May the God of our fathers keep you and teach you and bless you is my prayer."

Lee was too deeply moved for words to reply. He pressed his old friend's hand, held it in silence and turned away.

The young people rode horseback. Never in his life had Phil seen anything to equal the easy grace with which these

Southern girls sat their horses. Their mothers before them had been born in the saddle. Their ease, their grace was not an acquirement of the teacher. It was bred in the bone.

When a boy challenged a girl for a race, the challenge was instantly accepted. Their saddles were made of the finest leather which the best saddle makers of England and America could find. Their girths were set with double silver buckles. A saddle never turned.

When the long procession reached the gates of Arlington, it seemed to Phil that half the congregation were going to stop for dinner. A large part of them did. Every friend and neighbor who pressed Colonel Lee's hand, or the hand of his wife, had been invited.

When they reached the Hall and Library to talk, their conversation covered a wide range of interest. The one topic tabooed was scandal. It might be whispered behind closed doors. It was never the subject of conversation in an assembly of friends and neighbors in the home. They talked of the rich harvest. They discussed the changes in the fortunes of their mutual friends. They had begun to demand better roads. They discussed the affairs of the County, the Church, the State. The ladies chatted of fashions, of course. But they also discussed the latest novels of George Eliot with keen interest and true insight into their significance in the development of English literature. They knew their Dickens, Thackeray and Scott almost by heart - especially Scott. They expressed their opinions of the daring work of the new author with enthusiasm. Some approved; others had doubts. They did not yet know that George Eliot was a woman.

The chief topic of conversation among the men was politics, State and National. The problems of the British Empire came in for a share of the discussion. These men not only read Burke and Hume, Dickens and Scott, they read the newspapers of England and they kept up with the program of English political parties as their fathers had. And they quoted their opinions as authority for a younger generation. On the shelves of the library could be seen the classics in sober bindings and sprinkled with them a few French authors of distinction.

Over all brooded the spirit of a sincere hospitality, gentle, cordial, simple, generous. They did not merely possess homes, they loved their homes. The two largest words in the tongue which they spoke were Duty and Honor. They were not in a hurry. The race for wealth had never interested them. They took time to play, to rest, to worship God, to chat with their neighbors, to enjoy a sunset. They came of a race of world-conquering men and they felt no necessity for hurrying or apologizing for their birthright.

It was precisely this attitude of mind which made the savage attack of the Abolitionists so far-reaching in its possible results.

# CHAPTER X

The morning of the departure dawned with an overcast sky, the prophecy of winter in the gray clouds that hung over the surface of the river. A chill mist, damp and penetrating, crept up the heights from the water's edge and veiled the city from view.

Something in the raw air bruised afresh the thought of goodbye to the Southland. The threat of cold in Virginia meant the piling of ice and snow in the North. Not a sparrow chirped in the hedges. Only a crow, passing high in the dull sky, called his defiance of wind and weather.

The Colonel made his final round of inspection to see that his people were provided against the winter. Behind each servant's cottage, a huge pile of wood was stacked. The roofs were in perfect order. The chimneys were pouring columns of smoke. It hung low at first but rolled away at the touch of the breeze from the North.

With Mrs. Lee he visited the aged and the sick. The thing that brought the smile to each withered mouth was the assurance of their love and care always.

Among the servants Sam held the center of interest. The wonderful, doubtful, yet fascinating thing had come to him. He had been set free. In each heart was the wish and with it fear of the future. The younger ones laughed and frankly envied him. The older ones wagged their heads doubtfully.

Thomas Dixon

Old Ben expressed the best feelings of the wiser as he took Sam's hand for a fatherly word. He had finished the packing in an old cowhide trunk which Custis had given him.

"We's all gwine ter watch ye, boy, wid good wishes in our hearts and a whole lot er misgivin's a playin' roun' in our min'."

"Don't yer worry 'bout me, Uncle Ben. I'se all right."

He paused and whispered.

"Ye didn't know dat Marse Robert done gimme five hundred dollars in gol' - did ye?"

"Five hundred dollars in gol'!" Ben gasped.

Sam drew the shining yellow eagles from the bag in his pocket and jingled them before the old man's eyes.

"Dar it is."

Ben touched it reverently.

"Praise God fer de good folks He give us."

"I'se er proud nigger, I is. I'se sorry fur dem dat b'longs to po' folks."

Ben looked at him benignly.

"Don't you be too proud, boy. You'se powerful young and foolish. Yer des barely got sense enough ter git outen a shower er rain. Dat money ain't gwine ter las yer always."

"No, but man, des watch my smoke when I git up North. Yer hear frum me, yer will."

"I hopes I hear de right news."

Sam replaced his coin with a touch of authority in possession.

"Don't yer worry 'bout me no mo'. I'se a free man now an' I gwine ter come into de Kingdom."

The last important task done by the Colonel before taking the train for New York was the delivery to his lawyers of instructions for the removal of the Doyles and the placing in his hands sufficient funds for their journey.

He spent a day in Washington investigating the chances of the new settler securing a quarter section of land in Miami County, Kansas, the survey of which had been completed. He selected this County on the Missouri border to please Mrs. Doyle. She wished to live as near the line of old Virginia's climate as possible and in a country with trees.

Doyle promised to lose no time in disposing of his goods. The father, mother, three sons and two little girls were at Arlington to bid the Colonel and his family goodbye. They were not a demonstrative people but their affection for their neighbor and friend could not be mistaken.

The mother's eyes followed him with no attempt to hide her tears. She wiped them away with her handkerchief. And went right on crying and wiping them again. The boys were too shy to press forward in the crowd and grasp the Colonel's hand.

On arrival in New York the party stopped at the new Hotel Astor on Broadway. Colonel Lee had promised to spend a day at Fort Hamilton, his old command. But it was inconvenient to make the trip until the following morning.

Besides, he had important business to do for Sam. He had sent two of the servants, whom he had emancipated, to Liberia, and he planned the same journey for Sam. He engaged a reservation for him on a steamer sailing for Africa, and returned to the hotel at nine o'clock ready to leave for Fort Hamilton.

He was compelled to wait for Sam's return from the boarding house for colored people on Water Street where he had been sent by the proprietor of the Astor. Not even negro servants were quartered in a first-class hotel in New York or any other Northern city.

Sam arrived at half-past nine, and the Colonel strolled down Broadway with him to the little park at Bowling Green. He found a seat and bade Sam sit down beside him.

The boy watched the expression on his old master's face with dread. He had a pretty clear idea what this interview was to be about and he had made up his mind on the answer. His uncle, who had been freed five years before, had written him a glowing letter about Liberia.

He dreaded the subject.

"You know, of course, Sam," the Colonel began, "that your life is now in your own hands and that I can only advise you as a friend."

"An' I sho's glad ter have ye he'p me, Marse Robert."

"I'm going to give you the best advice I can. I'm going to advise you to do exactly what I would do if I were in your place."

"Yassah."

"If I were you, Sam, I wouldn't stay in this country. I'd go back to the land of my black fathers, to its tropic suns and rich soil. You can never be a full-grown man here. The North won't have you as such. The hotel wouldn't let you sleep under its roof, in spite of my protest that you were my body-servant. In the South the old shadow of your birth will be with you. If you wish to lift up your head and be a man it can't be here. No matter what comes in the future. If every black man, woman and child were set free to-morrow, there are not enough negroes to live alone. The white man will never make you his equal in the world he is building. I've secured your passage to Liberia and I will pay for it without touching the money which I gave you. What do you think of it?"

Sam scratched his head and looked away embarrassed. He spoke timidly at first, but with growing assurance.

"I'se powerful 'fraid dat Liberia's a long way frum home, Marse Robert."

"It is. But if you wish to be a full-grown man, it's your chance to-day. It will be the one chance of your people in the future as well. Can you make up your mind to face the loneliness and build your home under your own vine and fig tree? There you can look every man in the face, conscious that you're as good as he is and that the world is yours."

"I'se feared I ain't got de spunk, Marse Robert."

"The gold in your pocket will build you a house on public lands. You know how to farm. Africa has a great future. You've seen our life. We've taught you to work, to laugh, to play, to worship God, to love your home and your people. You're only twenty years old. I envy you the wealth of youth. I've reached the hilltop of life. Your way is still upward for a quarter of a century. It's the morning of life, boy, and a new world calls you. Will you hear it and go?"

"I'se skeered, Marse Robert," Sam persisted, shaking his head gravely.

Lee saw the hopelessness of his task and changed his point of appeal.

"What do you think of doing?"

"Who, me?"

"Who else? I can't think for you any longer."

"Oh, I'll be all right, sah. I foun' er lot er good colored friends in de bordin' house las' night. Wid dat five hundred dollars, I be livin' in clover here, sah, sho. I done talk wid a feller 'bout goin' in business."

"What line of business?"

"He gwine ter sho me ter-day, sah."

"You don't think you might change your mind about Liberia?"

"Na sah. I don't like my uncle dat's ober dar, nohow."

"Then I can't help you any more, Sam?"

"Na sah, Marse Robert. Y'u been de bes' master any nigger eber had in dis worl' an' I ain't nebber gwine ter fergit dat. When I feels dem five hundred dollars in my pocket I des swells up lak I gwine ter bust. I'se dat proud o' myse'f an' my ole marster dat gimme a start. Lordee, sah, hit's des gwine ter be fun fer me ter git long an' I mak' my fortune right here. Ye see ef I don't -"

Lee smiled indulgently.

"Watch out you don't lose the little one I gave you."

"Yassah, I got hit all sewed up in my close."

The old master saw that further argument would be useless. He rose wondering if his act of emancipation were not an act of cowardice - the shirking of responsibility for the boy's life. His mouth closed firmly. That was just the point about the institution of Slavery. No such responsibility should be placed on any man's shoulders.

Sam insisted on ministering to the wants of the family until he saw them safely on the boat for West Point. He waved each member a long goodbye. And then hurried to his new chum at the boarding house on Water Street. This dusky friend had won Sam's confidence by his genial ways on the first night of their acquaintance. He had learned that Sam had just been freed. That this was his first trip to New York though he spoke with careless ease of his knowledge of Washington.

But the most important fact revealed was that he had lately come into money through the generosity of his former master. The sable New Yorker evinced no curiosity about the amount.

After four days of joy he waked from a sickening stupor. He found himself lying in a filthy alley at dawn, bareheaded, his coat torn up the back, every dollar gone and his friend nowhere to be found.

Colonel Lee had given him the address of three clergymen and told him to call on them for help if he had any trouble. He looked everywhere for these cards. They couldn't be found. He had been so cocksure of himself he had lost them. He couldn't make up his mind to stoop to blacking boots and cleaning spittoons. He had always lived with aristocrats. He felt himself one to his finger tips.

There was but one thing he could do that seemed to be needed up here. He could handle tobacco. He could stem the leaf. He had learned that at Arlington in helping Ben superintend the curing of the weed for the servants' use.

He made the rounds of the factories only to find that the larger part of this work was done in tenement homes. He spent a day finding one of these workshops.

They offered to take him in as a boarder and give him sixty cents a day. He could have a pallet beside the six children in the other room and a place to put his trunk. Sixty cents a day would pay his room rent and give him barely enough food to keep body and soul together.

He hurried back to his boarding house, threw the little trunk on his back and trudged to the tobacco tenement. When he arrived no one stopped work. The mother waved her hand to the rear. He placed his trunk in a dark corner, came out and settled to the task of stemming tobacco.

He did his work with a skill and ease that fascinated the children. He took time to show them how to grip the leaf to best advantage and rip the stem with a quick movement that left scarcely a trace of the weed clinging to it. He worked with a swinging movement of his body and began to sing in soft, low tones.

The wizened eyes brightened, and when he stopped one of them whispered:

"More, black man. Sing some more!"

He sang one more song and choked. His eye caught the look of mortal weariness in the tired face of the little girl of six and his voice wouldn't work.

"Goddermighty!" he muttered, "dese here babies ought not ter be wukkin lak dis!"

When lunch time came the six children begged Sam to live in the place and take his meals with them.

Their mother joined in the plea and offered to board him for thirty cents a day. This would leave him a few cents to spend outside. He couldn't yet figure on clothes. It didn't seem right to have to pay for such things. Anyhow he had enough to last him awhile.

He decided to accept the offer and live as a boarder with the family. The lunch was discouraging. A piece of cold bread and a glass of water from the hydrant. Sam volunteered to bring the water.

The hydrant was the only water supply for the six hundred people whose houses touched the alley. It stood in the center. The only drainage was a sink in front of it. All the water used had to be carried up the stairs and the slops carried down. The tired people did little carrying downstairs. Pans and pails full of dishwater were emptied out the windows with no care for the passer below. Scarcely a day passed without a fight from this cause. A fight in the quarter was always a pleasure to the settlement.

Sam munched his bread and sipped his water. He watched the children eat their pieces ravenously. He couldn't finish his. He handed it to the smallest one of the children who was staring at him with eyes that chilled his heart. He knew the child was still hungry. Such a lunch as a piece of bread and a tin cup of water must be an accident, of course. He had heard of jailers putting prisoners on bread and water to punish them. He had never known human beings living at home to have such food. They would have a good dinner steaming hot. He was sure of that.

A sudden commotion broke out in the alley below. Yells, catcalls, oaths and the sound of crashing bricks, coal, pieces of furniture, and the splash of much water came from the court.

The mother rushed to the window and hurled a stone. There was a pile of them in the corner of the room.

Sam tried to look out.

"What's de matter, ma'm? Is dey er fight?"

"No - nothin' but a rent collector." The woman smiled.

It was the first pleasant thought that had entered her mind since Sam had come.

The dinner was as rude a surprise as the lunch. He watched the woman fumble over lighting the fire in the stove until he could stand it no longer.

"Lemme start de fire fer ye, ma'm," he offered at last.

"I wish you would," she sighed. "I married when I wuz seventeen and I never had made a fire before. I don't believe I'll ever learn."

The negro was not long in observing that she knew no more about cooking than she did about lighting a fire. The only cooking utensils in the place were a pot and a frying pan. The frying pan was in constant use. For dinner she fried a piece of tough beef without seasoning. She didn't know how to make bread. She bought the soggy stuff at the grocer's. There was no bread for dinner at all. They had boiled potatoes, boiled in plain water without even a grain of salt or pepper. The coffee was so black and heavy and bitter he couldn't drink it.

The father had a cup of beer with his coffee. A cup of beer was provided for Sam. The girl of twelve had rushed the growler to the corner saloon. The negro had never tasted beer before and he couldn't drink it. The stuff was horrible. It reminded him of a dose of quinine his mistress had once made him take when he had a chill.

He worked harder than usual next day to forget the fear that haunted him. At night he was ill. He had caught cold and had a fever. He dropped on his pallet without dinner and didn't get up for three weeks.

He owed his landlady so much money now, he felt in honor bound to board with her and give her all his earnings. He felt himself sinking into an abyss and he didn't have the strength to fight his way out.

The thing that hurt him more than bad food and air when he got to his work again was the look of death in the faces of the children. Their eyes haunted him in the dark as they slept on the same floor. He would get out of there when he was strong again. But these children would never go except to be hauled in the dead wagon to the Potter's Field. And he heard the rattle of this black wagon daily.

In a mood of desperation he walked down Water Street past the boarding house. In front of the place he met a boarder who had spoken to him the last day of his stay. He seized Sam by the coat, led him aside and whispered:

"Has ye heard 'bout de old man, name John Brown, dat come ter lead de niggers ter de promise' lan'?"

"No, but I'se waitin' fur somebody ter lead me."

"Come right on wid me, man. I'se a-goin' to a meetin' to-night an' jine de ban'. Will ye jine us?"

"I jine anything dat'll lead me to de promise' lan'."

"Come on. Hit's over in Brooklyn but a nigger's gwine ter meet me at de ferry and take me dar."

Sam felt in his pocket for the money for the ferry. Luckily he had twenty cents. It was worth while to gamble that much on a trip to the promised land.

An emissary of the prophet met them on the Brooklyn side and led them to a vacant store with closed wooden shutters. No light could be seen from the street. The guide rapped a signal and the door opened. Inside were about thirty negroes gathered before a platform. Chairs filled the long space. A white man was talking to the closely packed group of blacks. Sam pressed forward and watched him.

He was old until he began to talk. And then there was something strange and electric in his tones that made him young. His voice was vaulting and metallic and throbbed with an indomitable will. There was contagion in the fierceness of his tones. It caught his hearers and called them in a spell.

His shoulders were stooped. His manner grim and impressive. There was a quick, wiry movement to his body that gave the idea that he was crouching to spring. It was uncanny. It persisted as his speech lengthened.

He was talking in cold tones of the injustice being done the black man in the South. Of the crimes against God and humanity which the Southern whites were daily committing.

The one feature of the strange speaker that fascinated Sam was the glitter of his shifting eyes. He never held them still. He did not try to bore a man through with them. They were restless, as if moved by hidden forces within. The flash of light from their depths seemed a signal from an unknown world.

Sam watched him with open mouth.

He was finishing his talk now in a desultory way more gripping in its deadly calm than the most passionate appeal.

"We are enrolling volunteers," he quietly announced. "Volunteers in the United States League of Gileadites. If you sign your names to the roll to-night understand clearly what you are doing. I have written for each member *Words of Advice* which he must memorize as the guide to his action."

He drew a sheet of paper from his pocket and read:

"No jury can be found in the Northern States, that would convict a man for defending his rights to the last extremity. This is well understood by Southern Congressmen, who insist that the right of trial by jury should not be granted to the fugitive slave. Colored people have more fast friends among the whites than they suppose. Just think of the money expended by individuals in your behalf in the past twenty years! Think of the number who have been mobbed and imprisoned on your account. Have any of you seen the branded hand? Do you remember the names of Lovejoy and Torrey? Should any of your number be arrested, you must collect together as quickly as possible so as to outnumber your adversaries who are taking an active part against you. Let no able-bodied man appear on the ground unequipped or with his weapons exposed to view; let that be understood beforehand. Your plans must be known only to yourself, and with the understanding that all traitors must die, wherever caught and proven to be guilty.

"'Whosoever is fearful or afraid, let him return and depart early from Mount Gilead' (Judges VII Chapter, 3rd verse; Deuteronomy XX Chapter, 8th verse). Give all cowards an opportunity to show it on condition of holding their peace. Do not delay one moment after you're ready: you will lose all your resolution if you do. Let the first blow be the signal for all to engage; and when engaged do not do your work by halves; but make clean work with your enemies -"

It was the slow way in which he spoke the last words that gave them meaning. Sam could hear in his tones the crash of steel into human flesh and the grating of the blade on the bone. It made him shiver.

Every negro present joined the League.

When the last man had signed, John Brown led in a long prayer to Almighty God to bless the holy work on which these noble men had entered. At the close of his prayer he announced that on the following night at the People's Hall on the Bowery in New York, the Honorable Gerrit Smith, the noblest friend of the colored men in the North, would preside over a mass meeting in behalf of the downtrodden. He asked them all to come and bring their friends.

The ceremony of signing over, Sam turned to the guide with a genial smile.

"I done jine de League."

"That's right. I knew you would."

"I'se a full member now, ain't I?"

"Of course."

"When do we eat?" Sam asked eagerly.

"Eat?"

"Sho."

"We ain't organizin' de Gileadites to eat, man."

"Ain't we?"

"No, sah. We'se organizin' - ter kill white men dat come atter runaway slaves."

"But ain't dey got nuttin ter eat fer dem dat's here?"

"You come ter de big meetin' ter-morrow night an' hear sumfin dat's good fer yo' soul."

"I'll be dar," Sam promised. But he hoped to find something at the meeting that was good for his stomach as well as his soul.

# CHAPTER XI

The negroes in New York and Brooklyn were not the only people in the North falling under the influence of the strange man who answered to the name of John Brown. There was something magnetic about him that drew all sorts and conditions of men.

The statesmen who still used reason as the guiding principle of life had no use for him. Henry Wilson, the new Senator from Massachusetts, met him and was repelled by the something that drew others. Governor Andrew was puzzled by his strange personality.

The secret of his power lay in a mystic appeal to the Puritan conscience. He had been from childhood afflicted with this conscience in its most malignant form. He knew instinctively its process of action.

The Puritan had settled New England and fixed the principles both of economic and political life. The civilization he set up was compact and commercial. He organized it in towns and townships. The Meeting House was the center, the source of all power and authority. No dwelling could be built further than two miles from a church and attendance on worship was made compulsory by law.

The South, against whose life Brown was organizing his militant crusade, was agricultural, scattered, individual. Individualism was a passion with the Southerner, liberty his battle

Thomas Dixon

cry. He scorned the "authority" of the church and worshipped God according to the dictates of his own conscience. The Court House, not the Meeting House, was his forum, and he rode there through miles of virgin forests to dispute with his neighbor.

The mental processes of the Puritan, therefore, were distinctly different from that of the Southerner. The Puritan mind was given to hours of grim repression which he called "Conviction of Sin." Resistance became the prime law of life. The world was a thing of evil. A morass of Sin to be attacked, to be reformed, to be "abolished." The Southerner perceived the evils of Slavery long before the Puritan, but he made a poor Abolitionist. The Puritan was born an Abolitionist. He should not only resist and attack the world; he should *hate* it. He early learned to love the pleasure of hating. He hated himself if no more promising victim loomed on the horizon. He early became the foremost Persecutor and Vice-Crusader of the new world. He made witch-hunting one of the sports of New England.

When not busy with some form of the witch hunt, the Puritan found an outlet for his repressed instincts in the ferocity with which he fought the Indians or worked to achieve the conquest of Nature and lay up worldly goods for himself and his children. Prosperity, therefore, became the second principle of his religion, next to vice crusading. When he succeeded in business, he praised God for his tender mercies. His goods and chattels became the visible evidence of His love. The only holiday he established or permitted was the day on which he publicly thanked God for the goods which He had delivered. Through him the New England Puritan Thanksgiving Day became a national festival and through him a religious reverence for worldly success has become a national ideal.

The inner life of the Puritan was soul-fear. Driven by fear and repression he attacked his rock-ribbed country, its thin soil, its savage enemies and his own fellow competitors with fury.

And he succeeded.

The odds against him sharpened his powers, made keen his mind, toughened his muscles.

The Southern planter, on the other hand, represented the sharpest contrast to this mental and physical attitude toward life. He came of the stock of the English Squire. And if he came from Scotland he found this English ideal already established and accepted it as his own.

The joy of living, not the horror of life, was the mainspring of his action and the secret of his character. The Puritan hated play. The Southerner loved to play. He dreamed of a life rich and full of spiritual and physical leisure. He enjoyed his religion. He did not agonize over it. His character was genial. He hated fear and drove it from his soul. He loved a fiddle and a banjo. He was brave. He was loyal to his friends. He loved his home and his kin. He despised trade. He disliked hard work.

To this hour in the country's life his ideal had dominated the nation.

The Puritan Abolitionists now challenged this ideal for a fight to the finish. Slavery was protected by the Constitution. All right, they burn the Constitution and denounce it as a Covenant with Death, an agreement with Hell. They begin a propaganda to incite servile insurrection in the South. They denounce the Southern Slave owner as a fiend. Even the greatest writers of the North caught the contagion of this mania. Longfellow, Lowell, Whittier and Emerson used their pens to blacken the name of the Southern people. From platform, pulpit and forum, through pamphlet, magazine, weekly and daily newspapers the stream of abuse poured forth in ever-increasing volume.

That the proud Southerner would resent the injustice of this wholesale indictment was inevitable. Their habit of mind, their born instinct of leadership, their love of independence, their hatred of dictation, their sense of historic achievement in the building of the republic would resent it. Their critics had not only been Slave holders themselves as long as it paid commercially, but their skippers were now sailing the seas in violation of Southern laws prohibiting the slave trade. Our early Slave traders were nearly all Puritans. When one of their ships came into port, the minister met her at the wharf, knelt in prayer and thanked Almighty God for one more cargo of heathen saved from hell.

Brown's whole plan of attack was based on the certainty of resentment from the South. He set out to provoke his opponents. This purpose was now the inspiration of every act of his life.

A group of six typical Northern minds had fallen completely under his power: Dr. Samuel G. Howe, Rev. Theodore Parker, Rev. Thomas Wentworth Higginson, Frank B. Sanborn, George L. Stearns and the Rev. Hon. Gerrit Smith.

Gerrit Smith was many times a millionaire, one of the great land owners of the country, a former partner in business with John Jacob Astor, the elder, and at this time a philanthropist by profession. He had built a church at Peterboro, New York, and had preached a number of years. In his growing zeal as an Abolitionist he had entered politics and had just been elected to Congress from his district.

He was a man of gentle, humane impulses and looked out upon the world with the kindliest fatherly eyes. It was one of the curious freaks of fate that he should fall under the influence of Brown. The stern old Puritan was his antithesis in every line of face and mental make-up.

Smith was the preacher, the theorist, and the dreamer.

Brown had become the man of Action.

And by Action he meant exactly what the modern Social anarchist means by *direct action*. The plan he had developed was to come to "close quarters" with Slavery. He had organized the Band of Gileadites to kill every officer of the law who attempted to enforce the provisions of the Constitution of the United States relating to Slavery. His eyes were now fixed on the Territory of Kansas.

There could be no doubt about the abnormality of the mind of the man who had constituted himself the Chosen Instrument of Almighty God to destroy chattel Slavery in the South.

He was pacing the floor of the parlor of the New Astor House awaiting the arrival of his friend, Congressman Gerrit Smith, for a conference before the meeting scheduled for eight o'clock. It was a characteristic of Brown that he couldn't sit still. He paced the floor.

The way he walked marked him with distinction, if not eccentricity. He walked always with a quick, springing step. He didn't swing his foot. It worked on springs. And the spring in it had a furtive action not unlike the movement of a leopard. His muscles, in spite of his fifty-four years, were strong and sinewy. He was five feet ten inches in height.

His head was remarkable for its small size. The brain space was limited and the hair grew low on his forehead, as if a hark back to the primitive man out of which humanity grew. His chin protruded into an aggressive threat. His mouth was not only stern, it was as inexorable as an oath.

His hair was turning gray and he wore it trimmed close to his small skull. His nose was an aggressive Roman type. The expression of his face was shrewd and serious, with a touch always of cunning.

A visitor at his house at North Elba whispered one day to one of his sons:

"Your father looks like an eagle."

The boy hesitated and replied in deep seriousness:

"Yes, or some other carnivorous bird."

The thing above all others that gave him the look of a bird of prey was his bluish-gray eye. An eye that was never still and always shone with a glitter. The only time this strange light was not noticeable was during the moments when he drew the lids down half-way. He was in the habit of holding his eyes half shut in times of deep thinking. At these moments if he raised his head, his eyes glowed two pin points of light.

No matter what the impression he made, either of attraction or repulsion, his personality was a serious proposition. No man looked once only. And no man ever attempted undue familiarity or ridicule. His life to this time had been a series of tragic failures in everything he had undertaken. A study of his intense Puritan face revealed at once his fundamental character. A soul at war with the world. A soul at war with himself. He was the incarnation of repressed emotions and desires. He had married twice and his fierce passions had made him the father of twenty children before fifty years of age. His first wife had given birth to seven in ten years and died a raving maniac during the birth of her last. Two of his children had already shown the signs of unbalanced mentality.

The grip of his mind on the individuals who allowed themselves to be drawn within the circle of his influence became absolute.

He was a man of earnest and constant prayer to his God. The God he worshipped was one whose face was not yet revealed to the crowd that hung on his strangely halting words. He spoke in mystic symbols. His mysticism was always the source of his power over the religious leaders who had gathered about him. They had not stopped to analyze the meaning of this appeal. They looked once into his shining blue-gray eyes and became his followers. He never stopped to reason.

He spoke with authority.

He claimed a divine commission for action and they did not pause to examine his credentials. He had failed at every enterprise he had undertaken. And then he suddenly discovered his power over the Puritan imagination.

To Brown's mind, from the day of his devotion to the fixed idea of destroying Slavery in the South, "Action" had but one meaning - bloodshed. He knew that revolutionary ideas are matters of belief. He asserted beliefs. The elect believed. The damned refused to believe.

Long before Smith had entered the room Brown had dropped into a seat by the window, his eyes two pin points. His abstraction was so deep, his absorption in his dreams so complete that when Smith spoke, he leaped to his feet and put himself in an attitude of defense.

He gazed at his friend a moment and rubbed his eyes in a dazed way before he could come back to earth.

In a moment he had clasped hands with the philanthropist. Smith looked into his eyes and his will was one with the man of Action. He had not yet grasped the full meaning of the Action. He was to awake later to its tremendous import - primitive, barbaric, animal, linking man through hundreds of thousands of years to the beast who was his jungle father.

Smith did not know that he was to preside at the meeting until Brown told him. He consented without a moment's hesitation.

# CHAPTER XII

On their way to the hall on the Bowery Gerrit Smith and John Brown passed through dimly lighted streets along which were drifting scores of boys and girls, ragged, friendless, homeless, shelterless in the chill night. The strange old man's eyes were fixed on space. He saw nothing, heard nothing of the city's roaring life or the call of its fathomless misery.

He saw nothing even when they passed a house with a red light before which little girls of twelve were selling flowers. Neither of the men, living for a single fixed idea, caught the accent of evil in the child's voice as she stepped squarely in front of them and said:

"What's ye hurry?"

When they turned aside she piped again:

"Won't ye come in?"

They merely passed on. The infinite pathos of the scene had made no impression. That this child's presence on the streets was enough to damn the whole system of society to the lowest hell never dawned on the philanthropist or the man of Action.

The crowd in the hall was not large. The place was about half full and it seated barely five hundred. The masses of the North as yet took no stock in the Abolition Crusade.

They felt the terrific pressure of the problem of life at home too keenly to go into hysterics over the evils of Negro Slavery in the South. William Lloyd Garrison had been preaching his denunciations for twenty-one years and its fruits were small. The masses of the people were indifferent.

But a man was pushing his way to the platform of the little hall to-night who was destined to do a deed that would accomplish what all the books and all the magazines and all the newspapers of the Crusaders had tried in vain to do.

Small as the crowd was, there was something sinister in its composition. Half of them were foreigners. It was the first wave of the flood of degradation for our racial stock in the North - the racial stock of John Adams and John Hancock.

A few workingmen were scattered among them. Fifty or sixty negroes occupied the front rows. Sam had secured a seat on the aisle. Gerrit Smith rose without ceremony and introduced Brown. There were no women present. He used the formal address to the American voter:

"Fellow Citizens:

"I have the honor to present to you to-night a man chosen of God to lead our people out of the darkness of sin, my fellow worker in the Kingdom, the friend of the downtrodden and the oppressed, John Brown."

Faint applause greeted the old man as he moved briskly to the little table with his quick, springing step.

He fixed the people with his brilliant eyes and they were silent. He was slow of speech, awkward in gesture, and without skill in the building of ideas to hold the imagination of the typical crowd.

It was not a typical crowd of American freemen. It was something new under the sun in our history. It was the beginning of the coming mob mind destined to use Direct Action in defiance of the Laws on which the Republic had been built.

There was no mistaking the message Brown bore. He proclaimed that the negro is the blood brother of the white man. The color of his skin was an accident. This white man with a black skin was now being beaten and ground into the dust by the infamy of his masters. Their crimes cried to God for vengeance. All the negro needed was freedom to transform him into a white man - your equal and mine. At present, our brothers and sisters are groaning in chains on Southern plantations. His vaulting metallic tones throbbed with a strange, cold passion as he called for Action.

The vibrant call for bloodshed in this cry melted the crowd into a new personality. The mildest spirit among them was merged into the mob mind of the speaker. And every man within the sound of his voice was a murderer.

The final leap of the speaker's soul into an expression of supreme hate for the Southern white man found its instant echo in the mob which he had created. They demanded no facts. They asked no reasons. They accepted his statements as the oracle of God. They were opinions, beliefs, dogmas, the cries of propaganda only - precisely the food needed for developing the mob mind to its full strength. Envy, jealousy, hatred ruled supreme. Liberty was a catchword. Blood lust was the motive power driving each heart beat.

Brown suddenly stopped. His speech had reached no climax. It had rambled into repetition. Its power consisted in the repetition of a fixed thought. He knew the power of this repeated hammering on the mind. An idea can be repeated until it is believed, true or false. He had pounded his message into his hearers until they were incapable of resistance. It was unnecessary for him to continue. He stopped so suddenly, they waited in silence for him to go on after he had taken his seat.

A faint applause again swept the front of the house. There was something uncanny about the man that hushed applause. They knew that he was indifferent to it. Hidden fires burned within him that lighted the way of life. He needed no torches held on high. He asked no honors. He expected no applause and he got little. What he did demand was submission to his will and obedience as followers.

Gerrit Smith rose with this thought gripping his gentle spirit. His words came automatically as if driven by another's mind.

"Our friend and leader has dedicated his life to the service of suffering humanity. It is our duty to follow. The first step is to sacrifice our money in his cause."

The ushers passed the baskets and Sam's heart warmed as he heard the coin rattle. His eyes bulged when he saw that one of them had a pile of bills in it that covered the coin. He heard the great and good man say that it was for the poor brother in black. He saw visions of a warm room, of clean food and plenty of it.

He was glad he'd come, although he didn't like the look in John Brown's eyes while he spoke. Their fierce light seemed to bore through him and hurt. Now that he was seated and his eyes half closed, uplifted toward the ceiling, he wasn't so formidable. He rather liked him sitting down.

The ushers poured the money on the table and counted it. Sam had not seen so much money together since he piled his five hundred dollars in gold in a stack and looked at it. He watched the count with fascination. There must be a thousand at least.

He was shocked when the head usher leaned over the edge of the platform, and whispered to Smith the total.

"Eighty-five dollars."

Sam glanced sadly at the two rows of negroes in front. There wouldn't be much for each. He took courage in the thought, however, that some of them were well-to-do and wouldn't ask their share. He was sure of this because he had seen three or four put something in the baskets.

Gerrit Smith announced the amount of the collection with some embarrassment and heartily added:

"My check for a hundred and fifteen dollars makes the sum an even two hundred."

That was something worth while. Smith and Brown held a conference about the announcement of another meeting as Sam whispered to the head usher:

"Could ye des gimme mine now an' lemme go?"

"Yours?"

"Yassah."

"Your share of the collection?"

The usher eyed him in scorn.

"To be sho," Sam answered confidently. "Yer tuk it up fer de po' black man. I'se black, an' God knows I'se po'."

"You're a poor fool!"

"What ye take hit up fer den?"

"To support John Brown, not to feed lazy, good-for-nothing, free negroes."

Sam turned from the man in disgust. He was about to rise and shamble back to his miserable pallet when a sudden craning of necks and moving of feet drew his eye toward the door.

He saw a man stalking down the aisle. He carried on his left arm a little bundle of filthy rags. He mounted the platform and spoke to the Chairman:

"Mr. Smith, may I say just a word to this meeting?"

The Philanthropist Congressman recognized him instantly as the most eloquent orator in the labor movement in America. He had met him at a Reform Convention. He rose at once.

"Certainly."

"Fellow Citizens, Mr. George Evans, the leading advocate of Organized Labor in America, wishes to speak to you. Will you hear him?"

"Yes! Yes! Yes!" came from all parts of the house.

The man began in quivering tones that held Sam and gripped the unwilling mind of the crowd:

"My friends: Just a few words. I have in my arms the still breathing skeleton of a little girl. I found her in a street behind this building within the sound of the voice of your speaker."

He paused and waved to John Brown.

"She was fighting with a stray cat for a crust of bread in a garbage pail. I hold her on high."

With both hands he lifted the dazed thing above his head.

"Look at her. This bundle of rags God made in the form of a woman to be the mother of the race. She has been thrown into your streets to starve. Her father is a workingman whom I know. For six months, out of work, he fought with death and hell, and hell won. He is now in prison. Her mother, unable to support herself and child, sought oblivion in drink. She's in the gutter to-night. Her brother has joined a gang on the East

Side. Her sister is a girl of the streets.

"You talk to me of Negro Slavery in the South? Behold the child of the White Wage Slave of the North! Why are you crying over the poor negro? In the South the master owns the slave. Here the master owns the job. Down there the master feeds, clothes and houses his man with care. Black children laugh and play. Here the master who owns the job buys labor in the open market. He can get it from a man for 75 cents a day. From a woman for 30 cents a day. When he has bought the last ounce of strength they can give, the master of the wage slave kicks him out to freeze or starve or sink into crime.

"You tell me of the white master's lust down South? I tell you of the white master's lust for the daughters of our own race.

"I see a foreman of a factory sitting in this crowd. I've known him for ten years. I've talked with a score of his victims. He has the power to employ or discharge girls of all ages ranging from twelve to twenty-five. Do you think a girl can pass his bead eyes and not pay for the job the price he sees fit to demand?

"If you think so, you don't know the man. I do!"

He paused and the stillness of death followed. Necks were craned to find the figure of the foreman crouching in the crowd. The speaker was not after the individual. His soul was aflame with the cause of millions.

"I see also a man in the crowd who owns a row of tenements so filthy, so dark, so reeking with disease that no Southern master would allow a beast to live in them. This hypocrite has given to John Brown to-night a contribution of money for the downtrodden black man. He coined this money out of the blood of white men and women who pay the rent for the dirty holes in which they die."

A moment of silence that was pain as he paused and a hundred eyes swept the room in search of the man. Again the speaker stood without a sign. He merely paused to let his message sink in the hearts of his hearers.

"My eyes have found another man in this crowd who is an employer of wage slaves. He is here to denounce Chattel Slavery in the South as the sum of all villainies while he practices a system of wage slavery more cruel without a thought morally wrong.

"I say this in justice to the man because I know him. He hasn't intelligence enough to realize what he is doing. If he had he would begin by abolishing slavery in his own household. This reformer isn't a bad man at heart. He is simply an honest fool. These same fools in England have given millions to abolish black slavery in the Colonies and leave their own slaves in the Spittalfield slums to breed a race of paupers and criminals. Why don't a Buxton or a Wilberforce complain of the White Slavery at home? Because it is indispensable to their civilization. They lose nothing in freeing negroes in distant Colonies. They would lose their fortunes if they dared free their own white
brethren.

"The master of the wage slave employs his victim only when he needs him. The Southern master supports his man whether he needs him or not. And cares for him when ill. The Abolitionist proposes to free the black slave from the whip. Noble work. But to what end if he deprives him of food? He escapes the lash and lands in a felon's cell or climbs the steps of a gallows.

"Your inspired leader, the speaker of this evening, has found his most enthusiastic support in New England.

"No doubt.

"In Lowell, Massachusetts, able-bodied men in the cotton mills are receiving 80 cents a day for ten hours' work. Women are receiving 32 cents a day for the same. At no period of the history of this republic has it been possible for a human being to live in a city and reproduce his kind on such wages. What is the result? The racial stock that made the Commonwealth of Massachusetts a civilized state is perishing. It is being replaced from the slums of Europe. The standard of life is dragged lower with each generation.

"The negro, you tell me, must work for others or be flogged. The poor white man at your door must work for others or be starved. The negro is subject to a single master. He learns to know him, if not to like him. There is something human in the touch of their lives. The poor white man here is the slave of many masters. The negro may lead the life of a farm horse. Your wage slave is a horse that hasn't even a stable. He roams the street in the snows of winter. He is ridden by anybody who wishes a ride. He is cared for by nobody. Our rich will do anything for the poor except to get off their backs. The negro has a master in sickness and health. The wage slave is honored with the privilege of slavery only so long as he can work ten hours a day. He is a pauper when he can toil no more.

"Your Abolitionist has fixed his eye on Chattel Slavery in the South. It involves but three million five-hundred thousand negroes. The system of wage slavery involves the lives of twenty-five million white men and women.

"Slavery was not abolished in the North on moral grounds, but because, as a system of labor it was old-fashioned, sentimental, extravagant, inefficient. It was abolished by the masters of men, not by the men.

"The North abolished slavery for economy in production. There was no sentiment in it. Wage slavery has proven itself ten times more cruel, more merciless, more efficient. The Captain of Industry has seen the vision of an empire of wealth beyond the dreams of avarice. He has seen that the master who cares for the aged, the infirm, the sick, the lame, the halt is a fool who must lag behind in the march of the Juggernaut. Only a fool stops to build a shelter for his slave when he can kick him out in the cold and find hundreds of fresh men to take his place.

"Two years ago the Chief of Police of the City of New York took the census of the poor who were compelled to live in cellars. He found that eighteen thousand five hundred and eighty-six white wage slaves lived in these pest holes under the earth. One-thirteenth of the population of the city lives thus underground to-day. Hundreds of these cellars are near the river. They are not waterproof. Their floors are mud. When the tides rise the water floods these noisome holes. The bedding and furniture float. Fierce wharf rats, rising from their dens, dispute with men, women and children the right to the shelves above the water line.

"There are cellars devoted entirely to lodging where working men and women can find a bed of straw for two cents a night - the bare dirt for one cent. Black and white men, women and children, are mixed in one dirty mass. These rooms are without light, without air, filled with the damp vapors of mildewed wood and clothing. They swarm with every species of vermin that infest the animal and human body. The scenes of depravity that nightly occur in these lairs of beasts are beyond words.

"These are the homes provided by the master who has established 'Free' Labor as the economic weapon with which he has set out to conquer the world.

"And he is conquering with it. The superior, merciless power of this system as an economic weapon is bound to do in America what it has done throughout the world. The days of Chattel Slavery are numbered. The Abolitionist is wasting his breath, or worse. He is raising a feud that may drench this nation in blood in a senseless war over an issue that is settled before it's raised.

"Long ago the economist discovered that there was no vice under the system of Chattel Slavery that could not be more freely gratified under the new system of wage slavery.

"You weep because the negro slave must serve one master. He has no power to choose a new one. Do not forget that the power to *choose* a new master carries with it power to discharge the wage slave and hire a new one. This power to discharge is the most merciless and cruel tyranny ever developed in the struggle of man from savagery to civilization. This awful right places in the hand of the master the power of life and death. He can deprive his wage slave of fuel, food, clothes, shelter. Life is the only right worth having if its exercise is put into question. A starving man has no liberty. The word can have no meaning. He must live first or he cannot be a man.

"The wage slave is producing more than the chattel slaves ever produced, man for man, and is receiving less than the negro slave of the South is getting for his labor to-day.

"Your system of wage slavery is the cunning trick by which the cruel master finds that he can deny to the worker all rights he ever had as a slave.

"If you doubt its power, look at this bundle of rags in my hands and remember that there are five thousand half-starved children homeless and abandoned in the streets of this city to-night.

"Find for me one ragged, freezing, starving, black baby in the South and I will buy a musket to equip an army for its invasion -"

He paused a moment, turned and gazed at the men on the platform and then faced the crowd in a final burst of triumphant scorn.

"Fools, liars, hypocrites, clean your own filthy house before you weep over the woes of negroes who are singing while they toil -"

A man on an end seat of the middle aisle suddenly sprang to his feet and yelled:

"Put him out!"

Before Gerrit Smith could reach Evans with a gift of five dollars for the sick child which he still held in his arms the crowd had become a mob.

They hustled the labor leader into the street and told him to go back to hell where he came from.

Through it all John Brown sat on the platform with his blue-gray eyes fixed in space. He had seen, heard or realized nothing that had passed. His mind was brooding over the plains of Kansas.

# CHAPTER XIII

It was October, 1854, before John Brown's three sons, Owen, Frederick and Salmon, left Ohio for their long journey to Kansas. In April, 1855, they crossed the Missouri river and entered the Territory.

John Brown decided to move his family once more to North Elba before going West. It was June before his people reached this negro settlement in Northern New York. He placed his wife and children in an unplastered, four-roomed house. Through its rough weatherboarding the winds and snows of winter would howl. It had been hurriedly thrown together by his son-in-law, Henry Thompson. Brown had never stayed on one of his little farms long enough to bring order out of chaos.

His restless spirit left him no peace. He was now in Boston, now in Springfield, Massachusetts, now in New York, again in Ohio, or Illinois.

He was giving up the work in Ohio to follow his sons into Kansas. He had planned to move there two years before and abandoned the idea. He had at last fully determined to go.

On October the sixth, his party reached the family settlement at Osawatomie. With characteristic queerness the old man did not enter with his sons, Oliver, Jason and John, Jr., and their caravan. He stopped alone on the roadside two miles away until next day.

The party on arrival had plenty of guns, swords and ammunition but their treasury held but sixty cents.

The family settlement were living in tents around which the chill autumn winds were howling. The poor crops they had raised had not been harvested. The men were ill and discouraged. There was little meat, except game and that was difficult to kill. Their only bread was made from corn meal ground at a hand-turned mill two miles away.

Brown's sons, who had preceded him, had lost all vigor. The old man was not slow to see the way out.

The situation called for Action. He determined to get it. He immediately plunged into Free Soil Politics without pausing to build his first shanty against the coming rains and snows of a terrible winter.

# CHAPTER XIV

The race for the lands of the new Territories of Kansas and Nebraska was on to the finish. Nebraska was far North. Kansas only interested the Southerner. The frontiersmen were crossing the boundary lines years before Congress formally opened them for settlement.

After a brief stop in West Tennessee the Doyles had succeeded in reaching Miami County, just beyond the Missouri border, in 1853. They had settled on a fertile quarter section on the Pottawattomie Creek in a small group of people of Southern feeling.

The sun of a new world had begun to shine at last for the humble but ambitious woman who had borne five strong children to be the athletic sons and daughters of a free country. Her soul rose in a triumphant song that made her little home the holy of holies of a new religion. Her husband was the lord of a domain of fertile land. His fields were green with wheat. She loved to look over its acres of velvet carpet. In June her man and three stalwart boys, now twenty, eighteen and fourteen years of age, would swing the reaper into that field and harvest the waving gold without the aid of a hired laborer. She and her little girls would help and sing while they toiled.

There was no debt on their books. They had horses, cows, sheep, pigs, chickens, ducks, turkeys. Their crib was bulging with corn. The bins in their barn were filled with grain.

Their house was still the humble cottage of the prairie pioneer, but her men had made it snug and warm against the winds and snows of winter. Their farm had plenty of timber on the Pottawattomie Creek which flowed through the center of the tract. They had wood for their fires and logs with which to construct their stable and outhouses.

The house they built four-square with sharp gables patterned after the home they had lost. There were no dormers in the attic, but two windows peeped out of the gable beside the stone chimney and gave light and air to the boys' room in the loft. A shed extension in the rear was large enough for both kitchen and dining room.

The home stood close beside the creek, and the murmur of its waters made music for a busy mother's heart.

There was no porch over the front door. But her boys had built a lattice work that held a labyrinth of morning glories in the summer. She had found the gorgeous wild flowers blooming on the prairies and made a hedge of them for the walks. They were sending their shoots up through the soil now to meet the sun of spring. The warm rays had already begun to clothe the prairie world with beauty and fragrance.

The mother never tired of taking her girls on the hill beyond the creek and watching the men at work on the wide sweeping plains that melted into the skyline miles beyond. Something in its vast silence, in its message of the infinite, soothed her spirit. All her life in the East she had been fighting against losing odds. These wide breathing plains had stricken the shackles from her soul.

She was free.

Sometimes she felt like shouting it into the sky. Sometimes she knelt among the trees and thanked God for His mercy in giving her the new lease of life.

The new lease on life had depth and meaning because she lived and breathed in her children. Her man had a man's chance at last. Her boys had a chance.

The one thing that gave her joy day and night was the consciousness of living among the men and women of her own race. There was not a negro in the county, bond or free, and she fervently prayed that there never would be. Now that they were free from the sickening dread of such competition in life, she had no hatred of the race. As a free white woman, the mother of free white men and women, all she asked was freedom from the touch of an inferior. She had always felt instinctively that this physical contact was poison. She breathed deeply for the first time.

There was just one cloud on the horizon which threatened her peace and future. Her husband, after the fashion of his kind, in the old world and the new, had always held political opinions and had dared to express them without fear or favor. In Virginia his vote was sought by the leaders of the county. He had been poor but he had influence because he dared to think for himself.

He was a Southern born white man, and he held the convictions of his birthright. He had never stopped to analyze these faiths. He believed in them as he believed in God. They were things not to be questioned.

Doyle had not hesitated to express his opinions in Kansas as in Virginia. The few Southern settlers on the Pottawattomie Creek were sympathetic and no trouble had come. But the keen ears of the woman had caught ominous rumors on the plains.

The father and mother sat on a rude board settee which John had built. The boy had nailed it against a black jack close beside the bend of the creek where the ripple of the hurrying waters makes music when the stream is low and swells into a roar when gorged by the rains.

The woman's face was troubled as she listened to the waters. She studied the strong lines of her husband's neck, shoulders and head, with a touch of pride and fear. His tongue was long in a political argument. He had a fatal gift of speech. He could say witty, bitter things if stung by an opponent.

She spoke with deep seriousness:

"I wish you wouldn't talk so much, John -"

"And why not?"

"You'll get in trouble."

"Well, I've been in trouble most of my life. There's no use livin' at all, if you live in fear. I ain't never knowed what it is to be afraid. And I'm too old to learn."

"They say, the Northern men that's passin' into the Territory have got guns and swords. And they say they're goin' to use 'em. They outnumber the Southerners five to one."

"What are they goin' to do with their guns and swords? Cut a man's tongue out because he dares to say who he's goin' to vote for next election?"

"You don't have to talk so loud anyhow," his wife persisted.

"Ole woman, I'm free, white, and twenty-one. I've been a-votin' and watchin' the elections in this country for twenty odd years. Ef I've got to tiptoe around, ashamed of my raisin', and ashamed of my principles, I don't want to live. I wouldn't be fit ter live."

"I want ye to live."

"You wouldn't want to live with a coward."

"A brave man can hold his tongue, John."

"I ain't never learnt the habit, Honey."

"Won't you begin?"

"Ye can't learn a old dog new tricks - can they, Jack?"

He stroked his dog's friendly nose suddenly thrust against his knee.

"You know, Honey," he went on laughingly, "we brought this yellow pup from Old Virginia. He's the best rabbit and squirrel dog in the county. I've taught him to stalk prairie chickens out here. I'd be ashamed to look my dog in the face ef I wuz ter tuck my tail between my legs and run every time a fool blows off his mouth about the South -"

He stopped and laughed, his white teeth gleaming through his fine beard.

"Don't you worry, Honey. Those fields are too purty this spring for worrying. We're goin' to send Colonel Lee our last payment this fall and we'll not owe a cent to any man on earth."

# CHAPTER XV

John Brown plunged into politics in Kansas under the impression that his will could dominate the rank and file of the Northern party. He quickly faced the fact that the frontiersmen had opinions of their own. And they were not in the habit of taking orders from a master.

His hopes were raised to their highest at the Free State Convention which met at Lawrence on Monday, the twenty-fifth of June, 1855. This Convention spoke in tones that stirred Brown's admiration.

It meant Action.

They elected him a vice president of the body. He had expected to be made president. However, his leadership was recognized. All he needed was the opportunity to take the Action on which his mind had long been fixed. The moment blood began to flow, there would be but one leader. Of that, he felt sure. He could bide his time.

The Convention urged the people to unite on the one issue of making Kansas a Free Soil State. They called on every member of the Shawnee Legislature who held Free Soil views to resign from that body, although it had been recognized by the National Government as the duly authorized law-making assembly of the Territory. They denounced this Legislature as the creature of settlers from Missouri who had crowded over the border before the Northerners could reach their destination. They urged all people to refuse to obey every law passed by the body.

The final resolution was one inspired by Brown himself. It was a bold declaration that if their opponents wished to fight, the Northerners were READY! The challenge was unmistakable. Brown felt that Action was imminent. Only a set of poltroons would fail to accept the gauge of battle thus flung in their faces.

To his amazement the challenge was not received by the rank and file of the Free Soil Party with enthusiasm. Most of these Northerners had moved to Kansas as bona fide settlers. They came to build homes for the women they had left behind. They came to rush their shacks into shape to receive their loved ones. They had been furnished arms and ammunition by enthusiastic friends and politicians in the older States. And they had eagerly accepted the gifts. There were droves of Indians still roaming the plains. There were dangers to be faced.

The Southern ruffians of whom they had heard so much had not materialized. Although the Radical wing of the Northern Party had made Lawrence its Capital and through their paper, the *Herald of Freedom*, issued challenge after challenge to their enemies.

The Northern settlers began to divide into groups whose purposes were irreconcilable. Six different conventions met in Lawrence on or before the fifteenth of August. Each one of these conventions was divided in councils. In each the cleavage between the Moderates and Radicals became wider.

Out of the six conventions of Northerners at Lawrence, out of resolution and counter resolution, finally emerged the accepted plan of a general convention at Big Springs.

The gathering was remarkable for the surprise it gave to the Radicals of whom Brown was the leader. The Convention adopted the first platform of the Free State party and nominated ex-Governor Reeder as its candidate for delegate to Congress.

For the first time the hard-headed frontiersmen who came to Kansas for honest purposes spoke in plain language. The first resolution settled the Slavery issue. It declared that Slavery was a curse and that Kansas should be free of this curse. But that as a matter of common sense they would consent to any reasonable adjustment in regard to the few slaves that had already been brought into the Territory.

Brown and his followers demanded that Slavery should be denounced as a crime, not a curse, as the sum of all villainies and the Southern master as a vicious and willful criminal. The mild expression of the platform on this issue wrought the old man's anger to white heat. The offer to compromise with the slave holder already in Kansas he repudiated with scorn. But a more bitter draught was still in store for him.

The platform provided that Kansas should be a Free White State. And in no uncertain words made plain that the accent should be on the word WHITE. The document demanded the most stringent laws excluding ALL NEGROES, BOND AND FREE, forever from the Territory.

The old man did not hear this resolution when read. So deep was his brooding anger, the words made no impression. Their full import did not dawn on him until John Brown, Jr., leaned close and whispered:

"Did you hear that?"

The father stirred from his reverie and turned a dazed look on his son.

"Hear what?"

"The infamous resolution demanding that Kansas be made a

white man's country and no negro, bond or free, shall ever be allowed to enter it?"

The hard mouth twitched with scorn. And his jaws came together with a snap.

"It doesn't matter what they add to their first maudlin plank on the Slavery issue."

"Will you sit here and see this vile thing done?"

A look of weariness came over the stern face with its deep-cut lines.

"It's a waste of words to talk to politicians."

John, Jr. was grasping at the next resolution which was one surpassing belief. He rubbed his ears to see if he were really hearing correctly.

This resolution denounced the charge that they were Radicals at all. It denounced the attempt of any man to interfere by violence with slaves or Slavery where protected by the supreme law of the land. It repudiated as stale and ridiculous the charge of Abolitionism against them. And declared that such an accusation is without a shadow of truth to support it.

Charles Stearns, the representative of the New England Society, leaped to his feet and denounced the platform in withering tones. He fairly shrieked his final sentence:

"All honest anti-slavery men, here and elsewhere, will spit on your platform!"

He paused and faced the leaders who had drafted it.

"And all pro-slavery men must forever despise the base sycophants who originated it!"

John Brown, Jr., applauded. The crowd laughed.

Old John Brown had paid no further heed to the proceedings of the Convention. His eyelids were drawn half down. Only pin points of glittering light remained.

The resolutions were adopted by an overwhelming majority.

In the East, Horace Greeley in the *Tribune* reluctantly accepted the platform: "Why free blacks should be excluded it is difficult to understand; but if Slavery can be kept out by compromise of that sort, we shall not complain. An error of this character may be corrected; but let Slavery obtain a foothold there and it is not so easily removed."

Brown's hopes were to be still further dashed by the persistence with which the leaders of this Convention followed up the program of establishing a white man's country on the free plains of the West.

When the Convention met at Topeka on the twenty-third of October, to form a Constitution, the determination to exclude all negroes from Kansas was again sustained. The majority were finally badgered into submitting the issue to a separate vote of the people. On the fifteenth of December, the Northern settlers voted on it and the question *was* settled.

Negroes were excluded by a three-fourths majority.

Three-fourths of the Free State settlers were in favor of a white man's country and the heaviest vote against the admission of negroes was polled in Lawrence and Topeka, where the Radicals had from the first made the most noise.

The Northern men who had come to Kansas merely to oppose the extension of Slavery were in a hopeless minority in their own party. The American voters still had too much common sense to be led into a position to provoke civil war.

John Brown spent long hours in prayer after the final vote on the negro issue had been counted. He denounced the leaders in politics in Kansas as trimmers, time servers, sycophants and liars. He walked beneath the star-sown skies through the night. He wrestled with his God for a vision.

There must be a way to Action.

He rose from prayer at dawn after a sleepless night and called for his sons, Owen, Oliver, Frederick and Salmon, to get ready for a journey. He had received a first hint of the will of God. He believed it might lead to the way.

He organized a surveyor's party and disguised himself as a United States Surveyor. He had brought to Kansas a complete outfit for surveying land. He instructed Owen and Frederick to act as chain carriers, Salmon as axeman and Oliver as marker. He reached the little Southern settlement on the Pottawattomie Creek the fifteenth of May.

He planted his compass on the bank of the creek near the Doyles' house and proceeded to run a base line.

The father and three boys were in the fields at work beyond the hill.

He raised his compass and followed the chainman to the Doyles' door. The mother and little girl trudged behind, delighted with the diversion of the party, so rare on the lonely prairies. Little could they dream the grim deed that was shaping in the soul of the Surveyor.

When they reached the house she turned to the old man with Southern courtesy:

"Won't you come in, sir, and rest a few minutes?"

The strange, blue-gray eyes glanced restlessly toward the hill and he signaled his sons:

"Rest awhile, boys."

Frederick and Oliver sat down on a pile of logs. Salmon and Owen, at a nod from their father, wandered carelessly toward the stable and outhouses.

Owen found the dog Doyle had brought from Virginia and took pains to make friends with him.

Brown's keen, restless eyes carefully inspected the door, its fastenings and the strength of its hinges. The iron of the hinges was flimsy. The fastening was the old-fashioned wooden shutters hung outside and closed with a single slide. He noted with a quick glance that there was no cross bar of heavy wood nor any sockets in which such a bar could be dropped.

The windows were small. There was no glass. Solid wooden shutters hung outside and closed with a single hook and eye for fastenings.

The sun was setting before the surveying party stopped work. They had run a line close to the house of every Southern settler on the Pottawattomie Creek, noting carefully every path leading to each house. They had carefully mapped the settlement and taken a census of every male inhabitant and every dog attached to each house. They also made an inventory of the horses, saddles and bridles.

Having completed their strange errand, they packed their instruments and rode toward Osawatomie.

# CHAPTER XVI

With the opening of the Territory of Kansas the first Regiment of United States Cavalry, commanded by Colonel E.V. Sumner, had been transferred to Fort Leavenworth.

The life of the barracks was young Lieutenant J.E.B. Stuart.

Colonel Lee had been transferred from West Point to the command of the Second United States Cavalry on the Mexican Border at the same time that Stuart's regiment was moved to Kansas.

The rollicking song-loving, banjo-playing Virginian had early distinguished himself as an Indian fighter. He had been dangerously wounded, but recovered with remarkable rapidity. His perfect health and his clean habits stood him in good stead on the day an Indian's bullet crashed through his breast.

He was a favorite with officers and men. As a cadet he had given promise of the coming soldier. At the Academy he was noted for his strict attendance to every military duty, and his erect, soldierly bearing. He was particularly noted for an almost thankful acceptance of a challenge to fight any cadet who might feel himself aggrieved. The boys called him a "Bible Class Man." He was never known to swear or drink. They also called him "Beauty Stuart," in good natured boyish teasing.

He was the best-looking cadet of his class, as he was the best-looking young officer of his regiment. His hair was a reddish brown. His eyes a deep steel blue, his voice clear and ringing.

In his voice the soul of the man spoke to his fellows. He was always singing - always eager for a frolic of innocent fun. Above all, he was always eager for a frolic with a pretty girl. He played both the banjo and the guitar and little he cared for the gathering political feud which old John Brown and his sons had begun to foment on the frontier.

As a Southerner the struggle did not interest him. It was a foregone conclusion that the country would be settled by Northern immigrants. They were pouring into the Territory in endless streams. A colony from New Haven, Connecticut, one hundred strong, had just settled sixty miles above Lawrence on the Kansas River. They knew how to plow and plant their fields and they had modern machinery with which to do it. The few Southerners who came to Kansas were poorly equipped. Lawrence was crowded with immigrants from every section of the North. The fields were white with their tents. A company from Ohio, one from Connecticut, and one from New Hampshire were camping just outside the town. Daily their exploring committees went forth to look at localities. Daily new companies poured in.

Stuart let them pour and asked no questions about their politics. He was keen on one thing only - the pretty girls that might be among them.

When exploring parties came to Fort Leavenworth, the young Lieutenant inspected them with an eye single to a possible dance for the regiment. The number of pretty girls was not sufficient to cause excitement among the officers as yet. The daughters of the East were not anxious to explore Kansas at this moment. The Indians were still troublesome at times.

A rumor spread through the barracks that the prettiest girl in Kansas had just arrived at Fort Riley, sixty-eight miles beyond Topeka. Colonel Phillip St. George Cooke of Virginia commanded the Fort and his daughter Flora had ventured all the way from Harper's Ferry to the plains to see her beloved daddy.

The news thrilled Stuart. He found an excuse to carry a message from Colonel Sumner to Colonel Cooke.

He expected nothing serious, of course. Every daughter of Virginia knew how to flirt. She would know that he understood this from the start. It would be nip and tuck between the Virginia boy and the Virginia girl.

He had always had such easy sailing in his flirtations he hoped Miss Flora would prove a worthy antagonist.

As a matter of course, Colonel Cooke asked the gallant young Virginian to stay as his guest.

"What'll Colonel Sumner say, sir?" Stuart laughed.

"Leave Sumner to me."

"You'll guarantee immunity?"

"Guaranteed."

"Thank you, Colonel Cooke, I'll stay."

Stuart could hardly wait until the hour of lunch to meet the daughter. He was impatient to ask where she was. The Colonel guessed his anxiety and hastened to relieve it, or increase it.

"You haven't met my daughter, Lieutenant?" he asked casually.

"I haven't that honor, Colonel, but this gives me the happy opportunity."

He said it with such boyish fun in his ringing voice that Cooke laughed in spite of his desire to maintain the strictest dignity. He half suspected that the young officer might meet his match in more ways than one.

"She'll be in at noon," the Commander remarked. "Off riding with one of the boys."

"Of course," Stuart sighed.

He began to scent a battle and his spirits rose. He went to his room, took his banjo out of its old leather strapped case and tuned it carefully. He made up his mind to give the young buck out riding with her the fight of his life while there.

He heard the ring of the girl's laughter as she bade her escort goodbye at the door. He started to go down at once and begin the struggle. Something in the ring of her young voice stopped him. There was a joyous strength in it that was disconcerting. A girl who laughed like that had poise. She was an individual. He liked, too, the tones of her voice before he had seen her.

This struck him as odd. Never in his life before had he liked a girl before meeting her just for a tone quality in her voice. This one haunted him the whole time he was changing his uniform.

He decided to shave again. He had shaved the night before very late. He didn't like the suggestion of red stubble on his face. It might put him at a disadvantage.

He resented the name of Beauty Stuart and yet down in his man soul he knew that he was vain.

He began to wonder if she were blonde or brunette, short or tall, petite or full, blue eyes or brown? She must be pretty. Her father was a man of delicate and finely marked features - the type of Scotch-Irish gentlemen who had made the mountains of Virginia famous for pretty women and brainy men.

He heard her softly playing a piano and wondered how on earth they had ever moved a piano to this far outpost of civilization. The cost was enormous. But the motive of her father in making such a sacrifice to please her was more important. His love for her must be unusual. It piqued his interest and roused again his impulse for a battle royal with another elusive daughter of his native state.

He made up his mind not to wait for the call to lunch. He would walk boldly into the reception room and introduce himself. She knew he was there, of course.

At the first sound of his footstep, her hand paused on the keys and she turned to greet him, rising quickly, and easily.

The vision which greeted Stuart stunned him for a moment. A perfect blonde with laughing blue eyes, exactly the color of his own, slim and graceful, a smile that was sunlight, and a step that was grace incarnate.

And yet her beauty was not the thing that stunned him. He had discounted her good looks from a study of her father's delicate face. It was the glow of a charming personality that disarmed him at the first glance.

She extended a slender hand with a smile.

"I'm so glad to meet you, Lieutenant Stuart."

He took it awkwardly, and blushed. He mumbled when he spoke and was conscious that his voice was thick.

"And I'm so glad to see you, Miss Flora."

They had each uttered the most banal greeting. Yet the way in which the words were spoken was significant.

Never in his life had he heard a voice so gentle, so tender, so appealing in its sincerity. All desire to flirt, to match wit against a charming girl vanished. He felt a resistless impulse to protect her from any fool who would dare try to start a flirtation. She was too straightforward, too earnest, too sincere.

She seemed a part of his own inmost thought and life.

It was easy to see that while she was the pet of her father, she was unspoiled. Stuart caught himself at last staring at her in a dazed, foolish way. He pulled himself together and wondered how long he had held her hand.

"Won't you play for me, Miss Flora?" he asked at last.

"If you'll sing," she laughed.

"How do you know I sing?"

"How do you know I play?"

"I heard you."

"I heard you, too."

"Upstairs?"

"Just before you came down."

"I had no idea I was so loud."

"Your voice rings. It has carrying power."

He started to say: "I hope you like it," and something inside whispered: "Behave."

She took the seat at the piano and touched the keys with an easy, graceful movement. She looked up and smiled. Her eyes blinded him. They were so bright and friendly.

"What will you sing?"

"*Annie Laurie*," he answered promptly.

Stuart sang with deep tenderness and passion. He outdid

himself. And he knew it. He never knew before that he could sing so well.

On the last stanza the girl softly joined a low, sweet voice with his. As the final note died away in Stuart's voice, hers lingered a caress. The man's heart leaped at its tenderness.

"Why didn't you join me at first?" he asked.

"Nobody axed me, sir!" she said.

"Well, I ask you now - come on - we'll do it together!"

"All right," was the jolly answer.

They sang it in duet to the soft accompaniment which she played.

Never had he heard such singing by a slip of a girl. Her voice was rich, full of feeling and caressing tenderness. He felt his soul dissolving in its liquid depths.

Throughout the lunch he caught himself staring at her in moments of long silence. He had for the first time in his life lost his capacity for silly gaiety.

He roused himself with an effort, and wondered what on earth had come over him. He was too deeply interested in studying the girl to attempt to analyze his own feelings. It never occurred to him to try. He was too busy watching the tender light in her eyes.

He wondered if she could be engaged to the fellow she went riding with? He resented the idea. Of course not. And when he remembered the care-free ring to her laughter when she said goodbye, he was reassured. No girl could laugh a goodbye like that to a man she loved. The tone was too poised and impersonal.

He asked her to ride with him that afternoon.

"On one condition," she smiled.

"What?"

"That you bring your banjo and play for me when I ask you."

"How'd you know I had a banjo?"

"Caught the final twang as you tuned it on my arrival."

"I'll bring it if you like."

"Please."

He hurried to his room, placed the banjo in its case and threw it over his shoulder. She had promised to be ready in ten minutes and have the horses at the door.

She was ready in eight minutes, and leaped into the saddle before he could reach her side. For the life of him he couldn't keep his eye off her exquisite figure.

She rode without effort. She had been born in the saddle.

She led him along the military road to the juncture of the Smoky Hill and Republican rivers. A lover at the Fort had built a seat against a huge rock that crowned the hill overlooking the fork of the rivers.

Stuart hitched the horses and found the seat. For two hours he played his banjo and they sang old songs together.

"I love a banjo - don't you?" she asked enthusiastically.

"It's my favorite music. There's no sorrow in a banjo. You can make it laugh. You can make it shout. You can make it growl and howl and snarl and fight. But you can't make a banjo cry.

There are no tears in it. The joy of living is all a banjo knows. Why should we try to know anything else anyhow?"

"We shouldn't," she answered soberly. "The other things will come without invitation sometime."

For an hour they talked of the deep things of life. He told of his high ambitions of service for his country in the dark days that might come in the future. Of the kind of soldier the nation would need, and the ideal he had set for his soul of truth and honor, of high thinking and clean living in the temptations that come to a soldier's daily life.

And she applauded his ideals. She told him they were big and fine and she was proud of him as a true son of Old Virginia.

The sun was sinking behind the dim smoky hills toward the West when she rose.

"We must be going!"

"I had no idea it was so late," he apologized.

It was not until he reached his room at eleven o'clock after three hours more of her in the reception room that he faced the issue squarely.

He stood before the mirror and studied his flushed face. A look of deep seriousness had crept into his jolly blue eyes.

"You're a goner, this time, young man!" he whispered. "You're in love."

He paused and repeated it softly.

"*In love* - the big thing this time. Sweeping all life before it. Blotting out all that's passed and gripping all that lies beyond - Glory to God!"

For hours he lay awake. The world was made anew. The beauty of the new thought filled his soul with gratitude.

He dared not tell her yet. The stake was too big. He was playing for all that life held worth having. He couldn't rush a girl of that kind. A blunder would be fatal. He had a reputation as a flirt. She had heard it, no doubt. He must put his house in order. His word must ring true. She must believe him.

He made up his mind to return to Fort Leavenworth next day and manage somehow to get transferred to Fort Riley for two weeks.

Thomas Dixon

# CHAPTER XVII

The Surveyor of the lands of Pottawattomie Creek was shaping the organization of a band of followers.

To this little group, composed as yet of his own sons in the main, he talked of his work, his great duty, his mission with mystic elation. A single idea was slowly fixing itself in his mind as the purpose of life.

It was fast becoming an obsession.

He slept but little. The night before he had slept but two hours. When the camp supper had been prepared, he stood with bare head in the midst of his followers and thanked God. The meal was eaten to-night in a grim silence which Brown did not break once. The supper over, he rose and again returned thanks to the Bountiful Giver.

And then he left the camp without a word. Alone he tramped the prairie beneath the starlit sky of a beautiful May night. Hour after hour he paused and prayed. Always the one refrain came from his stern lips:

"Give me, oh, Lord God, the Vision!"

And he would wait with eyes set on the stars for its revelation. He crouched at last against the trunk of a tree in a little ravine near the camp. It was past three o'clock. William Walker, who was acting his second in command, was still waiting his orders for the following day. He saw Brown enter the ravine at one o'clock. Impatient of his endless wandering, tired and sleepy, he decided to follow his Chief and ask his orders.

He found him in a sitting posture, leaning against a blackjack, his rifle across his knees. Walker called softly and received no response. He approached and laid his hand on his shoulder.

Instantly he leaped to his feet, his rifle at his follower's breast, his finger on the trigger.

"My God!" Walker yelled.

His speech was too late to stop the pressure of the finger. Walker pushed the muzzle up and the ball grazed his shoulder. The leader gripped his follower's arm, stared at him a moment and merely grunted:

"Oh!"

When the day dawned a new man was found to act as second in command. Walker had deserted his queer chieftain.

The old man entered the camp at dawn, the light of determination in his eyes and a new set to his jaw. His first plan of the Pottawattomie was right. The turn toward Lawrence had been a waste of time. He selected six men to accompany him on his mission, his four sons who had made up the Surveyor's party, his son-in-law, Henry Thompson, and Theodore Weiner. Owen, Salmon, Oliver and Frederick Brown knew every foot of the ground. They had carried the chain, set the markers and flags and kept the records.

He called his men in line and issued his first command:

"To the house of James Townsley."

Townsley belonged to the Pottawattomie Rifles of which organization his son, John Jr., was the Captain.

Arrived at the house, Brown drew Townsley aside and spoke in a vague, impersonal manner.

"I hear there is trouble expected on the Pottawattomie."

"Is there?"

"We hear it."

"What are you going to do?"

"March to their rescue. Will you help us?"

"How?"

"Harness your team of grays and take our party to Pottawattomie."

"All right."

The old man found a grindstone and ordered the ugly cutlasses which he had brought from Ohio to be sharpened. He stood over the stone and watched it turned until each edge was as keen as a butcher's blade.

It began to dawn on the two younger sons before the grinding of the swords was finished what their father had determined.

Frederick asked Oliver tremblingly:

"What do you think of this thing?"

"It looks black to me."

"It looks hellish to me."

"I'm not going."

"Nor am I."

They promptly reported the decision to their father.

His eyes flamed.

"It's too late to retreat now!"

"We're not going," was the sullen answer in chorus.

The father gripped the two with his hard hands and held them as in a vise.

"You will not put me to shame now before these men. You will go with me - do you hear?"

His tones rang with the quiver of steel and the boys' wills weakened.

Frederick said finally:

"We'll go with you then, but we'll take no part in what you do."

"Agreed," was the stern answer.

He turned to Oliver and said:

"Give me your revolver. I may need it."

"It's mine," the boy replied. "I'll not give it up."

The old man looked the stalwart figure over in a quick glance of appraisement. Brown had been a man of iron strength in his day but his shoulders were stooped and he knew he was no match for the fierce strength of youth. Yet his hesitation was only for an instant.

With the sudden spring of a panther he leaped on the boy and attempted to take the pistol by force. The son resisted with fury.

Thomas Dixon

Frederick, alarmed lest the pistol should be discharged in the struggle, managed to slip it from his brother's belt.

The match was not equal.

Youth was master in the appeal to brute strength. At North Elba the father had once thrown thirty lumbermen in a day, one after the other, in a wrestling match. He summoned the last ounce of strength now to subdue his rebellious son.

Frederick watched the contest with painful anxiety. His own mind was not strong. He had already given evidences of insanity that had distressed his brother. If Oliver should kill his father or the old man should kill the brother! He couldn't face the hideous possibility. Yet he couldn't stop them.

Fortunately there were no other witnesses to the fight. Townsley was busy at the stable with the team. Weiner and Thompson had gone into the house to complete their packing of provisions for the journey.

In tones of blind anguish Frederick followed the two desperate struggling men.

"Don't do this, Father!"

The old man made no answer save to swing his agile son's frame to one side in another futile effort to throw him to the ground.

Not a word escaped his lips. His eyes flashed and glittered with the uncertain glare of a maniac in the moments when the iron muscles of the son pinned his arms and held his wiry body rigid.

Again Frederick's low pleading could be heard. This time to his brother:

"Can't you stop it, Oliver?"

"How can I?"

"For God's sake stop it - stop it!"

"I can't stop it. Don't ye see he's got me and I've got to hold him."

The consciousness of failing strength drove the father to fury. His breath was coming now in shorter gasps. He knew his chances of success were fading. He yielded for a moment, and ceased to struggle. A cunning look crept into his eyes.

The boy relaxed his vigilance. The old man felt the boy's grip ease. With a sudden thrust of his body he summoned the last ounce of strength, and threw his son to the ground.

The boy laughed a devilish cry of the strong with the weak as he fell. Before he touched the ground he had deftly turned the father's body beneath his and the full weight of his two hundred pounds fairly crushed the breath from the older man.

A groan of rage and despair was wrung from his stern lips. But no word escaped him. Frederick rushed to the prostrate figures, seized Oliver by the shoulders and tore his grip loose.

"This is foolish!" he stormed.

No sooner had Brown risen than he plunged again at his son. The boy had been playing with him to this time. The half of his strength was yet in reserve. A little angry grunt came from his lips, and his father was a child in his hands. With sure, quick movement he pinioned both arms and jammed him against the wheel of the wagon. He held him there for an instant helpless to resist or move.

The last cry of despairing command came from Brown's soul.

"Let go of me, sir!"

The boy merely growled a bulldog's answer.

"Not till you agree to behave yourself."

Another desperate contraction of muscles and the order came more feebly.

"Will you let go of me, sir?"

"Will you behave yourself?"

"Yes," came the sullen answer.

The boy relaxed his grip and stood ready for action.

"All right, then."

"You can keep your pistol."

"I intend to."

"But you are not to use it, sir, without my orders."

"I am not going to use it at all, except in self-defense."

"You will not be called upon to defend yourself. I am going on a divine mission. God has shown me the way in a Vision. I wish no man's help who must be driven."

"You'll not get any help, sir. I wouldn't have gone on that survey with you if I'd known what was in your mind."

Brown searched his son's eyes keenly.

"You will not betray me to my enemies?"

"I can't do that. You're my father."

He turned to Frederick.

"Nor you?"

The tears were streaming down the boy's face. He was hysterical from the strain of the fight.

"You heard me, sir," the father stormed.

"What did you say?" Frederick stammered.

Oliver explained.

"He asked if you were going to betray his plans to those people on the Pottawattomie."

A far-away expression came into his eyes.

"No - no - not that."

"Then you'll both follow and keep out of my way until we have finished the work and then come back with me?"

"Yes," Oliver answered.

"Yes," Frederick echoed vaguely.

Townsley and Weiner were coming with the pair of grays to be hitched to the wagon. Weiner led his own pony already saddled. When they reached the wagon all signs of rebellion had passed.

"Are you ready?" Townsley asked.

"Ready." Brown's metallic voice rang.

The horses were hitched to the wagon, the provisions and equipment loaded. Brown turned to his loyal followers:

"Arm yourselves."

Thomas Dixon

Owen, Salmon, Henry Thompson, Theodore Weiner and John Brown each buckled a loaded revolver about his waist, and seized a rifle and cutlass.

Weiner mounted his pony as an outpost rider and the others climbed into the wagon. Oliver and Frederick agreed to follow on foot. The expedition moved toward the Southern settlement on Pottawattomie Creek.

Brown crouched low in the wagon as it moved slowly forward and a look of cunning marked his grim face.

He was the Witch Hunter now. The chase was on. And the game was human.

As the sun was setting behind the Western horizon in a glow of orange and purple glory the strange expedition drove down to the edge of the timber between two deep ravines and camped a mile above Dutch Henry's Crossing of the Pottawattomie.

The scene was one of serene beauty. The month of May - Saturday, the twenty-third. Nature was smiling in the joy of her happiest hour. Peace on earth, plenty, good will and happiness breathed from every bud and leaf and song of bird.

The broad prairies of the Territory were fertile and sunny. They stretched away in unbroken, sublime loveliness until the land kissed the infinite of the skies. Unless one had the feeling for this suggestion of an inland sea the view might be depressing and the eye of the traveler weary.

The spot which John Brown picked for his camp was striking in its beauty and picturesque appeal. Winding streams, swelling hills, and steep ravines broke the monotony of the plains.

The streams were bordered by the rich foliage of noble trees. The streams were called "Creeks." In reality, they were beautiful rivers in the month of May - the Marais des Cygnes and the Pottawattomie. They united near Osawatomie to form the Osage River, the largest tributary to the Missouri below its mountain sources. Each river had its many tributaries winding gracefully along wood-fringed banks.

Beyond these ribbons of beautiful foliage stretched the gorgeous carpet of the grass-matted, flower-strewn prairies.

The wild flowers were in full bloom, pushing their red, white, yellow,blue and pink heads above the grass. The wind was blowin g a steady life-giving gale. The fields of flowers bowed and swayed and rose again at its touch. Their perfume filled the air. The perfume of the near-by fields was mingled with the odor of thousands of miles of prairie gardens to the south and west. A peculiar clearness in the atmosphere gave the widest range to vision. Brown climbed the hill alone while his men were unpacking. From the hilltop, even in the falling twilight, he could see clearly for thirty or forty miles.

He swept the horizon for signs of the approach of a party which might interfere with his plan.

He knelt again and prayed to his God, as the twilight deepened into darkness. The stars came out one by one and blinked down at his bent figure still in prayer, his eyes uplifted in an uncanny glare.

As he slowly moved back to his camp he met Townsley.

Frederick and Oliver had reached camp and Townsley had caught a note of the sinister in their whispered talk. He didn't like the looks of it. Brown had told him there was trouble brewing on the Pottawattomie. He had supposed, as a matter of course, that it was the long-threatened attack of enemies on Weiner's store. Weiner, a big, quarrelsome Austrian, had been in more than one fist fight with his neighbors.

Brown studied Townsley and decided to give him but a hint of his true purpose. He didn't like this sign of weakness on the eve of great events.

Townsley took the hint with a grain of salt, but what he heard was enough to bring alarm. The thing Brown had hinted was incredible.

But as Townsley looked at the leader he realized that he was not an ordinary man. There was something extraordinary about him. He either commanded the absolute obedience of men who came near him or he sent them from him with a repulsion as strong as the attraction to those who liked him.

He felt the smothering power of this spell over his own mind now and tried to break it.

"Mr. Brown," Townsley began haltingly, "I've brought you here now. You are snug in camp. I'd like to take my team back home."

"To-night?"

"To-night."

"It won't do."

"Why not?"

"I won't allow this party to separate until the work to which God has called me is done."

"I've done my share."

"No. It will not do for you to go yet."

"I'm going -"

"You're not!"

Brown faced the man and held him in a silent look of his

blue-gray eyes.

Townsley quailed before it.

"Whatever happens, you brought me here. You are equally responsible with me."

Townsley surrendered.

The threat was unmistakable. He saw that he was trapped. Whether he liked it or not, he had packed his camp outfit, harnessed his horses and driven over the trail on a hunting expedition. He knew now that they were stalking human game. It sent the chills down his spine. But there was no help for it. He had to stick.

Brown spent the night alone reconnoitering the settlement of the Pottawattomie, marking the place of his game and making sure that no alarm could be given. All was still. There was nowhere the rustle of a leaf along a roadway that approached the unsuspecting quarry.

Saturday dawned clear and serene. His plans required that he lie concealed the entire day. He could stalk his prey with sure success on the second night. The first he had to use in reconnoitering.

When breakfast had been eaten and Brown had finished his morning prayers, he ordered his men to lie low in the tall grass and give no sign of life until the shadows of night should again fall. They were not allowed to kindle another fire. The fires of the breakfast had been extinguished at daylight.

The wind rose with the sun and the tall wild flowers swayed gracefully over the dusty figures of the men. They lay in a close group with Brown in the center leading the low-pitched conversation which at times became a debate.

As the winds whispered through the moving masses of flowers, the old man would sometimes stop his talk suddenly and an ominous silence held the group. He had the strange power of thus imposing his will on the men about him. They watched the queer light in his restless eyes as he listened to the voices within.

Suddenly he awaked from his reverie and began an endless denunciation of both parties in Kansas. Northern and Southern factions had become equally vile. The Southerners were always criminals. Their crime was now fully shared by the time servers, trimmers and liars in the Free State party.

His eyelids suddenly closed halfway and his eyes shone two points of light as his metallic voice rang without restraint:

"They're all crying peace, peace!"

He paused and hissed his words through the grass.

"There shall be no peace!"

## CHAPTER XVIII

Brown lay flat on his belly the last hour of the day catching moments of fitful sleep. At sunset he lifted his small head above the grass and scanned the horizon. There might be the curling smoke of a camp in sight. A relief party might be on his trail.

He breathed a sigh of satisfaction. All was well. The sun was fast sinking beneath the hills, the prey was in sight and no hand could be lifted to help.

The moment the shadows closed over the ravine he rose, stretched his cramped body and turned to Thompson.

"Build your fire for supper."

Thompson nodded.

"And give our men all they can eat."

"Yes, sir."

"They'll need their strength to-night."

"I understand."

The supper ready, Brown gathered his band around the camp fire and offered thanks to his God. The meal was eaten in silence. The tension of an imperious mind had gripped the souls of his men. They moved as if stalking game at close quarters.

And they were doing this exactly.

The last pot and pan had been cleaned and packed. The fire was extinguished. Brown issued his first order of the deed.

"Lie down flat in the grass now."

The men dropped one by one. Brown was the last.

"When I give the word, see that your arms are in trim and march single file fifty yards apart and beat the brush as you go. If you come on a cabin in our path not marked in our survey, it is important. Do not pass it. Report to me immediately."

There was no response. He had expected none. The order was final.

The first move in the man hunt was carefully planned.

The instinct to kill is the elemental force, beneath our culture, which makes the hunter. The strongest personalities of our world-conquering race of Nordic freemen are always hunters. If they do not practice the chase the fact is due to an accident of position in life. The opportunity has not been given.

Beneath the skin of the man of the College, the Council Table, the Forum, the Sacred Altar, of Home, and the Church slumbers this elemental beast.

Culture at best is but a few hundred years old and it has probably skipped several generations in its growth. The Archaic instinct in man to kill reaches back millions of years into the past. The only power on earth to restrain that force is Law. The rules of life, embodied in law are the painful results of experience in killing and the dire effects which follow, both to the individual and the race. Law is a force only so long as reverence for law is made the first principle of man's social training. The moment he lifts his individual will against the embodied experience of humanity, he is once more the elemental beast of the prehistoric jungle - the Hunter.

And when the game is human and the hunter is a man of prayer, we have the supreme form of the beast, the ancient Witch Hunter. It is a fact that the pleasure of killing is universal in man. Our savage ancestors for millions of years had to kill to live. We have long ago outgrown this necessity in the development of civilization. But the instinct remains.

We are human as we restrain this instinct and bring it under the dominion of Law. We still hunt the most delicate and beautiful animals, stalk and kill them, driven by the passionate secret pleasure of the act of murder. With bated breath and glittering eyes we press our advantage until the broken wing ceases to flutter and the splintered bone to crawl.

This imperious atavism the best of us cannot or will not control in the pursuit of animals. When man has lifted his arm in defiance of Tradition and Law, this impulse is the dominant force which sweeps all else as chaff before it.

John Brown was the apostle of the sternest faith ever developed in the agonies of our history. To him life had always been a horror.

There was no hesitation, no halting, no quiver of maudlin pity, when he slowly rose from his grass-covered lair in the darkness and called his men at ten o'clock:

"Ready!"

Single file, moving silently and swiftly they crept through the night, only the sharpened swords clanking occasionally broke the silence. Their tread was soft as the claws of panthers. The leader's spirit gripped mind and body of his followers.

They moved northward from the camp in the ravine and crossed the Mosquito Creek just above the home of the Doyles. Once over the creek, the hunters again spread out single file fifty yards apart.

They had gone but two hundred yards when the signal to halt was whispered along the line. Owen Brown reported to his father:

"There's a cabin just ahead."

"We haven't charted it in our survey?"

"No."

"It will not do to pass it," said Brown.

"They might give the alarm."

"Surround it and do your duty," was the stern command.

Owen called three men, cautiously approached the door and knocked.

Something moved inside and a gun was suddenly rammed through a chink in the walls. The muzzle line could be seen in the flash of a star's light.

The four men broke and scattered in the brush. They reported to the leader.

"We want no fight with this fool. No gun play if we can avoid it. We'll take our chances and let him alone. He'll think we're a bunch of sneak thieves. I don't see how we missed this man's place. It can't be five hundred yards from the Doyles'. Back to your places and swing round his cabin."

Owen quickly gave the order and the hunters passed on. The first one of the marked prey had shown teeth and claws and the hunters slipped on under the cover of the darkness to easier game.

The Doyles were not armed.

At least the chances were the old shotgun was not loaded, as it was used only for hunting.

The hunters crouched low and circled the Doyle house, crawling through the timber and the brush.

A hundred yards from the stable, a dog barked. Owen had carefully marked this dog on the day of the survey. He was merely a faithful yellow cur which Doyle had brought from Virginia. He looked about seven years old. If crossed he might put up a nasty fight. If approached with friendly word by a voice he had once heard, the rest would be easy.

The signal was given to halt. The hunters paused and stood still in their tracks. Owen had taken pains to be friendly with this dog on the day of the survey. He had called him a number of times and had given him a piece of bread from his pocket. He was sure he could manage him.

In a low tone he whistled and called the dog by name. He had carefully recalled it.

"Jack!"

He listened intently and heard the soft step of a paw rustling the leaves. The plan was working.

The dog pushed his way into an open space in the brush and stopped.

The hunter called softly:

"Jack, old boy!"

The dog wagged his tail. The man could see the movement of kindly greeting in the starlight, and ventured close. He bent low and called again:

"Come on, boy!"

The dog answered with a whine, wagged his tail, came close and thrust his nose against the man's arm in a welcome greeting. With his left hand the man stroked the warm, furry head, while his right slowly slipped the ugly sharpened cutlass from its scabbard.

Still stroking the dog's head and softly murmuring words of endearment, he straightened his body:

"Bully old dog! Fine old doggie -"

The dog's eyes followed the rising form with confidence, wagging his tail in protest against his going.

The hand gripped the brass hilt of the cutlass, the polished steel whizzed through the air and crashed into the yellow mass of flesh and bones.

His aim was bad in the dark. He missed the dog's head and the sword split the body lengthwise. To the man's amazement a piercing howl of agony rang through the woods.

He dropped his sword and gripped the quivering throat and held it in a vise of steel until the writhing body was still at last.

Inside the darkened cabin, the mother stirred from an uneasy sleep. She shook her husband and listened intently. The only sound that came from without was the chirp of crickets and the distant call of a coyote from the hill across the creek.

She held her breath and listened again. The man by her side slept soundly. She couldn't understand why her heart persisted in pounding. There wasn't the rustle of a leaf outside. The wind had died down with the falling night. It couldn't be more than eleven o'clock.

Her husband's breathing was deep and regular. His perfect rest and the sense of strength in his warm body restored her poise. She felt the slender forms of her little girls in the trundle bed and tried to go back to sleep.

It was useless. In spite of every effort her eyes refused to close. Again she was sure she had heard the dog's cry in the night. She believed that it was an ugly dream. The dawn of a beautiful Sunday morning would find all well in the little home and her faithful dog again wagging his tail at the door asking for breakfast.

She listened to the beating of her foolish heart. Wide awake, she began to murmur a prayer of thanks to God for all His goodness and mercy in the new home He had given.

As Owen's hands slowly relaxed from the throat of the lifeless body he seized a handful of leaves and wiped the blood from the blade and replaced it in the scabbard.

He rose quickly and gave the signal to advance. Again crouching low, moving with the soft tread of beasts of prey, the hunters closed in on the settler's home.

The keen ears of the mother, still wide awake, caught the crunch of feet on the gravel of the walk. With a heart pounding again in alarm she raised her head and listened. From the other side of the house came the rustle of leaves stirred by another swiftly approaching footstep. It was so still she could hear her own heart beat again. There could be no mistake about it this time.

She gripped her husband's arm:

"John!"

He moaned drowsily.

"John - John -"

"What's matter?" he murmured without lifting his head from the pillow.

"Get up quick!"

"What for?" he groaned.

"There's somebody around the house."

"Na."

"I tell you - yes!"

"Hit's the dawgs."

"I heard a man's step on the path, I tell you."

"Yer dreamin', ole woman - "

"I'm not, I tell ye."

"Go back to sleep."

The man settled again and breathed deeply.

The woman remained on her elbow, listening with every nerve strained in agony.

Again she heard a step on the gravel. This time another footfall joined the first. She gripped her husband's shoulders and shook him violently.

"John, John!" she whispered.

He had half roused himself this time, shocked into

consciousness by her trembling grip on his shoulders. But above all by the tremor in her whispered call.

"What is it, Mahala?"

"For God's sake, get up quick and call the boys down outen the loft."

"No!" he growled.

"I tell you, there's somebody outside -"

They were both sitting on the edge of the bed now, speaking in whispers.

"You're dreamin', ole 'oman," he persisted.

"I heard 'em. There's more'n one. I heard some on the other side of the house. I heard two in front. Call the boys down -"

"Don't wake the boys up fer nothin -"

"Is yer gun loaded?"

"No."

"Oh, my God."

"I ain't got no powder. I don't kill game in the springtime."

They both listened. All was still. They could hear the breathing of the little girls in the trundle bed.

The crunch of feet suddenly came to the doorstep. The woman's hand gripped her husband's arm in terror. He heard it now.

"That's funny," he mused.

Thomas Dixon

"Call the boys!" the mother pleaded.

"*Wait* till we find out what it is -"

A firm knock on the door echoed through the darkened room.

"God save us!" the woman breathed.

Doyle rose and quietly walked to the door.

"What is it?" he called in friendly tones.

"We're lost in the woods," a voice answered.

His wife had followed and gripped his arm.

"Don't open that door."

"Wait, Mother -"

"We're trying to find the way to Mr. Wilkinson's - can you tell us?"

"Sure I can."

He moved to open the door. Again his wife held him.

"Don't do it!"

Doyle brushed her aside.

"Don't be foolish, Mahala," he protested indignantly. "I'm a poor sort o' man if I can't tell a lost traveler the way out of the woods."

"They're lyin'!"

"We'll see."

He raised the latch and six men crashed their way through the door. John Brown led the assault. He held a dim lantern in his hand which he lifted above his head, as he surveyed the room. He kept his own face in shadow.

With a smothered cry, the mother backed against the trundle bed instinctively covering the sleeping figures of the girls.

Brown pointed a cocked revolver at Doyle's breast and said in cold tones:

"Call those three boys down."

Doyle hesitated.

Brown's eye glanced down the barrel of his revolver:

"Quick!"

The man saw he had no chance.

He mounted the ladder, the revolver following him. The mother's terror-stricken eyes saw that each man was armed with two revolvers, a bowie knife and cutlass.

"Don't you scare 'em," Brown warned.

"I won't."

"Tell 'em to come down and show us the way to Wilkinson's."

"Boys!" the father called.

There was no answer at first, and the father wondered if they had heard and gotten weapons of some kind. He hoped not. It would be a useless horror to try to defend themselves before a mother's eyes, and those little girls screaming beside her.

He hastened to call a second time and reassure their fears.

"Boys!"

William, the older one, answered drowsily:

"Yessir -"

"Come down, all of you. Some travelers are here who've lost the way. They want you to help them get to Mr. Wilkinson's."

"All right, sir."

The boys hastily slipped on their trousers and shoes.

"Tell 'em to hurry," Brown ordered.

"Jest slip on yer shoes and britches," Doyle called.

The Surveyor held the lantern behind his body until the three sons had come down the ladder and he saw that they were unarmed.

He stepped to the fireplace, took the shotgun from the rack and handed it to Weiner.

The boys, startled at the group of stern armed men, instinctively moved toward their father, dazed by the assault.

Brown faced the group.

"You four men are my prisoners."

The mother left the trundle bed and faced the leader.

"Who are you?"

Brown dropped his lantern, fixed her with his eyes.

"I am the leader of the Northern Army."

"What are you doing here to-night?"

"I have come on a divine mission."

"Who sent you?"

"The Lord of Hosts in a Vision -"

"What are you going to do?"

"The will of God."

"What are you going to do?" she fairly screamed in his face.

"That is not for your ears, woman," was the stern answer. "I have important business with Southern settlers on the Pottawattomie to-night."

The woman's intuition saw in a flash the hideous tragedy. With a cry of anguish she threw her arms around her husband's neck, sobbing.

"Oh, John, John, my man, I told ye not to talk - but ye would tell folks what ye believed. Why couldn't ye be still? Oh, my God, my God, it's come to this!"

The man soothed her with tender touch.

"Hush, Mother, hush. You mustn't take on."

"I can't help it - I just can't. God have mercy on my poor lost soul -"

She paused and looked at her boys.

With a scream she threw herself first on one and then on the other.

"Oh, my big fine boy! I can't let you go! Where is God

to-night? Is He dead? Has He forgotten me?"

The father drew her away and shook her sternly.

"Hush, Mother, hush! Yer can't show the white feather like this!"

"I can't help it. I can't give up my boys!"

She paused and looked at Doyle.

"And I can't give you up, my man - I just can't!"

"Don't, don't -" the husband commanded. "We've got to be men now."

She fought hard to control her tears. The little girls began to sob. She rushed to the trundle bed and soothed them.

"Keep still, babies. They won't hurt you. Keep still!"

The children choked into silence and she leaped toward Brown and tried to seize his hand. He repulsed her and she went on frantically.

"Please, for God's sake, man, have mercy on a wife and mother, if you ain't got no pity in your heart for my men! Surely you have women home. Their hearts can break like mine. My man's only been talkin' as politicians talk. It was nothing. Surely it's no crime."

Brown drew a notebook from his pocket and held it up.

"I have the record in this book of your husband's words against the men of our party, Madame. He stands convicted of murder in his heart. His sons are not of age. Their opinions are his."

For a moment the mother forgot her pleading and shrieked her defiance into the stern face before her.

"And who made you a judge o' life and death for my man and my sons? I bore these boys of the pains of my body. God gave them to me. They are mine, not yours!"

Brown brushed her aside.

"That's enough from you. Those men are my prisoners. Bring them on!"

He moved toward the door and the guards with drawn swords closed in on the group.

The mother leaped forward and barred the way to the door. She faced Brown with blanched face. Her breath came in short gasps. She fought desperately for control of her voice, failed to make a sound, staggered to the old man, grasped blindly his body and sank to her knees at his feet.

At last she managed to gasp:

"Just one of my boys - then - my baby boy! He's a big boy - but look at his smooth face - he ain't but fourteen years old. Hit don't seem but yistiday that he wuz just a laughin' baby in my arms! And I've always been that proud of him. He's smart. He's always been smart - and God forgive me - I've loved him better'n all the others - hit - wuzn't - right - fer - a - mother - to - love one of her - children - more - than - the - others - but I couldn't help it! If ye'll just spare him - hit's all I'll ask ye now" - her voice sank into a sob as her face touched the floor.

The dark figure above her did not move and she lifted her head with desperate courage.

"I'll be all alone here - a broken-hearted woman with two little gals and nobody to help me - or work fer me - ef you'll just spare my baby boy -"

She sprang to her feet and threw her arms around the youngest boy's neck.

"Oh, my baby, my baby, I can't let ye go - I can't - I can't!"

She lifted her tear-streaming eyes to the dark face again.

"Please, please, for the love of God - you - say - you - believe - in - God - leave me this one!"

Brown moved his head in a moment's uncertainty. He turned to Owen.

"Leave him and come on with the others."

With a desperate cry, the mother closed her eyes and clung to the boy.

She dared not lift them in prayer for the others as they passed out into the night.

The armed men had seized her husband and her two older sons, William and Drury, and hustled them through the door. The mother drew the boy back on the trundle bed and held him in her arms. The little girls crouched close and began to sob.

"Hush - don't make a noise. They won't hurt you. I want to hear what they do - maybe -"

The mother stopped short, fascinated by the horror of the tragedy she knew would take place outside her door. The darkness gave no token of its progress. A cricket was chirping in the chimney just awakened by the noise.

She held her breath and listened. Not a sound. The silence was unbearable. She sprang to her feet in a moment's fierce rebellion against the crime of such an infamous attack. A roused lioness, she leaped to the mantel to seize the shotgun.

John followed and caught her.

"The gun's gone, Ma," he cried.

"Yes, yes, I forgot," she gasped. "They took it, the damned fiends!"

"Ma, Ma, be still!" the boy pleaded. He was horror-stricken at the oath from her lips. In all his life he had never heard her use a vulgar word.

"Yes, of course," she faltered. "I mustn't try to do anything. They might come back and kill you - my baby boy!"

She pressed him again to her heart and held him. She strained her ears for the first signal of the deed the darkness shrouded.

The huntsmen dragged the father and two sons but a hundred and fifty yards from the door and halted beside the road. Brown faced the father in the dim starlight.

"You are a Southern white man?"

"I am, sir."

"You are pro-Slavery?"

"I hate the sight and sound of a slave."

"But you believe in the institution?"

"I hate it, I tell you."

Brown paused as if his brain had received a shock. The answer had been utterly unexpected. The man was in earnest. He meant what he said. And he was conscious of the solemnity of the trial on which his life hung.

Brown came back to his cross examination, determined to convict him on the grounds he had fixed beforehand.

"What do you mean when you say that you hate the institution of Slavery?"

"Exactly what I say."

"You do not believe in owning slaves?"

"I do not."

"Did you ever own one?"

"No!"

"And you never expect to own one?"

"Never."

"Why did you rush into this Territory among the first to cross the border?"

"I come West to get away from niggers, and bring my children up in a white man's country."

Quick as a flash came the crucial question from lips that had never smiled. It was the triumphant scream of an eagle poised to strike. He had him at last.

"Then you don't believe the negro to be your brother and your equal - do you?"

The poor white man's body suddenly stiffened and his chin rose:

"No, by God, I don't believe that!"

John Brown lifted his hand in a quick signal and Owen stepped stealthily behind Doyle. The sharpened cutlass whistled through the air and crashed into Doyle's skull. His helpless hands were lifted instinctively as he staggered. The swift descending blade split the right hand open and severed the left from the body before he crumpled in a heap on the ground. The assassin placed his knee on the prostrate figure and plunged his knife three times in the breast, - once through the heart and once through each lung. He had learned the art in butchering cattle.

Fifty yards away the mangled bodies of William and Drury Doyle lay on the ground with the dim figure of the assassin bending low to make sure that no sign of life remained.

John Brown raised the wick of his lantern and walked coolly up to the body of the elder Doyle. He flashed the lantern on the distorted features. A look of religious ecstasy swept the stern face of the Puritan and his eyes glittered with an unearthly glare.

He uttered a sound that was half a laugh and half a religious shout, snatched his pistol from his belt, placed the muzzle within an inch of the dead skull and fired. The brains of the corpse splashed the muzzle of the revolver.

The trembling mother inside the cabin uttered a low cry of horror and crumpled in the arms of her son.

The boy dragged her to the bed and rushed to the kitchen for a cup of water. He dashed it in her face and cried for joy when she breathed again. He didn't mind the moans and sobs. The thought that she, too, might be dead had stopped his very heartbeat.

He soothed her at last and sat holding her hand in the dark. The girls nestled against her side. The mother gave no sign that she was conscious of their presence.

Her spirit was outside the cabin now, hovering in the darkness mourning her dead. Through the dread hours of the night she sat motionless, listening, dreaming.

No sounds came from the darkness. The coyote had ceased to call. The cricket in the chimney slept at last.

# CHAPTER XIX

The dark figures secured the horses, bridles and saddles and moved to the next appointed crime.

The stolen horses were put in charge of the two sons, who had refused to take part in the events of the night. They were ordered to follow the huntsmen carefully.

Again they crept through the night and approached the home of Wilkinson, the member of the Legislature from the County. Brown had carefully surveyed his place and felt sure of a successful attack unless the house should be alarmed by a surly dog which no member of his surveying party had been able to approach.

When they arrived within two hundred yards of the gate, it was one o'clock. Brown carefully watched the house for ten minutes to see that no light gleamed through a window or a chink. The wife had been sick with the measles when the survey was made. There was no sign of a light.

Salmon and Owen Brown were sent by the men on a protest to Brown.

Salmon was spokesman.

"We've got something to say to you, Father, before we take out Wilkinson -"

"Well?" the old man growled.

"You gave every man strict orders to fire no guns or revolver unless necessary - didn't you?"

"I did."

"You fired the only shot heard to-night."

"I'll not do it again. I didn't intend to. I don't know why I did it. Stick to my order."

"See that *you* stick to it," the boy persisted.

"I will. Use only your knives and cutlasses. The cutlass first always."

The men began to move slowly forward.

Brown called softly.

"Just a minute. This dog of Wilkinson's is sure to bark. Don't stop to try to kill him. Rush the house double quick and pay no attention to his barking -"

"If he bites?" Owen asked.

"Take a chance, don't try to kill him - Wilkinson might wake. Now, all together - rush the house!"

They rushed the, house at two hundred yards. They had taken but ten steps when the dog barked so furiously Brown called a halt. They waited.

Then, minutes later the dog raged, approaching the house and retreating. His wild cry of alarm rang with sinister echo through the woods. The faithful brute was calling his master and mistress to arms.

Still the man inside slept. The Territory of Kansas to this time had been as free from crime as any state on its border. The lawmaker had never felt a moment's uneasiness.

Footsteps approached the door. The sick woman saw the shadow of a man pass the window. The starlight sharply silhouetted his face against the black background.

Some one knocked on the door.

The woman asked:

"Who's that?"

No one answered.

"Henry, Henry!" she called tensely.

"Well?" the husband answered.

"There's somebody knocking at the door."

Wilkinson half raised in bed.

"Who is that?"

A voice replied:

"We've lost the road. We want you to tell us the way to Dutch Henry's."

Wilkinson began to call the directions.

"We can't understand -"

"You can't miss the way."

"Come out and show us!"

The request was given in tones so sharp there could be no mistake. It was a command not a plea.

"I'll have to go and tell them," he said to his wife.

"For God's sake, don't open that door," she whispered.

"It's best."

She seized and held him.

"You shall not go!"

Wilkinson sought to temporize.

"I'm not dressed," he called. "I can tell you the way as well without going outdoors."

The men stepped back from the door and held a consultation. John Brown at once returned and began his catechism:

"You are Wilkinson, the Member of the Legislature?"

"I am, sir."

"You are opposed to the Free Soil Party?"

"I am."

The answers were sharp to the point of curtness and his daring roused the wrath of Brown to instant action.

"You're my prisoner, sir."

He waited an instant for an answer and, getting none, asked:

"Do you surrender?"

"Gentlemen, I do."

Thomas Dixon

"Open the door!"

"In just a minute."

"Open it -"

"When I've made a light."

"We've got a light. Open that door or we'll smash it!"

Again the sick woman caught his arm.

"Don't do it!"

"It's better not to resist," he answered, opening the door.

Brown held the lantern in his face.

"Put on your clothes."

Wilkinson began to dress.

The men covered him with drawn revolvers. The sick woman sank limply on the edge of the bed.

"Are there any more men in this house?" Brown asked sharply.

"No."

"Have you any arms?"

"Only a quail gun."

"Search the place."

The guard searched the rooms, ransacking drawers and chests. They took everything of value they could find, including the shotgun and powder flask.

The sick woman at length recovered her power of speech and turned to Brown.

"If you've arrested my husband for anything, he's a law-abiding man. You can let him stay here with me until morning."

"No!" Brown growled.

"I'm sick and helpless. I can't stay here by myself."

"Let me stay with my wife, gentlemen," Wilkinson pleaded, "until I can get some one to wait on her and I'll remain on parole until you return or I'll meet you anywhere you say."

Brown looked at the woman and at the little children trembling by her side and curtly answered:

"You have neighbors."

"So I have," Wilkinson agreed, "but they are not here and I cannot go for them unless you allow me."

"It matters not," Brown snapped. "Get ready, sir."

Wilkinson took up his boots to pull them on when Brown signaled his men to drag him out.

Without further words they seized him and hurried into the darkness. They dragged him a few yards from the house into a clump of dead brush.

Weiner was the chosen headsman. He swung his big savage figure before Wilkinson and his cutlass flashed in the starlight.

The woman inside the darkened house heard the crash of the blade against the skull and the dying groan from the lips of the father of her babies.

When the body crumpled, Weiner knelt, plunged his knife into the throat, turned it and severed the jugular vein.

Standing over the body John Brown spoke to one of his men.

"The horses, saddles and bridles from the stable - quick!"

The huntsman hurried to the stable and took Wilkinson's horse.

It was two o'clock before they reached the home of James Harris on the other side of the Pottawattomie. Harris lived on the highway and kept a rude frontier boarding place where travelers stopped for the night.

With him lived Dutch Henry Sherman and his brother, William.

Brown had no difficulty in entering this humble one-room house. It was never locked. The latch string was outside.

Without knocking Brown lifted the latch and sprang into the room with his son, Owen, and another armed huntsman.

He surveyed the room. In one bed lay Harris, his wife and child. In two other beds were three men, William Sherman, John Whitman and a stranger who had stopped for the night and had given no name.

"You are our prisoners," Brown announced. "It is useless for you to resist."

The old man stood by one bed with drawn saber and Owen stood by the other while Weiner searched the room. He found two rifles and a bowie knife which he passed through the door to the guard outside.

Brown ordered the stranger out first. He kept him but a few minutes and brought him back. He next ordered Harris to follow him.

Brown confronted his prisoner in the yard. A swordsman stood close by his side to catch his nod.

"Where is Dutch Henry Sherman?"

"On the plains hunting for lost cattle."

"You are telling me the truth?" Brown asked, boring him through with his terrible eyes.

"The truth, sir!"

He studied Harris by the light of his lantern.

"Have you ever helped a Southern settler to enter the Territory of Kansas?"

"No."

"Did you take any hand in the troubles at Lawrence?"

"I've never been to Lawrence."

"Have you ever done the Free State Party any harm?"

"No. I don't take no part in politics."

"Have you ever intended to do that party any harm?"

"I don't know nothin' about politics or parties."

"What are you doing living here among these Southern settlers?"

"Because I can get better wages."

"Any horses, bridles, or saddles?"

"I've one horse."

"Saddle him and bring him here."

A swordsman walked by his side while he caught and saddled his horse and delivered him to his captors.

Brown went back into the house and brought out William Sherman. Harris was ordered back to bed, and a new guard was placed inside until the ceremony with Sherman should be ended.

It was brief.

Brown had no questions to ask this man. He was the brother of Henry Sherman, the most hated member of the settlement. Brown called Thompson and Weiner and spoke in tones of quick command.

"Take him down to the Pottawattomie Creek. I want this man's blood to mingle with its waters and flow to the sea!"

The doomed man did not hear the sentence of his judge. The two huntsmen caught his arms and rushed him to the banks of the creek. He stood for a moment trembling and dazed. Not a word had passed his lips. Not one had passed his guards.

They loosed their grip on his arms, stepped back and two cutlasses whistled through the air in a single stroke. The double blow was so swiftly and evenly delivered that the body stood erect until the second stroke of the sharpened blades had cut off one hand and split open the breast.

When the body fell at the feet of the huntsmen they seized the quivering limbs and hurled them into the creek.

They reported at once to their Captain. He stood in front of the house with his restless gaze sweeping the highway for any possible, belated traveler. The one hope uppermost in his mind was that Dutch Henry Sherman might return with his lost cattle in time.

He raised his lantern and looked at his watch. The men who had butchered William Sherman stood with red swords for orders.

Brown had not yet uttered a word. He knew that the work on the bank of the Pottawattomie was done. The attitude of his swordsmen was sufficient.

He asked but one question.

"You threw him into the water?"

"Yes."

"Good."

He closed his silver watch with a snap.

"It's nearly four o'clock. We have no more time for work to-night. Back to camp."

The men turned to repeat his orders.

"Wait!"

His order rang like vibrant metal.

The men stopped.

"We'll mount the horses we have taken, and march single file. I'll ride the horse taken here. Bring him to the door."

With quick springing step Brown entered the house where the husband and wife and the two lodgers were still shivering under the eye of the guard with drawn sword.

The leader's voice rang with a note of triumph.

"You people whose lives have been spared will stay in this house until sunrise. And the less you say about what's happened to-night the longer you'll live."

He turned to his guard.

"Come on."

Brown had just mounted his horse to lead the procession back to the camp in the ravine, when the first peal of thunder in a spring shower crashed overhead.

He glanced up and saw that the sky was being rapidly overcast by swiftly moving clouds. A few stars still glimmered directly above.

The storm without was an incident of slight importance. The rain would give him a chance to test the men inside. He ordered his followers to take refuge in the long shed under which Harris stabled the horses and vehicles of travelers.

He stationed a sentinel at the door of the house.

His orders were clear.

"Cut down in his tracks without a word, the man who dares to come out."

The swordsman threw a saddle blanket around his shoulders and took his place at the doorway.

The storm broke in fury. In five minutes the heavens were a sea of flame. The thunder rolled over the ravine, the hills, the plains in deafening peals. Flash after flash, roar after roar, an endless throb of earth and air from the titanic bombardment from the skies. The flaming sky was sublime - a changing, flashing, trembling splendor.

Townsley was the only coward in the group of stolid figures standing under the shed. He watched by the lightning the expression of Brown's face with awe. There was something terrible in the joy that flamed in his eyes. Never had he seen such a look on human face. He forgot the storm and forgot his fears of cyclones and lightning strokes in the fascination with which he watched the seamed, weather-beaten features of the man who had just committed the foulest deed in the annals of American frontier life. There was in his shifting eyes no shadow of doubt, of fear, of uncertainty. There was only the look of satisfaction, of supreme triumph. The coward caught the spark of red that flashed from his soul.

For a moment he regretted that he had not joined the bloody work with his own hand. He was ashamed of his pity for the stark masses of flesh that still lay on the deluged earth. In spite of the contagion of Brown's mind which he felt pulling him with resistless power, his own weaker intellect kept playing pranks with his memory.

He recalled the position of the bodies which they had left in the darkness. He had seen them by the light of the lantern which Brown had flashed each time before leaving. He remembered with a shiver that the two Doyle boys had died with their big soft blue eyes wide open, staring upward at the starlit skies. He wondered if the rain had beaten their eyelids down.

A blinding flash filled the sky and lighted every nook and corner of the woods and fields. He shook at its glare and put his hand over his eyes. For a moment he could see nothing but the wide staring gaze upward of those stalwart young bodies. He shivered and turned away from the leader.

The next moment found him again watching the look of victory on the terrible face.

As the lightning played about Brown's form he wondered at the impression of age he gave with his face turned away and his figure motionless. He was barely fifty-seven and yet he looked seventy-five, until he moved.

The moment his wiry body moved there was something uncanny in the impression he gave of a wild animal caught in human form.

Brown had tired waiting for the shower to pass and had begun to pace back and forth with his swinging, springy step. When he passed, Townsley instinctively drew aside. He knew that he was a coward and yet he couldn't feel the consciousness of cowardice in giving this man room. It was common sense.

The storm passed as swiftly as it came.

Without a word the leader gave the signal. His men mounted the stolen horses. With Townsley's grays and Weiner's pony the huntsmen returned to the camp in the ravine, a procession of cavalry.

The eastern sky was whitening with the first touch of the coming sun when they dismounted.

The leader ordered the fire built and a hearty breakfast cooked for each man. As was his custom he wandered from the camp alone, his arms gripped behind his stooped back. He climbed the hill, stood on its crest and watched the prairie.

The storm had passed from west to east. On the eastern horizon a low fringe of clouds was still slowly moving. They lay in long ribbons of dazzling light. The sun's rays flashed through them every color of the rainbow. Now they were a deep purple, growing brighter with each moment, until every flower in the waving fields was touched with its glory. The purple melted into orange; the waving fields were set with dazzling buttercups; the buttercups became poppies. And then the mounting sun kissed the clouds again. They blushed scarlet, and the fields were red.

The grim face gave no sign that he saw the glory and beauty of a wonderful Sabbath morning. His figure was rigid. His eyes set. A sweet odor seemed to come from the scarlet rays of the sun. The man lifted his head in surprise to find the direction from which the perfume came.

He looked at the ground and saw that he was standing in a bed of ripening wild strawberries.

He turned from the sunrise, stooped and ate the fruit. He was ravenously hungry. His hunger satisfied, he walked deliberately back to camp as the white light of day flooded the clean fields and woods.

He called his men about the fire and searched for marks of the night's work. As the full rim of the sun crept over the eastern hills and its first rays quivered on the surface of the water, the huntsmen knelt by the bank of the Pottawattomie and washed the stains from their swords, hands and clothes.

Breakfast finished, the leader divided among his headsmen the goods stolen from his victims and called his men to Sunday prayers.

With folded hands and head erect in the attitude of victory he read from memory a passage from the old Hebrew prophet, singing in triumph over the enemies of the Lord. From the scripture recitation, given in tones so cold and impersonal that they made Townsley shiver, his voice drifted into prayer:

"We thank thee, oh, Lord, God of Hosts, for the glorious victory Thou hast given us this night over Thy enemies. We have heard Thy voice. We have obeyed Thy commands. The wicked have been laid low. And Thy glory shines throughout the world on this beautiful Sabbath morning. Make strong, oh, God, the arms of Thy children for the work that is yet before them. Thou art a jealous God. Thou dost rejoice always in blood offerings on Thy altars. We have this night brought to Thee and laid before Thy face the five offerings which the sins of man have demanded. May this blood seem good in Thy sight, oh, God, as it is glorious in the eyes of Thy servant whom Thou hast anointed to do Thy will. May it be as seed sown in good ground. May it bring forth a harvest whose red glory shall cover the earth, even as the rays of the sun have baptized our skies this morning. We wait the coming of Thy Kingdom, oh, Lord, God of Hosts. Speed the day we humbly pray. Amen."

Townsley's eyes had gradually opened at the tones of weird, religious ecstasy with which the last sentences of the prayer were spoken. He was staring at Brown's face. It was radiant with a strange joy. He had not smiled; but he was happy for a moment. His happiness was so unusual, so sharply in contrast with his habitual mood, the sight of it chilled Townsley's soul.

# CHAPTER XX

Stuart succeeded in securing from Colonel Sumner a leave of absence of two weeks to visit Fort Riley. The Colonel suspected the truth and teased the gallant youngster until he confessed.

He handed Stuart the order with a hearty laugh.

"It's all right, my boy. I've been young myself. Good luck."

Stuart's laughter rang clear and hearty.

"Thank you, Colonel. You had me scared."

He had just turned to leave the room when a messenger handed Sumner a telegram.

Stuart paused to hear the message.

"Bad news, Lieutenant."

"What, sir?"

"An attack has been made on the Southern settlement on the Pottawattomie."

"A drunken fight -"

"No. Wilkinson, the member of the Legislature from Miami

Thomas Dixon

County, was taken from his house in the night and murdered."

"The story's a fake," Stuart ventured.

"The man who sent this message doesn't make such mistakes."

He paused and studied the telegram.

"No. This means the beginning of a blood feud. The time's ripe for it."

"We'll have better news to-morrow," Stuart hoped.

"We'll have worse. I've been looking for something like this since the day I heard old Brown harangue a mob at Lawrence."

He stopped short.

"You'll have to give me back that order, my boy."

Stuart's face fell.

"Colonel, I've just got to see that girl, if it's only for a day -"

He slowly handed the order back to the Commandant. Sumner watched the red blood mount to Stuart's face with a look of sympathy.

"Is it as bad as that, boy?"

"It couldn't be worse, sir," Stuart admitted in low tones. "I'm a goner."

"All right. You've no time to lose, I'll give you three days -"

"Thank you!"

"This regiment will be on the march before a week has passed or I miss my guess."

"I'll be here, sir!" was the quick response.

Stuart grasped the leave of absence and hurried out before another messenger could arrive.

He reached Fort Riley the following day and had but twenty-four hours in which to crowd the most important event of his life.

He paced the floor in Colonel Cooke's reception room awaiting Flora's appearance with eager impatience. What on earth could be keeping her? He asked himself the question fifty times and looked at his watch a dozen times before he heard the rustle of organdy on the stairs.

A vision of radiant youth! She had taken time to make her beauty still more radiant with the daintiest touches to her blonde hair.

The simple dress she wore was a poem. The young cavalier was stunned anew. There was no doubt about the welcome in her smile and voice. It thrilled him to his fingertips. He held her hand until she drew it away with a little self-conscious laugh that was confusing to Stuart's plan of direct action.

There was a touch of the Southern girl's conscious poise and coquetry in the laugh. There was something aloof in it that meant trouble. He felt it with positive terror. He didn't have time to fence for position. He was in no mood for a flirtation. He had come to speak the deep things.

She led him to a seat with an air of dignity and reserve that alarmed him still more. He had taken too much for granted perhaps. There might be another man. Conceited fool! He hadn't thought it possible. Her manner had been so frank, so utterly sincere.

She sat by his side smiling at him in the bewitching way so many pretty girls had done before, when they merely wished to play with love.

He spoke in commonplaces and studied her with increasing panic. Her tactics baffled him. Until at last he believed he had solved the riddle! She had suddenly waked to the fact, as he had, that she had met her fate. She was drawing back for a moment in fright at the seriousness of surrender.

"Yes, that's it!" he murmured half aloud.

"What did you say?" she asked archly.

And his heart sank again. She asked the question with a tone of teasing that made him blush in spite of himself.

With sudden resolution he decided to make the plunge.

# CHAPTER XX

Stuart succeeded in securing from Colonel Sumner a leave of absence of two weeks to visit Fort Riley. The Colonel suspected the truth and teased the gallant youngster until he confessed.

He handed Stuart the order with a hearty laugh.

"It's all right, my boy. I've been young myself. Good luck."

Stuart's laughter rang clear and hearty.

"Thank you, Colonel. You had me scared."

He had just turned to leave the room when a messenger handed Sumner a telegram.

Stuart paused to hear the message.

"Bad news, Lieutenant."

"What, sir?"

"An attack has been made on the Southern settlement on the Pottawattomie."

"A drunken fight -"

"No. Wilkinson, the member of the Legislature from Miami

Thomas Dixon

County, was taken from his house in the night and murdered."

"The story's a fake," Stuart ventured.

"The man who sent this message doesn't make such mistakes."

He paused and studied the telegram.

"Dee double dare you."

"He said that you're a sad product of Sir Walter Scott's novels, a singing, rollicking, flirting, lazy young cavalier."

"Didn't say lazy."

"No."

"I thought not."

"I added that for good measure."

"I thought so."

"And he warned me that there might be a streak of the old Stuart purple blood in your veins that might make you silly for life -"

"Didn't say silly."

"No, I added that, too."

Stuart again seized the hand she had deftly withdrawn. He pressed it tenderly and sought the depths of her blue eyes.

"Ah, honey girl," he cried passionately, "don't tease me any more, please! I've got to leave you in a few hours. My regiment is going to march. It may be a serious business. You're a brave soldier's daughter and you're going to be a soldier's bride."

The girl's lips quivered for the first time and her voice trembled the slightest bit as she fought for self-control.

"I'll never marry a soldier."

"You will!"

"My daddy's never at home. I promised my mother never to look at a soldier."

"You're looking at me, dear heart!"

She turned quickly.

"I won't -"

Stuart drew her suddenly into his arms and kissed her.

"I love you, Flora! And you're mine."

She looked into his eyes, smiled, slipped both arms around his neck and kissed him.

"And I love you, my foolish, singing, laughing boy!"

"Always?"

"Always."

"And you'll marry me?"

"You couldn't get away from me if you tried."

She drew him down and kissed him again.

"The shadow will always be in my heart, dear soldier man. The shadow of the day I shall lose you! But it's life. I'll face it with a smile."

Through the long, sweet hours of the day and deep into the night they held each other's hand, and talked and laughed and dreamed and planned.

What mattered the shadow that was slowly moving across the sunlit earth? It *was* the morning of life!

# CHAPTER XXI

The eight men engaged in the remarkable enterprise on the Pottawattomie, led by their indomitable Captain, mounted their stolen horses and boldly rode to the camp of the military company commanded by John Brown, Jr. The father planned to make his stand behind these guns if pursued by formidable foes.

Brown reached the camp of the Rifles near Ottawa Jones' farm at midnight. The fires still burned brightly. To his surprise he found that the news of the murders had traveled faster than the stolen horses.

The camp was demoralized.

John Brown, Jr., had been forced to resign as Captain and H. H. Williams had been elected in his stead.

The reception which the County was giving his inspired deed stunned the leader. He had expected a reign of terror. But the terror had seized his own people. He was compelled to lie and deny his guilt except to his own flesh and blood. Even before his sons he was arraigned with fierce condemnation.

On the outer edge of the panic-stricken camp his sons, Jason and John, Jr., faced him with trembling and horror in their voices.

Jason had denounced the first hint of the plan when the

surveyor's scheme was broached. John, Jr. had refused to move a step on the expedition. The two sons confronted their father with determined questions. He shifted and evaded the issue.

Jason squared himself and demanded:

"Did you kill those men?"

"I did not," was the sharp answer.

The son held his shifting eye by the glare of the camp fire.

"Did you have *anything* to do with the killing of those men?"

To his own he would not lie longer. It wasn't necessary. His reply was quick and unequivocal.

"I did not do it. But I approved it."

"It was the work of a beast."

"You cannot speak to me like that, sir!" the old man growled.

"And why not?"

"I am your father, sir!"

"That's why I tell you to your face that you have disgraced every child who bears your name - now - and for all time. What right had you to put this curse upon me? The devils in hell would blush to do what you have done!"

The father lifted his hand as if to ward a blow and bored his son through with a steady stare.

"God is my judge - not you, sir!"

John Brown, Jr., sided with his brother in the attack but with less violence. His feebler mind was already trembling on the verge of collapse.

"It cuts me to the quick," the old man finally answered, "that my own people should not understand that I had to make an example of these men -"

Jason finally shrieked into his ears:

"Who gave you the authority of Almighty God to sit in judgment upon your fellow man, condemn him without trial and slay without mercy?"

The father threw up both hands in a gesture of disgust and walked from the scene. He spent the night without sleep, wandering through the woods and fields.

Three days later while Brown and his huntsmen were still hiding in the timber, the people of his own settlement at Osawatomie held a public meeting which was attended by the entire male population. They unanimously adopted resolutions condemning in the bitterest terms the deed.

When the old man heard of these resolutions he ground his teeth in rage. He had thought to sweep the Territory with a Holy War in a Sacred Cause. He expected the men who hated Slavery to applaud his Blood Offering to the God of Freedom. Instead they had hastened to array themselves with his foes.

Something had gone wrong in the execution of his divine vision. His mind was stunned for the moment. But he was wrestling again with God in prayer, while the avengers were riding to demand an eye for an eye and a tooth for a tooth.

When the true history of man is written it will be the record of mind not the story of the physical acts which follow the mental process.

The dangers of society are psychological, not physical. The crucial moments of human history are not found in the hours in which armies charge. They are found in the still small voices that whisper in the silence of the night to a lone watcher by the fireside. They are found in the words of will that follow hours of silent thought behind locked doors or under the stars.

The story of man's progress, his relapses to barbarism, his victories, his failures, his years of savage cruelties, his eras of happiness and sorrow, must be written at last in terms of mental states.

John Brown's mind had conceived and executed the series of murders that shocked even a Western frontier. His mind enacted the tragedy days before the actual happening.

And it was the state of mind created by the deed that upset all his calculations. The reaction was overwhelming. He was correct in his faith that a blood feud once raised, all appeal to reason and common sense, all appeal to law, order, tradition, religion would be vain babble. But he had failed to gauge the moral sense of his own party. They had not yet accepted the theory which he held with such passionate conviction.

Brown's moral code was summed up in one passage from the Bible which he quoted and brooded over daily:

"WITHOUT THE SHEDDING OF BLOOD THERE IS NO REMISSION OF SINS."

But he had made a mistake in the spot chosen for rousing the Blood Feud. Men had instantly seen red. They sprang to their arms. They leaped as tigers leap on their prey. But his own people were the prey. He had miscalculated the conditions of frontier life, though he had not yet realized it. His stubborn, restless mind clung to the idea that the stark horror of the crimes which he had committed in the name of Liberty would call at last all men who stood for Freedom.

He held his armed band in camp under the sternest discipline to await this call of the blood.

The Southern avengers who swarmed across the Missouri border into the region of Osawatomie accepted Brown's standards of justice and mercy without question. A few men of education among them were the only restraining influence.

Through these exciting days the old man would show himself at daylight in different places removed from his camp in the woods. While squadrons of avengers were scouring the ravines, the river bottoms and the tangled underbrush, he was lying quietly on his arms. Sometimes his pursuers camped within hearing and got their water from the same spring.

With all his indomitable courage he was unable to rally sufficient men to afford protection to his people. He was a fugitive from justice with a price on his head. Yet, armed and surrounded by a small band of faithful followers, he led a charmed life.

His deed on the Pottawattomie made murder the chief sport of the unhappy Territory. The life of the frontier was reduced to anarchy. Outrages became so common it was impossible to record them. Murder was a daily incident. Many of them passed in secret. Many were not revealed for days and weeks after they had been committed - then, only by the discovery of the moldering remains of the dead. Two men were found hanging on a tree near Westport. They were ill-fated Free State partisans who had fallen by the hand of the avengers. The troops buried them in a grave so shallow that the prairie wolves had half devoured them before they were again found and re-buried.

The Free Soil men organized guerrilla bands for retaliation. John E. Cook, a daring young adventurer, the brother-in-law of Governor Willard of Indiana, early distinguished himself in this work. He put himself at the head of a group of twenty young "Cavalry Scouts" who ranged the country, asking no quarter and giving none.

A squadron of avengers invaded Brown's settlement at

Osawatomie, sacked and partly destroyed it, and killed his son, Frederick, whose mind had been in a state of collapse since the night of the murders on the Pottawattomie.

John Brown rallied a group of sympathizers and fought a pitched battle with the invaders but was defeated with bloody losses and compelled to retreat.

He was followed by Deputy United States Marshal, Henry C. Pate. Brown turned and boldly attacked Pate's camp and another battle ensued. The Deputy Marshal, wishing to avoid useless bloodshed, sent out a flag of truce and asked an interview with the guerrilla commander. Brown answered promptly, advanced and sent for Pate.

Pate, trusting the flag of truce, approached the old man.

"I am addressing the Captain in command?" Pate asked.

"You are, sir."

"Then let me announce that I am a Deputy United States Marshal."

"And why are you fighting us?"

"I have no desire for bloodshed, sir. I am acting under the orders of the Marshal of the Territory."

"And what does the Marshal demand?"

"The arrest of the men for whom I have warrants."

Pate had never seen John Brown and had no idea that he was talking to the old man himself.

"I have a proposition to make," he went on.

"I'll have no proposals from you, sir," Brown announced

shortly. "I demand your surrender."

"I am an officer of the law. I cannot surrender to armed outlaws."

Brown's metallic voice quivered.

"I demand your immediate and unconditional surrender!"

"I have the right to retire under a flag of truce and consider your proposition with my men - "

Pate started to go and Brown stood in front of him.

"You're not going."

"You will violate a flag of truce?"

Brown signaled his men to advance and surround Pate.

"You're not going, sir," he repeated.

"I claim my rights under a flag of truce accepted by you for this parley. An Indian respects that flag."

Brown pointed to his men who were standing within the sound of their voices.

"Order those men to surrender."

Pate folded his arms and remained silent.

Brown placed his revolver at the Deputy Marshal's breast and shouted.

"Tell your men to lay down their arms!"

Pate refused to speak. There was a moment's deadly silence and the Marshal's posse, to save the life of their Captain, threw down their guns and the whole party were made prisoners.

The United States Cavalry at Fort Leavenworth were ordered to the scene to rescue the Deputy Marshal and his men.

# CHAPTER XXII

The bugles at Fort Leavenworth sounded Boots and Saddles for the march on Brown and his guerrillas. The barracks were early astir with the excitement. Stern work might be ahead. Outlaws who would dare violate a flag of truce, to take a United States Marshal and his posse would have no more respect for cavalry. The men and officers were tired of disorder. They were eager for a stand up and knock down fight. They expected it and they were ready for it.

Stuart's bride was crying. In spite of her young husband's gay banter, she persisted in being serious.

"There's no danger, honey girl!" he laughed.

She touched the big cavalry pistol in its holster, her lips still trembling.

"No - you're just galloping off on a picnic."

"That's all it will be -"

"Then you can take me with you."

Stuart's brow clouded.

"Well, no, not just that kind of a picnic."

"There may be a nasty fight and you know it."

Thomas Dixon

"Nonsense."

"It may, too."

"Don't be silly, little bride," he pleaded. "You're a soldier's wife now. The bullet hasn't been molded that's going to get me. I feel it. I know it."

She threw her arms around his neck and held him in a long silence. Only a sob broke the stillness. He let her cry. His arms merely tightened their tender hold, as he caressed her fair head and kissed it.

"There, there, now. That's enough. It's hard, this first parting. It's hard for me. You mustn't make it harder."

"We've just begun to live, dearest," she faltered. "I can't let you go. I can't stand it for an hour and you'll be gone for days and days -"

She paused and sobbed.

"Why did I marry a soldier-man?"

"You had to, honey. It was fate. God willed it."

He spoke with deep reverence. She lifted her lips for his goodbye kiss.

He turned quickly to go and she caught him again and smothered him with kisses.

"I can't help it, darling man," she sobbed. "I didn't mean to make it hard for you - but - I've an awful presentiment that I shall lose you -"

Her voice died again in a pathetic whisper.

Stuart laughed softly and kissed the tears from her eyes.

"So has every soldier's wife, honey girl. The silly old presentiment is overworked. It will pass bye and bye - when you see me coming home so many, many times to play that old banjo for you and sing our songs over again."

She shook her head and smiled.

"Go now - quick," she said, "before I break down again."

He swung out the door, his sword clanking and his arm waving. She watched him from the window, crying. She saw him mount his horse with a graceful swing. His figure on horseback was superb. Horse and man seemed one.

He looked over his shoulder, saw her at the window and waved again. She ran to her room, closed the door, took his picture to bed with her and cried herself to sleep.

The thing that had so worried her was that Colonel Sumner was taking Major Sedgwick with him for conference and a single squadron of fifty men under Stuart's command. The little bride had found out that he was the sole leader of the fifty fighting men and her quick wit had sensed the danger of the possible extermination of such a force in a battle with desperadoes. She was ashamed of her breakdown. But she knew her man was brave and that he loved a fight. She would count the hours until his return.

Brown rallied a hundred and fifty men when the squadron of cavalry was ordered to the rescue of Pate and his posse. He entrenched himself on an island in Middle Ottawa Creek and from this stronghold raided and robbed the stores within range of his guerrillas. On June 3rd, he successfully looted the store of J. M. Bernard at Centropolis and secured many valuables, particularly clothing.

The raiding party was returning from the looted store as Stuart's cavalry troop was approaching Brown's camp.

The cavalry arrived in the nick of time. A battle was imminent that might have ended in a massacre. Within striking distance of Brown's island Colonel Sumner encountered General Whitfield, a Southern Member of Congress, at the head of a squadron of avengers, two hundred and fifty strong, heavily armed and well mounted.

Sumner acted with quick decision. He confronted Whitfield and spoke with a quiet emphasis not to be mistaken:

"By order of the President of the United States and the Governor of the Territory, I am here to disperse all armed bodies assembled without authority."

"May I see the order of the President, sir?" Whitfield asked.

"You may."

The telegraphic order was handed to the leader. He read it in silence and handed it back without a word.

Colonel Sumner continued:

"My duty is plain and I'll do it."

He signaled Stuart to draw up his company for action. The Lieutenant promptly obeyed. Fifty regulars wheeled and faced two hundred and fifty rugged horsemen of the plains.

Whitfield consulted his second in command and while they talked Colonel Sumner again addressed him:

"Ask your people to assemble. I wish to read to them the President's order and the Governor's proclamation."

Whitfield called his men. In solemn tones Sumner read the documents. Whitfield saw that his men were impressed.

"I shall not resist the authority of the General Government.

My party will disperse."

He promptly ordered them to disband. In five minutes they had disappeared.

On the approach of the company of cavalry, John Brown, with a single guard, walked boldly forward to meet them.

Colonel Sumner heard his amazing request with rising wrath. He spoke as one commanding a body of coordinate power.

"I have come to suggest the arrangement of terms between our forces," Brown coolly suggested.

"No officer of law, sir," Sumner sternly replied, "can make terms with lawless, armed men. I am here to execute the orders of the President. You will surrender your prisoners immediately, disarm your men and disperse or take the consequences."

Brown turned without a word and slowly walked back to his camp. The United States cavalry followed close at his heels with drawn sabers, Stuart at their head.

Colonel Sumner summoned Brown before Sedgwick and Stuart and made to him an announcement which he thought but fair.

"I must tell you now that there is with my company a Deputy United States Marshal, who holds warrants for several men in your camp. Those warrants will be served in my presence."

Brown's glittering eye rested on the Deputy Marshal. He moved uneasily and finally said in a low tone:

"I don't recognize any one for whom I have warrants."

The grim face of the man of visions never relaxed a muscle.

Sumner turned to the Deputy indignantly.

"Then what are you here for?"

He made no answer. And Stuart laughed in derision.

During this tense moment the keen blue eyes of the Lieutenant of cavalry studied John Brown with the interest of a soldier in the man who knows not fear.

At first glance he was a sorry figure. He was lean and gaunt and looked taller than he was for that reason. His face was deeply sun tanned and seamed. He looked a rough, hard-working old farmer. The decided stoop of his shoulders gave the exaggerated impression of age. His face was shaved. He wore a coarse cotton shirt, a clean one that had just been stolen from Bernard's store. It was partly covered by a vest. His hat was an old slouched felt, well worn. In general appearance he was dilapidated, dusty, and soiled.

The young officer was too keen a judge of character to be deceived by clothes on a Western frontier. The dusty clothes and worn hat he scarcely saw. It was the terrible mouth that caught and held his imagination. It was the mouth of a relentless foe. It was the mouth of a man who might speak the words of surrender when cornered. But he could no more surrender than he could jump out of his skin.

Stuart was willing to risk his life on a wager that if he consented to lay down his arms, he had more concealed and that he would sleep on them that night in the brush.

The low forehead and square, projecting chin caught and held his fancy. It was the jaw and chin of the fighting animal. No man who studied that jaw would care to meet it in the dark.

But the thing that had put the Deputy out of commission as warrant officer of the Government was the old man's strange, restless eyes. Stuart caught their steel glitter with a sense of the uncanny. He had never seen a human eye that threw at an enemy a look quite so disconcerting. He had laughed at the

Deputy's fear to move with fifty dragoons to back him. There was some excuse for it. Back of those piercing points of steel-blue light were one hundred and fifty armed followers. What would happen if he should turn to these men and tell them to fight the cavalry of the United States? It was an open question.

The old man walked toward his men with wiry, springing step.

The prisoners were released.

Stuart shook hands with Pate, who was a Virginian and a former student of the University.

Brown's men laid down their arms and dispersed.

True to Stuart's surmise he did not move far from his entrenched camp. He anticipated a fake surrender to the troops. He had concealed weapons for the faithful but half a mile away. With Weiner he built a new camp fire before Stuart's cavalry had moved two miles.

# CHAPTER XXIII

The man with the slouched hat and coarse cotton shirt lost no time in grieving over the dispersal of his one hundred and fifty men. It was the largest force he had ever assembled. His experience in the three days in which he had acted as their commander had greatly angered him. The frontiersman who failed to come under the spell of Brown's personality by direct contact generally refused to obey his orders.

The crowd of free rangers which his fight with Pate had gathered proved themselves beyond control. They raided the surrounding country without Brown's knowledge.

They stole from friend and foe with equal impartiality. There was one consolation in his surrender to the United States troops. He got rid of these troublesome followers. They had already robbed him of the spoils of his own successful raids and not one of them had shown any inclination to bring in the enemies' goods for common use.

He began to choose the most faithful among them for a scheme of wider scope and more tragic daring. He was not yet sure of his plan. But God would reveal it clearly.

He spent a week at his new camp in the woods wandering alone, dreaming, praying, weighing this new scheme from every point of view.

His mind came back again and again to the puzzle of the

failure to raise a National Blood Feud.

For a moment his indomitable Puritan soul was discouraged. He had obeyed the command of his God. He could not have been mistaken in the voice which spoke from Heaven:

"WITHOUT THE SHEDDING OF BLOOD THERE IS NO REMISSION OF SINS."

He had laid the Blood Offering on God's altar counting his own life as of no account in the reckoning and from that hour he had been a fugitive from justice, hiding in the woods. He had escaped arrest only by the accidental assembling of a mob of a hundred and fifty disorderly fools who had stolen his own goods before they had been dispersed.

Instead of the heroic acclaim to which the deed entitled him, his own flesh and blood had cursed him, one of his sons had been shot and another was lying in prison a jibbering lunatic.

Would future generations agree with the men who had met in his own town and denounced his deed as cruel, gruesome and revolting?

His stolid mind refused to believe it. Through hours of agonizing prayer the new plan, based squarely on the vision that sent him to Pottawattomie, began to fix itself in his soul.

This time he would chose his disciples from the elect. Only men tried in the fires of Action could be trusted. Of five men he was sure. His son, Owen, he knew could be depended on without the shadow of turning. Yet Oliver was the second disciple chosen. He had forgiven the boy for the fight over the pistol and had taken pains to regain his complete submission. John Henry Kagi was the third chosen disciple, a young newspaper reporter of excellent mind and trained pen. He had been captured by United States troops in Kansas as a guerrilla raider and was imprisoned first at Lecompton and then at Tecumseh. The fourth disciple selected was Aaron Dwight

Stevens, an ex-convict from the penitentiary at Fort Leavenworth. Stevens was by far the most daring and interesting figure in the group. His knowledge of military tactics was destined to make him an invaluable aide. The uncanny in Brown's spirit had appealed to his imagination from the day he made his escape from the penitentiary and met the old man. The fifth disciple chosen was John E. Cook, a man destined to play the most important role in the new divine mission with the poorest qualification for the task. Born of a well-to-do family in Haddon, Connecticut, he had studied law in Brooklyn and New York. He dropped his studies against the protest of his people in 1855, and, driven by the spirit of adventure, found his way into Kansas and at last led his band of twenty guerrillas into John Brown's camp. Brown's attention was riveted on him from the day they met. He was a man of pleasing personality and the finest rifle shot in Kansas. He was genial; he was always generous; He was brave to the point of recklessness; and he was impulsive, indiscreet and utterly reckless when once bent on a purpose. His sister had married Willard, the Governor of Indiana.

Brown's new plan required a large sum of money. With the prestige his fighting in Kansas had given him, he believed the Abolition philanthropists of the East would give this sum. He left his disciples to drill and returned East to get the money.

In Boston his success was genuine, although the large amount which he asked was slow in coming.

The old man succeeded in deceiving his New England friends completely as to the Pottawattomie murders. On this event he early became a cheerful, consistent and successful liar. This trait of his character had been fully developed in his youth. Everywhere he was acclaimed by the pious as, "Captain Brown, the old partisan hero of Kansas warfare."

His magnetic, uncanny personality rarely failed to capture the dreamer and the sentimentalist. Sanborn, Howe, Theodore Parker, Thomas Wentworth Higginson, George L. Stearns and

Gerrit Smith became his devoted followers. He even made Wendell Phillips and William Lloyd Garrison his friends.

Garrison met him at Theodore Parker's. The two men were one on destroying Slavery: Garrison, the pacifist; Brown, the man who believed in bloodshed as the only possible solution of all the great issues of National life. Brown quoted the Old Testament; Garrison, the New.

He captured the imagination of Thoreau and Ralph Waldo Emerson.

He was raising funds for another armed attack on Slavery in Kansas. The sentimentalists asked no questions. And if hard-headed business men tried to pry too closely into his plans, they found him a past master in the art of keeping his own counsel.

He struck a snag when he appealed to the National Kansas Committee for a gift of rifles and an appropriation of five thousand dollars. They voted the rifles on conditions. But a violent opposition developed against giving five thousand dollars to a man about whose real mind they knew so little.

H. B. Hurd, the Chairman of the Committee, had suspected the purpose back of his pretended scheme for operations in Kansas. He put to Brown the pointblank question and demanded a straight answer.

"If you get these guns and the money you desire, will you invade Missouri or any slave territory?"

The old man's reply was characteristic. He spoke with a quiet scorn.

"I am no adventurer. You all know me. You are acquainted with my history. You know what I have done in Kansas. I do not expose my plans. No one knows them but myself, except perhaps one. I will not be interrogated. If you wish to give me anything, I want you to give it freely. I have no other purpose but to serve the cause of Liberty."

His answer was not illuminating. It contained nothing the Committee wished to know. The statement that they knew him was a figure of speech. They had read partisan reports of his fighting and his suffering in Kansas - through his own letters, principally. How much truth these letters contained was something they wished very much to find out. He had given no light.

He declared that they knew what he had done in Kansas. This was the one point on which they needed most light.

The biggest event in the history of Kansas was the deed on the Pottawattomie. In the fierce political campaign that was in progress its effects had been neutralized by denials. Brown had denied his guilt on every occasion.

Yet as they studied his strange personality more than one member of the Committee began to suspect him as the only man in the West capable of the act.

The Committee refused to vote the rifles and compromised on the money by making a qualification that would make the gift of no service. They voted the appropriation, "in aid of Captain John Brown in any *defensive* measures that may become necessary." He was authorized to draw five hundred dollars when he needed it for this purpose.

The failure rankled in the old man's heart and he once more poured out the vials of his wrath on all politicians, - North and South.

For months he became an incessant and restless wanderer throughout New York and the New England States.

He finally issued a general appeal for help through the *New York Tribune* and other friendly papers.

The contributions came slowly. The invitations to speak came slower. At Collinsville, Connecticut, however, after his lecture he placed with Charles Blair, a blacksmith and forge-master, an important secret order for a thousand iron pikes. Blair pledged his loyalty. He received his first payment on account, for a stand of weapons destined to become souvenirs in marking the progress of civilization in the new world.

In the midst of his disappointing canvas for funds he received a letter from his son, Jason, that a Deputy United States Marshal had passed through Cleveland on the way East with a warrant for his arrest for the Pottawattomie murders.

On the receipt of this news he wrote his friend, Eli Thayer:

"One of the U. S. hounds is on my track: and I have kept myself hid for a few days to let my track get cold. I have no idea of being taken: *and intend* (if God *will*) to go back with Irons *in* rather than *upon* my hands. I got a *fine lift* in Boston the other day; and hope Worcester will not be *entirely behind*. I do not mean *you*; or *Mr. Alien & Company*."

So dangerous was the advent of the U. S. Marshal from Kansas that Brown took refuge in an upper room in the house of Judge Russell in Boston and remained in hiding an entire week. Mrs. Russell acted as maid and allowed no one to open the front door except herself during the time of his stay.

The Judge's house was on a quiet street and his connection with the Abolition movement had been kept secret for political reasons. His services to their cause were in this way made doubly valuable.

Brown daily barricaded his door and told his hostess that he would not be taken alive. He added with the nearest approach to a smile ever seen on his face:

"I should hate to spoil your carpet, Madame."

While in hiding at Judge Russell's he composed a sarcastic farewell to New England. It is in his best style and true character as a poseur:

"Old Brown's *Farewell*: to the Plymouth Rock; Bunker Hill Monument; Charter Oaks; and *Uncle Tom's Cabins*.

"Has left for Kansas. Was trying since he came out of the Territory to secure an outfit; or, in other words, the means of arming and equipping thoroughly, his regular minute men, who are mixed up *with the People of Kansas*: and *he leaves the States*, with a *deep feeling of sadness*: that after exhausting *his own* small means: and with his *family and his brave men*: suffered hunger, nakedness, cold, sickness, (and some of them) imprisonment, with most barbarous and cruel treatment: *wounds and death*: that after laying on the ground for months; in the most unwholesome *and* sickly as well as uncomfortable places: with sick and wounded destitute of any shelter part of the time; dependent in part on the care, and hospitality of the Indians: and hunted like Wolves: that after all this; in order to sustain a cause, which *every Citizen* of this *Glorious Republic*, is under equal moral obligation to do: (*and for the neglect of which HE WILL be held accountable TO GOD:) in which every Man, Woman and Child of the human family;* has a deep and awful interest; and that *no wages are asked or expected:* he cannot secure (amidst all the wealth, luxury and extravagance of this *'Heaven exalted'* people) even the necessary supplies for a common soldier. HOW ARE THE MIGHTY FALLEN?

"JOHN BROWN."

Following his usual tactics of interminable delays and restless, aimless wandering, it was the 7th of August before he reached Tabor, Iowa, the appointed rendezvous of his disciples.

Two days after his arrival the Free State election of the ninth of August was held in Kansas and the heavy vote polled was a complete triumph of the men of peace within the party. Kansas, in his absence, had settled down to the tried American plan of the ballot box for the decision of political disputes. Brown wrote Stearns a despairing letter. He was discouraged and utterly without funds. He begged for five hundred to one thousand dollars immediately for secret service and no questions asked. He promised interesting times in Kansas if he could secure this money. Of his disciples for the great coming deed but one had arrived at Tabor, his faithful son Owen. The old man lingered at Tabor with his religious friends until November before starting for Kansas.

Higginson, his chief backer in Massachusetts, was growing angry over his repeated delays and senseless inaction. Sanborn, always Brown's staunch defender, wrote Higginson a letter begging patience:

"You do not understand Brown's circumstances. He is as ready for revolution as any other man, and is now on the border of Kansas safe from arrest, prepared for action. But he needs money for his present expenses and active support.

"I believe that he is the best Dis-union champion you can find, and with his hundred men, when he is put where he can raise them and drill them (for he has an expert drill officer with him) WILL DO MORE TO SPLIT THE UNION than a list of 50,000 names for your Convention, good as that is.

"What I am trying to hint at is that the friends of Kansas are looking with strange apathy at a movement which has all the elements of fitness and success - a good plan, a tried leader, and a radical purpose. If you can do anything for it *now*, in God's name do it - and the ill results of the new policy in Kansas may be prevented."

The new policy in Kansas must be smashed at all hazards, of course. To the men who believed in bloodshed as the only rational way to settle political issues, the ballot box and the council table were the inventions of the Devil. It was the duty of the children of Light to send the Lord's Anointed with the Sword of Gideon to raise anew the Blood Feud.

It is evident from this letter of F. B. Sanborn to Higginson that even Sanborn had not penetrated the veil of the old Puritan's soul. The one to whom he had revealed his true plan was his faithful son in Kansas. The Territory was not the objective of this mission. It was only a feint to deceive friend and foe.

And he succeeded in doing it.

That his purpose was the disruption of the Union in a deluge of blood, Sanborn, of course, understood and approved. He was utterly mistaken as to the time and place and method which the Man of Visions had chosen for the deed.

On entering the Territory, now as peaceful as any State in the Union, Brown gathered his disciples, Oliver, Kagi, Stevens, and Cook and despatched them to Tabor, Iowa. Here they were informed for the first time of the real purpose of their organization - the invasion of Virginia and the raising of a servile insurrection in which her soil would be drenched in blood within sight of the Capitol at Washington. With Stevens, as drill master, they began the study of military tactics. They moved to Springdale and established their camp for the winter.

# CHAPTER XXIV

Suddenly the old man left Springdale. He ordered his disciples to continue their drill until he should instruct them as to their next march.

Two weeks later he was in Rochester, New York, with Frederick Douglas. In a room in this negro's house Brown composed a remarkable document as a substitute for the Declaration of Independence and the Constitution of the United States.

He hurried with his finished manuscript to the home of Gerrit Smith at Peterboro for a consultation with Smith, Sanborn, Higginson and Stearns.

Only Sanborn and Smith appeared. Brown outlined to them in brief his plan of precipitating a conflict by the invasion of the Black Belt of the South and the establishment of a negro empire. Its details were as yet locked in his own breast.

Smith and Sanborn discussed his plans and his Constitution for the Government of the new power. In spite of its absurdities they agreed to support him in the venture. Smith gave the first contribution which enabled him to call the convention of negroes and radicals at Chatham, Canada, to adopt the "Constitution."

Brown went all the way to Springdale, Iowa, to escort the entire body of his disciples to this convention. And they came

Thomas Dixon

across a continent with him - Stevens, Kagi, Cook, Owen Brown, and six new men whom he had added - Leeman, Tidd, Gill, Taylor, Parsons, Moffit and Realf.

Thirty-four negroes gathered with them. Among the negroes were Richard O. P. Anderson and James H. Harris of North Carolina.

The presiding officer was William C. Monroe, pastor of a negro church in Detroit. Kagi, the stenographer, was made Secretary of the Convention.

Brown addressed the gathering in an unique speech:

"For thirty years, my friends, a single passion has pursued my soul - to set at liberty the slaves of the South. I went to Europe in 1851 to inspect fortifications and study the methods of guerrilla warfare which have been successfully used in the old world. I have pondered the uprisings of the slaves of Rome, the deeds of Spartacus, the successes of Schamyl, the Circassian Chief, of Touissant L'Overture in Haiti, of the negro Nat Turner who cut the throats of sixty Virginians in a single night in 1831.

"I have developed a plan of my own to sweep the South. You must trust me with its details. I shall depend on the blacks for the body of my soldiers. And I expect every freedman in the North to flock to my standard when the blow has fallen. I know that every slave in the South will answer my call. The slaveholders we will not massacre unless we must. We will hold them as hostages for our protection and the protection of any prisoners who may fall into their hands."

The men listened in rapt attention and when he read his "Constitution and Preamble," it was unanimously adopted.

The Constitution which they adopted was a piece of insanity in the literal sense of the word, a confused medley of absurd, inapplicable forms.

The Preamble, however, which contained the keynote of Brown's philosophy of life, was expressed in clear-cut, logical ideas.

He read it in a cold, vibrant voice:

"Whereas, Slavery, throughout its entire existence in the United States is none other than a most barbarous, unprovoked and unjustifiable war of one portion of its citizens upon another portion: the only conditions of which are perpetual imprisonment, and hopeless servitude or absolute extermination, in utter disregard and violation of those eternal and self-evident truths set forth in our Declaration of Independence: *Therefore*, we CITIZENS OF the UNITED STATES, and the OPPRESSED PEOPLE who by a RECENT DECISION of the SUPREME COURT ARE DECLARED to have NO RIGHTS WHICH the WHITE MAN is BOUND to RESPECT; TOGETHER WITH ALL OTHER PEOPLE DEGRADED by the LAWS THEREOF, DO, for the TIME BEING ORDAIN and ESTABLISH for OURSELVES, the FOLLOWING PROVISIONAL CONSTITUTION and ORDINANCES the BETTER to protect, our PERSONS, PROPERTY, LIVES and LIBERTIES: and to GOVERN our ACTION."

The first result of his Radical Convention was the exhaustion of his treasury. He had used his last dollar to bring his men on from the West and no money had been collected to pay even their return fares.

They were compelled to go to work at various trades to earn their bread. Brown determined to return to Kansas and create a sensation that would again stir the East and bring the money into his treasury. He would at the same time test the first principle of his plan by an actual raid into a neighboring Southern State. In the meantime, he issued his first order of the Great Deed. He selected John E. Cook as his scout and spy and dispatched him to Harper's Ferry, Virginia, to map its roads, study its people and reconnoiter the surrounding territory.

He raised the money to pay Cook's fare and saw him on the train for Virginia before he started for Kansas to spring his second national sensation.

# CHAPTER XXV

Brown's scout reached the town of Harper's Ferry on June 5, 1858. The magnificent view which greeted his vision as he stepped from the train took his breath. The music of trembling waters seemed a grand accompaniment to an Oratorio of Nature.

The sensitive mind of the young Westerner responded to its soul appeal. He stood for half an hour enraptured with its grandeur. Two great rivers, the Potomac and the Shenandoah, rushing through rock-hewn gorges to the sea, unite here to hurl their tons of foaming waters against the last granite wall of the Blue Ridge Mountains.

Beyond the gorge, through which the roaring tide has cut its path, lies the City of Washington on the banks of the Potomac, but sixty miles away - a day's journey on a swift horse; an hour and a half by rail.

Cook at first had sharply criticized Brown's selection of such a place for the scene of the Great Deed. As he stood surveying in wonder the sublimity of its scenery he muttered softly:

"The old man's a wizard!"

The rugged hills and the rush of mighty waters called the soul to great deeds. There was something electric in the air. The town, the rivers, the mountains summoned the spirit to adventure. The tall chimneys of the United States Arsenal and

Rifle Works called to war. The lines of hills were made for the emplacement of guns. The roaring waters challenged the skill of generals.

The scout felt his heart beat in quick response. The more he studied the hills that led to High Knob, a peak two thousand four hundred feet in height, the more canny seemed the choice of Brown. From the top of this peak stretches the county of Fauquier, the beginning of the Black Belt of the South. Fauquier County contained more than ten thousand Slaves and seven hundred freed negroes. There were but nine thousand eight hundred whites. From this county to the sea lay a series of adjoining counties in which the blacks outnumbered the whites. These counties contained more than two hundred and sixty thousand negroes.

The Black Belt of Virginia touched the Black Belts of North Carolina, South Carolina and Georgia - an unbroken stretch of overwhelming black majority. In some counties they out-numbered the whites, five to one.

This mountain gorge, hewn out of the rocks by the waters of the rivers, was the gateway into the heart of the Slave System of the South. And it could be made the highroad of escape to the North if once the way were opened.

Another fact had influenced the mind of Brown. The majority of the workmen of Harper's Ferry were mechanics from the North. They would not be enthusiastic defenders of Slavery. They were not slave owners. In a fight to a finish they would be indifferent. Their indifference would make the conquest of the few white masters in town a simple matter.

Cook felt again the spell of Brown's imperious will. He had thought the old man's chief reason for selecting Harper's Ferry as the scene was his quixotic desire to be dramatic. He knew the history of the village. It had been named for Robert Harper, an Englishman. Lord Fairfax, the friend of George Washington, had given the millwright a grant of it in 1748.

Washington, himself, had made the first survey of the place and selected the Ferry, in 1794, as the site of a National Armory.

Colonel Lewis Washington, the great-grandson of Washington's brother, lived on the lordly plantation of Bellair, four miles in the country. Brown had learned that the sword which Frederick the Great had given to Washington, and the pistols which Lafayette had given him hung on the walls of the Colonel's library.

He had instructed Cook to become acquainted with Colonel Washington, and locate these treasures. He had determined to lead his negro army of insurrection with these pistols and sword buckled around his waist.

Cook was an adventurer but he had no trace of eccentricity in his character. He thought this idea a dangerous absurdity. And he believed at first that it was the one thing that had led his Chief to select this spot. He changed his mind in the first thirty minutes, as he stood studying the mountain peak that stood sentinel at the gateway of the Black Belt.

With a new sense of the importance of his mission he sought a boarding house. He was directed by the watchman at the railroad station, a good-looking freedman, an employee of the Mayor of the town, to the widow Kennedy's. Her house was situated on a quiet street just outside the enclosure of the United States Arsenal.

Cook was a man of pleasing address, twenty-eight years old, blue-eyed, blond, handsome, affable, genial in manner and a good mixer. Within twenty-four hours he had made friends with the widow and every boarder in the house.

They introduced him to their friends and in a week he had won the good opinion of the leading citizens of the place. A few days later the widow's pretty daughter arrived from boarding school and the young adventurer faced the first problem of his mission.

She was a slender, dark-eyed, sensitive creature of eighteen. Shy, romantic, and all eyes for the great adventure of every Southern girl's life - the coming of the Prince Charming who would some day ride up to her door, doff his plumed hat, kiss her hand and kneel at her feet?

Cook read the eagerness in her brown eyes the first hour of their meeting. And what was more serious he felt the first throb of emotion that had ever distressed him in the presence of a woman.

He had never made love. He had tried all other adventures. He had never met the type that appealed to his impulsive mind. He was angry with himself for the almost resistless impulse that came, to flirt with this girl.

It could only be a flirtation at best and, it could only end in bitterness and hatred and tragedy in the end. He had done dark deeds on the Western plains. But they were man deeds. No delicate woman had been involved in their tangled ethics.

There was something serious in his nature that said no to a flirtation of any kind with a lovely girl. He had always intended to take women seriously. He did take them seriously. He wouldn't hesitate to kill a man if he were cornered. But a woman - that was different. He tried to avoid the eyes of Virginia. He couldn't. In spite of all, seated opposite at the table, he found himself looking into their brown liquid depths. They were big, soulful eyes, full of tenderness and faith and wonder and joy. And they kept saying to him:

"Come here, stranger man, and tell me who you are, where you came from, where you're going, and what's your hurry."

There was nothing immodest or forward in them. They just kept calling him.

She was exactly the type of girl he had dreamed he would like to marry some day when life had quieted down. She was of the spirit, not the flesh. Yet she was beautiful to look upon. Her hair was a dark, curling brown, full of delicate waves even on the top of her head. Her hands were dainty. Her body was a slender poem in willowy, graceful lines. Her voice was the softest Southern drawl.

The Kennedys were not slave holders. The pretty daughter joyfully helped her mother when she came home from school. Her sentiments were Southern without the over emphasis sometimes heard among the prouder daughters of the old regime. These Southern sentiments formed another impassable barrier. Cook said this a hundred times to himself and sought to make the barrier more formidable by repeating aloud his own creed when in his room alone.

The fight was vain. He drifted into seeing her a few minutes alone each day. She had liked him from the first. He felt it. He knew it. He had liked her from the first, and she knew it.

Each night he swore he'd go to bed without seeing her and each night he laughed and said:

"Just this once more and it won't count."

He felt himself drifting into a tragedy. Yet to save his life he couldn't lay hold of anything that would stand the strain of the sweet invitation in those brown eyes.

To avoid her he spent days tramping over the hills. And always he came back more charmed than ever. The spell she was weaving about his heart was resistless.

Thomas Dixon

# CHAPTER XXVI

Brown returned to Kansas with Stevens and Kagi, his two bravest and most intelligent disciples.

If he could make the tryout of his plan sufficiently sensational, his prestige would be restored, his chief disciples become trained veterans and his treasury be filled.

When he arrived, the Free State forces had again completely triumphed at the ballot box. They had swept the Territory by a majority of three to one in the final test vote on the new Constitution. The issue of Slavery in Kansas was dead. It had been settled for all time.

Such an inglorious end for all his dreams of bloodshed did not depress the man of visions. Kansas no longer interested him except as a rehearsal ground for the coming drama of the Great Deed.

He had carefully grown a long gray beard for the make-up of his new role. It completely changed his appearance. He not only changed his make-up, but he also changed his name. The title he gave to the new character which he had come to play was, "Shubel Morgan."

The revelation of his identity would be all the more dramatic when it came.

When his men and weapons had been selected, he built his

camp fire on the Missouri Border. His raid was carefully planned in consultation with Stevens, Kagi and Tidd. With these trusted followers he had rallied a dozen recruits who could be depended on to obey orders. Among them was a notorious horse thief and bandit known in the Territory by the title of "Pickles."

As they entered the State of Missouri on the night of the twenty-fifth of January, Brown divided his forces. Keeping the main division under his personal command, he despatched Stevens with a smaller force to raid the territory surrounding the two plantations against which he was moving.

Between eleven and twelve o'clock Brown reached the home of Harvey G. Hicklin, the first victim marked on his list.

Without the formality of a knock he smashed his door down and sprang inside with drawn revolver.

Hicklin surrendered.

"We have come to take your slaves and such property as we need," the old man curtly answered.

"I am at your mercy, gentlemen," Hicklin replied.

Gill was placed in charge of the robbers who ransacked the bureau drawers, closets and chests for valuables.

Brown collected the slaves and assured them of protection. When every watch, gun, pistol, and every piece of plate worth carrying had been collected, and the stables stripped of every horse and piece of leather, the old man turned to his victim and coolly remarked:

"Now get your property back if you can. I dare you and the whole United States Army to follow me to-night. And you tell this to your neighbors to-morrow morning."

Hicklin kept silent.

Brown knew that his tongue would be busy with the rising sun. He also knew that his message would be hot on the wires to the East before the sun would set. He could feel the thrill it would give his sentimental friends in Boston. And he could see them reaching for their purses.

The men were still emptying drawers on the floor in a vain search for cash. Hicklin never kept cash over night in his house. He lived too near the border.

Brown called his men from their looting and ordered them to the next house which he had marked for assault - the house of James Lane, three-quarters of a mile away.

They smashed Lane's door and took him a prisoner with Dr. Erwin, a guest of the family.

From Hicklin he had secured considerable booty and his men were keen for richer spoils. The first attack had netted the raiders two fine horses, a yoke of oxen, a wagon, harness, saddles, watches, a fine collection of jewelry, bacon, flour, meal, coffee, sugar, bedding, clothing, a shotgun, boots, shoes, an overcoat and many odds and ends dumped into the wagon.

From Lane they expected more. They were sore over the results. They got six good horses, their harness and wagons, a lot of bedding, clothing and provisions, but no jewelry except two plain silver watches.

Brown added five negroes to his party and told them he would take them to Canada. Thus far no blood had been shed. The attacks had been made with such quiet skill, the surprise was complete. In spite of all the talk and bluster of frontier politicians no sane man in the State of Missouri could conceive of the possibility of such a daring crime. The victims were utterly unprepared for the assault. And no defense had been attempted.

Stevens had better luck. His party had encountered David Cruise, a man who was rash enough to resist. He was an old man, too, of quiet, peaceable habits and exemplary character. He proved to be the man who didn't know how to submit to personal insult.

He owned but one slave who did the cooking for his family. When Stevens broke into his house and demanded the woman, he indignantly refused to surrender his cook to a gang of burglars.

The ex-convict, who had served his term for an assault with intent to kill, didn't pause to ask Cruise any questions.

His revolver clicked, a single shot rang out and the old man dropped on the floor with a bullet through his heart.

Passing the body, Stevens looted the house. He made the largest haul of the night. He secured four oxen, eleven mules, two horses, and a wagon load of provisions. Incidentally he picked up a valuable mule from a neighbor of Cruise as they passed his house on the way to join Brown.

When Stevens reported the murder and gave the inventory of the valuable goods stolen, "Shubel Morgan" stroked his long gray beard and spoke but one word:

"Good."

In his grim soul he knew that the blood stain left on Cruise's floor would be worth more to his cause than all the stolen jewelry, horses and wagons. Its appeal to the East would be the one secret force needed to rouse the archaic instincts of his pious backers. They would deny with indignation the accusation of murder against his men. They would invent the excuse of self-defense. He did not need to make it. From the deeps of their souls would come the shout of the ancient head-hunter returning with the bloody scalp of a foe in his hand. Brown felt this. He knew it, because he felt it in his own heart. He was a

Puritan of Puritans.

With deliberate daring the caravan moved back into the Territory. For the moment the audacity of the crime stunned the frontier. He had figured on this hour of uncertainty and amazement to make good his escape. He knew that he could depend on the people along the way to Iowa to protect the ten slaves which he had brought out of Missouri.

The press of Kansas unanimously condemned the outrage. Brown knew they would. He could spit in their faces now. He was done with Kansas. His caravan was moving toward the North; his eyes were fixed on the hills of Virginia.

His experiment had been a success.

The President of the United States, James Buchanan, offered a reward of $250 for his arrest. The Governor of Missouri raised the reward to $3,000. The press flashed the news of the daring rescue of ten slaves by old John Brown. He regained in a day his lost prestige. The stories of the robberies which accompanied the rescue were denied as Border Ruffian lies, as "Shubel Morgan" knew they would be denied.

His enterprise had met every test. He got his slaves safely through to Canada and started a reign of terror. The effect of the raid into a Slave State had tested his theory of direct, bloodstained action as the solution and the only solution of the problem.

The occasional frowns of pious people on his methods caused him no uneasiness or doubt. He was a man of daily prayer. He was on more intimate terms with God than his critics.

The one fly in the ointment of his triumph was the cold reception given him by the religious settlement at Tabor, Iowa. These good people had treated him as a prophet of God in times past and his caravan had headed for Tabor as their first resting place.

He entered the village with a song of triumph. He would exhibit his freed slaves before the Church and join with the congregation in a hymn of praise to God.

But the news of his coming had reached Tabor before his arrival. They had heard of the stealing of the oxen, the horses, the mules, the wagons.

They had also heard of the murder of David Cruise. Brown had denied the Pottawattomie crimes and they had believed him. This murder he could not deny. They had not yet reached the point of justifying murder in an unlawful rescue. These pious folks also had a decided prejudice against a horse thief, however religious his training and eloquent his prayers.

When his caravan of stolen wagons, horses and provisions, moved slowly into the village, a curious but cold crowd gazed in silence. He placed the negroes in the little school house and parked his teams on the Common.

The next day was Sunday and the old Puritan hastened to church with his faithful disciples. Amazed that he had received from the Rev. John Todd no invitation to take part in the services, he handed Stevens a scribbled note:

"Give it to the preacher when he comes in."

Stevens gave the minister the bit of paper without a word and resumed his seat in the House of God.

The Rev. John Todd read the scrawl with a frown:

"John Brown respectfully requests the church at Tabor to offer public thanksgiving to Almighty God in behalf of himself and company: *and of their rescued captives, in particular,* for His gracious preservation of their lives and health: and His signal deliverance of all out of the hands of the wicked. 'Oh, give thanks unto the Lord; for He is good: for His mercy endureth forever.'"

The Rev. Dr. King was in the pulpit with the militant preacher Todd that day and the perplexed man handed the note to King.

The two servants of Christ were not impressed with the appeal. The words Brown had marked in italics and his use of the Psalms failed to rouse the religious fervor of the preachers. They knew that somewhere in the crowd sat the man who had murdered Cruise and stolen those horses. They also knew that John Brown had approved the deeds of his followers.

Todd rose and announced that he had received a petition which he could not grant. He announced a public meeting of the citizens of the town in the church the following day to take such action as they might see fit.

When Brown faced this meeting on Monday he felt its hostility from the moment he rose. He made an excuse for not speaking by refusing to go on when a distinguished physician from Missouri entered the church.

Brown demanded that the man from Missouri be expelled. The citizens of Tabor refused. And the old man sullenly took his seat.

Stevens, the murderer, sprang to his feet and in his superb bass voice shouted:

"So help me, God, I'll not sit in council with one who buys and sells human flesh."

Stevens led the disciples out of the church.

At the close of the discussion the citizens of Tabor unanimously adopted the resolution:

"*Resolved*, That while we sympathize with the oppressed and will do all that we conscientiously can to help them in their efforts for freedom, nevertheless we have no sympathy with those who go to slave states to entice away slaves and take property or life, when necessary, to attain this end.

"J. SMITH, *Sec. of Meeting.*" Tabor, Feb. 7, 1857.

John Brown shook the dust of Tabor from his feet after a long prayer to his God which he took pains to make himself.

At Grinnell, Iowa, his reception was cordial and he began to feel the confidence which his exploit would excite in the still more remote East. His caravan had moved Eastward but fourteen days' journey from Tabor and he had been received with open arms. The farther from the scene of action Brown moved, the more heroic his rugged patriarchal figure with its flowing beard loomed.

On reaching Boston his triumph was complete. Every doubt and fear had vanished. Sanborn, Higginson, Stearns, Howe, and Gerrit Smith, in a short time, secured for him more than four thousand dollars and the Great Deed was assured.

Thomas Dixon

# CHAPTER XXVII

While Brown was at work in the North collecting money, arms and ammunition, Cook was quietly completing his work at the Ferry. He fought the temptation to take Virginia with him on his trips and then succumbed.

The thing that decided it was the fact that she knew Colonel Louis Washington and had been to Bellair. She promised to introduce him.

To make sure of Brown's quixotic instructions about the sword and pistols he must make the trip. The drive in the snug little buggy along the river bank was a red letter experience in the young Westerner's life.

Seated beside the modest slip of a Southern girl chatting with vivacity and a happiness she couldn't conceal, the man forgot that he was a conspirator in a plot to deluge a nation in blood. He forgot the long nights of hiding in woods and ravines. He forgot dark deeds of sacking and robbery. He was just a boy again. The sun was shining in the glory of a sweet spring morning in the mountains. The flowers were blooming in the hedges. He smelled the wild cherry, blackberry and dewberry bushes. Birds were singing. The new green of the leaves was dazzling in its splendor. The air was pure and sweet and sent the blood bounding to the tips of his fingers.

He glanced at the soft red cheeks of the girl beside him and a great yearning for a home and babies and peace overwhelmed him. His lips trembled and his eyes filled with tears. He rebelled against the task to which he had put his hand.

"Why so pensive?" she asked with a laugh.

"Am I?"

"You haven't spoken for a mile."

"I'm just so happy, I reckon," he answered seriously.

He remembered his grim task and threw off the spell. He must keep a cool head and a strong hand. He remembered the strange old man to whose "Constitution" he had sworn allegiance in Canada and began to talk in commonplaces.

To the girl's romantic ears they had meaning. Every tone of his voice fascinated her. The mystery about him held her imagination. She was sure it was full of thrilling adventure. He would tell her some day. She wondered why he had waited so long. He had been on the point of telling his love again and again and always stopped with an ugly frown. She wondered sometimes if his life had been spoiled by some tragedy. A thousand times she asked herself the question whether he might be married and separated from a wife. He had lived in the North. He had told her many places he had seen. People were divorced sometimes in the North. She dismissed the thought as absurd and resigned herself again to the charms of his companionship.

Colonel Washington was delighted to see again the daughter of an old friend. Her father had been his companion on many a hunting and fishing trip.

Virginia introduced her companion.

"My friend, Mr. John Cook, Colonel Washington."

The colonel extended his hand cordially.

Thomas Dixon

"Glad to meet you, young man. A friend of Virginia's is a friend of mine, sir."

"Thank you."

"Walk right in, children, sit down and make yourselves at home. I'll find that damned old lazy butler of mine and get you some refreshments."

"Let's sit outside," Virginia whispered.

"No," Cook protested. "I want to see the inside of a Washington home."

The Colonel waved his arm toward the house.

"With you in a minute, children. Walk right in."

"Of course, if you wish it," the girl said softly.

They entered the fine old house, and sat down in the hall. Cook smiled at the easy fulfillment of his task. Directly in front of the door, set in a deep panel, was the portrait of the first President. On the right in a smaller panel hung the sword which Frederick the Great had given him. On the other side, the pistols from the hands of Lafayette. A tiny, gold plate, delicately engraved, marked each treasure.

Virginia showed him these souvenirs of her country's history. She spoke of them with breathless awe. She laughed with girlish pride.

"Aren't they just grand?"

Cook nodded.

He felt guilty of treachery. A betrayal of Southern hospitality in this sweet girl's presence! He ground his teeth at the thought of his weakness the next moment.

Colonel Washington appeared through the door from the dining room. He was followed by his ancient butler, bearing a tray filled with drinks.

The Colonel served them with his own hand. The negro grinned his welcome to the guests. At the sight of a slave, Cook was himself again. His jaw closed and his eye flashed. He was once more the disciple of the Man of the Blood-Feud.

Washington handed a tall glass to Virginia.

"Your lemonade, young lady. I know your taste and approve."

He bowed low and gave her the drink.

He took two glasses of mint juleps, one in each hand.

"Mr. Cook, the favorite drink of these mountains, sir, as pure as its dews, as refreshing as its air - the favorite drink of old Virginia. To your good health, sir!"

Cook's head barely moved and he drank in silence.

He held his mood of reserve on the drive home. In vain the girl smiled and coaxed his dreary spirits. He refused to respond. They passed the same wonderful views, the same birds were singing, the same waters foaming and laughing over the rocks below. The man heard nothing, saw nothing, save a vision inside his raging soul. He saw men riding through the night to that house. He saw black hands grip iron pikes and knock at the door of its great hall.

There was a far-away look in his keen eyes - eyes that could sight a rifle with deadly aim.

The slender girl nestled closer in wonder at the veil that had suddenly dropped between them. The fires of youth and passion responded for a moment to this instinctive stir of his mate. Resistance was agony. His arm moved to encircle her waist. He turned in an impulse to kiss her lips and whisper the mad things his heart was saying.

He caught himself in time.

What had he to do with this eternal call of the human heart to love and be loved? It meant home, it meant tenderness. It meant peace and good will to every living thing. He had come to kill, not to love; to destroy, not build homes.

Again he rebelled against his hideous task. And then he remembered John Brown and all for which he stood. His oath crashed through his memory. He resolved to put every thought of tenderness, beauty, and love under his feet and trample them. It was the only way to save himself and this girl.

It would be hard - but he would do it. For an entire week he did not speak to her except in monosyllables. He made no effort to hide his decision. He wanted her to see and know the firm purpose within his heart.

Her eyes followed him with a look of dumb anguish. If she had spoken in reproaches he would have fought and withstood her. Her silence was more than he could bear.

On the sixth day of his resolution he saw that she had been crying. She smiled and tried to hide it, but he knew. He would go for a walk to the Heights and cheer her up a bit. It wasn't necessary to be brutal.

Her brown eyes began to smile again. They walked over the Heights and down a steep pathway among the rocks to the river's edge and sat down on a boulder worn smooth by the waters of the spring floods.

The ripple of the current made soft music. They were silent for a long time and then she turned toward him a tender, questioning gaze. In spite of her effort to be strong a tear stole down the firm young cheek.

"What have I done to make you angry?"

"Nothing," he answered in a whisper.

"What's the matter, then?"

He took her hand and held it in a cruel grip before he spoke. His words came at last in passionate pleading.

"Oh, dear little girl, can't you see how I've been fighting this thing for months - how I've tried to keep away from you and couldn't?"

"Why?"

She breathed the question leaning so close that her lips framed a kiss.

"I can't tell you," he said.

"But you must! You must!" she pleaded.

Tears were in his eyes now. He looked away.

"A gulf separates us, child."

"How can it?" she whispered tenderly.

"It's just there!"

"Can't you cross it?"

"No."

She drew her slender body erect with an effort. She tried to speak twice before she succeeded.

"You - are - married - then?"

"Oh - no - no - not that - no!"

She bent close again, a sweet smile breaking through her tears.

"Then you can tell me what it is."

"I couldn't tell it, even to my wife."

Her brow contracted in a puzzled look.

"It's nothing low or dishonorable?"

"No. And it belongs to the big things of life-and death."

"And I cannot know this secret?"

"You cannot know. I have taken an oath."

"And it separates us?"

"Yes."

"But why - if - you - love - me - and I love - you -"

She paused and blushed scarlet. She had told a man her love before he had spoken. But he *had* spoken! His voice, his tears, his tones had told her.

He looked at her a moment, trembling. He spoke one word at a time as if he had no breath to finish the sentence.

"It's - sweet - to - hear - your - dear - lips - say - that - you - love - me - God knows I love you - you-dear-little-angel-sent-from heaven! I'm not worthy to touch your hand and yet I'm crushing it - I can't help it - I can't-I can't."

She slipped into his arms and he crushed her to his heart.

"I love you," she whispered. "I can trust you. I'll never ask your secret until you wish to tell me. Just love me, forever. That's all I ask."

"I can do that, and I will!" he answered solemnly.

They were married the next night in the parsonage of the Methodist Church of which she was a member. And the foundation was laid for a tragedy involving more lives than one.

# CHAPTER XXVIII

From an old log farmhouse on the hills of Maryland, - overlooking the town of Harper's Ferry, the panther was crouching to spring.

For four months in various disguises Brown had reconnoitered the mountains around the gorge of the two rivers. He had climbed the peak and looked into the county of Fauquier with its swarming slave population. Each week he piloted his wagon to the town of Chambersburg, Pennsylvania, thirty-five miles back in the hills.

The Humanitarians through their agents were shipping there, day by day, the powder, lead, guns, knives, torches and iron pikes the Chosen One had asked.

These pious men met him for a final conference in the home of Gerrit Smith, the preacher philanthropist of Peterboro.

The canny old huntsman revealed to them just enough to excite the unconscious archaic impulse beneath the skin of culture. He told them that he was going to make a daring raid into the heart of the Old South and rescue as many of the "oppressed" as possible. They knew that the raid into Missouri had resulted in murder and that he rode back into Kansas with the red stains on his hands.

Brown gained their support by this carefully concealed appeal to their subconscious natures. As the crowd of eager faces bent close to catch, the details of his scheme, the burning eyes of the leader were suddenly half closed. Silence followed and they watched the two pin points of light in vain.

Each pious man present caught the smell of human blood. Yet each pious man carefully concealed this from himself and his neighbor until it would be approved by all. Had the bald facts behind the enterprise been told in plain English, religion and culture would have called a halt. The elemental impulse of the Beast must therefore be carefully concealed.

Every man present knew that they were sending Brown on a man-hunt. They knew that the results might mean bloodshed. They knew, as individuals, exactly what was being said and what was being planned. Its details they did not wish to know. The moral significance - the *big* moral significance of the deed was something apart from the bloody details. The Great Deed could be justified by the Higher Law, the Greater Glory of God. They were twisting the moral universe into accord with the elemental impulse of the brute that sleeps beneath every human skin.

The Great Deed about to be done would be glorious, its actors heroes and martyrs of a Divine Cause. They knelt in prayer and their Chosen Leader invoked the blessings of the Lord of Hosts upon them and upon his disciples in the Divine Cause.

The hour of Action was now swiftly approaching. Cook had become a book agent. With his pretty Virginia wife his figure became familiar to every farm, in the county. He visited every house where a slave was to be found. He sold maps as well as books. He also sketched maps in secret when he reached the quiet of his home while his happy little bride sang at her work.

He carefully compiled a census of slaves at the Ferry and in the surrounding country. So sure had he become of the success of the blow when it should fall, that he begged his Chief to permit him to begin to whisper the promise of the uprising to a few chosen men among the slaves.

The old man's eyes; flamed with anger.

"You have not done this already?" he growled.

"No - no."

"You swear it?"

Brown had seized Cook by both arms and searched his eyes for the truth. The younger man was amazed at the volcanic outburst of anger.

"A hundred times I've told you, Cook, that you talk too much," he went on tensely. "You mean well, boy, but your marriage may prove a tragedy in more ways than one."

"It has proven my greatest weapon."

"If you're careful, if you're discreet, if you can control your foolish impulses. I've warned you again and again and yet you've been writing letters -"

Cook's eyes wavered.

"I only wrote one to an old girl friend in Tabor."

"Exactly. You told of your marriage, your happiness, your hopes of a great career - and I got a copy of the letter."

"How?"

"No matter. If I got it, somebody else could get one. Now will you swear to me again to obey my orders?"

The burning eyes pierced his soul and he was wax.

"Yes. I swear!"

"Good. I want a report from you daily from now on. Stop

your excursions into the country, except to meet me in broad daylight in the woods this side of our headquarters. You understand?"

"Yes. You can depend on me."

Brown watched him with grave misgivings. He was the one man on whom he depended least and yet his life and the life of every one in his enterprise was in his hands. There were more reasons than one why he must hasten the final preparations for the Deed.

The suspicions of the neighbors had been roused in spite of the utmost vigilance. He had increased his disciples to twenty men. He had induced his younger son, Watson, to leave North Elba and join them. His own daughter, Annie, and Oliver's wife had come with Watson, and the two women were doing the work for his band - cooking, washing, and scrubbing without a murmur.

The men were becoming restless in their close confinement. Five of them were negroes. Brown's disciples made no objections to living, eating and sleeping with these blacks. Such equality was one of the cardinal principles of their creed.

But the danger of the discovery of the presence of freed negroes living in this farmhouse with two white women and a group of white men increased each day.

The headquarters had a garrulous old woman for a neighbor. Gradually, Mrs. Huffmeister became curious about the doings at the farm. She began to invent daily excuses for a visit. They might be real, of course, but the old man's daughter became uneasy. As she cleaned the table, washed the dishes and swept the floors of the rooms and the porch, she was constantly on the lookout for this woman.

The thing that had fascinated her was the man whom this girl called father. His name was "Smith," but it didn't seem to fit him. She was an illiterate German and knew nothing of the stirring events in Kansas. But her eyes followed the head huntsman with fascinated curiosity.

At this time his personal appearance was startling in its impressive power, when not on guard or in disguise. His brilliant eyes, his flowing white beard and stooped shoulders arrested attention instantly and held it. He was sixty years old by the calendar and looked older. And yet always the curious thing about him was that the impression of age was on the surface. It was given only when he was still. The moment he moved in the quick, wiry, catlike way that was his habit, age vanished. The observer got the impression of a wild beast crouching to spring.

It was little wonder that Mrs. Huffmeister made excuses to catch a glimpse of his figure. It was little wonder that she had begun to talk to her friends about "Mr. Smith" and his curious ways.

She had talked to him only once. She was glad that he didn't talk much. There was an expression to his set jaw and lips that was repulsive. Especially there was something chill in the tones of his voice. They never suggested tenderness or love, or hope or happiness - only the impersonal ring of metal. The agile and alert body of a man of his age was an uncanny thing, too. The woman's curiosity was roused anew with each glimpse she got of him until her coming at last became a terror to the daughter.

She warned her father and he hastened his preparations. If the world below once got a hint of what was going on behind those rough logs there would be short shrift for the men who were stalking human game.

It became necessary for the entire party of twenty men to lie concealed in the low attic room the entire day. Not more than two of them could be seen at one time.

The strange assortment of ex-convicts, dreamers, theorists, adventurers and freed negroes were kept busy by their leader until the eve of the Great Deed. They whittled into smooth shape the stout hickory handles for a thousand iron pikes, which Blair, the blacksmith of Collinsville, Connecticut, had finally delivered. To these rude weapons the fondest hopes of the head-huntsman had been pinned from the first. The slave was not familiar with the use of firearms. His strong, black arm could thrust these sharp pieces of iron into human breasts with deadly accuracy. Brown saw that every nail was securely set in the handles.

Each day he required the first stand of rifles to be burnished anew. The swords and knives were ground and whetted until their blades were perfect.

There was not work enough to stop discussion toward the end. Cook had finally whispered to Tidd that the leader intended to assault and take the United States Arsenal and Rifle Works. Cook's study of law revealed the fact that this act would be high treason against the Republic.

The men had all sworn allegiance to Brown under his Constitution but the rank and file of the little provisional army did not understand that he intended to attack the National authority by a direct assault.

A violent discussion broke out in the attack led by Tidd. At the end of the argument Tidd became so infuriated by Brown's imperious orders for submission to his will that he left the place in a rage, went down to the Ferry and spent the week with Cook.

Brown tendered his resignation as Commander in Chief. There was no other man among them who would dare to lead. A frank discussion disclosed this fact and the disciples were compelled to submit. They voted submission and authorized Owen to put it in writing which he did briefly but to the point:

Harper's Ferry, Aug. 18, 1859.

DEAR SIR,

We have all agreed to sustain your decisions, until you have *proved incompetent*, and many of us will adhere to your decisions as long as you will.

Your friend, OWEN SMITH.

The rebellion was suppressed within the ranks and the leader's authority restored. But the task of watching and guarding became more and more trying and dangerous.

One of the women remained on guard every moment from dawn to dusk. When washing dishes she stood at the end of the table where she could see the approach to the house. The meals over, she took her place on the porch or just inside the door. Always she was reading or sewing. She not only had to watch for foes from without, but she was also the guard set over the restless "invisible" upstairs. In spite of her vigilance, Hazlett and Leeman would slip off into the woods and wander for hours. Hazlett was a fine-looking young fellow, over-flowing with good nature and social feelings. The prison life was appalling to him. Leeman was a boy from Saco, Maine, the youngest man among the disciples. He smoked and drank occasionally and chafed under restraint.

In spite of the women's keen watch these two fellows more than once broke the rules by slipping into Harper's Ferry in broad daylight and spending the time at Cook's house. They loved to watch the slender, joyous, little wife at her work. They envied Cook, and, while they watched, wondered at the strange spell that had bound their souls and bodies to the old man crouching on the hill to strike the sleeping village.

The reports of these excursions reached Brown's ears and increased his uneasiness. The thing that hastened the date for the Great Deed to its final place on the calendar was the fact that a traitor from ambush had written a letter to the Secretary of War, John B. Floyd, revealing the whole plot and naming John Brown of Kansas as the leader.

The Secretary of War was at the time in the mountains of Virginia on a vacation. The idea of any sane human being organizing a secret association to liberate the slaves of the South by a general insurrection was too absurd for belief - too puerile for attention. The letter was tossed aside.

If this were not enough, his friend and benefactor, Gerrit Smith, had made an unfortunate speech before a negro audience in which he had broadly hinted of his hope of an early slave insurrection.

It was the last straw. He was awaiting recruits but he dare not delay. He summoned his friend, Frederick Douglas, from Rochester to meet him at Chambersburg. If he could persuade Douglas to take his place by his side on the night the blow would be struck, he would need no other recruits. Brown knew this negro to be the foremost leader of his race and that the freedmen of the North would follow him.

The old man arranged through his agent in Chambersburg that the meeting should take place in an abandoned stone quarry just outside of town.

The watcher on the hill over Harper's Ferry was disguised as a fisherman. His slouch hat, and also rod and reel, rough clothes, made him a typical farmer fisherman of the neighborhood. He reached the stone quarry unchallenged.

With eager eloquence he begged for the negro's help.

Douglas asked the details of his attack.

Brown bared it, in all its daring. He did not omit the Armory or the Rifle Works.

Douglas was shocked.

With his vivid eloquence as a negro orator, he possessed far more common sense than the old Puritan before whom he stood. He opposed his plea as the acme of absurdity. The attack on the Federal Arsenal would be treason. It would array the whole Nation against him. It would hurl the army of the United States with the militia of Virginia on his back in an instant.

Brown; boldly faced this possibility and declared that with it he could still triumph, if once he crossed the line of Farquier county and thrust his pikes into the heart of the Black Belt.

All day Saturday and half the day on Sunday the argument between the two men continued. At noon on Sunday the old man slipped his arm around the negro and pressed it close. His voice was softer than Douglas had ever heard it and it sent the cold chills down his spine in spite of his firm determination never to yield.

"Come with me, Douglas, for God's sake," he begged. "I'll defend you with my life. I want you for a special purpose. I'll capture Harper's Ferry in two hours. They'll be asleep. When I cross the line on the mountain top and call the ten thousand slaves in Fauquier County - the bees will swarm, man! Can't you see them? Can't you hear the roar when I've placed these pikes in their hands? - *I want you* to hive them."

Douglas hesitated for only a moment. His vivid imagination had seen the flash of the hell-lit vision of the slave insurrection and his soul answered with a savage cry. But he slipped from Brown's arms, rubbed his eyes and flung off the spell.

"My good friend," he said at last, "you're walking into a steel trap. You can't come out alive."

He turned to Shields Green, the negro guard who was now one of the old man's disciples. Green had been a friend of

Douglas' in Rochester. He had introduced him to the Crusader. He felt responsible for his life. He had a duty to perform to this ignorant black man and he did it, painful as it was.

"Green, you have heard what I've just said to my friend. He has changed his plans since you volunteered. You understand, now. You can go with him or come home with me to Rochester. What will you do?"

His answer was coolly deliberate.

"I b'lieve I go wid de ole man!"

With a heavy heart Brown saw Douglas leave. It was the shattering of his most dramatic dream of the execution of the Great Deed. When the black bees should swarm he had seen himself at the head of the dark, roaring tide of avengers, their pikes and rifles flashing in the Southern sun. Around his waist was the sword of George Washington and the pistols of Lafayette. His Aide of Honor would ride, this negro, once a fugitive slave. Side by side they would sweep the South with fire and sword.

On arrival at his headquarters on the hill he learned that a revival of religion was going on in the town below and he fixed Sunday, the seventeenth of October, as the day of the Deed. Harper's Ferry would not only be asleep that night - every foe would be lulled in songs of praise to God.

# CHAPTER XXIX

At eight o'clock on Sunday night, the sixteenth of October, 1859, John Brown drove his one-horse wagon to the door of the rude log house in which he had hidden with his disciples for four months.

It was a damp, chill evening of mid fall. Heavy rain clouds obscured the stars and not a traveler ventured along the wind-swept roads. From the attic were loaded into the wagon crowbars, sledge hammers, iron pikes and oil-soaked faggots.

The crowbars and sledge hammers might be used on the gates or doors. There could be no doubt about the use to which the leader intended to put the pikes and torches.

When the wagon had been loaded the old man summoned his faithful son, Owen.

"Captain Owen Brown," the steel voice rang, "you will take private Barclay Coppoc and F.J. Merriam and establish a guard over this house as the headquarters of our expedition. Hold it at all hazards. You are guarding the written records of our work, the names of associates, the reserves of our arms and ammunition. We will send you reinforcements in due time."

Owen saluted his commander and the two privates under his command took their places beside him.

Brown waved to the eighteen men standing around the wagon.

"Get on your arms, and to the Ferry!"

They had been ready for hours, eager for the Deed. Not one among them in his heart believed in the wisdom of this assault, yet so grim was the power of Brown's mind over the wills of his followers, there was not a laggard among them.

Brown drove the wagon and led the procession down the pitch-black road toward the town. The men fell in line two abreast and slowly marched behind the team.

Cook and Tidd, raised to the rank of Captains, their commissions duly signed, led the tramping men. There were many captains in this remarkable army of twenty-one. There were more officers than privates. The officers were commissioned to recruit their black companies when the first blow had been struck.

The enterprise on which these twenty-one veteran rangers had started in the chill night was by no means so foolhardy as appears on the surface. The leader was leaving his base of supplies with a rear guard of but three men. Yet the army on the march consisted of but eighteen. He knew that the United States Arsenal had but one guarded gate and that the old watchman had not fired a gun in twenty-five years. It would be the simplest thing to force this gate and the Arsenal was in their hands. The Rifle Works had but a single guard. They could be taken in five minutes. Once inside these enclosures, he had unlimited guns and ammunition at his command.

The town would be asleep at ten o'clock when he arrived at the Maryland end of the covered bridge across the Potomac. Eighteen armed men were an ample force to capture the unsuspecting town. Not a single policeman was on duty after ten. The people were not in the habit of locking their doors.

The one principle of military law which the leader was apparently violating was the failure to provide a plan of retreat. But retreat was the last thing he intended to face.

The one thing on which he had staked his life and the success of his daring undertaking was the swarming of the black bees. His theory was reasonable from the Abolitionist's point of view. He believed that negro Chattel Slavery as practiced in the South was the sum of all villainies. And the Southern slave holders were the arch criminals and oppressors of human history. In his Preamble of the new "Constitution" to which his men had sworn allegiance, he had described this condition as one of "perpetual imprisonment, and hopeless servitude or absolute extermination." If the negroes of the South were held in the chains of such a system, if they were being beaten and exterminated, the black bees *would* swarm at the first call of a master leader and deluge the soil in blood.

John Brown believed this as he believed in the God to whom he prayed before he loaded his pikes and torches on the wagon. These black legions would swarm to-night! He could hear their shouts of joy and revenge as they gripped their pikes and swung into line under his God imposed leadership.

The whole scheme was based on this faith. If Garrison's words were true, if the Southern slave holder was a fiend, if Mrs. Stowe's arraignment of Slavery on the grounds of its inhuman cruelty was a true indictment, his faith was well grounded.

His thousand pikes in the hands of a thousand determined blacks led by the trained Captains whom he had commissioned was a force adequate to hold the town of Harper's Ferry and invade the Black Belt beyond the Peak.

The moment these black legions swarmed and weapons were placed in their hands the insurrection would spread with lightning rapidity. The weapons were in the Arsenal. The massacres would be sweeping through Virginia, North and South Carolina before an adequate force could reach this mountain pass. And when they reached it, he would be at the head of a black, savage army moving southward with resistless power.

The only question was the swarming of this dark army. Cook, who had spent nearly a year among the people and knew these slaves best, was the one man who held a doubt. For this reason he had begged Brown a second time to let him sound the strongest men among the slaves and try their spirit. Brown refused. He knew a negro. He was simply a white man in a black skin by an accident of climate. He knew exactly what he would do when put to the test. To discuss the subject was a waste of words. And so with faith serene in the success of the Deed, he paused but a moment at the entrance of the bridge.

He ordered Captains Kagi and Stevens to advance and take as prisoner William Williams, the watchman. The two rangers captured Williams without a struggle.

"A good joke, boys," he laughed.

"You'll find it a good one before the night's over," Stevens answered.

When he attempted to move, a revolver at his breast still failed to convince him.

"Go 'way, you boys, with your foolishness. It's a dark night, but I'm used to being scared!"

It was not until Kagi gave him a rap over the head with his rifle that he sat down in amazement and wiped the sweat from his brow. He forgot the chill of the night air. His brain was suddenly on fire.

Brown waited at the entrance of the bridge until the watchman had been captured and Cook and Tidd had cut the line on the Maryland side of the river.

He then advanced across the covered way to the gate of the Arsenal hut a few yards beyond the Virginia entrance.

He captured Daniel Whelan, the watchman at the Arsenal

entrance. Dumbfounded but stubborn, he refused to betray his trust by surrendering the keys.

"Open the gate!" Brown commanded.

"To hell wid yez!"

A half dozen rifles were thrust at his head.

He folded his arms and stood his ground.

They pushed a lantern into his face and Brown studied him a moment. He didn't wish a gun fired yet. The town was asleep and he wanted it to sleep.

"Get a crowbar," he ordered.

They got a crowbar from the wagon, jammed it into the chain which held the wagon gate and twisted the chain until it snapped. He drove the wagon inside, closed the gate and the United States Arsenal was in his hands.

Brown placed the two watchmen in charge of his men, Jerry Anderson and Dauphin Thompson.

He spoke to the prisoners in sharp command.

"Behave yourselves, now. I've come here to free all the negroes in this State. If I'm interfered with I'll burn the town and have blood."

Every man who passed through the dark streets was accosted, made prisoner and placed under guard.

Hazlett and Edwin Coppoc were ordered to hold the Armory. Oliver Brown and William Thompson were sent to seize the Shenandoah bridge, the direct line of march into the slave-thronged lower valley.

Stevens was sent to capture the Rifle Works which was accomplished in two minutes.

The program had worked exactly as Brown had predicted. Not a shot had been fired and they were masters of the town, its two bridges, the United States Arsenal, Armory and Rifle Works.

The men were now despatched through the town for the real work of the night - the arming of the black legion with pikes and torches.

It was one o'clock before the first accident happened. Patrick Higgins, the second night watchman, came to relieve Williams on the Maryland bridge.

Oliver Brown, on guard, cried:

"You're my prisoner, sir."

The Irishman grinned.

"Yez don't till me!"

Without another word he struck Oliver a blow. The crack of a rifle was the answer. In his rage young Brown was too quick with the shot. The bullet plowed a furrow in Higgins' skull but failed to pierce it.

He ran into the shadows.

Once inside the Wager House, he gave the alarm. The train from the West pulled into the station and was about to start across the bridge when Higgins, his face still streaked with blood, rushed up to the conductor and told him what had happened. He went forward to investigate, was fired on and backed his train out to the next station.

As the train pulled out Shepherd Haywood, a freedman, the

baggage master of the station, walked toward the bridge to find the missing watchman. The raiders shot him through the breast and he fell mortally wounded. The first victim was a faithful colored employee of Mayor Beekham, the station master of the Baltimore and Ohio Railroad Company.

The shot that killed him roused a man of action. Dr. John D. Starry lived but a stone's throw from the spot where Haywood had fallen. Hearing the shot and the groans of the wounded man, the doctor hastened to his rescue and carried him into the station. He could give no coherent account of what had happened and was already in a dying condition.

The doctor investigated. He approached two groups of the raiders, was challenged and retreated. Satisfied of the seriousness of the attack when he saw two armed white men lead three negroes holding pikes in their hands into the Armory gate, he saddled his horse and rode to his neighbors in town and country and gave the alarm.

While this dangerous messenger was on his foam-flecked horse, Brown, true to his quixotic sense of the dramatic, sent a raiding party of picked men to capture Colonel Washington and bring to his headquarters in the Arsenal the sword and pistols. On this foolish mission he despatched Captains Stevens, Cook and Tidd, with three negro privates, Leary, Anderson and Green. He gave positive orders that Colonel Washington should be forced to surrender the sword of the first President into the hands of a negro.

Day was dawning as the strange procession on its return passed through the Armory gate. In his own carriage was seated Colonel Washington and his neighbor, John H. Allstead. Their slaves and valuables were packed in the stolen wagons drawn by stolen horses.

Brown stood rifle in hand to receive them.

"This," said Stevens to Washington, "is John Brown."

"Osawatomie Brown of Kansas," the old man added with a stiffening of his figure.

He then handed a pike to each of the slaves captured at Bellair and Allstead's:

"Stand guard over these white men."

The negroes took the pikes and held them gingerly.

At sunrise Kagi sent an urgent message to his Chief advising him that the Rifle Works could not be held in the face of an assault. He begged him to retreat across the Potomac at the earliest possible moment.

Retreat was a word not in the old man's vocabulary. He sent Leary to reinforce him, with orders to hold the works.

He buckled the sword and pistols of Washington about his gaunt waist and counted his prisoners. He had forty whites within the enclosure. He counted the slaves whom he had armed with pikes. He had enrolled under his banner less than fifty. They stood in huddled groups of wonder and fear.

The black bees had failed to swarm.

He scanned the horizon and not a single burning home lighted the skies. It had begun to drizzle rain. Not a torch had been used.

He had lost four precious hours in his quixotic expedition to capture Colonel Washington, his sword and slaves. He could not believe this a mistake. God had shown him the dramatic power of the act. He held a Washington in his possession. He was being guarded by his own slaves, armed. The scene would make him famous. It would stir the millions of the North. It would drive the South to desperation.

The thing that stunned him was the failure of the black legions to mobilize under the Captains whom he had appointed to lead them.

It was incredible.

He paced the enclosure, feverishly recalling the histories of mobs which he had studied, especially the fury of the French populace when the restraints of Law and Tradition had been lifted by the tocsin of the Revolution. The moment the beast beneath the skin of religion and culture was unchained, the massacres began. Every cruelty known to man had been their pastime.

And these beasts were white men. How much more should he expect of the Blacks? Haiti had given him assurance of darker deeds. The world was shivering with the horrors of the Black uprising in Haiti when he was born. He had drunk the story from his Puritan mother's breast. From childhood he had brooded with secret joy over its bloody details.

The Black Bees had swarmed there and Toussaint L'Overture had hived them as he had asked Frederick Douglas to hive them here. They seized the rudest weapons and wiped out the white population. They butchered ten thousand French men, women and children. And not a cry of pity or mercy found an echo in a savage breast.

What was wrong here?

He had proclaimed the slave a freeman. He had placed an iron pike in his right hand and a torch in his left. Why had they not answered with a shout of triumph?

His somber mind refused to believe that they would not rise. Even now he was sure they were mobilizing in a sheltered mountain gorge. Before noon he would hear the roar of their coming and see the terror-stricken faces of the whites fleeing before their rush.

He had repeated to his Northern crowds the fable of negro suffering in the South until he believed the lie himself. He believed it with every beat of his stern Puritan heart. And he had repeated and shouted it until the gathering Abolitionist mob believed it as a message from God. The fact that the system of African slavery, as actually practiced in the South, was the mildest and most humane form of labor ever fixed by the masters of men, they refused to consider. The mob leader never allows his followers to consider facts.

He knows that his crowd prefers dreams to facts. Dreams are the motives of crowd action. The dream, the illusion, the unreality have ever been the forces that have shaped human history in its hours of crisis when Fate has placed the future in the hands of the mob.

The fact that Slavery in the South had lifted millions of black savages - half of them from cannibal tribes - into the light of human civilization - that it had been their school, their teacher, their church, their inspiration - did not exist, because it was a fact. They did not deal in facts.

And so again Brown lifted his burning eyes toward the hills reflected in the mirror of the rivers. Down one of those rocky slopes the Black Legion would sweep before the day was done!

He had boldly despatched Cook across the Potomac bridge with the wagons, horses and treasures stolen from Colonel Washington's house to be stored at headquarters. There was still no doubt or shadow of turning in his imperious soul.

With each passing moment the swift feet of the avengers were closing the trap into which he had walked.

By ten o'clock the terror-stricken people of the town and county had seized their weapons and the fight began. Bullets were whistling from every street corner and every window commanding a glimpse of the Arsenal and Armory.

Brown's handful of men began to fall. The Rifle Works surrendered first and his guard of three men were all dead or wounded. By three o'clock his forces had been cut to pieces and he had taken refuge in the Engine House of the Armory. The bridges were held by the people. Owen, Cook and his guard at the old log house on the Maryland side were cut off and could not come to his rescue.

The amazing news of an Abolition invasion of Virginia and the capture of the United States Arsenal and Rifle Works had shaken the nation. President Buchanan hastily summoned from Arlington the foremost soldier of the Republic and despatched Colonel Robert E. Lee to the scene with the only troops available at the Capital, a company of marines. Lieutenant J. E. B. Stuart volunteered to act as his aide. The young cavalier was in the East celebrating the birth of a baby boy.

# CHAPTER XXX

When the marines arrived from Washington it was past midnight. The town swarmed with armed men from every farm and fireside. Five companies of militia from Maryland and Virginia were on the ground and Henry Wise, the Governor of Virginia, was hurrying to take command.

Stuart had established Colonel Lee's headquarters behind the brick wall of the Arsenal enclosure. Not more than fifty yards from the gate stood the Engine House in which Brown had barricaded himself with his two sons, Oliver and Watson, and four of his men. He held forty white hostages.

A sentinel of marines covered the entrance to the enclosure. The militia had yielded command to the United States troops.

As Stuart stood awaiting Colonel Lee's arrival, Lieutenant Green, in command of the marines, stepped briskly to the aide's side to report the preliminary work.

As yet no one in the excited town knew the identity of the mysterious commander "John Smith" who led the invasion. No one could guess the number of men he had in his army nor how many he held in reserve on the Maryland hills.

Stuart's blue eyes flashed with excitement.

"The marines have the Arsenal completely surrounded?" he asked.

"A rat couldn't get through, Lieutenant Stuart."

"The bridges leading into Harper's Ferry guarded?"

"Three picked men at each end, sir."

"Any signs of the Abolitionists on the hills at dawn?"

"A shot from a sniper on the Maryland side nipped one of the guards -"

"Then their headquarters and the reserves are back in those hills."

"I'm sure of it. I've sent a squad to get the sniper."

"All right, it's daylight. Keep your marines away from the Arsenal gate. It's barely fifty yards to the Engine House. We've got the Abolitionists penned inside. But they're good shots."

"I've warned them, sir."

"No fighting now until Colonel Lee takes command. His train has just pulled in."

"Why the devil didn't he come with us?" Green asked suddenly.

"Called to the White House for a conference with President Buchanan, in such haste that he couldn't stop to put on his uniform. The Capital's agog over this affair. The wildest rumors are afloat."

"Nothing to the rumors afloat here among these militiamen and dazed citizens."

"Colonel Lee will straighten them out in short order -"

Stuart suddenly stiffened to attention as he saw the soldierly figure of the Colonel approaching from the station with quick, firm step. Over his civilian suit he had hastily thrown an army overcoat and looked what he was, the bronzed veteran commander of the Texas plains.

He saluted the two young officers and quickly turned to his aide.

"No sign of a slave uprising, of course?"

"The invaders did their best to bring it on. They've taken about fifty negroes from their masters."

"Armed them?"

"With pikes and rifles."

"The invaders have robbed houses as reported?"

"Taken everything they could get their hands on. They forced their way into Colonel Washington's home, dragged him from bed, stole his watch, silver, wagons, horses, saddles and harness. They hold him a prisoner with four of his slaves."

"Colonel Washington is now their prisoner?"

"With others they are holding as hostages."

"Hostages?"

"They swear to murder them all at the first sign of an attack."

"They won't!" he answered sharply.

"I think they will, sir. They shot an unarmed negro porter at the depot and murdered the Mayor to-day as he was passing through the streets. They are expecting reinforcements at any minute."

"The militia are ready for duty?"

"Some are. Some are drinking."

Lee turned to Lieutenant Green.

"Close every barroom in town."

Green saluted.

"At once, sir."

Green turned to execute the order. The only problem that gave Lee concern was the use the invaders might make of the prisoners they held. That they would not hesitate to expose them to death as a protection to their own lives he couldn't doubt. Men who would dare the crime of raising a slave insurrection would not hesitate to violate the code of military honor.

He saw Stuart was restless. There was something on his mind. He half guessed the trouble and paused.

"Well, Lieutenant?"

Stuart laughed.

"I suppose, Colonel, you couldn't possibly let me lead the assault on the Engine House, could you?"

Lee's eyes twinkled at the eager look. The Colonel was a man as well as a soldier. And he was a father. He loved the shouts of children more than he loved the shouts of armies. In the pause he saw a vision. A little blue-eyed mother crooning over a baby which she had named for her sweetheart. The great heart forgot the daring soldier before him eager for a fight. He saw only the handsome husband and a wife at home praying God for his safe return. He could see her pressing the pink bundle of flesh to her heart, singing a lullaby that was a prayer. There would be no glory in such an assault. There was only the possibility of a bloody tragedy before a handful of desperadoes could be overcome. He faced his aide with a frown.

"Lieutenant Green is in command of the marines, sir. You are only my voluntary aide. You will act strictly within the rules of war."

Stuart saluted. He knew that his commander was a stern disciplinarian. Argument was out of the question. He made up his mind, however, to watch for a chance to join in the attack, once it was begun.

Green returned from his errand leading an old negro who held one of Brown's iron pikes.

The lieutenant thrust the trembling figure before the Colonel.

Lee studied him, and suppressed the smile that began to play about his lips.

"Well, uncle, this looks bad for you," he said finally.

"Lordee, Master, don't you blame me!" the old negro protested.

"They found him hiding in the bushes," Green explained.

"Yassah," the old man broke in. "I wuz kivered up in de leaves!"

"That's right, sir," Green agreed. "The pike was standing beside a tree. They raked the leaves and found him in a hole."

"An' I tried ter git under de hole, too."

"The raiders took you by force?" Lee asked.

"Yassah! Dey pulls me outen bed, make me put on my close,

gimme dis here han' spike, an' tells me I kin kill my ole marster an' missis when I feels like it -"

"Did you try to kill them?" Lee asked seriously.

"Who? Me?"

"Yes."

"Man! I drawed dat han' spike on dem Abolishioners an' I says: 'You low doun stinkin' po' white trash. Des try ter lay de weight er yo' han' on my marster er missis, - an' I'll lan' yo' in de middle of er spell er sickness' -"

"And they took you prisoner."

"Yassah."

"I see."

"Dey starts ter shoot me fust! But den dey say I wuzn't wuf de powder an' lead hit'ud take ter kill me."

"And you escaped?"

"Na sah, not den. Dey make me go wid 'em, wher er no. But I git loose byme bye an' crawl inter dat patch er trees doun dar by de ribber -"

"We found him there," Green nodded.

"Yassah, I mak' up my min' dat dey's have ter burn de woods an' sif de ashes for' dey ebber see me ergin."

Stuart's boyish laughter rang without restraint.

"All right, uncle," Lee responded cordially. "You can leave that pike with me."

"Yassah, you kin sho have it. God knows I ain't got no use fur it."

He threw the pike down and brushed his hands as if to get rid of the contagion of its touch.

"You're safe," Lee added. "The United States Marines are in command of Harper's Ferry now."

"Yassah. De Lawd knows I doan wanter 'sociate wid no slu-footed, knock-kneed po' whites. I'se er ristercrat, I is. Yassah, dat's me!"

"I'm glad to help you, uncle."

"Thankee, sah."

"Hurry back to your home now and help your people in their troubles."

"Yassah, right away, sah - right away!"

The old man hurried home, bowing right and left to his white friends and muttering curses on the heads of the Abolitionists, who had dragged him from his bed and caused him to lose four square meals.

Lee examined the pike carefully. He measured its long stiletto-like blade, projecting nine inches from its fastenings in the hickory handle. He observed the skill and care with which the rivets had been set.

"An ugly piece of iron," he said at last.

"I'll bet they've thousands of them somewhere back in these hills," Stuart added.

"And not a negro has lifted his hand against his master?"

"Not one."

Lee ran his fingers along the edges of the blade and a dreamy look came into his thoughtful eyes.

"My boy, such people deserve their freedom. But not this way - not this way! God save us from the horrors of the mob and the fanatic who leads them! Slavery is surely and swiftly dying. It cannot survive the economic pressure of the century. If only we can be saved from such madness."

His voice died away as in a troubled dream. He looked up suddenly and turned to his aide.

"I must summon their leader to surrender. You have not yet learned his name?"

"He calls himself John Smith, sir. They've been here all summer in an old farmhouse on the Maryland side."

"Strange that their purpose should not have been discovered. Their work has been carefully and secretly planned."

"Beyond a doubt."

"They could not have done it without big backing some-where."

"They've had it. They've had plenty of money. They have rifles of the finest make. And they're not the type made in this Arsenal."

"They expected to use the rifles in the Armory, of course. And they expect reinforcements. Any sign of their reserves?"

"Not yet, sir. We have the roads guarded for ten miles."

"We'll settle it before they can get help," Lee said sharply.

He hastily wrote a summons to surrender and handed it to Stuart.

"Approach the Engine House under a flag of truce. Ask for a parley with their leader and give him this."

Stuart saluted.

"At once, sir."

He attached his handkerchief to his sword and entered the gate. A loud murmur rose from the crowd of excited people who had pressed close to see the famous commander of the Marines.

Lee turned to the sentinel.

"Push that crowd back."

The crowd had pressed closer, watching Stuart with increasing excitement.

The sentinel clubbed his musket and pressed against the front men savagely.

"Stand back!"

The people slowly retreated. Lee turned to Lieutenant Green.

"Your men are ready for action?"

"They await your orders, sir."

"I suppose you wish the honor of leading the troops in taking these men out of the Engine House?"

Green smiled and bowed.

"Thank you, Colonel!"

"Pick a detail of only twelve men, with a reserve of twelve more. When Lieutenant Stuart gives you the signal, assault the Engine House and batter down the doors with sledge hammers -"

Green saluted.

"Yes, sir."

Lee spoke his next command in sharp emphasis.

"The citizens inside whom the raiders are holding must not be harmed. See to this when you gain an entrance. Once inside, pick your enemies. You understand?"

"Perfectly, sir."

"Hold your men in check until the signal to attack. I hope it will not be necessary to give it. I shall do my best to avoid further bloodshed."

"All right, sir."

Green saluted and stood at attention awaiting the arrival of Stuart.

Lee's aide had approached the Engine House, watched in breathless suspense by a crowd of more than two thousand people. In spite of the efforts of the sentinels they had jammed every inch of space commanding a view of the enclosure.

When Stuart reached the bullet-marked door he called:

"For Mr. Smith, the commander of the invaders, I have a communication from Colonel Lee!"

Brown opened the door about four inches and placed his body against the crack. Stuart could see through the opening his hand gripping a rifle.

He refused to open it further and the parley was held with the door ajar.

He at last allowed Stuart to enter.

His first look at the man's face startled him. The full gray beard could not mask the terrible mouth which he had studied one day in Kansas. And nothing could dim the flame that burned in his blue-gray eyes.

He recognized him instantly.

"Why, aren't you old Osawatomie Brown of Kansas, whom I once held there as my prisoner?"

"Yes, but you didn't keep me."

"I have a written communication from Colonel Lee."

"Read it."

Stuart drew the sheet of paper from his pocket and read in his clear, ringing voice:

"Headquarters Harper's Ferry,

October 18, 1859.

Colonel Lee, United States Army, commanding the troops sent by the President of the United States to suppress the insurrection at this place, demands the surrender of the people in the Armory buildings."

"If they will peaceably surrender themselves and return the pillaged property, they shall be kept in safety to await the orders of the President. Colonel Lee reports to them, in all frankness, that it is impossible for them to escape, that the Armory is surrounded by troops, and that if he is compelled to take them by force he cannot answer for their safety.

R. E. LEE, *Colonel Commanding U. S. Troops.*"

Stuart waited and Brown made no reply.

"You will surrender?"

"I will not," was the prompt answer.

In vain the young officer tried to persuade the stubborn old man to submit without further loss of life.

"I advise you to trust to the clemency of the Government," Stuart urged.

"I know what that means, sir. A rope for my men and myself. I prefer to die just here."

"I'll give you a short time to think it over and return for your final answer."

Brown at once began to barricade the doors and windows. And Stuart reported to his commander.

Lee met him at the gate.

"Well?"

"A little surprise for us, Colonel -"

"He refuses to surrender?"

"Absolutely. Captain 'John Smith' turns out to be Old John Brown of Osawatomie, Kansas, sir."

"You're sure?"

"I couldn't be mistaken. I had him a prisoner on the plains once when our troops were ordered out to quell the disturbances."

"That man's been here all summer planning this attack?"

"And not a soul knew him."

Lee was silent a moment and spoke slowly:

"It can only mean a conspiracy of wide scope to drench the South in blood -"

"Of course."

"He refuses to yield without a fight?"

Stuart laughed.

"He don't know how to surrender. I left him with two pistols and a bowie knife in his belt and a rifle in each hand."

"How many men were with him?"

"I saw but six besides the prisoners he holds as hostages. The prisoners begged for an interview with you, sir. I told them to be quiet - that you knew what you were doing."

"It's incredible!" Lee exclaimed.

He paused in deep thought and went on as if talking to himself.

"Strange old man - I must see him."

"I wouldn't, Colonel. He's a tough customer."

"I hate to order an assault on six men. He must be insane."

"No more than you are, unless the pursuit of a fixed idea for a lifetime makes a man insane."

Lee turned suddenly to his aide.

"Press that crowd back into the next street and ask him to come here under a flag of truce."

"I warn you, Colonel," Stuart protested. "He violated a flag of truce in Kansas. He won't hesitate to shoot you on sight if he takes a notion."

Lee smiled.

"He didn't try to shoot you on sight, did he?"

"No -"

"Go back and bring him here. I must find out some things from him if I can. He may not survive the assault."

Stuart again fixed his flag of truce and returned to the Engine House. This time the Colonel called a cordon of marines and pressed the crowd into the next street.

He beckoned to a sentinel.

"Ask Lieutenant Green to step here."

The sentinel called a marine to take his place and went in search of the commander of the company.

Lee lifted his eyes to the hills of Maryland. But a few miles beyond the first range lay the town of Sharpsburg, where Destiny was setting the stage for the bloodiest battle in the history of the republic. A little farther on lay the town of Gettysburg, over whose ragged hills Death was hovering in search of camping ground.

Did his prophetic soul pierce the future? Never had he been more profoundly depressed. The event he was witnessing was but the prelude to a tragedy he felt to be from this hour inevitable.

Green saluted in answer to his summons.

"I want you to witness an interview which I will have with John Brown, and receive my final orders!"

"The leader is old John Brown?"

"Lieutenant Stuart has identified him."

A shout from a crowd of boys who had climbed the trees of the next street caused Lee to turn toward the gate as the invader and Stuart passed through.

As Lee confronted Brown no more startling contrast could be presented by two men born under the same flag. John Brown with his bristling, unkempt beard, his two revolvers and sword hanging and dangling on his gaunt frame, his eyes glittering and red from the loss of two nights' sleep, the incarnation of Lawlessness; Lee, the trained soldier, the inheritor of centuries of constructive genius, the aristocrat in taste, the humblest and gentlest Christian in spirit, the lover of Peace, of Order.

The commander of the forces of Law spoke in friendly tones.

"You are John Brown of Osawatomie, Kansas?"

"Yes!"

"You are in command of the invaders who have killed four citizens of Harper's Ferry and seized the United States Arsenal?"

"I am in command."

"Would you mind telling me why you have invaded Virginia?"

"To free your slaves."

"How many men were under your command when you entered?"

"Seventeen white men and five colored freedmen."

"With an armed force of twenty-two you have invaded the South to free three million slaves?"

"I expected help -" He paused and his burning eyes flashed toward the hills. "And I still expect it!"

"From whom could you expect it?"

"From here and elsewhere."

"From blacks as well as whites?"

"From both."

"You have been disappointed in not getting it from either?"

"Thus far - yes."

Lee studied him with increasing wonder. There was a quiet daring in his attitude, an utter disregard of the tragic forces that had closed in on his ill-fated venture that was astounding. What could be its secret? It was something more than the coolness and poise of a brave Ulan. His manner was not cool. His mind was not poised.

There was a vibrant ring to his metallic voice which betrayed the profoundest emotion. His daring came from some mysterious source within. It was a daring that was the contradiction of reason and experience. It was uncanny.

Lee asked his questions in measured tones.

"You were disappointed, I take it, particularly in the conduct of the blacks?"

"Yes."

"Exactly. If negro Slavery in the South were to-day the beastly thing which you and Garrison have so long proclaimed, you could not have been disappointed. Had your illusion of abuse and cruelty been true the negroes *would* have risen to a man, put their masters to death, and burned their homes. Yet, not a black man has lifted his hand. There must be something wrong in your facts -"

Brown lifted his head solemnly.

"There can be nothing wrong in my faith, Colonel Lee. It comes from God."

"I didn't say your faith, my friend. I said your facts -" He paused and picked up the pike.

"These unused pikes bear witness to your error. This is an ugly weapon, Mr. Brown!"

"It was meant to kill."

"We found it in the hands of a negro."

"I wish to conceal nothing, sir -" The old man paused, lifted his stooped shoulders and drew a deep breath. "I armed fifty blacks with them and I had many more which I hoped to use."

Lee touched the point of the two-edged blade,

"This piece of iron, then, placed in the hands of a negro was meant for the breasts of Southern white men, women and children?"

"I came to proclaim your slaves free and give them the weapons to make good my orders."

"Who gave you the authority to issue orders of life and death?" Lee asked with slow, steady emphasis.

Brown's eyes flashed.

"I gave it to myself, sir. By the authority of my conscience and what I believe to be right."

"Suppose all took the same orders? Every man who differs with his neighbor, gets his gun, proclaims himself the mouthpiece of God and kills those who disagree with him. Civilization is built on an agreement not to do this thing. We have placed in the hands of the officer of the law the task of executing justice. The moment we dare as individuals to take this into our own hands, the world becomes a den of wild beasts -"

"The world's already a den of wild beasts," Brown interrupted sharply. "They have snarled and snapped long enough. It's time to clinch and fight it out."

There could be no doubt of the savage earnestness of the man who spoke. There was the ring of steel in every word. Lee looked at him curiously.

"May I ask how many people you know in the North who feel that way toward the South?"

"Millions, sir."

"And they back you in this attack?"

"A few chosen prophets - yes - thank God."

"And these prophets of the coming mob of millions have furnished you the money to arm and equip this expedition?"

"They have."

"It's amazing -"

"The millions are yet asleep," Brown admitted. He shook his gray locks as his terrible mouth closed with a deep intake of breath. "But I'll awake them! The thunderbolt which I have launched over Harper's Ferry will call them. And they will follow me. I hope to hear the throb of their drums over the hills before you have finished with me to-day!"

Lee was silent again, looking at the face with flaming eyes in a new wonder.

"And you invade to rob and murder at will?"

"I have not robbed!"

"No?"

"I have confiscated the property of slaveholders for use in a divine cause."

"Who gave you the right to confiscate the property of others in any cause?"

"Again I answer, my conscience."

"So a common thief can say."

"I am no common thief."

"Yet when you forced your way into Colonel Washington's home at night you committed a felony, known as burglary."

"I did it in a holy crusade, sir."

"The highwayman on the plains might plead the same necessity."

"You know, Colonel Lee, that I am neither felon, nor highwayman. I am an Abolitionist. My sole aim in the invasion of the South is to free the slave -"

"At any cost?"

"At any cost. I see, feel, know but one thing-that you are guilty of a great wrong against God and humanity. I have the right to interfere with you. To free those whom you hold in bondage."

"Even though you deluge the world in blood?"

"Yes. That is why I am here. I have no personal hate. No spirit of revenge. I have killed only when I thought I had to. I have protected your citizens whom hold as prisoners."

"You had no right to take those men prisoners."

Brown ignored the interruption.

"I ordered my men to fire only on those who were trying to stop our work."

"And yet you placed these pikes in the hands of negroes and gave them oil-soaked torches?"

Brown threw his hand high over his head as if to waive an irrelevant remark.

"I am here, sir, to aid those suffering a great wrong."

"And you begin by doing a greater wrong!"

The old man pursued his one idea without a break in thought. Lee's words made not the slightest impression.

"This question of the negro, Colonel Lee, you must face. You may dispose of me now easily. But this question is still to be settled. The end of that is not yet!"

"I, too, believe that Slavery is wrong, my friend. Yet surely this is not the way to bring to the slave his freedom. On pikes to be driven into the breasts of unoffending men and women! Two wrongs have never yet made a right."

The old man lifted his head towards the hills and a look of religious rapture overspread his furrowed face. His soul's deepest faith breathed in his words:

"Moral suasion is a vain thing, sir. This issue can be settled in blood alone."

The Colonel watched him with a growing feeling of futility.

"I have taken pains in this interview, Mr. Brown, to clear the way for your surrender without bloodshed. I cannot persuade you?"

"Upon what terms?"

"Terms?"

"I said so, sir."

The Colonel marveled at his audacity. Yet he was in dead earnest. His suggestion was not bravado.

"The only possible terms I can offer I suggested in my first message. I will protect you and your men from this infuriated crowd and guarantee you a fair trial by the civil authorities."

"I can't accept," Brown answered curtly. "You must allow me to leave this place with my men and the prisoners I hold as hostages until I reach the canal locks on the Maryland side. There I will release your citizens, and as soon as this is done your troops may fire on us, and pursue us."

"Such an offer is a waste of words. You must see that further resistance is useless."

"You have the numbers on us, sir," Brown answered defiantly. "But we are not afraid of death. I'd as lief die by a bullet as on the gallows. I can do more now by dying than by living. I came here to destroy the institution of Slavery by the sword -"

Lee's answer came with clean-cut emphasis.

"The law which protects Slavery is going to be repealed in God's own time. I am, myself, working toward that end as well as you, sir, and the end is sure. But at this moment the Constitution of the United States to which we owe liberty, justice, order, progress, wealth and power, guarantees this institution. Until its repeal it is my duty and it is your duty to obey the law. Will you submit?"

Brown's answer came like the crack of a rifle.

"The laws of the United States I have burned in a public square, sir. The Constitution is a covenant with Death, an agreement with Hell. I loathe it. I despise it. I spit upon it -"

Lee lifted his hand in gesture of command.

"That will do, sir!"

He faced Stuart with quick decision.

"Take him back to his men and give the signal of assault."

"Good!"

Stuart turned to Green.

"I'll wave my cap."

Stuart led Brown through the gate to the Engine House.

Lee summoned Green.

"Your troops are raw men, I understand."

"They have never been under fire, sir. But they're soldiers - never fear."

"All right. We'll put them to the test. Assault and take the Engine House without firing a shot. No matter how severe the fire on you, we must protect our citizens held inside. Use the bayonet only. Give each of your twelve men careful instructions. When fired on, they must not return that fire!"

Green saluted and passed to the head of his detail of twelve men. A shout from the boys in the tree tops was the signal of Stuart's return.

"Watch that crowd," Lee ordered the sentinel. "Use the reserves to hold them out of range."

Stuart returned with his eyes flashing.

"Ready, sir!"

"Give your signal."

Stuart stepped into the open, and waved his cap.

Green's detail of twelve men, the commander at their head, rushed to the Engine House with a shout. The crowd of two thousand people answered with a roar.

A volley rang from the besieged and a moment's silence followed. Their first shots had gone wild and not a marine had fallen. They had reached the door and their sledge hammers were raining blows on its solid timbers. An incessant fire poured from the portholes which Brown had cut through the walls. The men were so close to the door his shots were not effective.

Brown ordered one of his prisoners, Captain Dangerfield, a clerk of the Armory Staff, to secure the fastenings. Dangerfield slipped the bolts to their limit and stood watching his chance to throw them and admit the marines.

Brown ordered him back. He retreated a few feet and watched

the bolts, as the blows rained on the door.

Stuart had slipped into the fight. He called to Green.

"The hammers are too light. There's a big ladder outside. Get it and use it as a battering ram."

With a shout the marines seized the ladder, five men on a side, and drove it with tremendous force against the door. The first blow shivered a panel.

Brown ordered the fire engine rolled against the door. Dangerfield sprang to assist. He slipped the bolt out instead of in! The next rush of the ladder drove the door against the engine, rolled it back a foot and made a small opening through which Lieutenant Green forced his way.

The marines crowded in behind him. Green sprang on the engine with drawn sword and looked for Brown. A shower of bullets greeted him. Yet the miracle happened. Not one touched him. He recognized Colonel Washington, leaped from the engine and rushed to his side.

On one knee, a few feet to his left, knelt a man with a carbine in his hand pulling the lever to reload.

Colonel Washington waved his arm.

"That's Osawatomie."

The Lieutenant sprang twelve feet at him. He gave a quick underthrust of his sword, struck him midway of the body and raised the old man completely from the ground. He fell forward with his head between his knees. Green clubbed his sword and rained blow after blow on his head.

The men who watched the scene supposed that he had split the skull. Yet he survived. Green's first sword thrust had struck the heavy leather belt and did not enter the body. The sword was bent double. The clubbed blade was too light. It had made only superficial wounds.

As the marines pressed through the opening the first man was shot dead. The second was wounded in the face. The men who followed made short work of the fight. They bayoneted a raider under the engine and pinned another to the wall.

The fight had lasted but three minutes.

Brown lay on the ground wounded. His son, Oliver, was dead. His son, Watson, was mortally wounded. All the rest were dead or prisoners, save seven who made good their escape with Cook and Owen Brown into the hills of Pennsylvania.

Colonel Lee entered the Engine House and greeted Washington.

"You are all right, sir?"

"Sound as a dollar, Colonel Lee. The damned old fool's had me penned up here for two days. I'm dry as a powder horn and hungry as a wolf. Nothing to eat, and nothing to drink, but *water out of a horse-bucket!*"

Green faced his Colonel and saluted. He glanced at the prostrate prisoners.

"See that their wounds are dressed immediately. Give them good food, and take them as quickly as possible to the jail at Charlestown under heavy guard. See that they are not harmed or insulted by the people."

Lee turned sadly to his friend.

"Colonel Washington, the thing we have dreaded has come. The first blow has been struck. The Blood Feud has been raised."

# CHAPTER XXXI

On the surface only was the Great Deed a failure. Not a single pike had been thrust into a white man's breast by his slave. Not a single torch had been applied to a Southern home. His chosen Captains never passed the sentinel peak into Fauquier county. The Black Bees had not swarmed. But the keen ear of the old man had heard the rumble of the swarming of twenty million white hornets in the North.

The moment he had lifted his head a prisoner in the hands of his courteous captor, he foresaw the power which the role of martyrdom would give to his cause. Instantly he assumed the part and played it with genius to the last breath of his indomitable body.

He had stained the soil of Virginia with the blood of innocent and unoffending citizens. He had raised the Blood Feud at the right moment, a few months before a Presidential campaign. He had raised it at the right spot in a mountain gorge that looked southward to the Capitol at Washington and northward to the beating hearts of the millions, who had been prepared for this event by the long years of the Abolition Crusade which had culminated in *Uncle Tom's Cabin*.

A wave of horror for a moment swept the nation, North and South. Frederick Douglas fled to Europe. Sanborn, the treasurer and manager of the conspiracy, hurried across the border into Canada. Howe and Stearns hid. Theodore Parker was already in Europe.

Poor, old, gentle, generous Gerrit Smith collapsed and was led to the insane asylum at Ithaca, New York.

Two men alone of the conspirators realized the tremendous thing that had been done - John Brown in jail at Charlestown, and Thomas Wentworth Higginson, the militant preacher of Massachusetts.

To Brown, life had been an unbroken horror. His tragic Puritan soul had ever faced it with scorn - scorn for himself and the world. He was used to failure and disaster. They had been his meat and drink. Bankruptcy, imprisonment, flight from justice and the death of half his children had been mere incidents of life.

He had cast scarcely a glance at his dying sons in the Engine House. He had not tried to minister to them. His hand was tightly gripped on his carbine.

His grim soul now rose to its first long flight of religious ecstasy. He saw that the Southerner's reverence for Law and Order would make his execution inevitable. His dark spirit shouted for joy. His own blood, if he could succeed in playing the role of martyr, would raise the Blood Feud to its highest power. No statesman, no leader, no poet, no seer could calm the spirit of the archaic beast in man, which this martyrdom would raise if skillfully played. He was sure he could play the role with success.

The one man in the North who saw with clear vision the thing which Brown's failure had done was the Worcester clergyman.

Higginson was a preacher by accident. He was a born soldier. From the first meeting with Brown his fighting spirit had answered his cry for blood with a shout of approval. Higginson not only refused to run, but also groaned with shame at the fears of his fellow conspirators. His first utterance was characteristic of his spirit.

"I am overwhelmed with remorse that the men who gave him money and arms could not have been by his side when he fell."

He stood his ground in Worcester and dared arrest. He did not proclaim his guilt from the housetop. But his friends and neighbors knew and he walked the streets with head erect.

He did more. He joined with John W. LeBarnes and immediately organized a plot to liberate Brown by force. He raised the money and engaged George H. Hoyt to go to Harper's Ferry, ostensibly to appear as his attorney at the trial, in reality to act as a spy, discover the strength of the jail and find whether it could be stormed and taken by a company of determined men.

At his first interview with Brown the spy revealed his purpose.

"I have come from Boston to rescue you," he whispered.

The old man's face was convulsed with anger. He spoke in the tones of final command which had always closed argument with friend or foe.

"Never will I consent to such a scheme."

"But listen -"

"You listen to me, young man. The bare mention of this thing again and I shall refuse to see or speak to you. Do you accept my decision, sir?"

Hoyt agreed at once. Only in this way could he keep in touch with the man whom he had come to save.

"The last thing on this earth I would ask," Brown continued sternly, "is to be taken from this jail except by the State of Virginia when I shall ascend the scaffold."

Hoyt looked longingly at the old-fashioned fireplace in his

prison room. Two men could have crawled up its flue at the same time.

His refusal did not stop Higginson's efforts. He appealed to the forlorn wife at North Elba, New York, to go to Harper's Ferry, ask to see her husband and whisper her plan into his ear. He sent the money and got Mrs. Brown as far as Baltimore on her journey when Brown heard of it and stopped her with a peremptory command.

The determined conspirator then worked up the proposition to buy a steam tug which could make 18 knots an hour, steam up the James River to Richmond, kidnap the Governor of the Commonwealth, Henry Wise, and hold him for ransom until Brown was released. The scheme only failed for the lack of money.

Higginson had seen one thing. Brown saw a bigger thing.

Higginson's refusal to flee was based on sound psychology. He knew that from the day John Brown struck his brutal blow at the heart of the South and blood had begun to flow, the Blood Feud would be the biggest living fact in the Nation's history.

He knew that he could remain in Worcester with impunity. The strength of a revolution lies in the fact that its first bloodletting releases the instincts of the animal in man hitherto restrained by law. He knew that Brown's cry of Liberty for the slave would become for millions the cloak to hide the archaic impulse to kill. He knew that while the purpose of civilization is to restrain and control these instincts of the beast in man - it was too late for the forces of Law and Order to rally in the North. The first outbursts of indignation against Brown would quickly pass. They would be futile.

He read them with a smile. The *New York Herald* said: "He has met with a fate which he courted, but his death and the punishment of all his criminal associates will be as a feather in the balance against the mischievous consequences which will probably follow from the rekindling of the slavery excitement in the South."

The *Tribune* took the lead in dismissing the act as the deed of a madman. The Hartford *Evening News* declared:

"Brown is a poor, demented, old man. The calamity would never have occurred had there been no lawless and criminal invasion of Kansas."

But the most significant utterance in the North came from the Pacifist leader of Abolition, William Lloyd Garrison, himself. Higginson read it with a cry of joy.

*The Liberator's* words of comment were brief but significant of the coming mob mind:

"The particulars of a misguided, wild, and apparently insane, through disinterested and well-intended effort by insurrection, to emancipate the slaves in Virginia, under the leadership of Captain John, alias 'Osawatomie' Brown, may be found on our third page. Our views of war and bloodshed even in the best of causes, are too well known to need, repeating here; *but let no one who glories in the revolutionary struggle of 1776, deny the right of slaves to imitate the example of our fathers.*"

Even the leader of the movement for Abolition by peaceful means had succumbed to the poison of the smell of human blood.

Higginson knew that the process of a revolution was always in the order of Ideas, Leaders, The Mob, The Tread of Armies. For thirty years Garrison and the Abolition Crusaders had spread the Ideas. The Inspired Leader had at last appeared. His right arm had struck the first blow. He could hear the roar of the coming mob whose impulse to murder had been roused. It would call their ancestral soul. The answer was a certainty. He could see no necessity for Brown's blood to be spilled in martyrdom.

The old man, walking with burning eyes toward his trial, knew better. His vision was clear. God had revealed His full purpose at last. He would climb a Virginia gallows and drag millions down, from that scaffold into the grave with him.

# CHAPTER XXXII

Never in the history of an American commonwealth was a trial conducted with more reverence for Law than the arraignment of John Brown and his followers in the stately old Court House at Charlestown, Virginia.

The people whom he had assaulted with intent to kill, the people against whom he had incited slaves to rise in bloody insurrection, the kinsmen of the dead whom his rifles had slain, stood in line on the street and watched him pass into the building manacled to one of his disciples. They did not hoot, nor hiss, nor curse. They watched him walk in silence between the tall granite pillars of the House of Justice.

The behavior of this crowd was highwater mark in the development of Southern character. The structure of their society rested on the sanctity of Law. It was being put to the supreme test.

A Northern crowd under similar conditions, had they followed the principles which John Brown preached, would have torn those prisoners to pieces without the formality of a trial.

It was precisely this trait of character in his enemies on which Brown relied for the martyrdom he so passionately desired. When the witnesses at the preliminary hearing had testified to his guilt and the Court had ordered the trial set, he was asked if he had counsel.

He rose from his seat and addressed the nation, not the Court:

"Virginians, I did not ask for any quarter at the time I was taken. I did not ask to have my life spared. The Governor of the State of Virginia tenders me his assurance that I shall have a fair trial, but under no circumstances whatever will I be able to have a fair trial. If you seek my blood, you can have it at any moment, without this mockery of a trial. I have no counsel. I am ready for my fate. I do not wish a trial. I have now little further to ask, other than that I may not be foolishly insulted, as cowardly barbarians insult those who fall into their power."

The posing martyr was courting insults which had not been offered him. He was grieved that he could not bring the charge of barbarous treatment. He had been treated by Colonel Lee with the utmost consideration. His wounds had been dressed. He had received the best medical care. He had eaten wholesome food. His jailer had proven friendly and sympathetic.

He went out of his way to insult the Court and the people and invite abuse. He demanded that he be executed without trial.

The Court calmly assigned him two of the ablest lawyers in the county, and ordered the trial to proceed.

At noon the following day the Grand Jury returned a true bill against each of the prisoners for treason to the commonwealth, and for conspiring with slaves to commit both treason and murder, and for murder.

Captain Avis, the kindly jailer, was ordered to bring his prisoners into Court. He found old Brown in bed, pretending to be ill. He refused to rise. He was determined to get the effect of an arraignment of his prostrate body in the court room. He had foreseen the effect of this picture on the imagination of the North. The crowd of eager reporters at the preliminary hearing had given him the cue.

He was carried into the court room exactly as he had desired, on a cot. While the hearing proceeded he lay with his eyes closed as if in deep suffering. He had carefully prepared a plea for delay which he knew would not be granted. Its effect on the mob mind of the North was what he sought. The press would give it wings.

He lifted himself on his elbow and asked Judge Parker to allow him to make a protest:

"I have been promised a fair trial. I am not now in circumstances that enable me to attend a trial, owing to the state of my health. I have a severe wound in the back, or rather in one kidney which enfeebles me very much. But I am doing well, and I only ask for a very short delay of my trial, that I may be able to listen to it! And I merely ask this that, as the saying is, the devil may have his dues, no more. I wish to say further that my hearing is impaired by wounds I have about my head. I could not hear what the Court said this morning. I would be glad to hear what is said at my trial. Any short delay would be all I would ask. I do not presume to ask more than a very short delay so that I may in some degree recover and be able at least to listen to my trial."

Dr. Mason the attending physician, swore that he had examined Brown, and that his wounds had effected neither his hearing nor his mind. He further swore that he was not seriously disabled.

Brown knew that this was true, but he had entered his plea. His words would flash over the nation. The effect was what he foresaw. Although he had defied the laws of God and man, he dared demand more than justice under the laws which he had spit upon. And, however inconsistent his position, he knew that as the poison of the Blood Feud which he was raising filled the souls of the people through the press, he would be glorified from day to day and new power given to every word he might utter.

He had already composed his last message destined to sway the minds of millions. The response of the radical press to his pose of illness was quick and sharp. The Lawrence, Kansas, *Republican* voiced the feelings of thousands:

"We defy an instance to be shown in any civilized community where a prisoner has been forced to trial for his life, when so disabled by sickness or ghastly wounds as to be unable even to sit up during the proceedings, and compelled to be carried to the judgment hall upon a litter. Such a proceeding shames the name of Justice, and only finds a congenial place amid the records of the bloody Inquisition."

Even so conservative a paper as the Boston *Transcript* said:

"Whatever may be his guilt or folly, a man convicted under such circumstances, and, especially, a man executed after such a trial, will be the most terrible fruit that Slavery has ever borne, and will excite the execration of the civilized world."

The canny old poseur was on his way to an immortal martyrdom. He knew that every article of the Virginia Code was being scrupulously obeyed. He knew that the Grand Jury was in session and that the trial was set at the first term of the court following the crime. There had been no haste. He also knew that the impartial Judge who was presiding was the soul of justice in his dealings both with the clamorous people, the prosecution and the counsel appointed for the defense. But he also knew that the mob mind to whom he was appealing would not believe that he knew this. In appeals to the crowd he was a past master. In this appeal he knew that facts would count for nothing - beliefs, illusions for everything.

He played each opportunity for all it was worth.

When the Court opened the following morning, his counsel, Mr. Botts, amazed the prisoner and the prosecution by reading a telegram from Ohio asking a delay on the ground that important affidavits were on the way to prove legally that John

Brown was insane. Before the old man could stop him he gave to the Court the substance of these sworn statements.

His friends and relatives in Ohio had sworn that Brown had been always a monomaniac and had been intermittently insane for twenty years. One swore that he had been plainly insane for a quarter of a century. On the family record of insanity the affidavits all agreed. His grandmother was hopelessly insane for six years and died insane. His uncles and aunts, two sons and two daughters had been intermittently insane for years, while one of his daughters had died a hopeless maniac. His only sister, her daughter and one of his brothers were insane at intervals. Two of his first cousins were occasionally mad. Two had been committed to the State Insane Asylum repeatedly and two others were at that time in close restraint.

Brown refused to allow this plea to be entered. He bitterly denounced the counsel assigned to him as traitors, and at their request the following day they were allowed to withdraw from the case. No sooner had he finished his denunciation of his counsel than Hoyt, the young alleged attorney, sent by Higginson to defend him, sprang to his feet and asked a delay, as he was unprepared to proceed without assistance.

The Judge adjourned the Court until the following morning at ten o'clock.

The young spy knew nothing of law but he bluffed it through until the arrival of two able attorneys, Samuel Chilton of Washington, and Hiram Grismer of Cleveland.

Botts, the dismissed counsel, who had sought to save Brown's life by the plea of insanity, put his notes and his office at the disposal of Hoyt and sat up all night with him preparing his work for the following day.

When the new lawyers appeared the old man made another play at illness to gain delay. The Court ordered him to be brought in on his cot. Again, the physician swore he was lying, that he was gaining in strength daily. The Judge, however, granted a delay of two days.

The moment the order was issued for an adjournment Brown deliberately rose from his cot and walked back to jail.

The trial was closed on Monday by the speeches of the prosecution and the defense. The judge charged the jury and in three-quarters of an hour they filed back into the jury box.

The crowd jammed every inch of space in the old Court House, the wide entrance hall, and overflowed into the street.

The foreman solemnly pronounced him guilty.

The old man merely pulled the covers of his cot up and stretched his legs, as if he had no interest in the verdict. Entirely recovered from every effect of his wounds, as able to walk as ever, he had refused to walk and had been carried again into the court room. He had determined to receive his sentence on a bed. He knew the effect of this picture on the gathering mob.

The silence of death fell on the crowded room. Not a single cry of triumph from the kindred of the dead. Not a single cheer from the men whose wives and children had been saved from the horrors of massacre.

Chilton made his motion for an arrest of judgment and the judge ordered the motion to stand over until the next day. Brown heard the arguments the following day again lying on his cot. The judge reserved his decision and the final scene of the drama was enacted on November second.

The clerk asked John Brown if he had anything to say concerning why sentence should not be pronounced upon him.

The crowd stared as they saw the wiry figure of the old man

quickly rise. He fixed his eagle eye on them, not on the judge.

Over their heads he talked to the gathering mob of his countrymen. Brown had been a habitual liar from boyhood. In this speech, made on the eve of the sentence of death, he lied in every paragraph. He lied as he had when he grew a beard to play the role of "Shubel Morgan." He lied as he had lied to his victims when posing as a surveyor on the Pottawattomie. He lied as he had done when he crept through the darkness of the night on his sleeping prey. He lied as he had a hundred times about those gruesome murders. He lied for his Sacred Cause.

He lied without stint and without reservation. He lied with such conviction that he convinced himself in the end that he was a hero - a martyr of human liberty and progress. And that he was telling the solemn truth.

"I have, may it please the court, a few words to say:

"In the first place I deny everything but what I have already admitted: of a design on my part to free slaves. I intended certainly to have made a clean thing of that matter, as I did last winter when I went into Missouri and there took slaves without the snapping of a gun on either side, moving them through the country and finally leading them into Canada. I designed to have done the thing again on a larger scale. That was all I intended. I never did intend murder or treason, or the destruction of property, or to excite or to incite slaves to rebellion, or to make insurrection.

"Now, if it is deemed necessary that I should forfeit my life for the furtherance of the ends of justice, and mingle my blood further with the blood of my children - and with the blood of millions in this slave country whose rights are disregarded by wicked, cruel and unjust treatment - I say let it be done."

David Cruise was not there to tell of the bullet that crashed through his heart in Missouri. Frederick Douglas was not there to tell that he abandoned Brown in the old stone quarry outside Chambersburg, precisely because he had changed the plan of carrying off slaves as in Missouri to a scheme of treason, wholesale murders and insurrection.

Cruise was in his grave and Douglas on his way to Europe. There was no one to contradict his statements. The mob mind never asks for facts. It asks only for assertions. John Brown gave them what he knew they wished to hear and believe.

They heard and they believed.

With due solemnity, the Judge pronounced the sentence of death and fixed the date on December the second, thirty days in the future.

The old man's eyes flamed with hidden fires at the unexpected grant of a month in which to complete the raising of the Blood Feud so gloriously begun. He was a master in the coming of mystic phrases in letters. He gloried in religious symbols. Within thirty days he could work with his pen the miracle that would transform a nation into the puppets of his will.

He walked beside the jailer, his eyes glittering, his head uplifted. The Judge ordered the crowd to keep their seats until the prisoner was removed. In silence he marched through the throng without a hiss or a taunt.

# CHAPTER XXXIII

The day of the Great Deed was one never to be forgotten by Cook's little bride. They had been married six months. Each hour had bound the girl's heart in closer and sweeter bonds. The love that kindled for the handsome blond the day of their first meeting had grown into the deathless passion of the woman for her mate.

He was restless Saturday night. Through the long hours she held her breath to catch his regular breathing. He did not sleep.

At last the terror of it gripped her. Her hand touched his brow and brushed the hair back from his forehead.

"What's the matter, John dear?"

"Restless."

"What is it?"

"Oh, nothing much. Just got to thinking about something and can't sleep. That's all. Go to sleep now, like a good girl. I'm all right."

The little fingers sought his hand and gripped it.

"I'll try."

She rose at dawn. He had asked an early breakfast to make a long trip into the country.

At the table she watched him furtively. She had asked to go with him and he told her he couldn't take her. She wondered why. A great fear began to steal into her soul. It was the first time she had dared to look into the gulf. She would never ask his secret. He must tell her of his own free will. Her eyes searched his. And he turned away without an answer.

He fought for self-control when he kissed her goodbye. A mad desire swept his heart to take her in his arms, perhaps for the last time.

It would be a confession at the moment the blow was about to fall. He would betray the lives of his associates. He gripped himself and left her with a careless smile.

All day she brooded over the odd parting, the constraint, the silence, the sleepless night.

She went to the services of the revival and sought solace in the songs and prayers of the people. At night the minister preached a sermon that soothed her. A warm glow filled her heart. If God is love as the preacher said, he must know the secrets of his heart and life. He must watch over and bring her lover safely back to her arms.

She reached home at a quarter to ten and went to bed humming an old song Cook had taught her. The tired body was ready for sleep. She did not expect her husband to return that night. He had gone as far as Chambersburg. He promised to come on Monday afternoon.

Through the early hours of the fatal night she slept as soundly as a child.

The firing at the Arsenal between three and four o'clock waked her. She sprang to her feet and looked out the window. The

Thomas Dixon

street lamps flickered fitfully in the drizzling rain. No one was passing. There were no shouts, no disturbances.

She wondered about the shots. A crowd of drunken fools were still hanging around the Galt House bar perhaps. She went back to bed and slept again.

It was eight o'clock before the crash of a volley from the Arsenal enclosure roused her. She leaped to her feet, rushed to the window and stood trembling as volley followed volley in a long rattle of rifle and shotgun and pistol.

A neighbor hurried past with a gun in his hand. She asked him what the fighting meant.

"Armed Abolitionists have invaded Virginia," he shouted.

Still it meant nothing to her personally. Her husband was not an Abolitionist. She had known him for more than a year. She had been with him day and night for six months in the sweet intimacy of home and love.

And then the hideous truth came crashing on her terror-stricken soul. Cook had been recognized by a neighbor as he drove Colonel Washington's wagon across the Maryland bridge at dawn. A committee of citizens came to cross-examine her.

She faced them with blanched cheeks.

"My husband, an Abolitionist!" she gasped.

"He's with those murderers and robbers."

She turned on the men like a young tigress.

"You're lying - I tell you!"

For an hour they tried to drag from her a confession of his

plans. They left at last convinced that she knew nothing, that she suspected nothing of his real life. She had fought them bravely to the last. In her soul of souls she knew the hideous truth. She recalled the strange yearning with which he had looked at her as he left Sunday morning. She saw the bottom of the gulf at last.

With a cry of anguish and despair she sank to the floor in a faint.

She stirred with one thought tearing at her heart. Had they killed or captured him? She rose, dressed and joined the crowd that surged through the streets. The Rifle Works had been captured, Kagi was dead, the other two wounded, one fatally, the other a prisoner. No trace of her husband had been found. He had not reentered the town from the Maryland side.

She walked to the bridge and found it guarded by armed citizens. Tears of joy filled her eyes.

"He can't get back now!" she breathed.

She hurried to her room, fell on her knees and prayed:

"Oh, dear Lord Jesus, I've tried to be a good and faithful wife. My man has loved me tenderly and truly. Save him, oh, Lord! Don't let him come back now into this den of howling beasts. They'll tear him to pieces. And I can't endure it. I can't. I can't. Have pity, Lord. I'm just a poor, heart-broken wife!"

Through six days of terror and excitement, of surging crowds and marching soldiers, the shivering figure watched through her window - and silently prayed. A guard had been set at her house to catch her husband if he dared to return. She laughed softly.

He would not return! She had asked God not to let him. She was asking him now with every breath she breathed. God would not forget her. He would answer her prayers. She knew it. God is love.

She had begun to sleep again at night. Her man was safe in the mountains of Pennsylvania. The Governor of Virginia had set a price on his head. Men were scouring the hills hunting, as they hunt wild beasts, but God would save him. She had seen His shining face in prayer and He had promised.

And then the blow fell.

Far down the street she caught the roar of a mob. Its cries came faintly at first and then they grew to fierce oaths and brutal shouts.

A man stopped in front of her house and spoke to the guard.

"They've got him!"

"Who?"

"Cook!"

"The damned beast, the spy, the traitor!"

"Where are they takin' him?"

"To the jail at Charlestown."

She had no time to lose. She must see him. Bareheaded she rushed into the street and fought her way to his side. His hands were manacled but his fair head was held erect until he saw the white face of his bride. And then his eyes fell.

Would she, too, turn and curse him?

He asked himself the hideous question once and dared not lift his head. He felt her coming nearer. The guard halted. His eyes were blurred. He could see nothing.

He only felt two soft arms slip round his neck. His own moved instinctively to clasp her but the manacles held them. She kissed his lips before the staring crowd and murmured inarticulate sounds of love and tenderness. She smoothed his blond hair back from his forehead and crooned over him as a mother over a babe.

"My little wife - my poor little girlie - my baby!" he murmured. "Forgive me - I tried to save you from this. But I couldn't. Love would have it so. Now you can forget me!"

The arms tightened about his neck, and gave the answer lips could not frame.

When his trial came she moved to Charlestown to sit by his side in the prison dock, touch his manacled hands and look into his eyes.

The trial moved to its certain end with remorseless certainty. Cook's sister, the wife of Governor Willard, sat beside her doomed brother, and cheered the desolate heart of the girl he had married. Governor Willard gave the full weight of his position and his sterling manhood to his wife in her grief.

He had employed the best lawyer in his state to defend Cook - Daniel W. Vorhees, whose eloquence had given him the title of "The Tall Sycamore of the Wabash."

When the great advocate rose, his towering figure commanded a painful silence in the crowded court room. The people, who packed every inch of its space, hated the man who had lived among them for more than a year as a spy. But he had a wife, he had a sister. And in this solemn hour he should have his day in court. The crowd listened to Vorhees' speech with rapt attention.

His appeal was not based on the letter of the law. He took broader, higher grounds. He sketched the dark days of blood-cursed Kansas. He saw a handsome prodigal son, lured by the spirit of adventure, drawn into its vortex of blind passions. He pictured the sinister figure of the grim Puritan leader condemned to death. He told of the spell this evil mind had thrown over a sensitive boy's soul. He pleaded for mercy and forgiveness, for charity and divine love. He pictured the little Virginia girl at his side drawn into the tragedy by a deathless love. He sketched in words that burned into the souls of his hearers the love of his sister, a love big and tender and strong, a love that had followed him in the far frontiers with prayers, a love that encircled him in the darkness of deeds of violence against the forms of law and order. He pleaded for her and the distinguished Governor of a great state, not because of their high position in life but because they had hearts that could ache and break.

When he had finished his remarkable speech, strong men who hated Cook were sobbing. The room was bathed in tears. The stern visaged judge made no effort to hide his.

The court charged the jury to do impartial justice under the laws of the commonwealth.

There could be but one verdict. It was solemnly given by the foreman and the judge pronounced the sentence of death.

Two soft arms stole around the doomed man's neck, and then, before the court, crowd and God as witnesses, the little wife tenderly cried:

"My lover - my sweetheart - my husband - through evil report and through good report, through life, through death, through all eternity - I - love - you!"

Again strong men wept and turned from one another to hide the signs of their weakness.

The wife walked beside her doomed lover back to the jail. As they went through the narrow passage to his cell, the tall, rough-looking prison guard who accompanied them brushed close, caught her hand and pressed it.

His eyes met hers in a quick look that said more plainly than words:

"I must see you alone."

She waited outside the jail until he reappeared.

He approached her boldly and spoke as if he were delivering a casual message.

"Keep your courage, young woman. And don't you be surprised at anything I'm going to say to you. There's people lookin' at us now. I'm just tellin' you a message your husband's told me - you understand."

"Yes - yes - go on - I understand," she answered quickly.

"I'm from Kansas. I'm a friend of John Cook's. I come all the way here to help him. I joined these guards to get to him. I'm goin' to get him out of here if I can."

"Thank God - thank God," she murmured.

"Keep a stiff upper lip and get your hand on some money to follow us."

"I will."

Another guard approached.

"Leave me now. My name's Charles Lenhart. Don't try to talk to me again. Just watch and wait."

She nodded, brushed the tears from her eyes and left quickly.

He was on the job without delay. Cook and Edwin Coppoc, condemned to die on the same day, occupied the same room in jail. They borrowed a knife from Lenhart as soon as he came on duty and "forgot" to return it. With this knife they worked at night for a week cutting a hole through the brick wall. Under their clothes in a corner they concealed the fragments of bricks.

When the opening had been completed, they cut teeth in the knife blade and made a small saw strong and keen enough to eat through a link in their shackles.

On the night fixed, Lenhart was on guard waiting in breathless suspense for the men to drop the few feet into the prison yard. A brick wall fifteen feet high could he scaled from his shoulders and the last man up could give him a lift.

Through the long, chill hours he paced his beat on the wall and waited to hear the crunching of the bodies slipping through the walls.

What had happened?

Something had gone wrong in the impulsive mind of the blue-eyed adventurer inside. The hole was open, the saw in his hand to cut the manacles, when he suddenly stopped.

"What's the matter?" Coppoc asked.

"We can't do this to-night."

"For God's sake, why?"

"My sister's in town with Governor Willard to tell me goodbye. They will put the blame of this on them. My sister might be imprisoned. The Governor would be in bad. I've caused them trouble enough - God knows -"

"When are they going?"

"To-morrow. We'll wait until to-morrow night - after

they've gone."

"But Lenhart may not be on guard."

"That's so," Cook agreed. "Coppoc, you can go alone. You'd better do it."

"No."

"You'd better."

"I'm not made out of that sort of goods," the boy answered.

"You've got a good old Quaker mother out in Springdale praying for you. It's your chance - go - I can't tonight."

Nothing could induce Coppoc to desert his comrade and leave him to certain death when his escape should be known.

They replaced the bricks, covered the debris and waited until the following night.

At eleven o'clock they cut the manacles and Coppoc crawled out first. He had barely touched the ground when Cook followed. They glanced about the yard and it was deserted. They strained their eyes to make out the figure of the guard who passed the brick wall. He was not in sight. It was a good omen. Lenhart had no doubt foreseen their escape and dropped to the street outside.

They saw that the timbers of the gallows on which they were to die had not all been fastened.

They secured two pieces of scantling and reached the top of the wall. Suddenly the dark figure of a guard moved toward them. Cook called the signal to Lenhart. But a loyal son of Virginia stood sentinel that night. The answer was a rifle shot. They started to leap and caught the flash of a bayonet below.

They walked back into the jail and surrendered to Captain Avis, their friendly keeper.

The little wife waited and watched in vain.

# CHAPTER XXXIV

All uncertainty at an end to his execution, John Brown set his hand to finish the work of his life in a supreme triumph. He entered upon the task with religious joy. The old Puritan had always been an habitual writer of letters. The authorities of Virginia allowed him to write daily to his friends and relatives. He quickly took advantage of this power. The sword of Washington which he grasped on that fatal Sunday night had proven a feeble weapon. He seized a pen destined to slay a million human beings.

His soul on fire with the fixed idea that he had been ordained by God to drench a nation in blood, he joyfully began the task of creating the mob mind.

No man in history had a keener appreciation of the power of the daily press in the propaganda of crowd ideas. The daily newspaper had just blossomed into its full radiance in the modern world. No invention in the history of the race has equaled the cylinder printing press as an engine for creating crowd movements.

The daily newspaper of 1859 spoke only in the language of crowds. They were, in fact, so many mob orators haranguing their subscribers. They wrote down to the standards of the mob. They were molders of public opinion and they were always the creatures of public opinion. They wrote for the masses. Their columns were filled with their own peculiar brand of propaganda, illusions, dreams, assertions, prejudices, sensations, with always a cheap smear of moral platitude. Our people had grown too busy to do their own thinking. The daily newspapers now did it for them. There was as little originality in them as in the machines which printed the editions. Yet they were repeated by the crowd as God-inspired truth.

We no longer needed to seek for the mob in the streets. We had it at the breakfast table, in the office, in the counting room. The process of crowd thinking became the habit of daily life.

John Brown hastened to use this engine of propaganda. From his comfortable room in the jail at Charlestown there poured a daily stream of letters which found their way into print.

A perfect specimen of his art was the concluding paragraph of a letter to his friend and fellow conspirator, George L. Stearns of Boston.

"I have asked to be *spared* from having any *mock or hypocritical prayers made over me* when I am publicly *murdered*; and that my only *religious attendants* be poor, *little, dirty, ragged, bareheaded and barefooted slave boys and girls*, led by old, *gray-headed slave mothers*,"

This message he knew would reach the heart of every Abolitionist of the North, of every reader of *Uncle Tom's Cabin*. On the day of his transfiguration on the scaffold he would deliver the final word that would sweep these millions into the whirlpool of the Blood Feud.

To his wife and children he wrote a message which hammered again his fixed idea into a dogma of faith:

"John Rogers wrote to his children, 'Abhor the arrant whore of Rome.' John Brown writes to his children to abhor with *undying hatred* also the 'sum of all villainies,' slavery."

Not only did these daily letters find their way into the hands of millions through the press, but the newspapers maintained a staff of reporters at Charlestown to catch every whisper from the prisoner. So brilliantly did these reports visualize his daily life that the crowds who read them could hear the clanking of the chains as he walked and the groans that came from his wounded body.

Thousands of letters began to pour into the office of the Governor of Virginia, threatening, imploring, pleading for his life. The leading politicians of all parties of the North were at length swept into this howling mob by the press. To every plea the Governor of the Commonwealth replied:

"Southern Society is built on Reverence for Law. The Law has been outraged by this man. It shall be vindicated, though the heavens fall."

In this stand he was immovable and the South backed him to a man. For exciting servile insurrection the King of Great Britain was held up to everlasting scorn by our fathers who wrote the Declaration of Independence. For this crime among others we rebelled and established the American Republic. Should John Brown be canonized for the same infamy? The Southern people asked this question in dumb amazement at the clamor from the North.

And so the Day of Transfiguration on the scaffold dawned.

Judge Thomas Russell and his good wife journeyed all the way from Boston to minister to the wants of their strange guest. There was in the distinguished jurist's mind a question which he must ask Brown before the rope should strangle him forever. His martyrdom had cleared every doubt and cloud from the mind of his friend save one. His fascinating letters, filled with the praise of God and the glory of a martyr's cause, had exalted him.

The judge had heard his speech in court on the day he was

Thomas Dixon

sentenced to death and had believed that each word was inspired. But the old man, who was now to die in glory, had spent a week in Judge Russell's house in Boston hiding from a deputy sheriff in whose hands was a warrant for plain murder - one of the foulest murders in the records of crime. The judge was a student of character, as well as Abolitionist.

He asked Brown for his last confidential statement as to these crimes on the Pottawattomie. There was no hesitation in his bold reply. Standing beneath the shadow of the gallows, the white hand of Death on his stooped shoulders, one foot on earth and the other pressing the shores of eternity, he lied as brazenly as he had lied a hundred times before. He assured his friend and his wife that he had nothing to do with those killings.

Mrs. Russell, weeping, kissed him.

And Brown said calmly: "Now, go."

As he ascended the scaffold he handed to one who stood near his final message, the supreme utterance over which he had prayed day and night to his God. Despatched from the scaffold, and sealed by his blood, he knew that its magic words would spread by contagion the Red Thought.

His face shone with the glory of his hope as his feet climbed the scaffold steps. On the scrap of paper he had written:

"I, JOHN BROWN, AM NOW QUITE CERTAIN THAT THE CRIMES OF THIS GUILTY LAND WILL NEVER BE PURGED AWAY BUT WITH BLOOD."

The trap fell, his darkened soul swung into eternity and the deed was done. He had raised the Blood Feud to the nth power. His message thrilled the world.

Bells were tolling in the North while crowds of weeping men and women knelt in prayer to his God. Had they but lifted the veil and looked, they would have seen the face of a fiend. But their eyes were now blinded with the madness which had driven him to his death.

In Cleveland, Melodeon Hall was draped in mourning at a meeting where thousands wept and cursed and prayed. Mammoth gatherings were held in New York, in Rochester and Syracuse. In Boston a crowd, so dense they were lifted from their feet by the pressure of thousands behind, clamoring for entrance, rushed into Tremont Temple.

William Lloyd Garrison, the Pacifist, declared the meeting was called to witness John Brown's resurrection. He flung the last shred of principle to the winds and joined the mob of the Blood Feud without reservation.

"As a peace man - an ultra peace man - I am prepared to say: 'Success to every Slave Insurrection in the South and in every Slave Country!'"

Wendell Phillips, believing Judge Russell's report of Brown's denial of the Pottawattomie murders, declared to the thousands who crowded Cooper Union that John Brown was a Saint - that he was not on the Pottawattomie Creek on that fateful night, that he was not within twenty-five miles of the spot!

Ralph Waldo Emerson, ignorant of the truth of Pottawattomie, hailed Brown as "the new Saint, than whom none purer or more brave was ever led by love of men into conflict and death - the new Saint who has achieved his martyrdom and will make the gallows glorious as the cross."

One great spirit among the anti-slavery forces refused to be swept in the current of insanity. Abraham Lincoln at Troy, Kansas, said on the day of Brown's death:

"Old John Brown has been executed for treason against a State. We cannot object, even though he agreed with us in thinking Slavery wrong. That cannot excuse violence, bloodshed and treason. It could avail him nothing that he might *think* himself right."

Lincoln's voice was drowned in the roar of the mob.

John Brown from the scaffold had set in motion forces of mind beyond control. Never before had men so little grasped the present, so stupidly ignored the past, so poorly divined the future. Reason had been hurled from her throne. Man had ceased to think.

Had Lieutenant Green's sword pierced Brown's heart he would have died the death of a mad dog. His imprisonment, his carefully staged martyrdom, his message of blood, and final, just execution by Law created the mob mind which destroyed reverence for Law.

As he swung from the gallows and his body swayed for a moment between heaven and earth Colonel Preston, standing beside the steps, solemnly cried:

"So perish all such enemies of Virginia! All such enemies of the Union! All such foes of the human race!"

Yet even as the trap was sprung, in the Capitol of the greatest State of the North, the leaders of the crowd were firing a hundred guns as a dirge for their martyr hero.

A criminal paranoiac had become the leader of twenty millions of people. The mob mind had caught the disease of his insanity and a nation began to go mad.

Robert E. Lee, in command of the forces of Law and Order, watched the swaying ghostly figure with a sense of deep foreboding for the future.

# CHAPTER XXXV

John Brown's body lay molderingin the grave but his soul was marching on. And his soul was a thousand times mightier than his body had ever been.

While living, his abnormal mind repelled men of strong personality. He had never been able to control more than two dozen people in any enterprise which he undertook. And in these small bands rebellions always broke out.

The paranoiac had been transfigured now into the Hero and the Saint through the worship of the mob which his insanity had created. His apparent strength of character was in reality weakness, an incapacity to master himself or control his criminal impulses. But the Jacobin mind of his followers did not consider realities. They only cherished dreams, illusions, assertions. The mob never reasons. It only believes. Reason is submerged in passion.

John Brown was a typical Jacobin leader. He was first and last a Puritan mystic. The God he worshipped was a fiend, but he worshipped Him with all the more passionate devotion for that reason. When he committed murder on the Pottawatt-omie he stalked his prey as a panther. He sang praises to his God as he paused in the brush before he sprang. His narrow mind, with a single fixed idea, was inaccessible to any influences save those which fed his mania. Nothing could loose the grip of his soul on this dream. He closed his glittering eyes and refused to consider anything that might contradict his faith.

He acted without reason, driven blindly forward by an impulse. When his cunning mind used reason it was never for the purpose of finding truth. It was only for the purpose of confounding his enemies. He never used it as a guide to conduct.

By the magic of mental contagion he had transferred from the scaffold this Jacobin mind to the soul of a nation. The contact of persons is not necessary to transfer this disease. Its contagion is electric. It moves in subtle thought waves, as a mysterious pestilence spreads in the night. The mob mind, once formed, is a new creation and becomes with amazing rapidity a resistless force. The reason for its uncanny power lies in the fact that when once formed it is dominated by the unconscious, not the conscious forces, of man's nature. Its credulity is boundless. Its passions dominate all life. The records of history are a sealed book. Experience does not exist.

Impulse rules the universe.

And this mob mind moves always as a unit. It devours individuality. Men who as individuals may be gentle and humane are swept into accord with the most beastly cry of the crowd. This mental unity grows out of the crushing power of contagion. Gestures, cries, deeds of hate and fury are caught, approved, repeated.

Any lie can be built into a religion if repeated often enough to a crowd by a mind on fire with its passions. Pirates have died as bravely as John Brown. The glorification of the manner of his dying was merely a phenomenon of the unity of the crowd mind. It was precisely the grip of his Puritan mysticism, his worship of the Devil, that gave to his insanity its most dangerous appeal.

For the first time in the history of the republic the mob mind had mastered the collective soul of its people. The contagion had spread both North and South. In the North by sympathy, in the South by a process of reaction even more violent and destructive of reason.

John Brown had realized his vision of the Plains. He had raised a
National Blood Feud.

No hand could stay the scourge. The Red Thought burst into a flame that swept North and South, as a prairie fire sweeps the stubble of autumn. *Uncle Tom's Cabin* had prepared the stubble.

From the Northern press began to pour a stream of vindictive abuse. A fair specimen of this insanity appeared in the New York *Independent*:

"The mass of the population of the Atlantic Coast of the slave region of the South are descended from the transported convicts and outcasts of Great Britain. Oh, glorious chivalry and hereditary aristocracy of the South! Peerless first families of Virginia and Carolina! Progeny of the highwaymen, the horse thieves and sheep stealers and pickpockets of Old England!"

The fact that this paper was a religious publication, the outgrowth of the New England conscience, gave its columns a peculiar power over the Northern mind.

The South retorted in kind. *De Bow's Review* declared:

"The basic framework and controlling inference of Northern sentiment is Puritanic, the old Roundhead rebel refuse of England, which has ever been an unruly sect of Pharisees, the worst bigots on earth and the meanest tyrants when they have the power to exercise it."

When the Conventions met a few months later to name candidates for the Presidency and make a declaration of principles, leaders had ceased to lead and there were no principles to declare.

The mob mind was supreme.

The Democratic Convention met at Charleston, South Carolina, to name the successor of James Buchanan. Their constituents commanded a vast majority of the voters of the Nation. The Convention became a mob. The one man, the one giant leader left in the republic, the one constructive mind, the one man of political genius who could have saved the nation from the holocaust toward which it was plunging was Stephen A. Douglas of Illinois. He could have been elected President by an overwhelming majority had he been nominated by this united convention. He was entitled to the nomination. He had proven himself a statesman of the highest rank. He had proven himself impervious to sectional hatred or sectional appeal. He was a Northern man, but a friend of the South as well as the North. He was an American of the noblest type.

But the radical wing of his party in the South were seeing Red. Old Brown's words to them meant the spirit of the North. They heard echoing and reechoing from every newspaper and pulpit:

"I, JOHN BROWN, AM NOW QUITE CERTAIN THAT THE CRIMES OF THIS GUILTY LAND WILL NEVER BE PURGED AWAY BUT WITH BLOOD."

If the hour for bloodshed had come they demanded that the South prepare without further words. And they believed that the hour had come. They heard the tread of swarming hosts. They were eager to meet them.

Reason was flung to the winds. Passion ruled. Compromise was a thing beyond discussion. Douglas was a Northern man and they would have none of him. He was hooted and catcalled until he was compelled to withdraw from the Convention.

The radical South named their own candidate for President.

He couldn't be elected. No matter. War was inevitable.

Let it come.

The Northern Democratic Convention named Douglas for President. He couldn't be elected. No matter. War was inevitable. Let it come.

In dumb amazement at the tragedy approaching - the tragedy of a divided Union and a bloody civil war - the Union men of the party nominated a third ticket, Bell of Tennessee and Everett of Massachusetts. They couldn't be elected. No matter. War was inevitable. It had to come. They would stand by their principles and go down with them.

When the new Republican party met at Chicago they were sobered by the responsibility suddenly thrust upon them of naming the next President of the United States. Fremont, a mere figurehead as their candidate, had polled a million votes in the campaign before. With three Democratic tickets in the field, success was sure.

They wrote a conservative platform and named for their candidate Abraham Lincoln, the one man in their party who had denounced John Brown's deeds, the man who had declared in his debates with Douglas that he did not believe in making negroes voters or jurors, that he did not believe in the equality of the races, that he did not believe that two such races could ever live together in a Democracy on terms of political or social equality.

Their candidate was the gentlest, broadest, sanest man within their ranks. Unless the nation had already gone mad they felt that in his triumph they would be safe from the Red Menace which stalked through their crowded hall. Their radical leaders were furious. But they were compelled to submit and fight for his election. The life of their party depended on it. Their own life was bound up in their party.

There was really but one issue before the nation - peace or war. The new party, both in its candidate and its platform, sought with all its power to stem the Red Tide of the Blood Feud which John Brown had raised.

Their well-meant efforts came too late.

War is a condition of mind primarily. Its causes are always psychological - not physical. The result of this state of mind is an abnormal condition of the nervous system, in which the thoughts and acts of men are controlled by the collective mind - the mob mind. Indians execute their war dances for days and nights to produce this mental state. Once it had been created, the war cry alone can be heard.

This mind, once formed, deliberative bodies cease to exist. The Congress of the United States ceased to exist as a deliberative body at the session which followed John Brown's execution.

The atmosphere of both the Senate and the House was electric with hatred and passion. Men who met at the last session as friends, now glared into each other's faces, mortal enemies.

L. Q. C. Lamar, the young statesman from Mississippi, threw a firebrand into the House on the day of its opening.

"The Republicans of this House are not guiltless of the blood of John Brown, his conspirators, and the innocent victims of his ruthless vengeance."

Keitt of South Carolina shouted:

"The South asks nothing but her rights. I would have no more, but as God is my judge I would shatter this republic from turret to foundation stone before I would take a little less!"

Old Thaddeus Stevens of Pennsylvania scrambled up on his club foot and with a face flaming with scorn replied:

"I do not blame gentlemen of the South for using this threat of rending God's creation from foundation to turret. They have tried it fifty times, and fifty times they have found weak and recreant tremblers in the North who have been affected by it, and who have retreated before these intimidations."

He turned to the group of conservative members of his own party with a look of triumphant taunting. He wanted war. He courted it. He saw its coming with a shout of joy.

The House was in an uproar. Members leaped from their seats and jammed the aisles, shouting, cheering, hissing, catcalling. The clerk was powerless to preserve order.

For two months the bedlam continued while they voted in vain to elect a Speaker. The new party was determined to have John Sherman. The opposition was divided but finally chose Mr. Pennington, a moderate of mediocre ability.

During these eight weeks of senseless wrangling the members began to arm themselves with revolvers. One of the weapons dropped from the pocket of a member from New York and he was accused of attempting to draw it for use against an opponent.

The sergeant at arms was summoned and pandemonium broke loose. For a moment it seemed that a pitched battle before the dais of the Speaker was inevitable.

John Sherman rose and made a remarkable statement - remarkable in showing how the mob mind will inevitably destroy the mind of the individual until its unity is undisputed. He spoke in tones of reconciliation.

"When I came here I did not believe that the Slavery question would come up; and but for the unfortunate affair of Brown's at Harper's Ferry I do not believe that there would have been any feeling on the subject. Northern members came here with kindly feelings, no man approving of the deed of John Brown, and every man willing to say so, every man willing to admit it an act of lawless violence."

It was true. And yet before that mad session closed they were Brown's disciples and he had become their martyr here. The mob mind devours individuality, and reduces all to the common denominator of the archaic impulse.

In the fierce conflict for Speaker four years before, when Banks had been chosen, Slavery was then the issue. Good humor, courtesy and reason ruled the contest which lasted three days longer than the fight over Sherman. Instead of courtesy and reason - hatred, passion, defiance, assertion were now the order of the day. Four years before a threat of disunion was made on the floor. The House received it with shouts of derision and laughter. Keitt's dramatic threat had thrown the House into an uproar which had to be quelled by the sergeant at arms. Envy, hate, jealousy, spite, passion were supreme. The favorite epithets hurled across the Chamber were:

"Slave driver!"

"Nigger thief!"

The newspapers no longer reported speeches as delivered. They were revised and raised to greater powers of vituperation and abuse. Instead of a convincing, logical speech, their champion hurled a "torrent of scathing denunciation," "withering sarcasm," and "crushing invective!"

At this historic session appeared the first suit of Confederate Gray, worn by Roger A. Pryor, the brilliant young member from Virginia.

Immediately a Northern member leaped to his feet. He had caught the significance of the Southern emblem. He gave a moment's silent survey to the gray suit and opened his address on the State of the Country by saying:

"Virginia, instead of clothing herself in sheep's wool, had better don her appropriate garb of sackcloth and ashes!"

The nation was already at war before Abraham Lincoln left Springfield for Washington to take his seat as President. It was deemed wise that he should enter the city practically in disguise.

In vain the great heart that beat within his lonely breast tried to stem the Red Tide in his first inaugural. With infinite pathos he turned toward the South and spoke his words of peace, reconciliation and assurance:

"I have no purpose directly or indirectly to interfere with the institution of Slavery in the States where it exists. I believe I have no lawful right to do so, and I have no inclination to do so."

His closing sentences were spoken with his deep eyes swimming in tears.

"I am loath to close. We are not enemies but friends. We must not be enemies. Though passion may have strained, it must not break our bonds of affection. The mystic chords of memory, stretching from every battlefield and patriot grave, to every living heart and hearthstone all over this broad land, will yet swell the chorus of the Union when again touched, as surely they will be, by the better angels of our nature."

The noblest men of North and South joined with the new President, pleading for peace. They knew by the light of reason that a war of brothers would be a wanton crime. They proved by irresistible logic that every issue dividing the nation could be settled at the Council Table.

They pleaded in vain. They pitched straws against a hurricane. From the deep, subconscious nature of man, the lair of the beast, came only the growl of challenge to mortal combat.

The new President is but a leaf tossed by the wind. The Union of which our fathers dreamed is rent in twain. With tumult and shout, the armies gather, blue and gray, brother against brother. A madman's soul now rides the storm and leads the serried lines as they sweep to the red rendezvous with Death.

# CHAPTER XXXVI

A little mother with a laughing boy two years old and baby in her arms was awaiting at a crowded hotel in Washington the coming of her father from the Western plains. Her men were going in opposite directions in these tragic days that were trying the souls of men. Colonel Phillip St. George Cooke was a Virginian. Lieutenant J. E. B. Stuart was a Virginian. The soul of the little mother was worn out with the question that had no answer. Why should her lover-husband and her fine old daddy fight each other?

She stood appalled before such a conflict. She had written to her father a letter so gentle, so full of tender appeal, he could not resist its call. She had asked that he come to see her babies and her husband and, face to face, say the things that were in his heart.

Her own sympathies were with her husband. He had breathed his soul into hers. She thought as he thought and felt as he felt. But her dear old daddy must have deep reasons for refusing to follow Virginia, if she should go with the South in Secession. She must hear these reasons. Stuart must hear them. If he could convince them, they would go with him.

In her girl's soul she didn't care which way they went, as long as they did not fight each other. She had watched the shadow of this war deepen with growing anguish. If her father should meet her husband in battle and one should kill the other! How could she live? The thought was too horrible to frame in, words, but it haunted her dreams. She couldn't shake it off.

That her rollicking soldier man would come out alive she felt sure somehow. No other thought was possible. To think that he might be killed in the pride and glory of his youth was nonsense. Her mind refused now to dwell on the idea. She dismissed it with a laugh. He was so vital. He lived to his finger tips. His voice rang with the joy of living. The spirit of eternal youth danced in his blue eyes. He was just twenty-eight years old. He was the father of a darling boy who bore his name and a baby that nestled in her arms to whom they had given hers.

Life in its morning of glory was his - wife, babies, love, youth, health, strength, clean living and high thinking. No, it was the thought of harm to her father that was eating her heart out. He has passed the noon-tide of life. His slender, graceful form lacked the sturdy power of youth. His chances were not so good.

The thing that sickened her was the certainty that both these men, father and husband, would organize the cavalry service and fight on horseback. They had spent their honeymoon on the plains. She had ridden over them with her joyous lover.

He would be a cavalry commander. She knew that he would be a general. Her father was a master of cavalry tactics and was at work on the Manuel for the United States Army.

The two men were born under the same skies. Their tastes were similar. Their clean habits of life were alike. Their ideals were equally high and noble. How could two such men fight each other to the death over an issue of politics when some wife or sister or mother must look on a dead face when the smoke has cleared?

Her soul rose in rebellion against it all. She summoned every power of her mind to the struggle with her father.

She brought them together at last in the room with her babies, asleep in their cradles. She sat down between the two and held a hand in each of hers.

"Now, daddy dear, you must tell me why you're going to fight Virginia if she secedes from the Union."

The gentle face smiled sadly.

"How can I make you understand, dear baby? It's foolish to argue such things. We follow our hearts - that's all."

"But you must tell me," she pleaded.

"There's nothing to tell, child. We must each decide these big things of life for himself. I'll never draw my sword against the Union. My fathers created it. I've fought for it. I've lived for it. And I've got to die for it, if must be, that's all -"

He paused, withdrew his hand from hers, rose and put it on Stuart's shoulder.

"You've chosen a fine boy for your husband, my daughter. I love him. I'm proud of him. I shall always be proud that your children bear his name. He must fight this battle of his allegiance in his own soul and answer to God, not to me. I would not dare to try to influence him."

Stuart rose and grasped the Colonel's hand. His eyes were moist.

"Thank you, Colonel. I shall always remember this hour with you and my Flora. And I shall always love and respect you, in life or death, success or failure."

The older man held Stuart's hand in a strong grip.

"It grieves me to feel that you may fight the Union, my son. I have seen the end in a vision already. The Union is indissoluble. The stars in their courses have said it."

"It may be, sir," Stuart slowly answered. "Who knows? We must do each what we believe to be right, as God gives us to see the right."

The little mother was softly crying. Her hopes had faded. There was the note of finality in each word her men had uttered. She was crushed.

For an hour she talked in tender commonplaces. She tried to be cheerful for her father's sake. She saw that he was suffering cruelly at the thought of saying a goodbye that might be the last.

She broke down in a flood of bitter tears. The father took her into his arms and soothed her with tender words. But something deep and strange had stirred in the mother heart within her.

She drew away from his arms and cried in anguish.

"It's wrong. It's wrong. It's all wrong - this feud of blood! And God will yet save the world from it. I must believe that or I'd go mad!"

The two men looked at each other in wonder for a moment and then at the mother's convulsed face. Into the older man's features slowly crept a look of awe, as if he had heard that voice before somewhere in the still hours of his soul.

Stuart bent and kissed her tenderly.

"There, dear, you're overwrought. Don't worry. Your work God has given you in these cradles."

"Yes, that's why I feel this way," she whispered on his breast.

# CHAPTER XXXVII

If reason had ruled, the Gulf States of the South would never have ordered their representatives to leave Washington on the election of Abraham Lincoln. The new administration could have done nothing with the Congress chosen. The President had been elected on a fluke because of the division of the opposition into three tickets. Lincoln was a minority President and was powerless except in the use of the veto.

If the Gulf States had paused for a moment they could have seen that such an administration, whatever its views about Slavery, would have failed, and the next election would have been theirs. The moment they withdrew their members of Congress, however, the new party had a majority and could shape the nation's laws.

The crowd mind acts on blind impulse, never on reason.

In spite of the President's humane purpose to keep peace when he delivered his first inaugural, he had scarcely taken his seat at the head of his Cabinet when the mob mind swept him from his moorings and he was caught in the torrent of the war mania.

The firing on Fort Sumter was not the first shot by the Secessionists. They had fired on the *Star of the West*, a ship sent to the relief of the Fort, weeks before. They had driven her back to sea. But the President at that moment had sufficient power to withstand the cry for blood. At the next shot he succumbed to the inevitable and called for 75,000 volunteers to invade the South. This act of war was a violation of his powers under Constitutional law. Congress alone could declare war. But Congress was not in session.

The mob had, in fact, declared war. The President and his Cabinet were forced to bow to its will and risk their necks on the outcome of the struggle.

So long as Virginia, North Carolina and Tennessee refused to secede and stood with the Border States of Maryland, Missouri and Kentucky inside the Union, the Confederacy organized at Montgomery, Alabama, must remain a mere political feint.

The call of the President on Virginia, North Carolina, Tennessee, Kentucky, Missouri and Maryland, all slave States, to furnish their quota of troops to fight the seceders, was in effect a declaration of war by a united North upon the South.

Virginia had refused to join the Confederacy before by an overwhelming majority. All eyes were again turned on the Old Dominion. Would she accept the President's command and send her quota of troops to fight her sisters of the South, or would she withdraw from the Union?

The darkest day of its history was dawning on Arlington. Lee had spent a sleepless night watching the flickering lights of the Capitol, waiting, hoping, praying for a message from the Convention at Richmond. On that message hung the present, the future, and the sacred glory of the past.

The lamp on the table in the hall was still burning dimly at dawn when Mary Lee came downstairs and pulled the old-fashioned bell cord which summoned the butler.

Ben entered with a bow.

"You ring for me, Missy?"

"Yes. You sent to town to see if an Extra had been issued?"

"Yassam. De boy come back more'n a hour ago."

"There was none?"

"Nomum."

"And he couldn't find Lieutenant Stuart?"

"Nomum. He look fur him in de telegraph office an' everywhar."

"Why don't he come - why don't he come?" she sighed.

"I spec dem wires is done down, an' de news 'bout Secesum come froo de country fum Richmon' by horseback, M'am."

The girl sighed again wearily.

"The coffee and sandwiches ready, Ben?"

"Yassam. All on de table waitin'. De coffee gittin' cold."

"I'll bring Papa down, if I can get him to come."

"Yassam. I hopes ye bring him. He sho must be wore out."

"It's daylight," she said, "open the windows and put out the lamp."

Mary climbed the stairs again to get her father to eat. Ben drew the curtains and the full light of a beautiful spring morning flooded the room. A mocking bird was singing in the holly. A catbird cried from a rosebush, a redbird flashed and chirped from the hedge and a colt whinnied for his mother.

The old negro lowered the lamp, blew it out and began to straighten the room. A soft knock sounded on the front door.

He stopped and listened. That was queer. No guest could be coming to Arlington at dawn. Lieutenant Stuart would come on horseback and the ring of his horse's hoofs could be heard for half a mile.

He turned back to his work and the knock was repeated, this time louder.

He cautiously approached the door.

"Who's dar?"

"Hit's me."

"Me who?"

"Hit's me - Sam."

"'Tain't no Sam nuther -"

"'Tis me."

"Sam's bin free mos' ten year now an' he's livin' in New York -"

"I done come back. Lemme come in a minute!"

Ben was not sure. He picked up a heavy cane, held it in his right hand and cautiously opened the door with his left, as Sam entered.

The old man dropped the cane and stepped back in dumb amazement. It was some time before he spoke.

"Name er Gawd, Sam - hit is you."

"Sho, hit's me!"

"What yer doin' here?"

"I come to see my old marster when I hears all dis talk 'bout war. Whar is he?"

Ben lifted his eyes to the ceiling and spoke in a solemn tone:

"Up dar in his room all night trampin' back an' forth lak er lion in de cage, waitin' fur Marse Stuart ter fetch de news fum Richmond 'bout secessun -"

"Secessun?"

Ben nodded - and raised his eyes in a dreamy look.

"Some say Ole Virginy gwine ter stay in de Union. Some say she's a gwine ter secede. De Convenshun in Richmon' wuz votin' on hit yestiddy. Marse Stuart gone ter town ter fetch de news ter Arlington."

Sam stepped close and searched Ben's face.

"What's my ole marster dat set me free gwine ter do?"

"Dat's what everybody's axin. He bin prayin' up dar all night."

Sam glanced toward the stairway and held his silence for a while. He spoke finally with firm conviction.

"Well, I'se gwine wid him. Ef he go wid de Union, I goes. Ef he go wid ole Virginy, I go wid ole Virginy. Whichever way *he* go, dat's de *right* way -"

"Dat's so, too!" Ben responded fervently.

Sam advanced to the old butler with the quick step of the days when he was his efficient helper.

"What ye want me ter do?"

Ben led him to the portico and pointed down the white

graveled way to Washington.

"Run doun de road ter de rise er dat hill an' stay dar. De minute yer see a hoss cross dat bridge - hit's Marse Stuart. Yer fly back here an' tell me -"

Sam nodded and disappeared. Ben hurried back into the hall, as Mary and her mother came down the stairs.

Mrs. Lee was struggling to control her fears.

"No sign of Lieutenant Stuart yet, Ben?"

"Nomum. I'se er watchin'."

"Look again and see if there's any dust on that long stretch beyond the river -"

Ben shook his head.

"Yassam, I look."

He passed out the front door still wagging his head in deep sympathy for the stricken mistress of the great house.

Mary slipped her arm around her mother, and used the pet name she spoke in moments of great joy and sorrow.

"Oh, Mim dear, you mustn't worry so!"

Her mother's lips trembled. She tried to be strong and failed. The tears came at last streaming down her cheeks.

"I can't help it, darling. Life hangs on this message - our home -"

She paused and her eyes wandered about the familiar room and its furnishings.

"You know how I love this home. It's woven into the very fiber of my heart. Our future - all that we have on earth - it's more than I can bear -"

The daughter drew the dear face to her lips.

"But why try to take it all on our shoulders, dearest? We must leave Papa to fight this out alone. We can't decide it for him."

The mother brushed her tears away and responded cheerfully.

"Yes, I know, dear. Your father didn't leave his room all day yesterday. He ate no dinner. No supper. All night the tramp of his feet overhead has only been broken when he fell on his knees to pray - "

Her voice wandered off as in a half dream. She paused, and then rushed on impetuously.

"Why, why can't we hear from Richmond? The Convention should have voted before noon yesterday. And we've waited all night - "

"The authorities may be holding back the news."

"But why should they suppress *such* news? The world must know."

She stopped suddenly - as if stunned by the thought that oppressed her. She seized Mary's hand, and asked tensely:

"What do you think, dear? Has Virginia left the Union?"

A quick answer was on the young lips. She had a very clear opinion. She had talked to Stuart. And his keen mind had seen the inevitable. She didn't have the heart to tell her mother. She feigned a mind blank from weariness.

"I can't think, honey. I'm too tired."

Ben came back shaking his gray head.

"Nomum. Dey ain't no sign on de road yet."

The waiting wife and mother cried in an anguish she could not control.

"Why - why - why?"

Ben sought to distract her thoughts with the habit of house control. He spoke in his old voice of friendly scolding.

"Ain't Marse Robert comin' doun to his coffee, M'am?"

"Not yet, Ben. I couldn't persuade him." The mistress caught the effort of her faithful servant to help in his humble way and it touched her. She was making a firm resolution to regain her self-control when a distant cry was heard from the roadway.

"Uncle Ben!"

"What's dat?" the old man asked.

"He's coming?" Mrs. Lee gasped.

"I dunno, M'am. I hears sumfin!"

Sam's cry echoed near the house now in growing excitement.

"Uncle Ben - Uncle Ben!"

"See, Ben, see quick -" Mary cried.

"Yassam. He's comin', sho. He's seed him."

The mother's face was uplifted in prayer.

"God's will be done!"

The words came in a bare whisper. And then as if in answer to the cry of her heart she caught new hope and turned to her daughter.

"You know, dear, the first Convention voted against Secession!"

Sam reached the door and met Ben.

"Uncle Ben - he's a comin' - Marse Stuart's horse! I seen him 'way 'cross de ribber fust - des one long, white streak er dust ez fur ez de eye can reach!"

The mother gripped Mary's arm with cruel force. The strain was again more than she could bear.

"Oh, dear, oh, dear, what have they done? What have they done?"

Ben entered the hall holding himself erect with the dignity of one who must bear great sorrows with his people. The mistress called to him weakly:

"Tell Colonel Lee, Ben."

The old man bowed gravely.

"Yassam. Right away, M'am."

Ben hurried to call his master as Sam edged into the front door and smiled at his mistress.

Mrs. Lee saw and recognized him for the first time. His loyalty touched her deeply in the hour of trial. She extended her hand in warm greeting.

"Why, *Sam*, you've come home!"

"Yassam. I come back ter stan' by my folks when dey

needs me."

Mary's eyes were misty as she smiled her welcome.

"You're a good boy, Sam."

"Yassam. Marse Robert teach me."

The echo of Stuart's horse's hoof rang under the portico and Sam hurried to meet him.

His clear voice called:

"Don't put 'im up, boy!"

Mary's heart began to pound. She knew he would be galloping down the white graveled way again in a few minutes. His next order confirmed her fear.

"Just give him some water!"

"Yassah!"

The two women stood huddled close in tense anxiety.

Lee hurried down the stairs and met Stuart at the door. Before the familiarity of a handshake or word of welcome he asked:

"What news, Lieutenant?"

Stuart spoke with deep emotion. On every word the man and the woman hung breathlessly.

"It has come, sir. Virginia has answered to the President's call to send troops against her own people. She has sacrificed all save honor. The vote of the Convention was overwhelming. She has withdrawn from the Union -"

A moment's deathly silence. And the cry of pain from a

woman's white lips. Mary caught her mother in her arms and held her firmly. The cry wrung her young heart.

"Oh, dear God, have mercy on us - and give us strength to bear it -"

Stuart hurried to her side and tried to break the blow with cheerful words.

"Don't worry, Mrs. Lee. The South is right."

Lee had not spoken. His brilliant eyes had the look of a man who walks in his sleep. They were in the world but not of it. The deep things of eternity were in their brooding. He waked at last and turned to Stuart sadly.

"God save our country, my boy."

He paused and looked out the doorway on the beautiful green of the lawn. The perfume from the rose garden stole in on the fresh breeze that stirred from the river.

"A frightful blow," he went on dreamily, "this news you bring."

Stuart's young body stiffened.

"You're the foremost citizen of Virginia, sir. Others may doubt and waver and be confused. I think I know what you're going to do, in the end -"

"It's hard - it's hard," the strong man cried bitterly.

The mother and daughter studied his face in eager, anxious waiting. On his word life hung. Stuart glanced at their tense faces and couldn't find speech. He turned and spoke briskly.

"I must hurry, sir. I'll be in Richmond before sunset."

The sound of carriage wheels grated on the road and a foaming pair of horses drew under the portico. A woman sprang out.

Mrs. Lee turned to the Colonel.

"It's your sister, Annie, Colonel."

"Yes," Stuart added, "I passed her on the way -"

Mrs. Marshall hurried to greet Mrs. Lee. The two women embraced and wept in silence.

"Mary!"

"Annie!"

The names were barely breathed.

Mary silently kissed her aunt as she turned from her mother. The Colonel's sister raised her eyes and saw Stuart. Her tones were sharp with the ring of a commander giving orders:

"Our army is marching, Lieutenant Stuart! You here in civilian clothes?"

The strong, young body stiffened.

"I have resigned my commission in the United States Army, Mrs. Marshall -"

Her finger rose in an imperious gesture.

"You will live to regret it, sir!"

Lee frowned and laid his hand on his sister's arm in a gesture of appeal.

"Annie, dear, please."

She regained her poise at the touch of his hand and turned to Mrs. Lee.

Stuart extended his hand briskly.

"Goodbye, sir. I hope to see you in Richmond soon -"

Lee's answer was gravely spoken.

"Goodbye, my boy. I honor you in your quick decision, with the clear vision of youth. We, older men, must halt and pray, and feel our way."

With a laugh in his blue eyes Stuart paused at the door half embarrassed at Mrs. Marshall's presence. He waved his hat to the group.

"Well, goodbye, everybody! I'm off to join the Cavalry!"

Outside as he hurried to his horse he waved again.

"Goodbye - !"

There was a moment's painful silence. They listened to the beat of his horse's hoof on the white roadway toward Washington. As the tall soldier listened he heard the roar of the hoofs of coming legions. And a warrior's soul leaped to the saddle. But the soul of the man, of the father and brother uttered a cry of mortal pain. He looked about the hall in a dazed way as if unconscious of the presence of the women of his home.

Mrs. Lee saw his deep anxiety and whispered to Mrs. Marshall.

"Come to my room, Annie, and rest before you say anything to Robert -"

She shook her head.

"No - no, my dear. I can't. My heart's too full. I can't rest. It's no use trying."

The wife took both her hands.

"Then remember, that his heart is even fuller than yours."

"Yes, I know."

"And you cannot possibly be suffering as he is."

"I'll not forget, dear."

Mrs. Lee pressed her hands firmly.

"And say nothing that you'll live to regret?"

"I promise, Mary."

"Please!"

With a lingering look of sympathy for brother and sister, Mrs. Lee softly left the room.

Lee stood gazing through the window across the shining waters of the river whose mirror but a few months ago had reflected the distorted faces of John Brown and his men at Harper's Ferry. It had come, the vision he had seen as he looked on the dark stains that fateful morning.

He dreaded this interview with his sister. He knew the views of Judge Marshall, her husband. He knew her own love for the Union.

She was struggling for control of Her emotions and her voice was strained.

"You've - you've heard this awful news from Richmond?"

"Yes," he answered quietly. "And I've long felt it coming. The first thunderbolt struck us at Harper's Ferry. The storm has broken now -"

"What are you going to do?"

She asked the question as if half afraid to pronounce the words. Lee turned away in silence. She followed him and laid a hand on his arm.

"You'll let me tell you all that's in my heart, my brother?"

The soldier was a boy again. He took his sister's hand and stroked it as he had in the old days at Stratford.

"Of course, my dear."

"And remember that we *are* brother and sister?"

"Always."

She clung to his hand and made no effort now to keep back the tears.

"And that I shall always believe in you and be proud of you -"

A sob caught her voice and she could not go on. He pressed her hand.

"It's sweet to hear you say this, Annie, in the darkest hour of my life -"

She interrupted him in quick, passionate appeal.

"Why should it be the darkest hour, Robert? What have you or I, or our people, to do with the madmen who are driving the South over the brink of this precipice?"

Lee shook his head.

"The people of the South are not being driven now, my dear -"

He stopped. His eyes flashed as his words quickened.

"They are rushing with a fierce shout as one man. The North thinks that only a small part of the Southern people are in this revolution, misled by politicians. The truth is, the masses are sweeping their leaders before them, as leaves driven by a storm. The cotton states are unanimous. Virginia has seceded. North Carolina and Tennessee will follow her to-morrow, and the South a Unit, the Union is divided."

The sister drew herself up with pride, and squarely faced him. She spoke with deliberation.

"Our families, Robert, from the beginning have stood for the glory of the Union. It is unthinkable that you should leave it. Such men as Edmund Ruffin - yes - the impulsive old firebrand has already volunteered as a private and gone to South Carolina. He pulled the lanyard that fired the first shot against Fort Sumter. We have nothing in common with such men - "

Lee lifted his hand in protest.

"Yes, we have, my dear. We are both sons of Virginia, our mother and the mother of this Republic."

"All the more reason why I'm begging to-day that you dedicate your genius, your soul and body to fight the men who would destroy the Union!"

Lee raised his eyes as if in prayer and drew a deep breath.

"There's but one thing for me to decide, Annie - my duty."

His sister clasped her hands nervously and glanced about the room. Her eyes rested on the portraits of Washington, and his wife and she turned quickly.

"Your wife is the grand-daughter of Martha Washington. Can you look on that portrait of the father of this country, handed down to the mother of your children, and dare draw your sword to destroy his work?"

"I've tried to put him in my place and ask what he would do -"

He stopped suddenly.

"What would Washington do if he stood in my place to-day?"

"My dear brother!"

"Remember now that you are appealing to me as my sister. Did Washington allow the ties of blood to swerve him from his duty? His own mother was a loyal subject of the King of Great Britain and died so -"

"Washington led an army of patriots in a sacred cause," she interrupted.

"Surely. But he won his first victories as a soldier fighting the French, under the British flag. He denounced that flag, joined with the French and forced Cornwallis to surrender to the armies of France and the Colonies of America. He was equally right when he fought under the British flag against the French, and when he fought with Lafayette and Rochambeau and won our independence. Each time he fought for his rights under law. Each time with mind and conscience clear, he answered the call of duty. The man who does that is always right, my sister, no matter what flag flies above him!"

"Oh, Robert, there is but one flag - the flag of Washington, and your father, Henry Lee -"

The brother broke in quickly.

"And yet, the first blood in this conflict was drawn by a man who cursed that flag, who again and again defied its authority, and gloried in the fact that he had trampled it beneath his feet. The North has proclaimed him a Saint. Their soldiers are now marching on the South singing a song of glory to John Brown and all for which he stood. What would Washington do if he were living, and these men were marching to invade Virginia, put his home at Mount Vernon to the torch, and place pikes in the hands of his slaves -"

Lee searched his sister's eyes and drove his question home.

"What would he do?"

The woman was too downright in her honesty to quibble or fence. She couldn't answer. She flushed and hesitated.

"I don't know - I don't know. I only know," she hastened to add, "that he couldn't be a traitor."

"Even so. Who is the traitor, my dear? The man who defies the Constitution and the laws of the Union? Or the man who defends the law and the rights of his fathers under it?"

Again she couldn't answer. She would not acknowledge defeat. She simply refused to face such a problem. It led the wrong way. With quick wit she changed her point of attack. She drew close and asked in passionate tenderness:

"Have you counted the cost? The frightful cost which you and yours must pay if you dare defend Virginia?"

Lee nodded his head sorrowfully.

"On my knees, I've tried to reckon it." He looked longingly over the wide lawn that rolled in green splendor toward the river.

"I know that if I cast my lot with Virginia, this home, handed down to us from Washington, will be lost, and its fields trampled under the feet of hostile armies. That my wife and children may wander homeless, dependent on the charity or courtesy of friends. The thought of it tears my heart!"

His voice sank to a whisper. And then he lifted his head firmly.

"But I must not allow this to swerve me an inch from my duty -"

The sound of horses' hoofs again echoed on the roadway, as Ben entered from the dining room to announce breakfast.

Lee listened.

"See who that is, Ben."

"Yassah."

As Ben passed out the door, Lee continued:

"I will not say one word to influence my three sons. I will not even write to them. They must fight this battle out alone, as I am fighting it out to-day."

His sister smiled wanly.

"Your sons will follow you, Robert. And so will thousands of the best men in Virginia. Your responsibility is terrible."

Ben announced from the door.

"Mr. Francis Preston Blair, ter see you, sir."

Lee waved the butler from the room.

"I'll receive him, Ben. You can go."

"Thank God!" Mrs. Marshall breathed. "He's the most influential man in Washington. He is in close touch with the President, and he is a Southerner -"

She looked at her brother pleadingly.

"You'll give him the most careful hearing, Robert?"

"I don't know the object of his visit, but I'll gladly see him."

"He's a staunch Union man. He can have but one object in coming!" she cried with elation.

With courtesy Lee met his distinguished visitor at the door and grasped his hand.

"Walk in, Mr. Blair. You know my sister, Mrs. Marshall of Baltimore?"

Blair smiled.

"I am happy to say that Mrs. Marshall and I are the best of friends. We have often met at the house of my son, Montgomery Blair, of Mr. Lincoln's Cabinet."

"Let me take your hat, sir," Lee said with an answering smile.

"Thank you."

The Colonel crossed the room to place it on a table.

Mrs. Marshall took advantage of the moment to whisper to Blair.

"I've done my best. I'm afraid I haven't convinced him. May God give you the word to speak to my brother to-day!"

Blair rubbed his hands and a look of triumph overspread his rugged face.

"He has, Madame. I have a message for him!"

"A message?"

"From the highest authority!"

"May I be present at your conference?" she pleaded eagerly.

"By all means, Madame. Stay and hear my announcement. He cannot refuse me."

Lee sought at once to put Blair at ease on his mission.

"From my sister's remark a moment ago, I may guess the purpose of your coming, Mr. Blair?"

His guest surveyed Lee with an expression of deep pleasure in the unfolding of his message.

"In part, yes, you may have guessed my purpose. But I have something to say that even your keen mind has not surmised -"

"I am honored, sir, in your call and I shall be glad to hear you."

Blair drew himself erect as if on military duty.

"Colonel Lee, I have come after a conference with President Lincoln, to ask you to throw the power of your great name into this fight now to put an end to chaos -"

"You have come from the President?"

"Unofficially -"

"Oh -"

"But with his full knowledge and consent."

"And what is his suggestion?"

Blair hesitated.

"He cannot make it until he first knows that you will accept his offer."

"His offer?"

Blair waited until the thought had been fully grasped and then uttered each word with solemn emphasis.

"His offer, sir, of the supreme command of the armies of the Union -"

A cry of joy and pride came resistlessly from the sister's lips.

"Oh, Robert - Robert!"

Lee was surprised and deeply moved. He rose from his seat, walked to the window, looked out, flushed and slowly said:

"You - you - cannot mean this - ?"

Blair hastened to assure him.

"I am straight from the White House. General Scott has eagerly endorsed your name."

"But I cannot realize this to me - from Abraham Lincoln?"

"From Abraham Lincoln, whose simple common sense is the greatest asset to-day which the Union possesses. His position is one of frank conciliation toward the South."

"Yet he said once that this Republic cannot endure half slave and half free and the South interpreted that to mean - war -"

"Exactly. Crowds do not reason. They refuse to think. They refuse, therefore, to hear his explanation of those words. He hates Slavery as you hate Slavery. He knows, as you know, that it is doomed by the process of time. To make this so clear that he who runs may read, he wrote in his inaugural address in so many words his solemn pledge to respect every right now possessed by the masters of the South under law.

*"'I have no purpose to interfere with the institution of Slavery in the States where it exists.'"*

"His sole purpose now is to save the Union, Slavery or no Slavery -"

"Surely, Robert," his sister cried, "you can endorse that stand!"

"Mr. Lincoln," Blair went on eagerly, "is a leader whose common sense amounts to genius. No threats or bluster, inside his own party or outside of it, can swerve him from his high aim. He is going to save this Union first and let all other questions bide their time."

Lee searched Blair with his keen eyes.

"But Mr. Lincoln, without the authority of Congress, has practically declared war. He has called on Virginia to furnish troops to fight a sister State. My State has decided that he had no power under the Constitution to issue such a call. It is, therefore, illegal. The organic law of the republic makes no provision for raising troops to fight a sister State."

Blair lifted both hands in a persuasive gesture.

"Let us grant, Colonel Lee, that in law you are right. The States are sovereign. The Constitution gives the General Government no power to coerce a State. Our fathers, as a matter of fact, never faced such a possibility. Grant all that in law. Even so, a mighty, united nation has grown through the years. It is now a living thing, immutable, indissoluble. It commands your obedience and mine."

Lee was silent and Mrs. Marshall cried:

"Surely this is true, Robert!"

"My dear Mr. Blair," Lee slowly began, "your claim is the beginning of the end of law - the beginning of anarchy. If under the law, Virginia is right, is it not my duty to defend her? Obedience to law is the cornerstone on which all nations are built if they endure. Reverence for law is to-day the force driving the South into revolution -"

"A revolution doomed to certain failure," Blair quickly interrupted. "The border slave states of Maryland, Kentucky and Missouri, under Mr. Lincoln's conservative leadership, will never secede. Without them the South must fail. You have served under the flag of the Union for thirty years. You know the North. You know the South. And you know that such a revolution based on a division of the Union without these border States is madness -"

"It is madness, Robert," Mrs. Marshall joined, "utter madness!"

"Right and duty, Mr. Blair, have nothing to do with success or failure,"Lee responded. "I know the fearful odds against the South. I know the indomitable will, the energy, the fertile resources, the pride of opinion of the North, once set in motion. I know that the South has no money, no army, no organized government, no standing in the Court of Nations. She will have a white population of barely five millions against twenty-two millions - and her ports will be closed by our Navy -"

Blair interrupted and leaned close.

"And let me add, that as our leader *you* will not only command the greatest army ever assembled under the American flag, backed by a great Navy - but that your victory will be but the beginning of a career. From your window you see the White House and the Capitol. The man who leads the Union armies will succeed Mr. Lincoln as President."

Lee's protest was emphatic.

"I aspire to no office, Mr. Blair. I'm fifty-four years of age. I am on the hilltop of life. The way leads down a gentle slope, I trust, to a valley of peace, love and happiness. Ambition does not lure me; I have lived. I have played my part as well as I know how. I am content. I love my Country, North and South, East and West. I am a trained soldier - I know nothing else."

"The highest honor of this Nation, Colonel Lee, is something no man born under our flag dares to decline. Few men in history have been so well equipped as you for such an honor, both by birth and culture. You must also remember that the President of the United States is Commander in Chief of the Army and Navy. You are proud of your profession. You would honor it in the highest office of the Republic. You are held in the highest esteem by every soldier in the army. The President calls you. The Nation calls you. All eyes are upon you."

Blair studied the effect of his appeal. He saw that Lee was profoundly moved. Yet his courteous manner gave no hint of the trend of his emotions. He did not reply for a moment and then spoke with tenderness.

"My dear friend, you must not think that I am deaf to such calls. They move me to the depths. But no honor can reconcile me to this awful war. It is madness. It is absolutely unnecessary. But for John Brown's insane act it could have been avoided. But it has come. Its glory does not tempt me. I wish peace on earth and good will to all men. I am a soldier, but a Christian soldier -"

His voice broke.

"I am one of the humblest followers of Jesus Christ. There is but a single question for me to decide - my duty -"

A horseman dashed under the portico, threw his reins to Sam and entered without announcement.

"Colonel Lee?" he asked.

"Yes."

He handed Lee a folded paper bearing the great seal of the State.

"A message, sir, from Richmond."

Lee's hand trembled as he broke the seal. He stared at its words as in a dream.

"You have important news?" Blair asked.

"Most important. I am summoned to Richmond by the Governor in obedience to a resolution of the Legislature."

Mrs. Marshall advanced on the dusty, young messenger, her eyes aflame with anger.

"How dare you enter this house unannounced, sir?"

The boy did not answer. He turned away with a smile. She repented her words immediately. They had sounded undignified, if not positively rude. But she had been so sure that Blair could not fail. This call from Richmond, coming in the moment of crisis, drove her to desperation. She looked at Blair helplessly and he rallied to the attack with renewed determination.

"A Nation is calling you. The Union your fathers created is calling you, Colonel Lee!"

Lee's figure stiffened the least bit, though his words were uttered in the friendliest tones.

"Virginia is also calling me, Mr. Blair. Your own State of Maryland has not seceded. For that reason you cannot feel this tragedy as I feel it. Put yourself in my place. I ask you the question, is not the command of a State that of a mother to a child? We are citizens of the State, not of the Union. There is no such thing as citizenship in the Union. We vote only as citizens of a State. We enlist as soldiers by States. I was sent to West Point as a cadet by the State of Virginia. Even President Lincoln's proclamation calling for volunteers to coerce a State, revolutionary as it is, is addressed, not to individual men, but to the States. He must call on each to furnish her quota of soldiers -"

"Yet the call is to every citizen of the Nation!"

Lee's hand was raised in a gesture of imperious affirmation.

"There is no such thing as citizenship of the Nation! We don't pay taxes to the Nation. We may yet become a Nation. We are as yet a Union of Sovereign States. Virginia has refused to furnish the troops called for by the President and has withdrawn from the Union. She reserved in her vote to enter, the right to withdraw. I am a Virginian. What is my duty?"

"To fight for the Union, Robert - always!" Mrs. Marshall answered.

"I love the Union, my dear sister, my heart aches at the thought of its division -"

He turned sharply to Blair.

"But is not the South to-day in taking her stand for the rights of the State asserting a principle as vital as the Union itself? All the great minds of the North have recognized that these rights are fundamental to our life. Bancroft declares that the State is the guardian of the security and happiness of the individual. Hamilton declares that, if the States shall lose their powers, the people will be robbed of their liberties. George Clinton says that the States are our *only* security for the liberties of the people against a centralized tyranny. These rights once surrendered, and I solemnly warn you, my friend, that your children and mine may live to see in Washington a centralized power that will dare to say what you shall eat, what you shall drink, and what you shall wear!"

Blair laughed incredulously.

"Surely it's a far cry to that, Colonel -"

"I'm not so sure, Mr. Blair. And the cry from Virginia rings through my heart. I see her in mortal peril. My father was three times Governor of the Commonwealth. Virginia gave America the immortal words of the Declaration of Independence. She gave us something greater. She gave us George Washington, a Southern slaveholder, whose iron will alone carried our despairing people through ten years of hopeless revolution and won at last our right to live. Madison wrote the Constitution. John Marshall of Virginia, as Chief Judge of the Supreme Court, established its power on the foundations of Justice and Law. Jefferson doubled our area in the Louisiana Territory. Scott and Taylor extended it to the Pacific Ocean from Oregon to the Gulf of California. Virginia in the generosity of her great heart gave the Northwest to the Union and forbade the extension of slavery within it -"

Blair leaped to make a point.

"Surely these proud recollections, of her gifts to the Union should form bonds too strong to be broken!"

"So say I, sir! Surely they should place the people of all sections under obligations too deep to permit the invasion of her sacred soil! Can I stand by as her loyal son and see this invasion begun? I regret that Virginia has withdrawn. But the deed is done. Her people through their Governor and their Legislature call me - command me to come to her defense. They may be wrong. They may be blinded by passion. They are still my people, my neighbors, my friends, my children - and I cannot -"

He drew a deep breath and rose to his full height.

"*I will not draw my sword against them!*"

"Glory to God!" the messenger exulted.

Blair spoke with despair.

"This is your final decision?"

"Final."

The messenger slipped close to Lee and spoke hurriedly.

"I came by special train, sir - an engine and coach. They wait you on a siding just outside of town. We're afraid the line may be cut. The Northern troops are bivouacing on the Capitol hill. They may stop us. We've no time to lose. I hope you can come at once."

The messenger walked quickly through the door and seized his horse's reins.

Lee turned to Blair.

"Troops are on the Capitol Hill?"

"A regiment of Pennsylvanians has just arrived, I believe."

Sam had edged through the door and stood smiling at his old master. The Colonel had not seen him to this moment.

"You here, Sam?" he said with feeling.

"Yassah. I come home ter stan' by you, Marse Robert."

"Saddle my horse, you can go with me!"

"Yassah. Thankee, sah!"

"Bring Sid to fetch our horses back from the train."

"Yassah, glory hallelujah!" Sam shouted as he darted for the stable.

The anxious mother, praying in her room upstairs, heard Sam's shout and hurried down with Mary. The other children happily were on the Pamunkey at the home of Custis.

The mother's heart was pounding. There was war in Sam's shout. She felt its savage thrill. She gripped herself for the ordeal. There should be no vain regrets, no foolish words. Her soul rose in the glory of sacrificial love.

"What is it, my dear?" she asked softly.

"I go to Richmond immediately. Northern troops are pouring into Washington. Send my things to me if you can."

His eyes wandered about the room he loved. He would never see it again. He felt this in his inmost soul. It would be but the work of an hour for the troops to sweep across the bridge, sack its rooms and leave its beautiful lawn a sodden waste.

The wife saw the anguish in his gaze and her words rang with exaltation.

"Then it is God's will. And I shall try to smile. You have reached this decision in deepest thought and prayer. And I know that you are right!"

Lee took her in his arms and held her in silence. Those who saw, wept. At last he kissed her tenderly and turned to the others.

His sister walked blindly toward him.

"Oh, Robert, you have broken my heart -"

"I know, Annie, that you'll blame me," he answered, gently.

She slipped her arms about his neck.

"No, I shall not blame you. I understand now. I only grieve -"

Her voice broke. She struggled to control herself.

"How handsome you are in this solemn hour, my glorious, soldier-brother -" Again her voice failed.

"The pity and horror of it all! My husband and my son will fight you - and - I - shall - pray - for - their - success - oh - how can God permit it! - Goodbye, Robert!"

Her arms tightened and his responded. His hand touched her hair and he said slowly:

"If dark hours come to us, my sister, we are children again roaming the fields hand in hand. We'll just remember that."

She kissed him tenderly.

"And success or failure, dear Annie," he continued, "shall be in God's hands - not ours. I go to lead a forlorn hope perhaps. But I must share the miseries of my people."

He slipped from her arms and silently embraced his daughter, and again her mother.

"Say goodbye to the other children for me when you see them, dear."

Blair took his extended hand.

"I know what you feel, Colonel Lee," he said solemnly. "I'm only sorry I could not hold you."

"Thank you, my friend. My people believe, and I believe that we have rights to defend. And we must do our best - even if we perish."

He strode quickly to the door, and paused. A sudden pain caught his heart as he crossed its threshold for the last time. He looked back, lifted his head as in prayer and passed out.

He mounted his horse and rode swiftly through the beautiful spring morning toward Richmond - and Immortality. The women stood weeping. The President's messenger watched in sorrow.

# CHAPTER XXXVIII

When John Brown cunningly surveyed the lines around those houses in Kansas, observed the fastenings of their doors, marked the strength of the shutters, learned the names of their dogs, crept under the cover of darkness on his prey as a wild beast creeps through the jungle and hacked his innocent victims to pieces, we know that he was a criminal paranoiac pursuing a fixed idea under the delusion that God had sent him.

Yet on the eighteenth of July, 1861, Colonel Fletcher Webster's regiment, the Twelfth Massachusetts, marched through the streets of Boston singing a song of glory to John Brown which one of its members composed. They were also marching Southward to kill. The only difference was they had a Commission.

War had been declared.

Why did the war crowd on the streets and in the ranks burst into song as they marched to kill their fellow men?

To find the answer we must go back to the dawn of human history and see man, as yet a savage beast, with but one impulse the dominant force in life, the archaic impulse to slay.

All wars are not begun in this elemental fashion. There are wars of defense forced on innocent nations by brutal aggressors. But the joy that thrills the soul of the crowd on the declaration of war is always the simple thing. It is the roar of the lion as he springs on his prey.

In this Song to the Soul of John Brown there was no thought of freeing a slave. War was not declared on that ground. The President who called them had no such purpose. The men who marched had no such idea. They sang "Glory, Glory Hallelujah! Glory, Glory Hallelujah!" because they saw Red.

The restraints of Law, Religion and Tradition had been lifted. The primitive beast that had been held in check by civilization, rose with a shout and leaped to its ancient task. The homicidal wish - fancy with which the human mind had toyed in times of peace in dreams and reveries - was now a living reality.

Not one in a thousand knew what the war was about. And this one in a thousand who thought he knew was mistaken. It had been made legal to kill. They were marching to kill. They shouted. They sang.

They were marching to the most utterly senseless and unnecessary struggle in the history of our race. The North in the hours of sanity which preceded the outburst did not wish war. The South in her sane moments never believed it possible. Yet the hell-lit tragedy of brothers marching to slay their brothers had come. Nothing could dampen the enthusiasm of this first joyous mob.

On the night of the twentieth of July the Army of the North was encamped about seven miles from Beaureguard's lines at Bull Run. The volunteers were singing, shouting, girding their loins for the fray. They had heard the firing on the first skirmish line. Fifteen or twenty men had been killed it was reported.

The Red Thought leaped!

At two o'clock before day on Sunday morning, the order came to advance against the foe. The deep thrill of the elemental man swept the crowd. They had come loaded down with baggage. They hurled it aside and got their guns.

What many of them were afraid of was that the whole rebel army would escape before they could get into the thick of it. Many had brought handcuffs and ropes along with which to manacle their prisoners and have sport with them after the fight, another ancient pastime of our half-ape ancestors. They threw down some of their blankets but held on to their handcuffs.

When the first crash of battle came these raw recruits on both sides fought with desperate bravery for nine terrible hours. They fought from dawn until three o'clock in the afternoon under the broiling Southern sun of July. Charge and counter charge left their toll of the dead and then the tired archaic muscles began to wonder when it would end. Why hadn't victory come? Where were the prisoners they were to manacle?

Both sides were sick with hunger and weariness. The Southerners were expecting reinforcements from Manassas Junction. The Northerners were expecting reinforcements. Their eyes were turned toward the same road which led from the Shenandoah Valley.

A dust cloud suddenly rose over the hill. A fresh army was marching on the scene. North and South looked with straining eyes. They were not long in doubt. The first troops suddenly swung in on the right flank of the Southern army and began to form their lines to charge the North.

Suddenly from this fresh Southern line rose a new cry. From two thousand throats came the shrill, elemental, savage shout of the hunter in sight of his game - the fierce Rebel Yell.

They charged the Northern lines and then pandemonium - blind, unreasoning wolf-panic seized the army that had marched with songs and shouts to kill. They broke and fled. They cut the traces of their horses, left the guns, mounted and rode for life.

The mob engulfed the buggies and carriages of Congressmen and picnickers who had come out from Washington to see the fun. A rebellion crushed at a blow!

Stuart at the head of his Black Horse Cavalry, his saber flashing, cut his way through this mob again and again.

When the smoke of battle lifted, the dazed, ill-organized ambulance corps searched the field for the first toll of the Blood Feud. They found only nine hundred boys slain and two thousand six hundred wounded. They lay weltering in their blood in the smothering heat and dust and dirt.

The details of men were busy burying the dead, some of their bodies yet warm.

The morning after dawned black and lowering and the rain began to pour in torrents. Through the streets of Washington the stragglers streamed. The plumes which waved as they sang were soaked and drooping. Their gorgeous, new uniforms were wrinkled and mud-smeared.

The President called for five hundred thousand men this time. The joy and glory of war had gone.

But war remained.

War grim, gaunt, stark, hideous - as remorseless as death.

# CHAPTER XXXIX

In a foliage-embowered house on a hill near Washington Colonel Jeb Stuart, Commander of the Confederate Cavalry, had made his headquarters.

Neighing horses were hitched to the swaying limbs. They pawed the ground, wheeled and whinnied their impatience at inaction. Every man who sat in one of those saddles owned his mount. These boys were the flower of Southern manhood. The Confederate Government was too poor to furnish horses for the Cavalry. Every man, volunteering for this branch of the service, must bring his own horse and equipment complete. The South only furnished a revolver and carbine. At the first battle of Bull Run they didn't have enough of them even for the regiments Stuart commanded. Whole companies were armed only with the pikes which John Brown had made for the swarming of the Black Bees at Harper's Ferry. They used these pikes as lances.

The thing that gave the Confederate Cavalry its impetuous dash, its fire and efficiency was the fact that every man on horseback had been born in the saddle and had known his horse from a colt. From the moment they swung into line they were veterans.

The North had no such riders in the field as yet. Brigadier-General Phillip St. George Cooke was organizing this branch of the service. It would take weary months to train new riders and break in strange horses.

Thomas Dixon

Until these born riders, mounted on their favorites, could be killed or their horses shot from under them, there would be tough work ahead for the Union Cavalry.

A farmer approached at sunset. He gazed on the array with pride.

He lifted his gray head and shouted:

"Hurrah for our boys! Old Virginia'll show 'em before we're through with this!"

A sentinel saluted the old man.

"I've come for Colonel Stuart. His wife and babies are at my house. He'll understand. Tell him."

The farmer watched the spectacle. Straight in front of the little portico on its tall staff fluttered the Commander's new, blood-red battle flag with its blue St. Andrew's cross and white stars rippling in the wind. Spurs were clanking, sabers rattling. A courier dashed up, dismounted and entered the house. Young officers in their new uniforms were laughing and chatting in groups before the door.

An escort brought in a Federal Cavalry prisoner on his mount. The boys gathered around him and roared with laughter. He was a good-natured Irishman who could take a joke. His horse was loaded down with a hundred pounds of extra equipment. The Irishman had half of it strapped on his own back.

A boy shouted:

"For the Lord's sake, did you take him with all that freight?"

An escort roared:

"That's why we took him. He couldn't run."

The boy looked at the solemn face of the prisoner and chaffed:

"And why have ye got that load on your own back, man?"

Without cracking a smile the Irishman replied:

"An' I thought me old horse had all he could carry!"

The boys roared, pulled him down, took off his trappings and told him to make himself at home.

Inside the house could be heard the hum of conversation, with an occasional boom of laughter that could come from but one throat.

Work for the day completed, he came to the door to greet his visitor. The farmer's eyes flashed at the sight of his handsome figure. He was only twenty-eight years old, of medium height, with a long, silken, bronzed beard and curling mustache.

He waved his hand and cried:

"With you in a minute!"

His voice was ringing music. He wore a new suit of Confederate gray which his wife had just sent him. His gauntlets extended nine inches above the wrists. His cavalry boots were high above the knee. His broad-brimmed felt hat was caught up on one side with a black ostrich plume. His cavalry coat fitted tightly - a "fighting jacket." It was circled with a black belt from which hung his revolver and over which was tied a splendid yellow sash. His spurs were gold.

A first glance would give the impression of a gay youngster over fond of dress. But the moment his blue eyes flashed there came the glint of steel. The man behind the uniform was seen, the bravest of the brave, the flower of Southern chivalry.

For all his gay dress he was from the crown of his head to the soles of his feet, every inch the soldier - the soldier with the big brain and generous, fun-loving heart. His forehead was extraordinary in height and breadth, bronzed by sun and wind. His nose was large and nostrils mobile. His eyes were clear, piercing, intense. His laughing mouth was completely covered by the curling mustache and long beard.

He had darted around the house on waving to his visitor and in a minute reappeared, followed by three negroes. He was taking his minstrels with him on the trip to see his wife.

The cavalcade mounted. He waved his aides aside.

"No escort, boys. See you at sunrise."

The farmer's house was only half a mile inside his lines. When the army of the North was hurled back into Washington he had sent for his wife and babies and arranged for their board at the nearest farmhouse.

The little mother's heart was fluttering with love and pride. Richmond was already ringing with the praises of her soldier man. They were recruiting the first brigade of Cavalry. He was slated for Brigadier-General of the mounted forces. And he was only twenty-eight!

Stuart sprang from his horse and rushed to meet his wife. She was waiting in the glow of the sunset, her eyes misty with joyous tears.

It was a long time as she nestled in his arms before she could speak. Her voice was barely a whisper.

"You've passed through your first baptism of blood safely, my own!"

"Baptism of blood - nothing!" He laughed. "It wasn't a fight at all. We had nothing to do till the blue birds flew. And then we flew after 'em. Oh, honey girl, it was just a lark. I laughed till I cried -"

She raised her eyes to his.

"And you didn't see my dear old daddy anywhere?"

"No. I wish I had! I'd have taken the loyal old rascal prisoner and made you keep him till the war's over."

"It *is* over, isn't it, dear?"

"No."

"Why, you've driven the army back in a panic on Washington. They'll ask for peace, won't they?"

"They won't, honey. I know 'em too well. They'll more than likely ask for a million volunteers."

"It's not over, then?"

"No, dear little mother. I'll be honest with you. Don't believe silly talk. We're in for a long, desperate fight - "

"And I've been so happy thinking you'd come home - "

"Your home will be with me, won't it?"

"Always."

"All right. This is the beginning of my scheme for the duration of the war. I'm going to get you a map of Virginia, showing the roads. I'll get you a compass. There'll always be a little farmhouse somewhere behind my headquarters. Our home will be in the field and saddle for a while."

He kissed his babies and ate his supper laughing and joking like a boy of nineteen. The table cleared, he ordered a concert for their entertainment.

Bob, the leader of his minstrels, was a dandified mulatto who played the guitar, the second was a whistler and the third a master of the negro dance, the back step and the breakdown.

Bob tuned his guitar, picked his strings and gazed at the ceiling. He was apparently selecting the first piece. It, was always the same, his favorite, "Listen to the Mocking Bird." He played with a plaintive, swaying melody that charmed his hearers. The whistler amazed them with his marvelous imitation of birds and bird calls. The room throbbed with every note of the garden, field and wood.

The mother's face was wreathed in smiles. The boy shouted. The baby crooned. The first piece done, the audience burst into a round of applause.

Bob gave them "Alabama" next, accompanied by the whistler and his bird chorus.

Stuart laughed and called for the breakdown. Bob begins a jig on his guitar, the whistler claps and the sable dancer edges his way to the center of the floor in little spasmodic shuffles. He begins with his heel tap, then the toe, then in leaps and whirls. The guitar swelled to a steady roar. The whistler quickens his claps. And Stuart's boyish laughter rang above the din.

"Go it, boy! Go it!"

The dancer's eyes roll. His step quickens. He cuts the wildest figures in a frenzy of abandoned joy. With a leap through the door he is gone. The guitar stops with a sudden twang and Stuart's laughter roars.

And then he gave an hour to play with his children before a mother's lullaby should put them to sleep. He got down on his all fours and little Jeb mounted and rode round the room to the baby's scream of joy. He lay flat on the floor with the baby on his breast and let her pull his beard and mustache until her strength failed.

The children were still sound asleep when they sat down and ate breakfast before day.

At the first streak of dawn he was standing beside his horse ready for the dash back to his headquarters and the work of the day.

The shadow had fallen across the woman's heart again. He saw and understood. He put his hand under her chin and lifted it.

"No more tears now, my sweetheart."

"I'll try."

"We may be here for weeks."

"There'll be another fight soon?"

"I think not."

"For a month?"

"Not for a long time."

"Thank God!"

A far-off look stole into his eyes.

"It will be a good one though when it comes, I reckon."

"There can be no *good* one - if my boy's in it."

"Well, I'll be in it!"

"Yes. I know."

She kissed him and turned back into the house, with the old fear gripping her heart.

# CHAPTER XL

The early months of the war were but skirmishes. The real work of killing and maiming the flower of the race had not begun.

The defeat had given the sad-eyed President unlimited power to draw on the resources of the nation for men and money. His call for half a million soldiers met with instant response. The fighting spirit of twenty-two million Northern people had been roused. They felt the disgrace of Bull Run and determined to wipe it out in blood.

Three Northern armies were hurled on the South in a well-planned, concerted movement to take Richmond. McDowell marched straight down to Fredericksburg with forty thousand. Fermont, with Milroy, Banks and Shields, was sweeping through the Shenandoah Valley. McClellan, with his grand army of one hundred and twenty thousand men, had moved up the Peninsula in resistless force until he lay on the banks of the Chickahominy within sight of the spires of Richmond.

To meet these three armies aggregating a quarter of a million men, the South could marshall barely seventy thousand. Jackson was despatched with eighteen thousand to baffle the armies of McDowell, Fremont, Milroy, Shields and Banks in the Valley and prevent their union with McClellan.

The war really began on Sunday, the second of June, 1862, when Robert E. Lee was sent to the front to take command of the combined army of seventy thousand men of the South.

The new commander with consummate genius planned his attack and flung his gray lines on McClellan with savage power. The two armies fought in dense thickets often less than fifty yards apart. Their muskets flashed sheets of yellow flame. The sound of ripping canvas, the fire of small arms in volleys, could no longer be distinguished. The sullen roar was endless, deafening, appalling. Over the tops of oak, pine, beech, ash and tangled undergrowth came the flaming thunder of two great armies equally fearless, the flower of American manhood in their front ranks, daring, scorning death, fighting hand to hand, man to man.

The people in the churches of Richmond as they prayed could hear the awful roar. They turned their startled faces toward the battle. It rang above the sob of organ and the chant of choir.

The hosts in blue and gray charged again and again through the tangle of mud and muck and blood and smoke and death. Bayonet rang on bayonet. They fought hand to hand, as naked savages once fought with bare hands. The roar died slowly with the shadows of the night, until only the crack of a rifle here and there broke the stillness.

And then above the low moans of the wounded and dying came the distant notes of the church bells in Richmond calling men and women again to the house of God.

There was no shout of triumph - no cheering hosts - only the low moan of death and the sharp cry of a boy in pain. The men in blue could have moved in and bivouaced on the ground they had lost. The men in gray had no strength left.

The dead and the dying were everywhere. The wounded were crawling through the mud and brush, like stricken animals; some with their legs broken; some with arms dangling by a thread; some with hideous holes torn in their faces.

Thomas Dixon

The front was lighted with the unclouded splendor of a full Southern moon. Down every dim aisle of the woods they lay in awful, dark heaps. In the fields they lay with faces buried in the dirt or eyes staring up at the stars, twisted, torn, mangled. The blue and the gray lay side by side in death, as they had fought in life. The pride and glory of a mighty race of freemen.

The shadows of the details moved in the moonlight. They were opening the first of those long, deep trenches. They were careful in these early days of war. They turned each face downward as they packed them in. The grave diggers could not then throw the wet dirt into their eyes and mouths. Aching hearts in far-off homes couldn't see; but these boys still had hearts within their breasts.

The fog-rimmed lanterns flickered over the fields peering into the faces on the ground.

The ambulance corps did its best at the new trade. It was utterly inadequate on either side. It's always so in war. The work of war is to maim, to murder - not to heal or save.

The long line of creaking wagons began to move into Richmond over the mud-cut roads. Every hospital was filled. The empty wagons rolled back in haste over the cobble stones and out on the muddy roads to the front again.

At the hospital doors the women stood in huddled groups - wives, sweethearts, mothers, sisters, praying, hoping, fearing, shivering. Far away in the field hospitals, the young doctors with bare, bloody arms were busy with saw and knife. Boys who had faced death in battle without a tremor stood waiting their turn trembling, crying, cursing. They could see the piles of legs and arms rising higher as the doctors hurled them from the quivering bodies. They stretched out their hands in the darkness to feel the touch of loved ones. They must face this horror alone, and then battle through life, maimed wrecks. They peered through the shadows under the trees where the dead were piled and envied them their sleep.

The armies paused next day to gird their loins for the crucial test. Jackson was still in the Shenandoah Valley holding three armies at bay, defeating them in detail. His swift marches had so paralyzed his enemies that McDowell's forty thousand men lay at Fredericksburg unable to move.

Lee summoned Stuart.

When the conference ended the young Cavalry Commander threw himself into the saddle and started Northward with a song. Determined to learn the strength of McClellan's right wing and confuse his opponent, Lee had sent Stuart on the most daring adventure in the history of cavalry warfare. Stuart had told him that he could ride around McClellan's whole army, cut his communications and strike terror in his rear.

With twelve hundred picked horsemen, fighting, singing, dare-devil riders, Stuart slipped from Lee's lines and started toward Fredericksburg.

On the second day he surprised and captured the Federal pickets without a shot. He dreaded a meeting with the Cavalry. His father-in-law, General Cooke, was in command of a brigade of blue riders. He thought with a moment's pang of the little wife at home praying that they should never meet. Let her pray. God would help her. He couldn't let such a thing happen.

He suddenly confronted a squadron of Federal Cavalry. With a yell his troops charged and cleared the field. They must ride now with swifter hoofbeat than ever. The news would spread and avengers would be on their heels. They were now far in the rear of McClellan's grand army. They had felt out his right wing and knew to a mile where its lines ended.

They dashed toward the York River Railroad which supplied the Northern army, surprised the company holding Tunstall's Station, took them prisoners, cut the wires and tore up the tracks.

On his turn toward Richmond when he reached the Chickahominy River, its waters were swollen and he couldn't cross. He built a bridge out of the timbers of a barn, took his last horse over and destroyed it, as the shout of a division of Federal Cavalry was heard in the distance.

With twelve hundred men he had made a raid which added a new rule to cavalry tactics. He had ridden around a great army, covering ninety miles in fifty-six hours with the loss of but one man. He had established the position of the enemy, destroyed enormous quantities of war material, captured a hundred and sixty-five prisoners and two hundred horses. He had struck terror to the hearts of a sturdy foe, and thrilled the South with new courage.

Jackson's victorious little army joined Lee at Gaines' Mill on the twenty-seventh of June, and on the following day McClellan was in full retreat.

On the first of July it ended at Malvern Hill on the banks of the James. Of the one hundred and ten thousand men who marched in battle line on Richmond, eighty-six thousand only reached the shelter of his gunboats.

The first great battle of the war had raged from the first of June until the first of July. Fifty thousand brave boys were killed or mangled on the red fields of death. Washington was in gloom. The Grand Army of more than two hundred thousand had gone down in defeat. It was incredible.

Richmond had been saved. The glory of Lee, Jackson and Stuart filled the South with a new radiance. But the celebration of victory was in minor key. Every home was in mourning.

Six days later Stuart once more clasped his wife to his heart. It had been a month since he had seen her. The thunder of guns she had heard without pause. She knew that both her father and her lover were somewhere in the roaring hell below the city. Stuart never told her how close they had come to a charge and counter charge at the battle of Gaines' Mill.

The old, tremulous question she couldn't keep back:

"You didn't see my daddy, did you, dear?"

Stuart shouted in derision at the idea.

"Of course not, honey girl. It's not written in the book of life. Forget the silly old fear."

"And they didn't even scratch my soldier man?"

"Never a scratch!"

She kissed him again.

"You know I've a little woman praying for me every day. I lead a charmed life!"

She gazed at his handsome, bronzed face.

"I believe you do, dearest!"

# CHAPTER XLI

McClellan fell before the genius of Lee, and Pope was put in his place.

They met at Second Manassas. The new general ended his brief campaign in a disaster so complete, so appalling that it struck terror to the heart of the Nation. Lee had crushed him with an ease so amazing that Lincoln was compelled to recall McClellan to supreme command. When the toll of the Blood Feud was again reckoned twenty-five thousand more of our brave boys lay dead or wounded beneath the blazing sun of the South.

The Confederate Government now believed its army invincible, led by Lee. In spite of poor equipment, with the men half clad and half barefooted, Lee was ordered to invade Maryland. It was a political move, undertaken without the approval of the Commander.

As the gray lines swept Northward to cross the Potomac into Maryland, Lincoln was jubilant. To Hay, his young secretary, he whispered:

"We've got them now, boy. We've got them! The war must speedily end. Lee can never get into Maryland with fifty thousand effective men. The river will be behind them. I'll have McClellan on him with a hundred thousand well-shod, well-fed, well-armed soldiers and the finest equipment of artillery that ever thundered into battle.

"McClellan's on his mettle. His army will fight like tigers to show their faith in him. They were all against me when I removed him. Now they'll show me something. Mark my words."

Luck was with McClellan. By an accident Lee's plan of campaign had fallen into his hands. Yet it was too late to forestall his first master stroke. In the face of a hostile army of twice his numbers Lee divided his forces, threw Jackson's corps on Harper's Ferry, captured the town, Arsenal and Rifle Works, twelve thousand five hundred prisoners and vast stores of war material. Among the booty taken were new blue uniforms with which Jackson promptly clothed his men.

Lee met McClellan at Antietam and waited for Jackson to arrive from Harper's Ferry.

When McClellan's artillery opened in the gray dawn, more than sixteen thousand of Lee's footsore men had fallen along the line of march unable to reach the battlefield. The Union Commander was massing eighty-seven thousand men behind his flaming batteries. Lee could count on but thirty-seven thousand. He gave McClellan battle with his little army hemmed in on one side by Antietam Creek and on the other by the sweeping Potomac.

The President in Washington received the news of the positions of the armies and their chances of success with exultation. As the sun rose a glowing dull red ball of fire breaking through the smoke of the artillery, Hooker's division swept into action and drove the first line of Lee's men into the woods. Here they rallied and began to mow down the charging masses with deadly aim. For two hours the sullen fight raged in the woods without yielding an inch on either side. Hooker fell wounded. He called for aid. Mansfield answered and fell dead as he deployed his men. Sedgwick's Corps charged and were caught in a trap between two Confederate brigades concealed and massed to meet them. Sedgwick was wounded and his command barely saved from annihilation.

While this struggle raged on the Union right, the center saw a bloodier tragedy. French and Richardson charged the Confederate position. A sunken road crossed the field over which they marched. For four tragic hours the men in gray held this sunken road until it was piled with their bodies. When the final charge of massed blue took it, they found to their amazement that but three hundred living men had been holding it for an hour against the assaults of five thousand. So perfect was the faith of those gray soldiers in Robert E. Lee they died as if it were the order of the day. It was simply fate. Their Commander could make no mistake.

Burnsides swung his reinforced division around the woods and pushed up the heights against Sharpsburg to cut Lee's only line of retreat. He forced the thin, gray lines before him through the streets of the village. On its outer edge he suddenly confronted a mass of men clad in their own blue uniform.

How had these men gotten here?

He was not long in doubt. The blue line suddenly flashed a red wave squarely in their faces. It was Jackson's Corps from Harper's Ferry in their new uniforms. The shock threw the Union men into confusion, a desperate charge drove them out of Sharpsburg, and Lee's army camped on the field with the dead.

For fourteen hours five hundred guns and a hundred thousand muskets thundered and hissed their message of blood. When night fell more than twenty thousand of our noblest men lay dead and wounded on the field.

Lee skillfully withdrew his army across the Potomac. Safe in Virginia he rallied his shattered forces while he sent Stuart once more in a daring ride around McClellan's army.

Again McClellan fell before the genius of Lee. Burnsides was put in his place.

They met at Fredericksburg. Burnsides, the courtly, polished gentleman, crossed the Rappahannock River and charged the hills on which Lee's grim, gray men had entrenched. His magnificent army marched into a death trap. Lee's batteries had been trained to rake the field from three directions.

Five times the Union hosts charged these crescent hills and five times they were rolled back in waves of blood. A fierce freezing wind sprang up from the North. The desperate Union Commander thought still to turn defeat into victory and ordered the sixth charge.

The men in blue pulled down their caps and charged once more into the jaws of death. The lines as they advanced snatched up the frozen bodies of their comrades, carried them to the front, stacked the corpses into long piles for bulwarks, dropped low and fought behind them. In vain. The gray hills roared and blazed, roared and blazed with increasing fury. Darkness came at last and drew a mantle of mercy over the scene.

The men in blue planted the frozen bodies of their dead along the outer line as dummy sentinels and crept through the shadows across the river shattered, broken, crushed. They left their wounded. Through the long hours of the freezing night the pitiful cries came to the boys in gray on the wings of the fierce North winds. They crawled out into the darkness here and there and held a canteen to the lips of a dying foe.

At dawn they looked and saw the piles of the slain wrapped in white shrouds of snow. The shivering, ragged, gray figures, thinly clad, swept down the hill, stripped the dead and shook the frost from the warm clothes.

Burnsides fell before the genius of Lee and Hooker was put in his place.

Fighting Joe Hooker they called him. At Chancellorsville a few months later he led his reorganized army across the same river and threw it on Lee with supreme confidence in the results. He led an army of one hundred and thirty thousand men in seven grand divisions backed by four hundred and forty-eight great guns.

Lee, still on the hills behind Fredericksburg, had sixty-two thousand men and one hundred and seventy guns. He had sent Longstreet's corps into Tennessee.

Hooker threw the flower of his army across the river seven miles above Fredericksburg to flank Lee and strike him from the rear while the remainder of his army crossed in front and between the two he would crush the Confederate army as an eggshell.

But the unexpected happened. Lee was not only a stark fighter. He was a supreme master of the art of war. He understood Hooker's move from the moment it began. His gray army had already slipped out of his trenches and were feeling their way through the tangled vines and underbrush with sure, ominous tread. In this wilderness Hooker's four hundred guns would be as useless as his own hundred and seventy. It would be a hand-to-hand fight in the tangled brush. The gray veteran was a dead shot and he was creeping through his own native woods. On this beautiful May morning, Lee, Jackson, and Stuart met in conference before the battle opened. The plan was chosen. Lee would open the battle and hold Hooker at close range. Jackson would "retreat." Out of sight, he would turn, march swiftly ten miles around their right wing and smash it before sundown.

At five o'clock in the afternoon while Lee held Hooker's front, Jackson's corps crept into position in Hooker's rear. The shrill note of a bugle rang from the woods and the yelling gray lines of death swept down on their unsuspecting foe. Without support the shattered right wing was crushed, crumpled and rolled back in confusion.

At eight o'clock Jackson, pressing forward in the twilight, was mortally wounded by his own men and Stuart took his command. The gay, young cavalier placed himself at the head of Jackson's corps and charged Hooker's disorganized army. Waving his black plumed hat above his handsome, bearded face, he chanted with boyish gaiety an improvised battle song:

"Old Joe Hooker,
Won't you come out o' the Wilderness?"

His men swept the field and as Hooker's army retreated Lee rode to the front to congratulate Stuart. At sight of his magnificent figure wreathed in smoke his soldiers went wild. Above the roar of battle rang their cheers:

"Lee! Lee! Lee!"

From line to line, division to division, the word leaped until the wounded and the dying joined its chorus.

The picket lines were so close that night in the woods they could talk to one another. The Southerners were chaffing the Yanks over their many defeats, when a Yankee voice called through the night his defense of the war to date:

"Ah, Johnnie, shut up - you make me tired. You're not such fighters as ye think ye are. Swap generals with us and we'll come over and lick hell out of you!"

There was silence for a while and then a Confederate chuckled to his mate:

"I'm damned if they mightn't, too!"

The morning dawned at last after the battle and they began to bury the dead and care for the wounded. Their agonies had been horrible. Some had fallen on Friday, thousands on Saturday. It was now Monday. Through miles of dark, tangled woods in the pouring rain they still lay groaning and dying.

Thomas Dixon

And over all the wings of buzzards hovered.

The keen eyes of the vultures had watched them fall, poised high as the battle raged. The woods had been swept again and again by fire. Many of the bodies were black and charred. Some of the wounded had been burned to death. Their twisted bodies and distorted features told the story. The sickening odor of roasted human flesh yet filled the air.

It was late at night on the day after, before the wounded had all been moved. The surgeons with sleeves rolled high, their arms red, their shirts soaked, bent over their task through every hour of the black night until legs and arms were piled in heaps ten feet high beside each operating table.

Thirty thousand magnificent men had been killed and mangled.

The report from Chancellorsville drifted slowly and ominously northward. The White House was still. The dead were walking beside the lonely, tall figure who paced the floor in dumb anguish, pausing now and then at the window to look toward the hills of Virginia.

Lee's fame now filled the world and the North shivered at the sound of it.

Volunteering had ceased. But the cannon were still calling for fodder. The draft was applied. And when it was resisted in fierce riots, the soldiers trained their guns on their own people. The draft wheel was turned by bayonets and the ranks of the army filled with fresh young bodies to be mangled.

Hooker fell before Lee's genius and Meade took his place.

The Confederate Government, flushed with its costly victories, once more sought a political sensation by the invasion of the North. Lee marched his army of veterans into Pennsylvania.

At Gettysburg he met Meade.

The first day the Confederates won. They drove the blue army back through the streets of the village and their gallant General, John F. Reynolds, was killed.

The second day was one of frightful slaughter. The Union army at its close had lost twenty thousand men, the Confederate fifteen thousand.

The moon rose and flooded the rocky field of blood and death with silent glory. From every shadow and from every open space through the hot breath of the night came the moans of thousands and high above their chorus rang the cries for water.

No succor could be given. The Confederates were massing their artillery on Seminary Ridge. The Union legions were burrowing and planting new batteries.

Fifteen thousand helpless, wounded men lay on the field through the long hours of the night.

At ten o'clock a wounded man began to sing one of the old hymns of Zion whose words had come down the ages wet with tears and winged with human hopes. In five minutes ten thousand voices, from blue and gray, had joined. Some of them quivered with agony. Some of them trembled with a dying breath. For two hours the hills echoed with the unearthly music.

At a council of war Longstreet begged Lee to withdraw from Gettysburg and pick more favorable ground. Reinforced by the arrival of Pickett's division of fifteen thousand fresh men and Stuart's Cavalry, he decided to renew the battle at dawn.

The guns opened at the crack of day. For seven hours the waves of blood ebbed and flowed.

At noon there was a lull.

Thomas Dixon

At one o'clock a puff of white smoke flashed from Seminary Ridge. The signal of the men in gray had pealed its death call. Along two miles on this crest they had planted a hundred and fifty guns. Suddenly two miles of flame burst from the hills in a single fiery wreath. The Federal guns answered until the heavens were a hell of bursting, screaming, roaring shells.

At three o'clock the storm died away and the smoke lifted.

Pickett's men were deploying in the plain to charge the heights of Cemetery Ridge. Fifteen thousand heroic men were forming their line to rush a hill on whose crest lay seventy-five thousand entrenched soldiers backed by four hundred guns.

Pickett's bands played as on parade. The gray ranks dressed on their colors. And then across the plain, with banners flying, they swept and climbed the hill. The ranks closed as men fell in wide gaps. Not a man faltered. They fell and lay when they fell. Those who stood moved on and on. A handful reached the Union lines on the heights. Armistead with a hundred men broke through, lifted his red battle flag and fell mortally wounded. The gray wave in sprays of blood ebbed down the hill, and the battle ended. Meade had lost twenty-three thousand men and seventeen generals. Lee had lost twenty thousand men and fourteen generals.

The swollen Potomac was behind Lee and his defeated army. So sure was Stanton of the end that he declared to the President:

"If a single regiment of Lee's army ever gets back into Virginia in an organized condition it will prove that I am totally unfit to be Secretary of War."

The impossible happened.

Lee got back into Virginia with every regiment marching to quick step and undaunted spirit. He crossed the swollen Potomac, his army in fighting trim, every gun intact, carrying thousands of fat Pennsylvania cattle and four thousand prisoners of war taken on the bloody hills of Gettysburg.

The rejoicing in Washington was brief. Meade fell before the genius of Lee, and Grant, the stark fighter of the West, took his place.

The new Commander was granted full authority over all the armies of the Union. He placed Sherman at Chattanooga in command of a hundred thousand men and ordered him to invade Georgia. He sent Butler with an army of fifty thousand up the Peninsula against Richmond on the line of McClellan's old march. He raised the army of the Potomac to a hundred and forty thousand effective fighting soldiers, placed Phil Sheridan in command of his cavalry, put himself at the head of this magnificent army and faced Lee on the banks of the Rapidan. He was but a few miles from Chancellorsville where Hooker's men had baptized the earth in blood the year before.

A new draft of five hundred thousand had given Grant unlimited men for the coming whirlwind. His army was the flower of Northern manhood. He commanded the best-equipped body of soldiers ever assembled under the flag of the Union. His baggage train was sixty miles long and would have stretched the entire distance from his crossing at the Rapidan to Richmond.

Lee's army had been recruited to its normal strength of sixty-two thousand. Again the wily Southerner anticipated the march of his foe and crept into the tangled wilderness to meet him where his superiority would be of no avail.

Confident of his resistless power Grant threw his army across the Rapidan and plunged into the wilderness. From the dawn of the first day until far into the night the conflict raged. As darkness fell Lee had pushed the blue lines back a hundred yards, captured four guns and a number of prisoners. At daylight they were at it again. As the Confederate right wing crumpled and rolled back, Long-street arrived on the scene and threw his corps into the breach.

Lee himself rode forward to lead the charge and restore his line. At sight of him, from thousands of parched throats rose the cries:

"Lee to the rear!"

"Go back, General Lee!"

"We'll settle this!"

They refused to move until their leader had withdrawn. And then with a savage yell they charged and took the field.

Lee sent Longstreet to turn Grant's left as Jackson had done at Chancellorsville. The movement was executed with brilliant success. Hancock's line was smashed and driven back on his second defenses. Wardsworth at the head of his division was mortally wounded and fell into Longstreet's hands. At the height of his triumph in a movement that must crumple Grant's army back on the banks of the river, Longstreet fell, shot by his own men. In the change of commanders the stratagem failed in its big purpose.

In two days Grant lost sixteen thousand six hundred men, a greater toll than Hooker paid when he retreated in despair.

Grant merely chewed the end of his big cigar, turned to his lieutenant and said:

"It's all right, Wilson. We'll fight again."

The two armies lay in their trenches watching each other in grim silence.

# CHAPTER XLII

In Lee's simple tent on the battlefield amid the ghostly trees of the wilderness his Adjutant-General, Walter Taylor, sat writing rapidly.

Sam, his ebony face shining, stood behind trying to look over his shoulder. He couldn't make it out and his curiosity got the better of him.

"What dat yer writin' so hard, Gin'l Taylor?"

Without lifting his head the Adjutant continued to write.

"Orders of promotion for gallantry in battle, Sam."

"Is yer gwine ter write one fer my young Marse Robbie?"

Taylor paused and looked up. The light of admiration overspread his face.

"General Lee never promotes his sons or allows them on his staff, Sam. General Custis Lee, General Rooney Lee, and Captain Robbie won their spurs without a word from him. They won by fighting."

"Yassah! Dey sho's been some fightin' in dis here wilderness. Hopes ter God we git outen here pretty quick. Gitten too close tergedder ter suit me."

Thomas Dixon

The clatter of a horse's hoofs rang out in the little clearing in front of the tent.

Taylor looked up again.

"See if that's Stuart. General Lee's expecting him."

Sam peered out the door of the tent.

"Dey ain't no plume in his hat an' dey ain't no banjo man wid him. Nasah. Tain't Gin'l Stuart."

"All right. Pull up a stool."

"Yassah!"

Sam unfolded a camp stool and placed it at the table. A sentinel approached and called:

"Senator William C. Rives of the Confederate Congress to see General Lee."

Taylor rose.

"Show him in."

The Senator entered with a quick, nervous excitement he could not conceal.

"Colonel Taylor -"

"Senator."

The men clasped hands and Taylor continued to watch the nervous manner of his caller.

"My coming from Richmond is no doubt a surprise?"

"Naturally. We're in pretty close quarters with Grant here

to-night -"

Rives raised his hand in a gesture of despair.

"No closer than our Government in Richmond is with the end at this moment, in my judgment. I couldn't wait. I had to come to-night. You have called an informal council as I requested?"

"The moment I got your message an hour ago."

Taylor caught his excitement and bent close.

"What is it, Senator?"

Rives hesitated, glanced at the doors of the tent and answered rapidly.

"The Confederate Congress has just held a secret session without the knowledge of President Davis -"

He drew from his pocket a letter and handed it to the Adjutant.

"You will see from this letter of the presiding officer my credentials. They have sent me as their agent on an important mission to General Lee."

He paused as Taylor carefully read the letter.

"How soon can I see him?"

"I'm expecting him in a few minutes," Taylor answered. "He's riding on the front lines trying to feel out Grant's next move. He is very anxious over it."

"This battle was desperate?" Rives asked nervously.

"Terrific."

"Our losses in the two days?"

"More than ten thousand."

"Merciful God - "

"Grant's losses were far greater," Taylor added briskly.

"No matter, Taylor, no matter!" he cried in anguish, springing to his feet. He fought for control of his emotions and hurried on.

"The maws of those cannon now are insatiate! We can't afford to lose ten thousand men from our thin ranks in two days. If your army suspected for one moment the real situation in Richmond, they'd quit and we'd be lost."

"They only ask for General Lee's orders, Senator. Their faith in our leader is sublime."

"And that's our only hope," Rives hastened to add. "General Lee may save us. And he is the only man who can do it."

He stopped and studied Taylor closely. He spoke with some diffidence.

"The faith of his officers in him remains absolutely unshaken?"

"They worship him."

"My appeal will be solely to him. But I may need help."

"I've asked Alexander and Gordon to come. General Gordon did great work to-day. It was his command that broke Hancock's lines and took prisoners. I've just slated him for further promotion. Stuart is already on the way here to report the situation on the right where his cavalry is operating."

The ring of two horses' hoofs echoed.

"If Stuart will only back me!" Rives breathed.

Outside the Cavalry Commander was having trouble with Sweeney, his minstrel follower, an expert banjo player.

Stuart laughed heartily at his fears.

"Come on, Sweeney. Don't be a fool."

The minstrel man still held back and Stuart continued to urge.

"Come on in, Sweeney. Don't be bashful. I promised you shall see General Lee and you shall. Come on!"

Taylor and Rives stood in the door of the tent watching the conflict.

"Never be afraid of a great man, Sweeney!" Stuart went on. "The greater the man the easier it is to get along with him. General Lee wears no scarlet in his coat, no plume in his hat, no gold braid on his uniform. He's as plain as a gray mouse -"

Stuart laughed and whispered:

"He's too great to need anything to mark his rank. But he never frowns on my gay colors."

"He knows," Taylor rejoined, "that it's your way of telling the glory of the cause."

"Sure! He just laughs at my foolishness and gives me an order to lick a crowd that outnumbers me, three to one."

He took hold of Sweeney's arm.

"Don't be afraid, old boy. Marse Robert won't frown on your banjo. He'll just smile as he recalls what the cavalry did in our last battle. Minstrel man, make yourself at home."

Sweeney timidly touched the strings, and Stuart wheeled toward Rives.

"Well, Senator, how goes it in Richmond?"

Rives answered with eager anxiety. His words were not spoken in despair but with an undertone of desperate appeal.

"Dark days have come, General Stuart. And great events are pending. Events of the utmost importance to the army, to the country, to General Lee."

"Just say General Lee and let it go at that," Stuart laughed. "He *is* the army *and* the country."

He turned to Taylor.

"Where's Marse Robert?"

"Inspecting the lines. He fears a movement to turn our flank at Spottsylvania Court House."

"My men are right there, watching like owls. They'll catch the first rustle of a leaf by Sheridan's cavalry."

"I hope so."

"Never fear. Well, Sweeney, while we wait for General Lee, Senator Rives needs a little cheer. We've medicine in that box for every ill that man is heir to. Things look black in Richmond, he tells us. All right. Give us the old familiar tune - *Hard Times and Wuss Er Comin'!* - Go it!"

Sweeney touched his strings sharply.

"You don't mind, sir?" he asked Taylor.

"Certainly not. I like it."

Sentinels, orderlies, aides and scouts gathered around the door as Sweeney played and sang with Stuart. The Cavalryman's spirit was contagious. Before the song had died away, they were all singing the chorus in subdued tones. Sweeney ended with Stuart's favorite - *Rock of Ages*.

General John B. Gordon joined the group, followed by General E.P. Alexander.

Taylor called the generals together.

"Senator Rives, gentlemen, is the bearer of an important message from the Confederate Congress to General Lee. I have asked you informally to join him in this meeting."

Rives entered his appeal.

"I am going to ask you to help me to-night in paying the highest tribute to General Lee in our power."

Gordon responded promptly.

"We shall honor ourselves in honoring him, sir."

"Always," Alexander agreed.

Rives plunged into the heart of his mission.

"Gentlemen, so desperate is the situation of the South that our only hope lies in our great Commander. The Confederate Congress has sent me to offer him the Dictatorship -"

"You don't mean it?" Stuart exploded.

"Will you back me?"

The Cavalry leader grasped his hand.

"Yours to count on, sir!"

"Yes," Gordon joined.

"We'll back you!" Alexander cried.

Rives' face brightened.

"If he will only accept. The question is how to approach him?"

"It must be done with the utmost care," Alexander warned.

"Exactly." Rives nodded. "Shall I announce to him it once the vote of Congress conferring on him the supreme power?"

"Not if you can approach him more carefully," Alexander cautioned.

"I can first propose that as Commanding General he might accept the peace proposals which Francis Preston Blair has brought from Washington -"

"What kind of peace proposals?" Gorden asked sharply.

"He proposes to end the war immediately by an armistice, and arrange for the joint invasion of Mexico by the combined armies of the North and South under the command of General Lee."

Alexander snapped at the suggestion.

"By all means suggest the armistice first. General Lee won his spurs in Mexico. The plan might fire his imagination - as it would have fired the soul of Caesar or Napoleon. If he refuses to go over the head of Davis, you can then announce the vote of Congress giving him supreme power."

The general suddenly paused at the familiar sound of Traveler's hoofbeat.

The officers stood and saluted as Lee entered. He was dressed in his full field gray uniform of immaculate cut and without spot. He wore his sword, high boots and spurs and his field glasses were thrown across his broad shoulders.

He glanced at the group in slight surprise and drew Stuart aside.

"I sent for you, General Stuart, to say that I am expecting a courier at any moment who may report that General Grant will move on Spottsylvania Court House."

He paused in deep thought.

"If so, Sheridan will throw the full force of his cavalry on your lines, to turn our right and circle Richmond."

Stuart's body stiffened.

"I'm ready, sir. He may reach Yellow Tavern. He'll never go past it."

In low, tense words Lee said:

"I'm depending on you, sir."

Stuart saluted in silence.

Lee turned back into the group and Taylor explained:

"I have called an informal meeting at the request of Senator Rives."

Lee smiled.

"Oh, I see. A council of both War and State."

Rives came forward and the Commander grasped his hand.

"Always glad to see *you*, Senator. What can we do for you?"

"Everything, sir. Can we enter at once into our conference?"

"The quicker the better. General Grant may drop in on us at any moment without an invitation."

Rives smiled wanly.

"General Lee, we face the gravest crisis of the war."

"No argument is needed to convince me of that, sir. Grant's men have gripped us with a ferocity never known before."

"And our boys," Alexander added, "in all the struggle have never been such stark fighters as to-day."

"I agree with you," Lee nodded. "But Grant is getting ready to fight again to-morrow morning - not next month. His policy is new, and it's clear. He plans to pound us to death in a series of quick, successive blows. His man power is exhaustless. We can't afford to lose many men. He can. An endless blue line is streaming to the front."

"And that's why I'm here to-night, General," Rives said gravely.

"Grant is now in supreme command of all the Armies of the Union. While he moves on Richmond, Butler is sweeping up the James and Sherman is pressing on Atlanta. We have lost ten thousand men in two-days' battle. In the next we'll lose ten thousand more. In the next ten thousand more -"

"We must fight, sir. I have invaded the North twice. But I stand on the defense now. I have no choice."

"That remains to be seen, General Lee," Rives said with a piercing look.

"What do you mean?"

"A few days ago, your old friend, Francis Preston Blair, entered our lines and came to Richmond on a mission of peace. He has now before Mr. Davis and his Cabinet a plan to end the war. He proposes that we stop fighting, unite and invade Mexico to defend the Monroe Doctrine. Maximilian of Austria has just been proclaimed Emperor in a conspiracy backed by Napoleon. The suggestion is that we join armies under your command, dethrone Maximilian, push the soldiers of Napoleon into the sea, and restore the rule of the people on the American Continent."

Lee looked at him steadily.

"Mr. Davis refuses to listen to this proposal?"

"Only on the basis of the continued division of our country. Lincoln naturally demands that we come back into the Union first, and march on Mexico afterwards. Mr. Davis refuses to come back into the Union first. And so we end where we began - unless we can get help from you, General Lee -"

"Well?"

"The Confederate Congress has sent me as their spokesman to make a proposition to you."

He handed Lee the letter from the Congress.

"Will you issue as Commanding General an order for an armistice to arrange the joint invasion of Mexico?"

"You mean take it on myself to go over the head of Mr. Davis, and issue this order without his knowledge?"

"Exactly. We could not take him into our confidence."

"But Mr. Davis is my superior officer and he is faithfully executing the laws."

"You will not proclaim an armistice, then?"

Lee spoke with irritation.

"How can you ask me to go over the head of my Chief with such an order?"

Alexander pressed forward.

"But you might consider a proclamation looking to peace under this plan - if you were in a position of supreme power?"

"I have no such power. I advised our people to make peace before I invaded Pennsylvania. I have urged it more than once, but they cannot see it. And I must do the work given me from day to day."

"We now propose to give to you the sole decision as to what that work shall be."

"How, sir?"

"I am here to-night, General, as the agent of our Government, to confer on you this power. The Congress has unanimously chosen you as Dictator of the Confederacy with supreme power over both the civil and military branches of the Government."

"And well done!" cried Gordon.

"We back them!" echoed Alexander.

"Hurrah for the Confederate Congress," shouted Stuart - "the first signs of brains they've shown in many a day -"

He caught himself at a glance from Rives.

"Excuse me, Senator - I didn't mean quite that."

Lee fixed Rives with his brilliant eyes.

"The Confederate Congress has no authority to declare &
Dictatorship."

"We have."

"By what law?"

"By the law of necessity, sir. The civil government in
Richmond has become a farce. I acknowledge it sorrowfully.
Your soldiers are ill clothed, half starved, and the power to
recruit your ranks is gone. The people have lost faith in their
civil leaders. Disloyalty is rampant. In the name of ultra State
Sovereignty, treason is everywhere threatening. Soldiers are
taken from your army by State authorities on the eve of battle.
Men are deserting in droves and defy arrest. You have justly
demanded the death penalty for desertion. It has been denied.
Bands of deserters now plunder, burn and rob as they please.
You are our only hope. You are the idol of our people. At your
call they will rally. Men will pour into your ranks, and we can
yet crush our enemies, or invade Mexico as you may decide."

"He's right, General," Gordon agreed. "The South will stand
by you to a man."

Alexander added with deep reverence:

"The people believe in you, General Lee, as they believe in
God."

A dreamy look overspread Lee's face.

"Their faith is misplaced, sir! God alone decides the fate of
nations. And God, not your commanding General, will decide
the fate of the South. The thing that appalls me is that we have
no luck. For in spite of numbers, resources, generalship - the
unknown factor in war is luck. The North has had it all. At
Shiloh at the moment of a victory that would have ended

Grant's career, Albert Sydney Johnson, our ablest general, was shot and Grant escaped. At the battle of Chancellorsville in these very woods, Jackson at the moment of his triumph-Jackson my right arm - was shot by his own men. To-day Longstreet falls in the same way when he is about to repeat his immortal deed -"

He paused.

"The South has had no luck!"

Alexander eagerly protested.

"I don't agree with you, sir. God has given the South Lee as her Commander. Your genius is equal to a hundred thousand men. And in all our terrible battles, at the head of your men, again and again, as you were to-day, with bullets whistling around you, you've lived a charmed life. You're here to-night strong in body and mind, without a scratch. Don't tell me, sir, that we haven't had luck!"

Stuart broke in.

"You're the biggest piece of luck that ever befell an army."

Lee rose.

"I appreciate your confidence and your love, gentlemen. But I've made many tragic mistakes, and tried to find an abler man to take my place."

"There's no such man!" Stuart boomed. "Give the word to-night and every soldier in this army would follow you into the jaws of hell!"

Lee's eyes were lifted dreamily.

"And you ask me to blot out the liberties of our people by a single act of usurpation?"

Alexander lifted his hand.

"Only for a moment, General, that we may restore them in greater glory. The truth is the Confederate Government is not fitted for revolution. Let's win this war and fix it afterwards."

"I do not believe either in military statesmen or political generals. The military should be subordinate always to the civil power -"

"But Congress," Rives broke in, "speaking for the people, offers you supreme power. Mr. Davis has not proven himself strong enough for the great office he holds."

Lee flared at this assertion.

"And if he has not, sir, who gave *me* the right to sit in judgment upon my superior officer and condemn him without trial? Mr. Davis is the victim of this unhappy war. I say this, though, that he differs with me on vital issues. I urged the abolition of Slavery. He opposed it. So did your Congress. I urged the uncovering of Richmond and the concentration of our forces into one great army for an offensive -"

Rives interrupted.

"We ask you to take the supreme power and decide these questions."

Lee replied with a touch of anger.

"But I may be wrong in my policies. Mr. Davis is a man of the highest character, devoted soul and body to the principles to which he has pledged his life. He is a statesman of the foremost rank. He is a trained soldier, a West Point graduate. He is a man of noble spirit - courageous, frank, positive. A great soul throbs within his breast. He has done as well in his high office as any other man could have done -"

He looked straight at Rives.

"We left the Union, sir, because our rights had been invaded. Our revolution is justified by this fact alone. You ask me to do the thing that caused us to revolt. To brush aside the laws which our people have ordained and set up a Dictatorship with the power of life and death over every man, woman and child. For three years we have poured out our blood in a sacred cause. We are fighting for our liberties under law, or we are traitors, not revolutionists. We are fighting for order, justice, principles, or we are fighting for nothing -"

A courier dashed to the door of the tent and handed Lee a message which he read with a frown.

"This discussion is closed, gentlemen. General Grant is moving on Spottsylvania Court House. My business is to get there first. My work is not to jockey for place or power. It is to fight. Move your forces at once!"

# CHAPTER XLIII

Lee hurried to Spottsylvania Court House and was entrenched before Grant arrived. The two armies again flew at each other's throat. True to Lee's prediction the Union Commander hurled Sheridan's full force of ten thousand cavalry in a desperate effort to turn the right and strike Richmond while the Confederate infantry were held in a grip of death.

From a hilltop Stuart saw the coming blue legions of Sheridan. They rode four abreast and made a column of flashing sabers and fluttering guidons thirteen miles long.

The young Cavalier waved his plumed hat and gave a shout. It was magnificent. He envied them the endless line of fine horses. He had but three small brigades to oppose them. But his spirits rose.

He ordered his generals to harass the advancing host at every point of vantage, delay them as long as possible and draw up their forces at Yellow Tavern for the battle.

He took time to dash across the country from Beaver Dam Station to see his wife and babies. He had left them at the house of Edmund Fontaine. He feared that the Federal Cavalry might have raided the section.

To his joy he found them well and happy, unconscious of the impending fight.

Thomas Dixon

For the first time in his joyous life of song and play and war he was worried.

His wife was in high spirits. She cheered him.

"Don't worry about us, my soldier man! We're all right. No harm has ever befallen us. We've had three glorious years playing lovers' hide-and-seek. I've ceased to worry about you. Your life is charmed. God has heard my prayers. You're coming home soon to play with me and the babies always!"

She was too happy for Stuart to describe the host of ten thousand riders which he had just seen. Their lives were in God's hands. It was enough.

He held her in his arms longer than was his wont at parting. And then with a laugh and a shout to the children he was gone.

At Jerrold's Mill, Wickham's brigade suddenly fell on Sheridan's rear guard and captured a company. Sheridan refused to stop to fight.

At Mitchell's Shop, Wickham again dashed on the rear guard and was forced back by a counter charge. As he retreated, fighting a desperate hand-to-hand saber engagement, Fitzhugh Lee and Stuart rushed to his aid and the blue river rolled on again toward Richmond.

At Hanover Junction Stuart allowed his men to sleep until one o'clock and then rode with desperate speed to Yellow Tavern. He reached his chosen battle ground at ten o'clock the following morning. He had won the race and at once deployed his forces to meet the coming avalanche.

Wickham he stationed on the right of the road, Lomax on the left. He placed two guns in the road, one on the left to rake it at an angle.

He dismounted his men and ordered them to fight as infantry. A reserve of mounted men were held in his rear.

He sent his aide into Richmond to inquire of its defenses and warn General Bragg of the sweeping legions. The Commandant at the Confederate Capital replied that he could hold his trenches. He would call on Petersburg for reinforcements. He asked Stuart to hold Sheridan back as long as possible.

On the morning of the eleventh of May, at 6:30, he wrote his dispatch to Lee:

"Fighting against immense odds of Sheridan. My men and horses are tired, hungry and jaded, *but all right!*"

It was four o'clock before Sheridan struck Yellow Tavern. With skill and dash he threw an entire brigade on Stuart's left, broke his line, rolled it up and captured his two guns. Stuart ordered at once a reserve squadron to charge the advancing Federals. With desperate courage they drove them back in a hand-to-hand combat, saber ringing on saber to the shout and yell of savages.

As the struggling, surging mass of blue riders rolled back in confusion, Stuart rode into the scene cheering his men. A man in blue, whose horse had been shot from under him, fired his revolver pointblank at Stuart. The shot entered his body just above the belt and the magnificent head with the waving plume drooped on his breast.

Captain Dorsey hurried to his assistance. There were but a handful of his men between him and the Federal line, The wounded Commander was in danger of being captured by a sudden dash of reserves. He was lifted off his horse and he leaned against a tree.

Stuart raised his head.

"Go back now, Dorsey, to your men."

Thomas Dixon

"Not until you're safe, sir."

As the ambulance passed through his broken ranks in the rear, he lifted himself on his elbow and rallied his men with a brave shout:

"Go back! Go back to your duty, men! And our country will be safe. Go back! Go back! I'd rather die than be whipped."

The men rallied and rushed to the firing line. They fought so well that Sheridan lost the way to Richmond and the Capital of the Confederacy was saved.

The wounded Commander was taken to the home of his brother-in-law, Dr. Charles Brewer, in Richmond. He had suffered agonies on the rough journey but bore his pain with grim cheerfulness.

He had sent a swift messenger to his wife. He knew she would reach Richmond the next day.

The following morning Major McClellan, his aide, rode in from the battlefield to report to General Bragg. Having delivered his message he hurried to the bedside of his beloved Chief.

The doctor shook his head gravely.

"Inflammation has set in, Major -"

"My God, is there no hope?"

"None."

The singing, rollicking, daring young Cavalier felt the hand of death on his shoulder. He was calm and cheerful. His bright words were broken by paroxysms of suffering. He would merely close his shining blue eyes and wait.

He directed his aide to dispose of his official papers.

He touched McClellan's hand and the Major's closed over it.

"I wish you to have one of my horses and Venable the other."

McClellan nodded.

"Which of you is the heavier?"

"Venable, sir."

"All right, give him the gray. You take the bay."

The pain choked him into silence again. At last he opened his eyes.

"You'll find in my hat a small Confederate flag which a lady in Columbia, South Carolina, sent me with the request that I wear it on my horse in a battle and return it to her. Send it."

Again the agony stilled the musical voice.

"My spurs," he went on, "which I have always worn in battle, I promised to Mrs. Lilly Lee of Shepherdstown, Virginia -"

He paused.

"My sword - I leave - to - my - son."

A cannon roared outside the city. With quick eagerness he asked:

"What's that?"

"Gracey's brigade has moved out against Sheridan's rear as he retreats. Fitz Lee is fighting them still at Meadow Bridge."

He turned his blue eyes upward and prayed:

"God grant they may win -"

He moved his head aside and said:

"I must prepare for another world."

He listened to the roar of the guns for a moment and signaled to his aide:

"Major, Fitz Lee may need you."

McClellan pressed his hand and hurried to the front.

As he passed out the tall figure of the President of the Confederacy entered. Jefferson Davis sat by his side and held his hand. He loved his daring young Cavalry Commander. He had made him a Major-General at thirty. He was dying now at thirty-one. The tragedy found the heart of the sorrowful leader of all the South.

When the Reverend Dr. Peterkin entered he said:

"Now I want you to sing for me the old song I love best -

"'Rock of Ages cleft for me,
Let me hide myself in thee -'"

With failing breath he joined in the song.

A paroxysm of pain gripped him and he asked the doctor:

"Can I survive the night?"

"No, General. The end is near."

He was silent. And then slowly said:

"I am resigned if it be God's will. But - I - would - like - to - see - my - wife -"

The beautiful voice sank into eternal silence.

So passed the greatest cavalry leader our country has produced. A man whose joyous life was a long wish of good will toward all of his fellow men.

The little mother heard the news as she rode in hot haste over the rough roads to Richmond. The hideous thing was beyond belief, but it had come. She had heard the roar of battle for three years and after each bloody day he had come with a smile on his lips and a stronger love in his brave heart. She had ceased to fear his death in battle. God had promised her in prayer to spare him. Only once had a bullet cut his clothes.

And now he was dead.

But yesterday he dashed across the country from his line of march, and, even while the conflict raged, held her in his arms and crooned over her.

The tears had flowed for two hours before she reached the house of death. She could weep no longer.

A sister's arm encircled her waist and led her unseeing eyes into the room. There was no wild outburst of grief at the sight of his cold body.

She stooped to kiss the loved lips, placed her hand on the high forehead and drew back at its chill. She stood in dumb anguish until her sister in alarm said:

"Come, dear, to my room."

The set, blue eyes never moved from the face of her dead.

"It's wrong. It's wrong. It's all wrong - this hideous murder of our loved ones! Why must they send my husband to kill my father? Why must they send my father to kill the father of my babies? Why didn't they stop this a year ago? It must end some time. Why did they ever begin it? Why must brother kill his brother? My father, thank God, didn't kill him. But little Phil Sheridan, his schoolmate, did. And he never spoke an unkind word about him in his life! His heart was overflowing with joy and love. He sang when he rode into battle -"

She paused and a tear stole down her cheeks at last.

"Poor boy, he loved its wild din and roar. It was play to his daring spirit."

A sob caught her voice and then it rose in fierce rebellion:

"Where was God when he fell? He was thirty-one years old, in the glory of a beautiful life -"

Her sister spoke in gentle sympathy.

"His fame fills the world, dear."

"Fame? Fame? What is that to me, now? I stretch out my hand, and it's ashes. My arms are empty. My heart is broken. Life isn't worth the living."

Her voice drifted into a dreamy silence as the tears streamed down her cheeks. She stood for half an hour staring through blurred eyes at the cold clay.

She turned at last and seized her sister's hands both in hers, and gazed with a strange, set look that saw something beyond time and the things of sense.

"My dear sister, God will yet give to the mothers of men the power to stop this murder. There's a better way. There's a better way,"

# CHAPTER XLIV

While Sheridan rode against Richmond, Lee and Grant were struggling in a pool of red at the "Bloody Angle" of Spottsylvania. The musketry fire against the trees came in a low undertone, like the rattle of a hail storm on the roofs of houses.

A company of blue soldiers were cut off by a wave of charging gray. The men were trying to surrender. Their officers drew their revolvers and ordered them to break through. A sullen private shouted:

"Shoot your officers!"

Every commander dropped in his tracks. And the men were marched to the rear. Hour after hour the flames of hell swirled in endless waves about this angle of the Southern trenches. Line after line of blue broke against it and eddied down its sides in slimy pools.

Color bearers waved their flags in each other's faces, clinched and fought, hand to hand, like devils. Two soldiers on top of the trench, their ammunition spent, choked each other to death and rolled down the embankment among the mangled bodies that filled the ditch.

In this mass of struggling maniacs men were fighting with guns, swords, handspikes, clubbed muskets, stones and fists. Night brought no pause to save the wounded or bury the dead.

For five days Grant circled his blue hosts in a whirlpool of death trying in vain to break Lee's trenches. He gave it up. The stolid, silent man of iron nerves watched the stream of wagons bearing the wounded, groaning and shrieking, from the field. Lee's forces had been handled with such skill the impact of numbers had made but little impression.

Thirty thousand dead and mangled lay on the field.

The stark fighter of the West was facing a new problem. The devotion of Lee's men was a mania. He was unconquerable in a square hand-to-hand fight in the woods.

A truce to bury the dead followed. They found them piled six layers deep in the trenches, blue and gray locked in the last embrace. Black wings were flapping over them unafraid of the living. Their red beaks were tearing at eyes and lips, while deep below yet groaned and moved the wounded.

Again Grant sought to flank his wily foe. This time he beat Lee to the spot. The two armies rushed for Cold Harbor in parallel columns flashing at each other deadly volleys as they marched. Lee took second choice of ground and entrenched on a gently sloping line of hills. They swung in crescent as at Fredericksburg.

With consummate skill he placed his guns and infantry to catch both flanks and front of the coming foe. And then he waited for Grant to charge. Thousands of men in the blue ranks were busy now sewing their names in their under-clothing.

With the first streak of dawn, at 4:30, they charged. They walked into the mouth of a volcano flaming tons of steel and lead in their faces. The scene was sickening. Nothing like it had, to this time, happened in the history of man.

*Ten thousand men in blue fell in twenty minutes.*

Meade ordered Smith to renew the assault. Daring a court martial, Smith flatly refused.

The story of the next seventy-two hours our historians have refused to record. Through the smothering heat of summer for three days and nights the shrieks and groans of the wounded rose in endless waves of horror. No hand could be lifted to save. With their last breath they begged, wept, cried, prayed for water. No man dared move in the storm-swept space. Here and there a heroic boy in blue caught the cry of a wounded comrade and crawled on his belly to try a rescue only to die in the embrace of his friend.

When the truce was called to clear the shambles every man of the ten thousand who had fallen was dead - save two. The salvage corps walked in a muck of blood. They slipped and stumbled and fell in its festering pools. The flies and vultures were busy. Dead horses, dead men, smashed guns, legs, arms, mangled bodies disemboweled, the earth torn into an ashen crater.

In the thirty days since Grant had met Lee in the wilderness, the Northern army had lost sixty thousand men, the bravest of our race.

Lee's losses were not so great but they were tragic. They were as great in proportion to the number he commanded.

Grant paused to change his plan of campaign. The procession of ambulances into Washington had stunned the Nation. Every city, town, village, hamlet and country home was in mourning. A stream of protest against the new Commander swept the North. Lincoln refused to remove him. And on his head was heaped the blame for all the anguish of the bitter years of failure.

His answer to his critics was remorseless.

"We must fight to win. Grant is the ablest general we have.

His losses are appalling. But the struggle is now on to the bitter end. Our resources of men and money are exhaustless. The South cannot replace her fallen sons. Her losses, therefore, are fatal!"

War had revealed to all at last that the Abolition crusade had been built on a lie. The negro had proven a bulwark of strength to the South. Had their theories been true, had the slaves been beaten and abused the Black Bees would surely have swarmed. A single Southern village put to the torch by black hands would have done for Lee's army what no opponent had been able to do. It would have been destroyed in a night. The Confederacy would have gone down in hopeless ruin.

Not a black hand had been raised against a Southern man or woman in all the raging hell. This fact is the South's vindication against the slanders of the Abolitionists. The negroes stood by their old masters. They worked his fields; they guarded his women and children; they mourned over the graves of their fallen sons.

And now in the supreme hour of gathering darkness came the last act of the tragedy - the arming of the Northern blacks and the training of their hands to slay a superior race.

In the first year of the war Lincoln had firmly refused the prayer of Thomas Wentworth Higginson that he be allowed to arm and drill the Black Legions of the North. Later the pressure could not be resisted. The daily murder of the flower of the race had lowered its morale. It had lowered the value set on racial trait and character. The Cavalier and Puritan, with a thousand years of inspiring history throbbing in their veins, had become mere cannon fodder. The cry for men and still more men was endless. And this cry must be heard, or the war would end.

Men of the white breed were clasping hands at last across the lines under the friendly cover of the night. They spoke softly through their tears of home and loved ones. The tumult and the shout had passed. The jeer and taunt, blind passion and sordid hate lay buried in the long, deep graves of a hundred fields of blood.

Grant's new plan of campaign resulted in the deadlock of Petersburg. The two armies now lay behind thirty-five miles of deep trenches with a stretch of volcano-torn, desolate earth between them.

The Black Legions were massed for a dramatic ending of the war. Grant, Meade, and Burnside had developed a plan. Hundreds of sappers and miners burrowed under the shell-torn ground for months, digging a tunnel under Lee's fortress immediately before Petersburg.

The tunnel was not complete before Lee's ears had caught the sound. A counter tunnel was hastily begun but Grant's men had reached the spot under the center of Elliot's salient before the Confederates could intercept them.

Grant skillfully threw a division of his army on the north side of the James and made a fierce frontal attack on Richmond while he gathered the flower of his army, sixty-five thousand men with his Black Legions, before the tunnel that would open the way into Petersburg.

Lee was not misled by the assault on Richmond. But it was absolutely necessary to meet it, or the Capital would have fallen. He was compelled, in the face of the threatened explosion and assault, to divide his forces and weaken his lines before the tunnel.

His men were on the ground beyond the James to intercept the column moving toward Richmond. When the assault failed, Hancock and Sheridan immediately recrossed the river to take part in the capture of Petersburg and witness the end of the Confederacy.

Thomas Dixon

The tons of powder were stored under the fort and the fuse set. The Black battalions stood ready to lead the attack and enter Petersburg first.

At the final council of war, the plan was changed. A division of New Englanders, the sons of Puritan fathers and mothers, were set to this grim task and the negroes were ordered to follow.

High words had been used at the Council. The whole problem of race and racial values was put to the test of the science of anthropology and of mathematics. The fuse would be set before daylight. The charge must be made in darkness with hundreds of great guns flaming, shrieking, shaking the earth. The negro could not be trusted to lead in this work. He had followed white officers in the daylight and under their inspiration had fought bravely. But he was afraid of the dark. It was useless to mince matters. The council faced the issue. He could not stand the terrors of the night in such a charge.

The decision was an ominous one for the future of America - ominous because merciless in its scientific logic. The same power which had given the white man his mastery of science and progress in the centuries of human history gave him the mastery of his brain and nerves in the dark. For a thousand years superstition had been trained out of his brain fiber. He could hold a firing line day or night. The darkness was his friend, not his enemy.

The New Englanders were pushed forward for the attack. The grim preparations were hurried. The pioneers were marshaled with axes and entrenching tools. A train pulled in from City Point with crowds of extra surgeons, their amputating tables and bandages ready. The wagons were loaded with picks and shovels to bury the dead quickly in the scorching heat of July.

The men waited in impatience for the explosion. It had been set for two o'clock. For two hours they stood listening. Their hearts were beating high at first. The delay took the soul out of them. They were angry, weary, cursing, complaining.

The fuse had gone out. Another had to be trained and set. As the Maine regiments gripped their muskets waiting for the explosion of the mine, a negro preacher in the second line behind them was haranguing the Black Battalions. His drooning, voodoo voice rang through the woods in weird echoes:

"Oh, my men! Dis here's gwine ter be er great fight. De greatest fight in all de war. We gwine ter take ole Petersburg dis day. De day er Juberlee is come. Yes, Lawd! An' den we take Richmon', 'stroy Lee's army an' en' dis war. Yas, Lawd, an' 'member dat Gen'l Grant an' Gen'l Burnside, an' Gen'l Meade's is all right here a-watch-in' ye! An' member dat I'se er watchin' ye. I'se er sargint in dis here comp'ny. Any you tries ter be a skulker, you'se gwine ter git a beyonet run clean froo ye - yas, Lawd! You hear me!"

He had scarcely finished his harangue when a smothering peal of thunder shook the world. The ground rocked beneath the feet of the men. Some were thrown backwards. Some staggered and caught a comrade's shoulder. A pillar of blinding flame shot to the stars. A cloud of smoke rolled upward and spread its pall over the trembling earth. A shower of human flesh and bones spattered the smoking ground.

The men in front shivered as they brushed the pieces of red meat from their hands and clothes.

The artillery opened. Hundreds of guns were pouring shells from their flaming mouths. The people of Petersburg leaped from their beds and pressed into the streets stunned by the appalling shock and the storm of artillery which followed.

The ground in front of the tunnel had been cleared of the abatis. Burnside's New England veterans rushed the crater. A huge hole had been torn in Lee's fortifications one hundred yards long and sixty feet wide and twenty-five feet in depth.

The hole proved a grave. The charging troops floundered in its spongy, blood-soaked sides. They stumbled and fell into its pit. The regiments in the rear, rushing through the smoke and stumbling over the mangled pieces of flesh of Elliott's three hundred men who had been torn to pieces, were on top of the line in front before they could clear the crumbling walls.

When the charging hosts at last reached the firm ground inside the Confederate lines, the men in gray were rallying. Their guns had been trained on the yawning chasm now a struggling, squirming, cursing mass of blue. Slowly order came out of chaos and Burnside's men swung to the right and to the left and swept Lee's trenches for three hundred yards in each direction. The charging regiments poured into them and found the second Confederate line. Elliott's men who yet lived, driven from their outer line by the resistless rush of the attack, retreated to a deep ravine, rallied and held this third line.

Lee reached the field and took command. Mahone's men came to the rescue marching with swift, steady tread. They took their position on the crest which commanded the open space toward the captured trenches.

As Wright's brigade moved into position, the Black Battalions were ordered to charge. They had been hurried through the crater and into the trenches on the right and left. At the signal they swarmed over the works, with a voodoo yell, and in serried black waves, charged the men in gray. In broad daylight the Southerners saw for the first time the plan of the dramatic attack.

The white men of the South shrieked an answer and gripped their muskets. The cry they gave came down the centuries from three thousand years of history. It came from the hearts of a conquering race of men. They had heard the Call of the Blood of the Race that rules the world.

Without an order from their commanders, with a single impulse, the whole Southern line leaped from their cover and dashed on the advancing Black Legions in a counter charge so swift, so terrible, there was but a single crash and the yell of white victory rang over the field. The Blacks broke and piled pell mell into the trenches and on into the hell hole of the crater.

Fifty of Lee's guns were now pouring a steady stream of shells into this pit of the damned.

The charging gray lines rolled over the captured trenches. They ringed the edge of the crater with a circle of flaming muskets. The writhing mass of dead, dying, wounded and living, scrambling blacks and whites, was a thing for devil's joy. At the bottom of the pit the heap was ten feet deep in moving flesh. In vain the terror-stricken blacks scrambled up the slippery sides through clouds of smoke. They fell backward and rolled down the crumbling walls.

Young John Doyle stood on the brink of this crater, his eyes aflame with revenge. His musket was so hot at last he threw it down, tore a cartridge belt from the body of a dead negro trooper, seized his rifle and went back to his task.

Sickened at last by the holocaust, the officers of the South ordered their men to cease firing. They had charged without orders. They refused to take orders. The officers began to strike them with their swords!

"Cease firing!"

"Damn you, stop it!"

Their orders rang around the flaming curve in vain. They seized the men by their collars and dragged them back. The gray soldiers tore away, rushed to the smoking rim and fired as long as they had a cartridge in their belts.

It was the poor white man who got beyond control at the sight of these yelling black troops wearing the uniform of the

Republic. Had their souls leaped the years and seen in a vision dark-skinned hosts charging the ranks of white civilization in a battle for supremacy of the world?

# CHAPTER XLV

When the smoke had lifted from the field of the Black Battalions, Lee stood in Richmond before a secret meeting of the leaders of the Confederacy. Jefferson Davis presided. The meeting was called by request of the Commander. He had an important announcement to make.

Facing the anxious group gathered around the Cabinet table he spoke with unusual emphasis:

"Gentlemen, the end is in sight unless I can have more men. So long as I can burrow underground my half-clothed and half-starved soldiers will hold Grant at bay. I may hold him until next spring. Not longer. The North is using negro troops. They have enrolled nearly two hundred thousand. Their man power counts. We can arm our negroes to meet them. They will fight under the leadership of their masters. I speak as a mathematician and a soldier. I do not discuss the sentimental side. I must have men and I must have them before spring or your cause is lost."

Robert Toombs of Georgia leaped to his feet. His words came slowly, throbbing with emotion.

"Any suggestion from General Lee deserves the immediate attention of this Government. He speaks to-night as an engineer and mathematician. He has told us the worst. It was his duty. I honor him for it.

"But I differ with him. He can see but one angle of this question. He is a soldier in field. It is our duty to see both the soldier's and the statesman's point of view. And our cause is not so desperate as the science of engineering and mathematics would tell us.

"The war of the revolution was won by Washington in spite of mathematics. The odds were all against him. We have our chance. This war is now in its fourth year. The outlook seems dark in Richmond. It is darker in Washington. What have they accomplished in these years of blood and tears? Nothing. Not a slave has been freed. Not a question at issue has found its solution. The millions of the North are in despair and they are crying for peace - peace at any price. The Presidential election is but a few weeks off. They have nominated Abraham Lincoln again for President. They had to, although he is the most unpopular man who ever sat in the White House. All the mistakes, all the agony, all the horrors of this war, they have unjustly heaped on his drooping shoulders.

"McClellan is his opponent *on a peace platform*.

"The Republican Party is split as ours was before the war. John C. Fremont is running on the Radical ticket against Lincoln. Unless a miracle happens General George B. McClellan will be elected the next President. If he is, the war ends in a draw.

"It's a fair chance. We can take it.

"But our chance of success is not the real question before us. It is a bigger one. The question before you is bigger than the South. It is bigger than the Republic. It is bigger than the Continent. It may involve the future of civilization.

"The employment of these negro troops, clothed in the uniform of the Union, marks the lowest tide mud to which its citizenship has ever sunk. The profoundest word in history is _race_. The ancestral soul of a people rules its destiny. What is the ancestral soul of the negro? The measurement of the skull of the Egyptian is exactly the shape and size of six thousand years ago. Has the negro moved upward? This republic was born of the soul of a race of pioneer white freemen who settled our continent and built an altar within its Forest Cathedral to Liberty and Progress. In the record of man has a negro ever dreamed this dream?

"The Roman Republic fell and Rome became a degenerate Empire. Why? Because of the lowering of her racial stock by slaves. The decline of the Roman spirit was due to a mixture of races. The flower of her manhood died on her far-flung battle lines. Slaves and degenerates at home bred her future citizens.

"Have we also placed our feet on the path of oblivion? History is littered with the wrecks of civilization. And always the secret is found in racial degeneracy - the lowering of the standard of racial values. Civilization is a name - an effect. Race is the cause. If a race maintains its soul, it must remain itself and it must breed its best. Race is the result of thousands of years of this selection. One drop of negro blood makes a negro. The inferior can always blot out the superior if granted equality.

"This uniform is the first step toward racial oblivion for the white man in America. It is the first step toward equality. A people of half breeds have no soul. They are always ungovernable. The negro is the lowest species of man. Through Slavery he has been disciplined into the family of humanity. We cannot yet grant him equality. Abraham Lincoln who has consented to arm these blacks against us has himself said:

*"'There is a physical difference between the white and black races which will forever forbid them living together on terms of political or social equality.'*

"How can he prevent social and political equality once these black men are clothed with the dignity of the uniform of a Nation? He has declared his intention of colonizing the negro race. General Lee also holds this as the solution. If Slavery falls, it *is* the *only* solution.

"In the meantime we hold fast to the faith within us. Dare to arm a negro, drill and teach him to kill white men, and we are traitors to country, traitors to humanity, traitors to civilization. Robert E. Lee himself is the supreme contradiction of the sentimental mush involved in the dogma of equality. His genius and character is a racial product.

"The man in gray stands for two things, Reverence for Law and the Racial Supremacy of the White Man.

"If we must clothe negroes in gray to save the Confederacy, let it go down in blood and ashes. We'll stand for this. And hand our ideal down to our children. If defeat shall come, we may yet live to save the Republic. We hold a message for Humanity."

There was no further discussion. The South chose death before racial treason.

# CHAPTER XLVI

The miracle which Toombs feared came to pass. In the blackest hour of the Lincoln administration, his own party despaired of his election. The National Republican Committee came to Washington and demanded that he withdraw from the ticket and allow them to name a candidate who might have a chance against General McClellan and his peace platform.

And then it happened.

Sherman suddenly took Atlanta and swung his legions toward the sea. A black pall of smoke marked his trail. The North leaped once more with the elemental impulse. A wave of war enthusiasm swept Lincoln back into the White House. And a new line of blue soldiers streamed to Grant's front.

The ragged men in gray were living on parched corn. Grant edged his blue legions farther and farther southward until he saw the end of the mortal trenches Lee's genius had built. The lion sprang on his exposed flank and Petersburg was doomed.

The Southern Commander sent his fated message to Richmond that he must uncover the Capital of the Confederacy, and staggered out of his trenches to attempt a union of forces with Johnston's army in North Carolina.

Grant's host were on his heels, his guns thundering, his cavalry destroying.

A negro regiment entered Richmond as the flames of the burning city licked the skies.

Lee paused at Appomattox to await the coming of his provision train. His headquarters were fixed beneath an apple tree in full bloom.

He bent anxiously over a field map with his Adjutant. His face was clouded with deep anxiety.

"Why doesn't Gordon report?" he cried. "We've sent three couriers. They haven't returned. Grant has not only closed the road to Lynchburg, he has pushed a wedge into our lines and cut Gordon off. If he has, we're in a trap -"

"It couldn't have happened in an hour!" Taylor protested.

"Order Fitzhugh Lee to concentrate every horse for Gordon's support and call in Alexander for a conference."

Taylor hastened to execute the command and Lee sat down under the flower-draped tree.

Sam approached bearing a tray.

"De coffee's all ready, Marse Robert - 'ceptin' dey ain't no coffee in it. Does ye want a cup? Hit's good, hot black water, sah!"

Lee's eyes were not lifted.

"No, Sam, thank you."

The faithful negro shook his head and walked back to his sorry kitchen.

Taylor handed his order to a dust-covered courier.

"Take this to Fitz Lee."

The courier scratched his head.

"I don't know General Fitz Lee, sir."

"The devil you don't. What division are you from?"

"Dunno, sir. Been cut to pieces so many times and changed commanders so much I dunno who the hell I belong to -"

"How'd you get here?"

"Detailed for the day."

"You know General John B. Gordon?"

The dusty figure stiffened.

"I'm from Georgia."

"Take this to him."

Taylor handed the man his order as the thunder of a line of artillery opened on the left.

"Which way is General Gordon?" the courier asked.

"That's what I want to know. Get to him. Follow the line of that firing. You'll find him where it's hottest. Get back here quick if you have to kill your horse."

Sam came back with his tray.

"I got yo' breakfus' an' dinner both now, Marse Robert."

Lee looked up with a smile.

"Too tired now. Eat it for me, Sam -"

Sam turned quickly.

Thomas Dixon

"Yassah. I do de bes' I kin fur ye."

As Sam went back to the kitchen he motioned to a ragged soldier who stood with his wife and little girl gazing at the General.

"Dar he is. Go right up an' tell him."

Sweeney approached Lee timidly. The wife and girl hung back.

He tried to bow and salute at the same time.

"Excuse me for coming, General Lee, but my company's halted there in the woods. You've stopped in a few yards of my house, sir. Won't you come in and make it your headquarters?"

"No, my good friend. I won't disturb your home."

The wife edged near.

"It's no trouble at all, sir. We'd be so proud to have you."

"Thank you. I always use my tent, Madame. I'll not be here long."

"Please come, sir!" the man urged.

Lee studied his face.

"Haven't I seen you before, my friend?"

"Yes, sir. I'm the man who brought the news that General Stuart had fallen at Yellow Tavern."

Lee grasped his hand.

"Oh, I remember. You're Sweeney - Sweeney whose banjo he loved so well. And this is your wife and little girl?"

"Yes, sir," Mrs. Sweeney answered.

The Commander pressed her hand cordially.

"I'm glad to know you, Mrs. Sweeney. Your husband's music was a great joy to General Stuart."

The little girl handed him a bunch of violets. He stooped, kissed her and took her in his arms.

"You'd like your papa to come back home from the war and stay with you always, wouldn't you, dear?"

"Yes, sir," she breathed.

"Maybe he will, soon."

"You see, General," Sweeney said, "when my Chief fell, I threw my banjo away and got a musket."

"If I only had Stuart here to-day!" Lee sighed.

"He'd cut his way through, sir, with a shout and a laugh," Sweeney boasted.

A courier handed Lee a dispatch and Sweeney edged away. The Commander read the message with a frown and crumpled the paper in his hand. The wagons at Appomattox had been cut to pieces. His army had nothing to eat. They had been hungry for two days and nights.

"It's more than flesh can bear, Taylor - and yet listen to those guns! They're still fighting this morning. Fighting like tigers. Grant's closing in with a hundred thousand men. Unless Gordon breaks through within an hour - he's got us -"

Lee gazed toward the sound of the guns on the left. His face was calm but his carriage was no longer quite erect. The agony of sleepless nights had plowed furrows in his forehead. His eyes were red. His cheeks were sunken and haggard. His face was colorless. And yet he was calmly deliberate in every movement.

An old man, flushed with excitement, staggered up to him.

Lee started.

"Ruffin - you here?"

"General Lee," he began, "will you hear me for just one moment?"

"Certainly."

Lee sprang to his feet.

"But how did you get into my lines - I thought I was surrounded?"

"I came out of Richmond with General Alexander's rear guard, sir, six days ago."

"Oh, I see."

"Ten years ago, General Lee, in your house, I predicted this war. Last week I saw the city in flames and I hope to God every house was in ashes before that regiment of negro cavalry galloped through its streets."

"I trust not, Ruffin. I left my wife and children there."

"I hope they're safe, sir."

"They're in God's hands."

A courier handed Lee a dispatch which he read aloud.

"President Davis has been forced to flee from Danville and all communication with him has been cut."

"General Lee," Ruffin cried excitedly, "this country is now in your hands."

"What would you have me do?"

"Fight until the last city is in ashes and the last man falls in his tracks. Fools at your headquarters have been talking for two days of surrender. It can't be done. It can't be done. If you surrender do you know what will happen?"

"I've tried to think."

"I'll tell you, sir. Thaddeus Stevens, the Radical Leader of Congress, has already prepared the bill to take the ballot from the Southern white man and give it to the negro. The property of the whites he proposed to confiscate and give to their slaves. He will clothe the negro with all power and set him to rule over his former masters."

Lee answered roughly.

"Nonsense, Ruffin. I am better informed. Senator Washburn, Mr. Lincoln's spokesman, entered Richmond with the Federal army. He says that the President will remove the negro troops from the United States as soon as peace is declared. He has a bill in Congress to colonize the negro race."

"Stevens is the master of Congress."

"If the North wins, Lincoln will be the master of Congress. We need fear no scheme of insane vengeance."

Lee took from Taylor two despatches.

"General Mahone has taken a thousand prisoners -"

"Glory to God!" Ruffin shouted. "Such men don't know how to surrender!"

"And our cavalry has captured. General Gregg and a squadron of his men -"

"Surrender!" the old man roared. "They'll never surrender, sir, unless you say so. Our wives, our daughters, our children, our homes, our cause, our lives, are in your hands. For God's sake, don't listen to fools. Don't give up, General Lee - don't - "

General Alexander sprang from his horse and approached his Commander.

Lee spoke in low, strained tones.

"I'm afraid we're caught."

He turned to the old man.

"Excuse me, Ruffin, I must confer with General Alexander."

Ruffin's reply came feebly.

"With your permission I will - stay - at - your headquarters for a little while."

"Certainly."

Taylor led the old man toward his baggage wagon.

"Come with me, sir. I'll find you a cot."

"Thank you. Thank you." His eyes were dim and he walked stumblingly. "Surrender, Taylor! Surrender? Why, there's no such word - there's no such word -"

Lee and Alexander moved down to the little field table.

"We must decide," the Commander began, "what to do in case Gordon can't break through. How many guns in your command?"

"More than forty, sir. We've just captured a section of Federal artillery in perfect order."

"Forty guns! And Grant is circling us with five hundred -"

"We have fought big odds before. We have ammunition. The artillery has done little on this retreat. They're eager for a fight, if you wish to give battle."

"I can rally but eight thousand men for a final charge. They are tired and hungry. What have we got to do?"

"This means but one thing, then -"

"Well, sir?"

"Order the army to scatter - each man for himself. They can slip through the brush to-night like quail, and reach Johnston's army."

"You think this best?"

"It's the only thing to do, sir. Surrender - never. Scatter. And when Grant closes in to-morrow his hands will be empty. He'll find a few broken guns and wagons. Our men will be safe beyond his lines and ready to fight again."

"That's the plan!" Taylor joined.

"We can beat Grant that way, General. The Confederacy may win by delay. At least by delay we can give the State Governments time to make their own terms as States. If you surrender, it's all over."

"I do not think the North will acknowledge the sovereignty of the States at this late day."

"It is reported that Lincoln has offered to accept the surrender of States and make terms -"

"This would, of course," Lee slowly answered, "prolong the war as long as one held out -"

"And don't forget, sir," Alexander urged stoutly, "that the single State of Texas is three times larger than France. She has countless head of cattle and horses on her plains. She can equip armies. Her warlike sons, with you to lead them, would laugh at conquest for the next ten years. The territory of the South is too vast to be held except at a cost the North cannot afford to pay -"

"Armies may march across it," Taylor interrupted, "a million soldiers could not hold it *unless you surrender!*"

"Guerrilla warfare is a desperate resort," Lee answered sadly.

"There are things worse," Alexander cried passionately. "This army is ready to die to a man before we will submit to unconditional surrender. The men who have fought under you for these three tragic years have the right to demand that you spare us this shame!"

"General Grant will not ask unconditional surrender. I have been in correspondence with him for two days. He has already put his terms in writing. They are generous. All officers may retain their swords and every horse go home for the spring plowing. He merely requires our parole not to take up arms again."

"He would offer no such terms," Alexander argued, "unless he knew you yet had a chance to win -"

Lee waved his hand.

"Our only chance is to continue the struggle by a fierce guerrilla war -"

"For God's sake, let's do it, sir!"

"Can we," the calm voice went on, "as Christian soldiers, choose such a course? We've fought bravely for what we believed to be right. If I enter a guerrilla struggle, what will be the result? Years of bloody savagery. Our own men, demoralized by war, would supply their wants by violence and plunder. I could not control them. And so raid and counter-raid. Houses pillaged and burned by friend and foe. Crops destroyed. All industry paralyzed. Women violated. We might force the Federal Government at last to make some sort of compromise. But at what a cost - what a cost!"

"You can control our men," Alexander maintained. "Your name is magic. The South will obey you."

Lee gazed earnestly into the face of his gallant young Commander of Artillery and said:

"If I wield such power over our people, is it not a sacred trust? Is it not my duty now to use it for their healing, and not their ruin?"

General John B. Gordon suddenly rode up and sprang from his horse.

Lee eagerly turned.

"General Gordon - you have cut through?"

"I have secured a temporary truce to report to you in person, I have fought my corps to a frazzle. The road is still blocked and I cannot move."

"What is your advice?" Lee asked.

"Your decision settles it, sir."

A courier plunged toward the group on a foaming horse.

"Fitzhugh Lee's cavalry's broken through!" he shouted. "The

Thomas Dixon

way's opened. The whole army can pass!"

"I don't believe it," Gordon growled.

"It's too good to be true," Taylor said.

"It's true!" Alexander exclaimed, "of course it's true!"

"You come from Longstreet?" Lee inquired.

"Yes, sir. He asks instructions."

"Tell him to use his discretion. He's on the spot."

The courier wheeled and rode back as the crash of a musket rang out beside the baggage wagon.

"What's that?" Taylor asked sharply.

"It can't be an attack," Gordon wondered. "A truce is in force."

Sam rushed to Lee.

"Hit's Marse Ruffin, sah," he whispered. "He put de muzzle er de gun in his mouf an' done blow his own head clean off!"

"See to him, Taylor," Lee ordered. "The old ones will quit, I'm afraid."

A courier rode up and handed him another dispatch. He read it slowly.

"Fitzhugh Lee says the message was a mistake, the road is still blocked. Only a company of raiders broke through."

"It's too bad," Gordon said.

"It's hell," Alexander groaned. "Let's scatter, sir! It's the only way. Issue the order at once -"

A sentinel saluted.

"Colonel Babcock, aide to General U.S. Grant, has come for your answer, sir."

All eyes were fixed on Lee.

"Tell Babcock I'll see him in a moment."

An ominous silence fell. Lee lifted his head and spoke firmly.

"We've played our parts, gentlemen, in a hopeless tragedy, pitiful, terrible. At least eight hundred thousand of our noblest sons are dead and mangled. A million more will die of poverty and disease. Every issue could have been settled and better settled without the loss of a drop of blood. The slaves are freed by an accident. An accident of war's necessity - not on principle. The manner of their sudden emancipation, unless they are removed, will bring a calamity more appalling than the war itself. It must create a Race Problem destined to grow each day more threatening and insoluble. Yet if I had to live it all over again I could only do exactly what I have done -"

He paused.

"And now I'll go at once to General Grant."

He took two steps to cross the stile over the fence, and turned as a cry of pain burst from Alexander's lips. He sank to a seat, bowed his face in his hands and groaned:

"Oh, my God, I can't believe it! I can't believe it. After all these years of blood. I can't believe it - my God - to think that this is the end!"

"I know, General Alexander," Lee spoke gently, "that my surrender means the end. It has come and we must face it. We must accept the results in good faith and turn our faces toward the east. Yesterday is dead. To-morrow is ours -"

His voice softened.

"I don't mind telling you now, that I had rather die a thousand deaths than go to General Grant. Dying is the easiest thing that I could do at this moment. I could ride out front along the lines for five minutes and it would be all over. But the men who know how to die must do harder things. I call you, sir, to this battle grimmer than death - to this nobler task - we've got to live now!"

Alexander slowly rose with Gordon and both men saluted.

Within an hour he was returning from the meeting with his brave and generous conqueror. A loud cheer rang over the Confederate lines.

"It's Lee returning along the road crowded with his men," Gordon explained.

Another cheer echoed through the forests.

Gordon smiled.

"Alexander the Great, when he conquered a world, never got the tribute which Lee is receiving from those men. There's not one in their ranks who wouldn't die for him."

Louder and louder rolled the cheers mingled now with the pet name his soldiers loved.

"Marse Robert! Marse Robert!"

Alexander's eyes flashed.

"The hour of his surrender, the supreme triumph of his life."

Lee rode slowly into view on Traveler's gray back. The men were crowding close. They cried softly. They touched his saddle, his horse and tried to reach his hands.

He lifted his right arm over their heads and they were still.

"My heart's too full for speech, my men. I have done for you all that was in my power. You have done your duty. We leave the rest to God. Go quietly to your homes now and work to build up our ruined country. Obey the laws and be as good citizens as you have been soldiers. I'm going to try to do this. Will you help me?"

"That we will!"

"Yes."

"Yes."

"Goodbye."

"Goodbye, Marse Robert!"

Grizzled veterans were sobbing like children.

The war had ended - the most futile and ferocious of human follies. When it shall cease on earth at last, then, and not until then, will the soul of man leap to its final triumph, for the energy of the universe will flow through the fingers of workmen, artists, authors, inventors and healers. On this issue the saving of a world awaits the word of the mothers of men.

# Choose from Thousands of 1stWorldLibrary Classics By

A. M. Barnard
Ada Leverson
Adolphus William Ward
Aesop
Agatha Christie
Alexander Aaronsohn
Alexander Kielland
Alexandre Dumas
Alfred Gatty
Alfred Ollivant
Alice Duer Miller
Alice Turner Curtis
Alice Dunbar
Ambrose Bierce
Amelia E. Barr
Amory H. Bradford
Andrew Lang
Andrew McFarland Davis
Andy Adams
Anna Sewell
Annie Besant
Annie Hamilton Donnell
Annie Payson Call
Annonaymous
Anton Chekhov
Arnold Bennett
Arthur Conan Doyle
Arthur M. Winfield
Arthur Ransome
Atticus
B.H. Baden-Powell
B. M. Bower
Baroness Emmuska Orczy
Baroness Orczy
Basil King
Bayard Taylor
Ben Macomber
Bertha Muzzy Bower
Bjornstjerne Bjornson
Booth Tarkington
Boyd Cable
Bram Stoker
C. Collodi
C. E. Orr
C. M. Ingleby
Carolyn Wells
Catherine Parr Traill
Charles A. Eastman
Charles Dickens

Charles Dudley Warner
Charles Farrar Browne
Charles Ives
Charles Kingsley
Charles Klein
Charles Amory Beach
Charles Hanson Towne
Charles Lathrop Pack
Charles Whibley
Charles Willing Beale
Charlotte M. Braeme
Charlotte M. Yonge
Charlotte Perkins Stetson
Clair W. Hayes
Clarence Day Jr.
Clarence E. Mulford
Clemence Housman
Confucius
Cornelis DeWitt Wilcox
Cyril Burleigh
D. H. Lawrence
Daniel Defoe
David Garnett
Dinah Craik
Don Carlos Janes
Donald Keyhoe
Dorothy Kilner
Dougan Clark
Douglas Fairbanks
E. Nesbit
E.P.Roe
E. Phillips Oppenheim
Earl Barnes
Edgar Rice Burroughs
Edith Van Dyne
Edith Wharton
Edward J. O'Biren
Edward S. Ellis
Edwin L. Arnold
Eleanor Atkins
Eliot Gregory
Elizabeth Gaskell
Elizabeth McCracken
Elizabeth Von Arnim
Ellem Key
Emerson Hough
Emilie F. Carlen
Emily Dickinson
Enid Bagnold

Enilor Macartney Lane
Erasmus W. Jones
Ernie Howard Pie
Ethel Turner
Ethel Watts Mumford
Eugenie Foa
Eugene Wood
Eustace Hale Ball
Evelyn Everett-green
Everard Cotes
F. H. Cheley
F. J. Cross
Federick Austin Ogg
Ferdinand Ossendowski
Francis Bacon
Francis Darwin
Frances Hodgson Burnett
Frances Parkinson Keyes
Frank Gee Patchin
Frank Harris
Frank Jewett Mather
Frank L. Packard
Frank V. Webster
Frederic Stewart Isham
Frederick Trevor Hill
Frederick Winslow Taylor
Friedrich Kerst
Friedrich Nietzsche
Fyodor Dostoyevsky
G.A. Henty
G.K. Chesterton
Gabrielle E. Jackson
Garrett P. Serviss
Gaston Leroux
George A. Warren
George Ade
Geroge Bernard Shaw
George Durston
George Ebers
George Eliot
George Gissing
George MacDonald
George Meredith
George Orwell
George Sylvester Viereck
George Tucker
George W. Cable
George Wharton James
Gertrude Atherton

| | | |
|---|---|---|
| Grace E. King | J. Henri Fabre | Katherine Stokes |
| Grace Gallatin | J. M. Barrie | L. A. Abbot |
| Grant Allen | J. Macdonald Oxley | L. T. Meade |
| Guillermo A. Sherwell | J. S. Fletcher | L. Frank Baum |
| Gulielma Zollinger | J. S. Knowles | Latta Griswold |
| Gustav Flaubert | J. Storer Clouston | Laura Lee Hope |
| H. A. Cody | Jack London | Laurence Housman |
| H. B. Irving | Jacob Abbott | Lawrence Beasley |
| H.C. Bailey | James Allen | Leo Tolstoy |
| H. G. Wells | James Andrews | Leonid Andreyev |
| H. H. Munro | James Baldwin | Lewis Carroll |
| H. Irving Hancock | James DeMille | Lewis Sperry Chafer |
| H. Rider Haggard | James Joyce | Lilian Bell |
| H. W. C. Davis | James Lane Allen | Lloyd Osbourne |
| Hamilton Wright Mabie | James Lane Allen | Louis Hughes |
| Hans Christian Andersen | James Oliver Curwood | Louis Tracy |
| Harold Avery | James Oppenheim | Louisa May Alcott |
| Harold McGrath | James Otis | Lucy Fitch Perkins |
| Harriet Beecher Stowe | James R. Driscoll | Lucy Maud Montgomery |
| Harry Houidini | Jane Austen | Lydia Miller Middleton |
| Helent Hunt Jackson | Janet Aldridge | Lyndon Orr |
| Helen Nicolay | Jens Peter Jacobsen | M. Corvus |
| Hendrik Conscience | Jerome K. Jerome | M. H. Adams |
| Hendy David Thoreau | John Burroughs | Margaret E. Sangster |
| Henri Barbusse | John Cournos | Margaret Vandercook |
| Henrik Ibsen | John F. Kennedy | Margret Penrose |
| Henry Adams | John Gay | Maria Edgeworth |
| Henry Ford | John Glasworthy | Maria Thompson Daviess |
| Henry Frost | John Habberton | Mariano Azuela |
| Henry James | John Joy Bell | Marion Polk Angellotti |
| Henry Jones Ford | John Kendrick Bangs | Mark Overton |
| Henry Seton Merriman | John Milton | Mark Twain |
| Henry W Longfellow | John Philip Sousa | Mary Austin |
| Herbert A. Giles | Jonas Lauritz Idemil Lie | Mary Catherine Crowley |
| Herbert N. Casson | Jonathan Swift | Mary Cole |
| Herman Hesse | Joseph A. Altsheler | Mary Hastings Bradley |
| Homer | Joseph Carey | Mary Roberts Rinehart |
| Honore De Balzac | Joseph Conrad | Mary Rowlandson |
| Horace Walpole | Joseph E. Badger Jr | M. Wollstonecraft Shelley |
| Horatio Alger Jr. | Joseph Hergesheimer | Maud Lindsay |
| Howard Pyle | Joseph Jacobs | Max Beerbohm |
| Howard R. Garis | Jules Vernes | Myra Kelly |
| Hugh Lofting | Julian Hawthrone | Nathaniel Hawthrone |
| Hugh Walpole | Julie A Lippmann | Nicolo Machiavelli |
| Humphry Ward | Justin Huntly McCarthy | O. F. Walton |
| Ian Maclaren | Kakuzo Okakura | Oscar Wilde |
| Inez Haynes Gillmore | Kenneth Grahame | Owen Johnson |
| Irving Bacheller | Kenneth McGaffey | P.G. Wodehouse |
| Israel Abrahams | Kate Langley Bosher | Paul and Mabel Thorne |
| Ivan Turgenev | Kate Langley Bosher | Paul G. Tomlinson |
| J.G.Austin | Katherine Cecil Thurston | Paul Severing |

Percy Brebner
Peter B. Kyne
Plato
R. Derby Holmes
R. L. Stevenson
R. S. Ball
Rabindranath Tagore
Rahul Alvares
Ralph Bonehill
Ralph Henry Barbour
Ralph Victor
Ralph Waldo Emmerson
Rene Descartes
Rex Beach
Rex E. Beach
Richard Harding Davis
Richard Jefferies
Richard Le Gallienne
Robert Barr
Robert Frost
Robert Gordon Anderson
Robert L. Drake
Robert Lansing
Robert Lynd
Robert Michael Ballantyne
Robert W. Chambers
Rosa Nouchette Carey
Rudyard Kipling
Samuel B. Allison

Samuel Hopkins Adams
Sarah Bernhardt
Sarah C. Hallowell
Selma Lagerlof
Sherwood Anderson
Sigmund Freud
Standish O'Grady
Stanley Weyman
Stella Benson
Stephen Crane
Stewart Edward White
Stijn Streuvels
Swami Abhedananda
Swami Parmananda
T. S. Ackland
T. S. Arthur
The Princess Der Ling
Thomas A. Janvier
Thomas A Kempis
Thomas Anderton
Thomas Bailey Aldrich
Thomas Bulfinch
Thomas De Quincey
Thomas H. Huxley
Thomas Hardy
Thomas More
Thornton W. Burgess
U. S. Grant
Valentine Williams

Various Authors
Vaughan Kester
Victor Appleton
Virginia Woolf
Walter Camp
Walter Scott
Washington Irving
Wilbur Lawton
Wilkie Collins
Willa Cather
Willard F. Baker
William Dean Howells
William le Queux
W. Makepeace Thackeray
William W. Walter
Winston Churchill
Yei Theodora Ozaki
Yogi Ramacharaka
Young E. Allison
Zane Grey

www.ingramcontent.com/pod-product-compliance
Lightning Source LLC
Chambersburg PA
CBHW020827030726
47496CB00001B/120